The
Dover Café
on the
Front Line

Ginny Bell went to school in Dover, never realising at the time what a fascinating and crucial role the town played in the Second World War. She is a freelance editor who lives in London with her three children.

Also by Ginny Bell:

The Dover Café at War

The Dover Café on the Front Line

Ginny Bell

ZAFFRE

First published in the UK in 2021 by
ZAFFRE
An imprint of Bonnier Books UK
4th Floor, Victoria House, Bloomsbury Square, London
WC1B 4DA
Owned by Bonnier Books
Sveavägen 56, Stockholm, Sweden

A CIP catalogue record for this book is
available from the British Library.

ISBN: 978-1-83877-374-8

Also available as an ebook and in audio

1 3 5 7 9 10 8 6 4 2

Typeset by IDSUK (Data Connection) Ltd
Printed and bound in Great Britain by Clays Ltd, Elcograf S.p.A.

Zaffre is an imprint of Bonnier Books UK
www.bonnierbooks.co.uk

For Daddy. Miss you every day.

Chapter 1

August 1940

Lily bounded down the two flights of stairs from her bedroom to the kitchen, her nose twitching as the familiar scents of breakfast at Castle's Café wafted towards her: sausages, toast, eggs and cigarette smoke. Opening the door at the bottom of the stairs that led into the kitchen, the muffled clink of cutlery and hum of conversation grew louder and the smell stronger. She wrinkled her nose, delighted that she no longer had to wash dishes and serve the dozens of rowdy servicemen who passed through the café. Much as she enjoyed the banter, she hated washing-up and she absolutely loathed being at her mother's beck and call.

She smiled at her sister, Marianne, who pushed a mug of tea across the oak table that stood in the centre of the room.

'How come you manage to look good even in a nurse's uniform?' Marianne said as she turned back to the range to flip the sausages that were sizzling in a frying pan.

1

'Are you joking?' Lily smoothed down the white apron pinned at the shoulders of her grey, short-sleeved dress. Though the tight belt showed off her waist and the colour made her blue eyes lighter, she wouldn't have said this was her best look. All the same, she felt a thrill every time she put on her uniform. Nursing was all she'd ever wanted to do, and though the hours were long and the work mostly involved cleaning at this stage, she had enjoyed every minute since she'd started a couple of weeks before.

'That Dr Toland was in here yesterday,' Marianne said as she slid eggs onto a plate. 'And it got me thinking – I reckon you'd be clever enough to be a doctor like her. What d'you think?'

'In my dreams,' Lily said wistfully. 'But it's out of reach for someone like me.'

'Too right it is!' A voice floated into the kitchen, and Lily's mother poked her head through the hatch, her purple scarf clashing with the green summer dress and pink apron she was wearing. 'Because who would end up paying for all those years of study? No point getting above your station.'

'And what station's that, Mum?' Lily asked. 'Café skivvy? You'd have me at that sink for the rest of my life if you could.'

'Oh, that's nice, that is. After letting you stay on at school when you could have been here helping with the family business. It's all take take take with you. Still—' her face softened into a smile as she squinted at her daughter '—at least you're making yourself useful.'

Nellie's head disappeared as laughter erupted from the café and a man shouted, 'If you'd wanted a bird, Jasper, all you had to do was pop down the Oak on a Friday night.'

'For the love of God, what the hell is that?' Nellie's voice rose above the hum of excitement.

Lily and Marianne went to the kitchen door and giggled at the sight of the tall, rotund man standing in the entrance. He was wearing dusty blue ARP overalls, and a black steel helmet with a white 'W' painted on the front was perched precariously on his bushy hair. His face was smudged and dirty, but though he looked tired, there was a broad grin on his face as he held up a large metal birdcage, inside which a grey parrot with bright red tail feathers sat on a perch, its head cocked to one side.

Marianne raised her eyebrows at her younger sister. Jasper Cane had been like a father to the six Castle children ever since their own father's death over twelve years before and he was almost always at the café for breakfast. Even after a night that had been disrupted by air raids, he still managed to make it in for his usual plate of sausage, egg and fried bread – although these days he had to make do with just the one sausage. But he'd never yet arrived with a parrot.

Jasper looked around the crowded room with its three rows of dark wood tables, each fully occupied, as they were every morning at breakfast time, and whispered something to the bird.

3

Immediately, the parrot stood up straight and stamped her feet, flapping her wings as she squawked, 'Bloody man! Bloody man!'

Jasper grinned triumphantly at the stunned faces around him, then winked at Nellie. 'It's a parrot, Nell,' he said. 'Goes by the name of Polly.'

'I can see what it is,' Nellie chided. 'What I want to know is, why have you brought her here?'

'Polly!' Lily laughed with delight as she threaded her way through the crowded tables towards Jasper. The parrot belonged to the barber on the High Street, and as far as she knew, it was older than her. When she was small, she and her friends would often pop by to say hello, just as her nephew Donny and his friends did now.

'Is Mr Headley all right?' she asked with a worried frown.

Jasper's face turned sober. 'Smashed windows and damaged roof,' he said. 'He's all right though, he'd taken shelter in Pencester along with Polly, here. Just it'll be a while before he's up and running again, so he asked me to find a home for this one. Just for a few weeks.' He looked at Nellie hopefully.

'So you brought her here for a visit before taking her back to yours, ain't that right, Jasper?' Nellie folded her arms.

Jasper shuffled his feet and inched forward. 'That'd be cruel, Nell. She's a bird as likes company, and she'd be alone all the time if I had her at mine. Gerald said when she gets lonely she starts pulling out her feathers. So, I says to myself, "Hmm," I says. "What's the liveliest place in Dover where folks come for a laugh and a chat and Polly won't be lonely?"'

Nellie raised an eyebrow, although her lips twitched.

Jasper grinned back at her winningly. 'Where there's always a warm welcome for those in need, and a spot of food for those as is hungry?'

Nellie gestured towards a group of soldiers who worked on the anti-aircraft guns beneath the castle. 'Lads? That sound like your barracks?'

One of the men held up his hands and shook his head. 'No way. Our commanding officer'd have something to say about that. Anyways, it'd be too noisy for the bird. What with that bastard Hitler's planes—'

There was a commotion from the cage. 'Bloody man!'

A man in sailor's uniform sitting at another table had just taken a gulp of tea, and he spat it out across the table.

'Did that bird—' He couldn't continue as he thumped the wooden table with the palm of his hand, making the plates and crockery rattle as he snorted with laughter.

Jasper threw his head back and guffawed. 'Mate! If you say Hitler—'

'Bloody man!'

'—anywhere near Polly, this is what she does. She's a very special bird, Nell. People love her and she'll bring in more custom.'

Nellie glanced around. 'If it's not escaped your notice, the place is heaving morning, noon and night.

5

And anyway, you can't have a bloody parrot in a café! All them germs and feathers and stink!'

Jasper put his face close to the bars. 'What do you think, Pol? You'll be a good girl for Nellie, won't you, love?' He stuck his fingers in the cage and Polly nipped the end of one of them gently.

'Good girl,' she repeated. Then she looked at Nellie and held her wings out, as if she was pleading.

'See? You reckon you can house a poor homeless parrot?' He walked over and put an arm around Nellie's plump shoulders, smiling down at her.

For a moment, Nellie smiled back, but then she pushed his hand away. 'No! I will not have that filthy thing in here creating havoc and more work!'

'Oh, come on, Mum. How can you not want Polly? It's not like you to turn a person in need away,' Lily pleaded.

'Maybe so, but *that* ain't no person.'

Just then, Marianne's son, Donny, ran through from the kitchen, stopping abruptly at the sight of Jasper.

'Polly!' he squealed excitedly. 'Hey, Polly, what do you think of Hitler?'

'Bloody man! Bloody man!' The parrot flapped her wings.

Donny ran to his mother. 'Mum, can Polly stay with us? Please!'

'You'll have to ask your gran,' said Marianne, smiling at her son's excitement. If it had been up to her, she'd have had a menagerie of parrots to stay if it made him happy. She couldn't deny him anything since she and her

6

mother had to rescue him just a few weeks before when his father kidnapped him from his evacuation billet in Wales.

'Gran?' Donny's grey eyes sparkled hopefully at his grandmother.

Nellie looked between him and the parrot, then glanced around the café.

The people sitting near the counter started to thump their hands on the table, as they began to chant, 'Let her stay. Let her stay.'

Soon the cry was taken up by the other customers, and Polly flapped her wings in approval, as Donny hopped from foot to foot, a pleading expression on his face.

The bell above the door tinkled then and Roger Humphries, the local police constable, walked in. 'Is there a problem here?' he asked, as the voices died away.

Lily glanced back at Marianne and pulled a face. Now there'd be fireworks for certain. Nellie despised Roger and deplored the fact that he still came into the café for his breakfast every day, despite her best efforts to deter him. They had both hoped that when Marianne announced her engagement to their brothers' friend Alfie, he'd stay away, but no such luck.

Taking off his helmet, Roger wrinkled his nose. 'I'm assuming the parrot is just visiting,' he said.

'And what's it got to do with you?' Nellie asked.

'I don't imagine having a parrot in a café is recommended by the health and hygiene standards that you are required to adhere to. Do you, Mrs Castle?'

7

Nellie bristled. 'Let's see what the customers think.' She looked around. 'All right, you lot, would you be worrying about your food if Polly were sitting over there on the counter?' She pointed to the long, dark-wood counter that stretched from the wall to the edge of the kitchen door at the back of the room.

'Are you kidding, Mrs C?' a Wren called out. 'We'll be making trips specially to see her. She'll be good for morale.'

'That's right, Mrs C. I'd say you'd be doing us a real service,' another soldier piped up.

The bell tinkled again and Nellie's friend Gladys walked in. Tall and thin, she was the opposite of Nellie with her dark clothes and tightly curled greying hair, but the two had been friends for years, and since Gladys's flower stall had had to close, she'd been working in the café.

'What do you think, Glad? How'd you feel if Polly came to stay?'

Gladys looked startled. 'Bloomin' heck, Nell,' she gasped. 'A parrot in here?'

Nellie caught her eye and nodded subtly at Roger, whose face was puce with indignation.

'Oh ... I'm sure she'd be most welcome?' she said tentatively.

'Well, now that's settled, I've got to love you and leave you,' Lily said, swinging her bag and gas mask onto her shoulder. 'There's floors that need cleaning and people that need tending up at the hospital.'

One of the soldiers wolf-whistled. 'You can come and tend my—'

He got no further as Nellie strode up and gave him a clip round the ear. 'You can keep your thoughts to yourself or take your custom elsewhere, lad. As a nurse our Lily deserves respect.'

'Hear hear.' Jasper caught Lily round the waist with his free arm. 'Prettiest nurse in Dover.' He stared down at her affectionately. 'After all your hard work, I'm proud of you.'

'Hey, Jasper, that's not a tear, is it?' Lily teased.

Jasper blushed. 'Just a bit of dust, love.'

'You big softy.' She stretched up and kissed his bristly cheek. 'And hopefully see you later, Polly Parrot,' she said, putting her fingers through the bars of the cage.

Polly put her head on one side and flapped her wings gently. 'See you later,' she repeated.

Lily laughed and pulled open the door, stepping out onto the pavement beside the market square. Then, pausing, she poked her head back inside the café. 'Oh, and don't forget I'll be bringing Pauline back to stay later, will you, Mum?'

'I've not forgotten, love. How long'll she be here?'

Lily shrugged. 'Couple of weeks, I think. That's if Hitler doesn't—' She laughed as, predictably, Polly let out a loud squawk. 'Bloody man!'

Giggling, she shut the door with a bang.

∞

As soon as the bell stopped tinkling, Roger announced loudly, 'If that bird stays here, I may be forced to report you to the relevant authorities.'

Nellie sighed loudly. 'Roger, if you don't like it, go somewhere else for your breakfast. Our Marianne is an engaged woman now, so there's no point hanging around here anyway, cos she won't be changing her mind.'

'So does that mean it's a yes, Nell?' Jasper said hopefully.

'I'm warning you, Mrs Castle, that it would not be advisable—'

Holding the hapless policeman's gaze, she said, 'Yes, I think it does, Jasper.' She smiled challengingly at Roger then turned and indicated the back of the room. 'Stick her behind the counter and me and Glad'll make a space for her by the wall. But any nonsense from you, Polly, and you're out on your beak, you hear me?'

Polly lifted her wings, as though she was shrugging.

Nellie gave a satisfied nod. 'Just so long as we understand each other.' She looked up at Jasper and sighed. 'The things you make me do.'

He bent down and planted a loud kiss on her cheek. 'Ah, Nell, and what you do to me!'

Nellie shook her head, but she couldn't help smiling.

''Ere, Jasper, I reckon you're well in there, mate. If I brought a parrot home to the missus, she'd give me what for,' a soldier said around a mouthful of sausage.

'And I'll give you what for if you ever refer to me as anyone's missus again. I'm my own woman, thank you very much.'

'Mrs Castle, as a member of His Majesty's constabulary, it's my duty to see that the people of this town can
eat free from the fear of poisoning. And you leave me no
alternative but to report this.' Roger tried again to assert
his authority.

'And you, Constable Humphries, leave me with no
alternative but to tell you to mind your own bloody
business.' She looked towards the bird. 'What do you
think of our constable, Polly? He's worse than Hitler,
wouldn't you say?'

'Bloody man!' the parrot replied.

As the room erupted into gales of laughter, Roger
jammed his helmet back on his head and, red-faced,
wrenched open the door and stalked out.

Jasper shook his head at Nellie. 'I reckon you'll come
to regret that, Nell. The man won't rest till he gets his own
back. And considerin' Marianne's an engaged woman
now, he's got no reason to stay on your good side.'

Nellie pursed her lips and folded her arms across her
chest. 'I won't be intimidated by that little runt of a man.
Let him try his worst.'

Chapter 2

Lily skipped up the street, relishing the warmth of the August day. Despite the early hour, the pavements around the market square was coming to life. Over the past few weeks, as they had adjusted to living under almost daily bombing raids, people had started to realise that the German planes usually arrived around mid-morning, so had taken to getting as much of their shopping as they could before then. On the opposite side of the square, Phyllis Perkins was arranging fish on ice in the large open window of Perkins' Fish. Next door, at Turners' Grocery Store, a queue of people had already formed. Through the window, Lily spotted Marianne's friend, Reenie, dropping some tins into a customer's string bag.

She glanced up at the clear blue sky, the sun shining brightly on the cobbles of the square, the gulls circling, ready to pounce on any scraps dropped by the shoppers. Although most stalls operated inside the covered market, the steps of which were already bustling with people, in the square itself, Lou Carter, who had recently taken over the whelk stall, was setting up her trays and buckets of cockles and mussels underneath the stall's cheerful green-and-white awning. Lily chuckled to herself, wondering what Lou and her mother would find to argue about today. The two women had a fractious relationship that apparently dated back to their schooldays, and barely a day went by when they didn't take a snipe at each other.

She took a deep breath, enjoying the tang of salt blowing in on the gentle sea breeze. If it wasn't for the criss-crossing of tape across the shop windows and the barrage balloon floating above the buildings that lined the seafront and glinting silver in the sun, Lily could almost forget there was a war on. But she knew the peace wouldn't last. Almost every day there was an air attack of some sort – whether bombarding the east and west harbours, or attacking one of the convoy of ships that frequently passed through the Channel. It seemed the German planes were breaking through with increasing regularity, sometimes strafing the streets with bullets. They'd already had a few civilian casualties, and Lily lived in fear of seeing one of her own family or friends brought in to the hospital. Especially as, after so many false alarms, people had started to ignore the air raid siren, preferring to trust their own instincts.

Hurrying past Woolworths on Biggin Street, Lily checked her watch. Her old schoolfriend, Pauline, would be waiting for her outside Turpenny's Furniture shop, and she'd be annoyed if Lily was late; Pauline had a fierce temper and it didn't take much to set her off. Still, she was glad to be doing her nurses' training with someone she knew. The other trainees were billeted together in the nurses' home, so Lily sometimes felt a bit of an outsider amongst them.

Passing the bakery, she paused momentarily, wondering if Mary and Jack Guthrie had had any news about their son, Colin. She could see Mary at the counter inside, looking tired and worn, though she was smiling bravely at the customer she was serving. Lily sighed as she thought of her brother Jimmy's best friend, who hadn't made it back from Dunkirk. The last time she'd seen her brother, before he rejoined his regiment, he'd been grim-faced and taciturn. It was almost, she thought, as though now his friend was gone, he no longer cared whether he lived or died.

She shook her head. Now wasn't the time for such thoughts; she needed to be positive and cheerful and if she thought too hard about her fears for her brother, she'd be in no state to help anyone at the hospital.

She walked past the bakery, head down, feeling ashamed that she wasn't taking the time to at least wave a greeting and nearly bumped into a middle-aged woman wearing a flowered housecoat, who was sweeping outside the hat shop.

'Oops, sorry, Mrs Owen. You all right?'

The woman took the cigarette from her mouth, her face creasing into a smile. 'All right, Lily, love?' She looked her up and down. 'Well, don't you look a treat. Hope you managed to get some sleep last night. Not a wink to be had in the shelter at Pencester. Still, managed to have a bit of a nose around while I was down there. Lived here all me life, and never realised the tunnel ran all the way to Snargate. Room for thousands of us down there.' She laughed. 'Things get too bad, we may as well move the town underground.'

'No way. I like to see the sun. And anyway, I'll be needed at the hospital.'

'That uniform suits you. Your mum must be proud.' As she was speaking, Mrs Owen was forced to raise her voice as a squadron of Spitfires flew overhead.

The women glanced up briefly then looked south towards the seafront. The sky was clear, but if they'd learnt anything over the past few weeks it was that when planes raced towards the sea, the Luftwaffe were on their way. Lily felt her heart rate increase; like everyone, she carried on as normally as possible, but the truth was, the drone of low-flying aircraft always made her stomach knot with tension.

'How's things at the café?'

Lily brought her gaze back down to Mrs Owens. 'Busy as usual. Jasper brought Mr Headley's parrot over. Mum's going to look after her till he gets back on his feet.'

'She never is!' Mrs Owens laughed.

'Oy, Lily! Get a bloody move on, will you?' A tall, slim, brown-haired girl dressed in a grey dress the same as Lily's waved to her impatiently from further up the street.

''Ere, Pauline, love,' Mrs Owens shouted, ''ow's your mum. I 'eard she was off up to London with your dad today.'

Pauline walked over, her expression defensive. 'She's all right, thanks, Mrs O. Her and me dad have gone off on one of his delivery trips, so I'll be staying at the café. Dad don't like me staying on me own.'

'Have they now?' Mrs Owen's eyes were sharp but sympathetic as she looked at Pauline. 'How is your dad?'

Pauline's eyes narrowed. 'Same as always.'

Mrs Owens patted Pauline's arm. 'Well, you enjoy your stay, won't you, love. And tell your mum I'm always here if she needs me.'

Pauline frowned at the woman. 'My mum's fine, thank you. And we don't need busybodies asking after our business.'

Lily stared at her friend in astonishment. 'All right, Paul. She was only asking.'

'Yeah, well. She shouldn't.'

But her response was drowned out as yet more planes flew out to join their comrades. Around them, people stopped, their necks craning and Pauline tugged at Lily's arm. 'We better get moving. If I'm not mistaken the siren will go any minute.'

Lily followed her friend, glancing back to give a brief wave over her shoulder to Mrs Owen, who was leaning on her broom, the cigarette clamped back between her lips and a look of pity on her face as she watched Pauline's retreating back.

'Why'd you have to be so rude to Mrs O?'

'She's a nosy old cow.'

'She was just being friendly.' Lily sighed. They'd always had a laugh and Pauline liked to dance as much as Lily did, but you never knew what would set her temper off. Sometimes it was like walking on eggshells when she was around. 'Anyway, you ready for another day?' Lily asked, wisely deciding to change the subject.

'Course. Can't wait to get down to some more scrubbing and cleaning,' Pauline said sarcastically.

'It won't be forever. Just while we learn the ropes.'

Pauline linked her arm through Lily's. 'Yeah, you're right. Once we get going, it's gonna be a right laugh; you and me on the wards with all those injured men thinking we're the dog's bollocks. Anyway, I don't plan to be there forever. I'm going to find a dashing pilot or a doctor and live a life of leisure, you see if I don't.' She grinned.

Lily laughed. 'The pilots aren't exactly up for romance while they're lying in the hospital injured.'

'Ahh, but that's where you're wrong. That's exactly when they're more likely to fall for your charms. Happens in all the romances I read. Doctors, pilots, soldiers, sailors . . . Hospitals is where it's at if you want to find a man.'

'If you say so. Stupid me thought you became a nurse cos you wanted to look after people.'

Pauline wrinkled her nose. 'Ugh. No way I'm gonna spend my life cleaning up other people's filth. This time next year, I'll be married and living in me own house, you just see if I'm not.'

The increase in the noise of the planes flying towards the seafront prevented Lily from answering. The girls briefly glanced up again, then, as one, they started to jog up the High Street towards Union Road. There was a loud boom and they jumped and spun round, their eyes straining to see what had happened. But the sea was hidden from view now and, with no other choice, they kept running as the air raid siren started to wail. An ARP warden ran towards them, flapping his hands.

'Take shelter now!' he shouted.

'What shall we do?' Pauline screamed.

Lily looked behind her and saw a plume of smoke rising above the rooftops beneath the castle, and her heart started to thud as she considered how close the café was to the seafront. But they had no choice; they had to get to the hospital. Lily knew that for Matron only death would be a good enough excuse for being late.

'I think they're bombing the harbour again!' she shouted. 'We should keep going; they won't come into town.'

Her words were brave, but inside, her stomach was clenched with fear as she thought about the merry scene in the café that morning. She knew they'd all have gone down to the basement, but would that be enough to keep them safe? If the planes continued inland, what chance did the little community round the market square have?

Pauline still looked undecided, so Lily grabbed her arm and the two girls started to run full tilt up London Road as the explosions behind them intensified. Lily was certain that she heard gunfire as well. Were they firing on people in the streets? she wondered frantically. In the distance they could hear the urgent ringing of the fire engines and as they turned left into Union Road, the girls were almost knocked down as a squadron of soldiers, rifles held tight to their chests, raced down the road from the barracks on Crabble Hill.

'Get to the shelter, you little fools!' one of them shouted.

But the girls kept running, their capes flying out behind them, their chests heaving, as the noise from the air battle intensified. Finally, they turned through the gates of a long, two-storey red-brick building with a large lawn in front of the entrance. Sandbags were piled to the first-floor windows and an ambulance raced down the driveway towards them, its bell ringing. They hopped back just in time as the driver made a rude gesture at them. Another one swiftly followed. They glanced at each other. It looked like today was going to be a busy day.

Chapter 3

The morning mist was just starting to clear over the Channel as Marge Atkinson enjoyed a quick cigarette before her shift started deep in the tunnels beneath Dover Castle.

Since Dunkirk, Marge had been recruited to the navy's plotting room. It was a difficult job, and one that required huge amounts of concentration. If she'd thought typing the messages in the communications room was headache-inducing, it was nothing compared to this. One small mistake could cost lives and while she was on duty there was no room in her mind for anything but tracking the ships' movements and moving the small models on the plotting table. The battle in the air seemed to intensify daily and the work had been relentless, as they had to keep careful watch of the battleships' movements, alerting and advising the crews whenever the RAF phoned through a warning that enemy aircraft were heading their way. During their breaks, she and her fellow Wrens had taken to standing outside watching as the planes engaged in terrifying dog-fights. Back in June, after the soldiers had been evacuated from Dunkirk, Churchill had predicted that the Battle of

Britain would now start and he hadn't been wrong, Marge reflected. They all knew that if the RAF failed to stem the steady tide of German aircraft, then it would only be a matter of time before Britain was invaded.

She became aware of a tall figure coming to stand beside her and she looked up and smiled into the serious blue eyes of Rodney Castle, sometime sparring partner and brother of one of her best friends, Marianne. Since Dunkirk, their relationship had mellowed into friendship, and to her surprise, she had discovered that his presence was comforting rather than irritating. 'Morning, Rodders. I don't usually see you out here.'

Rodney sighed as he lit his own cigarette. 'It's been a bit of a night,' he said, blowing out a long plume of smoke.

Marge knew that Rodney was involved with some sort of secret operation, but she didn't ask what it was. They weren't allowed to talk about what they did, not even to each other, but she knew that every person at the castle was crucial to the war effort; she was just glad that she wasn't the one who had to keep an eye on the overall picture. 'Operation not going well?' she asked sympathetically.

Rodney sighed. 'You could say that. Bloody shambles, if you want the truth.' He was staring out over the Channel, the water sparkling like crystals in the morning sun. As he raised his arm to take another drag, he paused suddenly. 'Bloody hell!' he exclaimed.

Marge followed his gaze and gasped. The sky above the sea had suddenly turned black as scores of enemy aircraft flew towards Dover like a deadly swarm of locusts.

'Jesus Christ,' she breathed. 'Where did they come from?'

Loud roars from the sky behind her made her turn as dozens of Spitfires and Hurricanes sped towards the German planes. She tried to count them, but there were too many. All she knew for certain was there didn't seem to be as many of them as there were German planes.

As the air raid siren began to wail from the town, the boom of the anti-aircraft batteries in the cliffs under the castle made the ground shake.

'Good shot! One down,' Rodney yelled as one of the Messerschmitts, its nose painted a venomous yellow, suddenly dropped out of the formation, grey smoke clearly showing its progression towards the water.

Marge grimaced. 'And the rest,' she shouted despairingly. 'I can't see how we can keep repelling them.'

'Have faith, Marge,' Rodney said. 'What we lack in numbers we more than make up for in sheer grit.'

Marge grunted, unconvinced. But then, looking at Rodney, his dark hair still neatly slicked back despite working all night, his navy blue jacket immaculate and buttoned up, his blue trousers without a crease, she supposed he should know. If ever there was a man who showed sheer determination, it was Rodney Castle. Throughout the endless days in May and June as they'd battled to bring back the soldiers, Rodney's calm and confidence had been one of the things that had given her hope.

A wisp of bright red hair blew into Marge's face and she brushed it away impatiently as she watched the stricken plane dive into the water. But despite the continued boom from the batteries and the appearance of the RAF, still the Luftwaffe kept coming, some of the planes diving at a convoy of ships in the middle of the Channel, causing gouts of water to erupt around the vessels. But while a dozen planes attacked the convoy, the rest continued to stream towards them, and suddenly all hell broke loose as the screeching of the Stuka dive-bombers competed with the rat-a-tat-tat of the Spitfire's guns and the boom of the AA batteries, as they desperately tried to shoot them down.

Above the noise they became aware of another voice screaming at them. 'Damn fools! Get inside!'

But they didn't move. Marge gripped Rodney's sleeve tightly as she followed the planes' progress through the blue sky, squinting against the sun. She squealed in despair as she watched one of the ships docked below the castle erupt into flames. Seconds later, the air reverberated to the sound of massive explosions and suddenly the harbour, which just moments before had been calm and orderly, was engulfed in smoke, blocking their view.

'What the hell is happening?' Marge screamed. 'It was as if they came out of nowhere!'

Rodney shook his head, looking shocked, which worried Marge even more. This was not the first raid on the harbour; over the past few weeks it had been continuous and every convoy that sailed across the Channel was accompanied by tankers and planes in an attempt to protect them. But they had never seen anything like this. It was as if the Luftwaffe had sent every plane they possessed to destroy the navy once and for all. How many people had already died in just the two minutes since the planes had appeared? Marge wondered in despair.

'Those bastards! Those bloody bastards! They won't get away with this! I won't let them!' she screamed. But in her heart of hearts it felt futile. Everyone was already doing everything they could. She wished she could train to be a pilot. She wished she could shoot the buggers down herself.

Rodney put his arm around her shoulders and bent to shout in her ear, 'Come on, Marge. Come inside now.'

Marge allowed him to lead her back to the entrance of the tunnel, but her eyes were fixed on the sky as more planes swept over them. Would there be anything left of the town by the end of the war? Frustrated and feeling like a coward, she ducked into the tunnel. She was safe here, deep underground, but her friends were facing death every day. Head down, she trailed her hand along the rough, whitewashed tunnel wall as she followed Rodney to the plotting room. They stopped outside the wooden door and stared at each other; Rodney's face was pale and he looked shaken.

Instinctively, she put her hand on his arm in a comforting gesture. 'Try not to worry about the café. Your mum will have got everyone down to the basement and right now they'll be having a sing-song and a cup of tea, and if the worst comes to the worst, Jasper will be digging them out with his bare hands. No way he'd let anything happen to your mum. Or any of them.'

Rodney stared at her hand on his arm for a moment, then back at her. Finally, he cleared his throat and said, 'You're right.' A loud rumble from outside made them pause and Rodney drew in a deep breath. 'Anyway, you best get on. I'll see you soon, Marge.'

Marge sighed as she watched him stride away, his back straight, his uniform immaculate and uncreased as always. She'd wanted to ask him if he'd be going to the dance at the town hall tonight, maybe hint that they could go together, but then he'd probably be on duty. It wasn't like her to hold back, but with Rodney she had the feeling she should wait for him to take the lead. But no matter how many hints she dropped, he seemed to remain oblivious to her. Shaking her head, she pushed Rodney to the back of her mind and opened the door. If this morning was anything to go by, today would be even busier than usual and she needed to keep her head, because if she lost it, it wouldn't just be her who'd suffer, but brave sailors who took their lives in their hands whenever they set out to sea.

Chapter 4

With the air raid siren still ringing in their ears and the sound of explosions being carried on the wind towards them, Lily and Pauline dashed through the staff entrance, pausing briefly to throw off their cloaks, before running out to the main entrance hall where Matron Watson, wearing a navy blue dress and with her brown hair pulled into a tight bun, was shouting orders. Around her several nurses were helping those who could walk down the stairs to the basement, while the porters carried the bed-bound patients on stretchers.

The hospital wasn't enormous, but since the flu outbreak a few months before, and then Dunkirk, it had expanded and now had the capacity to treat close to eight hundred people. Having spent the last couple of years volunteering at the hospital, Lily felt lucky to have been accepted as one of only a handful of trainees. For all her independent ways, she didn't want to be too far from her family, especially when they were so close to the firing line.

Seeing that Matron was too busy to speak to them, the girls went down a corridor to their right that led to the men's ward. There, Sister Sally Murphy, who Lily had got to know well during the Dunkirk crisis, was helping a man wearing blue-and-white striped pyjamas out of bed. His head was swathed in bandages and it was clear the sister was struggling to hold him upright. Dr Ramsay limped over to help her. He was young, with dark hair brilliantined back from his broad forehead, and Lily supposed he hadn't been called up on account of the calliper on his right leg. She didn't much like him, if she was honest; he might be young, but he was pompous and self-important, and spoke with an exaggeratedly posh accent. Anyone would think he was the only doctor at the hospital the way he swanned around shouting orders.

Dr Ramsay stumbled slightly under the weight of the patient and cursed. Lily's eyebrows rose. *That* hadn't sounded very posh, she thought with a small smile. A soldier in khaki uniform rushed into the corridor.

'I need help in the prisoners' hut!' he shouted. 'Bloody prisoner won't budge.'

'Leave him there,' one of the patients shouted. 'He deserves to die. Bastards!'

Sister Murphy ignored him. 'Nurse Castle, go with Corporal Stanmore to help, will you?'

'A man would be better. He's a big blighter!'

'I've no men to spare, Corporal! The porters and orderlies are busy looking to our own injured.'

With a grimace at Lily, the soldier grabbed her arm. 'Come on then, girl. Maybe you can use your charms to get him out of there!'

Lily could guess exactly who would be causing the trouble. Felix Muller was one of the first German pilots to be shot down and had been at the hospital longer than she had. He was due to have the plaster removed from his broken leg soon, but since he'd been there, it had become clear that something else was wrong. So while the other prisoners were generally treated before being removed to the prisoner-of-war camp at St Radigunds, Felix had stayed. Dr Ramsay had diagnosed stomach cancer, as the man couldn't seem to keep any food down, and suggested the prisoner remained for a while longer while he treated him. It was odd, Lily thought. Surely he should just be sent with the others, but apparently the POW camp didn't have the resources to treat such a serious illness.

They emerged into the gardens at the back of the hospital. The noise was louder here, but Lily could tell it was still concentrated at the seafront, so, pushing her fear aside, she ran towards the low, corrugated iron building that had been erected beneath the steep bank behind the hospital. It was painted khaki to blend in with the surroundings and the arched doorway opened into a long room, with narrow cots lining each side. The walls inside had been covered with plasterboard and painted white to try to achieve some sort of insulation, but she knew these places could be perishingly cold in winter, despite the large black boiler that stood at the end of the room.

In the bed to the right, nearest the door, a thin, blond man, wearing the regulation blue-and-white striped pyjamas, lay calmly smoking a cigarette. He glanced up

28

when they entered and raised his eyebrows, for all the world as if they'd just come to visit.

Corporal Stanmore looked at her and rolled his eyes. 'Bloody Kraut,' he muttered. 'I'd leave him to rot if I could.'

Lily nodded. She understood where Stanmore was coming from, although in truth she wouldn't be able to forgive herself if Felix was killed because of her. Together, they walked over to the man and the corporal grabbed his arm, tugging at him.

'*Nein!*' the patient barked.

Despite his thinness, he was strong, and Stanmore, who was several inches shorter, was no match for him physically.

Lily doubted they'd be able to remove him by force, so decided to use a different tactic. Giving him her best smile, she said, 'Come on, mister. You don't want to be killed by one of your own bombs, do you?' She pulled the covers back and indicated that he should get out of bed.

The man stared at her expressionlessly as he blew smoke in her face. She coughed and waved it away. 'If you don't move, I'll be blown up with you,' she said angrily. She couldn't help noticing that his eyes were thickly lashed and a striking navy blue and his dark-blond hair seemed to have been carefully styled despite the fact that he was a prisoner.

His eyes raked over her, taking in every inch, and if the situation hadn't been urgent, she'd have given him a piece of her mind – not that he would have understood her. She glanced at the corporal, who was watching, arms folded across his chest, eyebrows raised, as if to say, 'I told you so.'

Lily's temper boiled over. 'For God's sake, you stupid man. We have to get out of here now!' she cried in frustration.

'Well, now that's sorted,' the corporal said sarcastically, starting to walk away, 'what say you and me leave here and see to the safety of our own people. Not our fault the bloke won't move. Stuff him.'

Lily stared at the man's retreating back and huffed out a sigh, blowing a stray strand of blonde hair away from her face. Maybe she should just follow him. Like he said, she didn't owe this man anything. But then again, she couldn't just leave someone in danger; she was here to help save lives after all. Finally, she flopped down into the chair beside his bed. 'Fine. If you stay—' she pointed at him '—I stay. And we both die.' She hoped he grasped what she was trying to say, and that he had enough humanity in him not to want to risk her life as well as his own. But he was a Nazi, so she wasn't holding her breath because, right at this moment, his countrymen were raining death and destruction down on her town.

But the thought of her brothers made her determined to get him out of there. If one of them was ever injured in enemy territory, she hoped that someone would show them the same compassion that she believed was due to everyone, regardless of race, religion or nationality.

The man continued to smoke, and Lily looked around desperately, trying to find something that might help her. Her eyes caught a crumpled photograph lying on the dresser. She picked it up and looked at it curiously. It was the pilot, looking smart in his Luftwaffe uniform, his arms around a short, plump, well-dressed woman and a tall, thin man. She presumed they were his parents, as they were beaming with pride at the camera. In front of them stood a small boy, his head tilted up, staring at the man with a huge gap-toothed smile on his face.

She held it up. 'And how would they feel? I expect your mother cries herself to sleep every night, wondering if you're safe. And then there's your little brother. Isn't he sweet?'

The man snatched the photograph from her hand, staring at the faces briefly before putting it aside.

'*Geh!*' he said, pointing towards the door.

Lily held his gaze. 'No,' she said, reaching her arm over to his cigarette case, and taking one out. Putting it to her lips, she looked at him, eyebrows raised, and mimed striking a match. Sighing, the man opened the drawer in the bedside table and pulled out a shiny gold cigarette lighter. She took it, attempting to light her cigarette, but her hands were trembling so much, she couldn't seem to get it to work.

He reached out and held her hand steady, observing her intently.

Avoiding his stare, she took a drag on the cigarette, blowing out smoke as she considered what to do next. A

31

loud explosion shook the walls, making her jump, and she stood decisively, stubbing out the cigarette in the over-flowing ashtray by his bed. 'Suit yourself.' She turned and stomped towards the entrance.

As she put her hand on the door handle, she became aware of the man grunting with effort. Turning, she was surprised to see that he was attempting to stand, but his illness had clearly weakened him, and he thumped back onto the bed.

He stared back at her, one eyebrow raised sardonically. '*Komm schon,*' he said, beckoning to her.

Lily hurried back and put her shoulder under his armpit. '*Verdammte frau,*' he muttered under his breath.

She had no idea what he was saying, so she ignored him, as she managed to get him upright. Lily was a tall girl, but this man was well over six foot and, despite his thinness, his frame was solid and well muscled. Once he was balanced, he grinned sardonically down at her, and Lily felt her cheeks colour. She couldn't deny that he was possibly one of the most handsome men she had ever seen, and if the situation had been different, then he was exactly the type of man she'd have had fun flirting with. She shook her head. If her mother was here she'd give her a clip round the ear for being foolish. And she'd deserve it.

Outside, the siren was still wailing, although she thought the sounds of explosions seemed to have lessened. Could it really only be half an hour since she and Pauline had been running up the street? It felt like a lifetime ago, and the attack had sounded intense. She hoped that not too many people had died. And that the café was safe.

Once they set off, she realised that Felix was proficient with his crutches and hadn't needed much help after all. She felt a surge of anger. She would have been much more usefully employed helping other patients.

'I see *you* managed to persuade him,' a disdainful voice called out. The corporal was standing at the top of the stone steps that led down to the basement, watching their progress through narrowed eyes.

'No thanks to you!'

'Couldn't see the point of staying. Looked like the two of you fancied a bit of time alone.' He stared at the German with hard eyes. 'I'm warning you, Kraut, keep your eyes and your hands to yourself.' He grabbed the man's arm and tugged him towards the steps. The pilot stumbled and would have fallen had Lily not caught his other arm.

'Hey, watch it!'

'What's it to you?'

'Seeing as *your* orders were to get the man to safety, and *I* am the one who managed it, the least you can do is show some gratitude!'

Stanmore snorted and took the man's crutches. 'Maybe if I was a pretty little blonde nurse, I'd have managed it sooner too.'

The German was looking between the two of them, and Lily noticed his eyes flash with anger. It made her wonder if he could understand them.

But there was no time to speculate on this further as they began to slowly descend the steps, the prisoner holding tightly to the metal stair rail, his other arm around Lily's shoulder. The corporal held the door at the bottom open for them and they made their way slowly along the short, dark corridor. Lily pushed open the swing doors at the end and stopped briefly as she took in the scene. It was controlled chaos. Men lying on stretchers lined both sides of the wall, while doctors and nurses paced up and down between them, checking they were all right. Some of the men were groaning, while others lay in silence, smoking calmy. Many of them, she knew, were pilots who'd been injured after either crashing into the sea or bailing out.

The basement had recently been expanded, and now with two operating theatres and several large wards running off either side of a long central corridor, Lily supposed that the situation could have been a lot worse if they hadn't managed to move most of the patients down to the recently prepared wards over the last couple of weeks – a task she and the other trainees had been helping with.

A short, stocky man in a porter's beige coat came up and grabbed the German none too gently by the arm. 'So you got him to come with you then.' He smirked as he looked Lily up and down, then winked at the corporal. 'Can't say as I blame him. I'd come for you any day.' He snickered as he pulled the man's arm from around Lily's shoulder. She shuddered as the porter's hand brushed her neck. 'Come on, man, get your filthy Kraut hands off her,' he snarled as he half carried, half dragged Felix down the corridor.

Staring after them, her cheeks flushed with anger, Lily suddenly became aware of a tall, dark man in khaki standing a few steps away. He'd clearly been watching the scene and he raised his eyebrows. 'Well, the man's got a point,' he said with a wink. 'I can't say as I blame him either. But next time, perhaps set your sights higher than a prisoner of war.'

Before Lily had a chance to give him a piece of her mind, he hurried past her to the stairs and bounded out of sight.

Lily stamped her foot. Why was everyone making insinuations? She was just doing her job, for God's sake. But before she could give in to her impulse to scream insults at the arrogant man's back, Pauline came rushing up to her. 'Why is it the best-looking men are either Krauts or married?' she said as she watched the porter open a door towards the end of the corridor and push the prisoner roughly inside, causing him to stumble and curse.

Lily started forward. 'Oy! Be careful.'

The porter shut the door and walked up to her. 'Why do you care, Nurse *Castle*?' he sneered. 'Oh, I see. Head turned by a pretty face, is it? One word of advice, girlie, don't go making eyes at the Krauts. They're dirty bastards, and if I catch you being too friendly, it's straight to Matron.' He looked at Pauline. 'All right there, Nurse Elliott,' he said, giving her a wink, before walking away.

Pauline shuddered. 'That man makes my skin crawl,' she said. 'And how come he knows our names already?' Though he'd only been working at the hospital for a few days, Dick Brown had quickly become known as Dirty Dick, as he was prone to copping a feel if he got close to the nurses.

Their conversation was interrupted by Sister Murphy's voice calling them over. Small, red-haired and freckled with a kindly face, the woman was standing in one of the wards with two of the other trainees, Dot and Vi.

'What a morning!' she exclaimed. 'But like I just said to Nurses Williams and Calloway, just because we're in the middle of an air raid doesn't mean the cleaning can be ignored, so, Lily – I mean, Nurse Castle—' She stopped short as an urgent shout from the end of the corridor diverted their attention.

'The ambulances are bringing in the wounded from the bombing. It's been bad.'

'I have to go,' Sister Murphy said hurriedly. 'Lily, could you organise everyone and get the rest of the patients in the corridor to beds. There are some fold-down cots if you need them. Ask Dick Brown, he knows where they are. And if anyone is in pain, get them some aspirin.'

With that, she rushed off to join several other nurses and a couple of doctors as they hurried up the stairs.

The feeling of urgency was infectious, and the girls got to work making the beds and, at the direction of the ward sisters, helping the patients into them. Once finished, they gathered in the corridor, curious to see what was happening.

The lift at the far end rattled open and Dr Ramsay limped out alongside a trolley bearing an unconscious man. 'Oy you, porter.' The doctor clicked his fingers at Dick Brown, who was emerging from a ward further down the corridor. 'Telephone lines are down. Get a message to Dr Toland at home. We need her here now. Tell her multiple casualties. Repeat. Multiple casualties!'

He continued on and disappeared through the swing doors that led to the operating theatres, his white coat flapping.

'Gordon Bennett, that didn't look good,' Pauline gasped. 'What the hell has happened out there?'

Dot Calloway, a short, plump girl with wiry dark curls poking out from under her white cap, put her hand on Pauline's arm. 'Try not to worry. Best thing for us all to do is keep working.'

Lily smiled at her. She had come to like Dot very much over the previous weeks; she was calm and competent, and not much seemed to faze her.

'I reckon we should see about serving tea to everyone,' Lily said decisively. 'Dot, Vi, could you sort the tea trolley. Me and Pauline'll ask if anyone needs painkillers.'

'What gives you the right to tell us what to do?' Vi muttered sulkily.

'I'm not. I'm just passing on Sister Murphy's orders, so if I was you, Vi Williams, I'd hop to it if you don't want a trip to Matron,' Lily snapped, doing her best impersonation of her mother. She was finding it hard to like Vi. But maybe at the dance tonight they could get to know each other better.

'Still don't seem right. What makes you so special?' Vi glared at Lily, arms folded tightly across her snow-white apron. Her blonde hair was pulled tightly back into a bun and her thin face seemed to wear a continual frown. If it wasn't for that, she'd be very pretty with her unusual, slanted green eyes and high cheekbones.

Lily was saved from answering when Sister MacDonald, a middle-aged woman who'd worked at the Victoria Hospital in the centre of Dover for years before she had moved to the Casualty, clapped her hands at them. 'Nurses! There is plenty for you to be doing. Please don't use the current emergency as an excuse to shilly-shally. Nurse Calloway, go to the kitchens and organise tea for the patients. Nurses Williams and Elliott make a start on cleaning the wards. Start on the men's surgical. I have a feeling there'll be some very sick men in there before too long and it needs to be spotless. Nurse Castle, come with me, I have a special job for you.'

'But that's not fair. Why do we have to clean while she—' Vi protested.

The sister fixed her with a stern glare and Vi shut her mouth. 'Nurse Williams, if you question my orders, you and I will not get along. Now chop-chop. I'll be round to inspect your work shortly.'

The girl lowered her eyes, though her cheeks were flushed. 'Yes, Sister,' she said sullenly, turning to follow Dot and Pauline.

Sister MacDonald turned back to Lily. 'Follow me,' she urged, rushing towards the swing doors at the end of the corridor. 'You're to help in the recovery room. Sister Murphy has only good things to say about you, and we can't spare anyone else right now. And, frankly, desperate times call for desperate measures.'

Lily followed the bustling little woman, narrowly avoiding yet another trolley bearing a badly injured man as it rushed past them. She couldn't deny that, despite the situation, she was excited to be selected for a special task. She'd expected to spend most of the day cleaning and emptying chamber pots, as she had for the previous few weeks, but it seemed the many hours she'd spent helping at the hospital had paid off. She just hoped that Vi wouldn't resent her too much because of it. She shrugged. Oh well, never mind if she did. Lily was more than capable of holding her own with a girl like that. She was Nellie Castle's daughter, after all.

Chapter 5

Even muffled by the thick walls of the café's basement, the noise outside was intense. Far worse than they had experienced so far.

'Jesus wept!' Nellie exclaimed. 'What the hell is going on?' She clattered her teacup on to the old wooden table in front of her, mortified to realise her hand was shaking.

The café was one of the only buildings around the square to have such a large basement, and so it had become a regular shelter for anyone caught out while shopping in the market square, and any nearby residents who preferred to go there rather than take their chances in their Anderson shelters. Not only was it more comfortable, with plenty of chairs arranged round a table in the middle of the room and some large, colourful cushions scattered along the wall, but, thanks to Marianne, there was usually a generous supply of snacks as well.

No one replied to Nellie's rhetorical question, though the parrot, whose cage was on the table by Nellie's elbow, gave a muted squawk and stamped her feet, as though she agreed. But even this didn't elicit a response from the huddled group listening to the noise outside. The light mood from earlier had entirely dissipated with the sudden cacophony from the harbour. The air raid siren had started up a minute after the first explosion had rocked the building, but by then, Nellie had grabbed Polly's cage and shouted to the customers to get downstairs, while Marianne went to stand at the back gate that led on to Church Street ushering in anyone who looked in need of shelter. Some of the servicemen, meanwhile, sensing that this was no normal raid, had rushed out of the door, promising to be back for tea – if they were still standing. Jasper, too, had run outside, whistle to his lips as he directed people to the shelters.

Marianne sat with her arms around her knees and watched Donny, who was sitting at the table, poking his fingers through the bars of Polly's cage. The bird was obligingly nipping at them gently, making him giggle. He seemed to be taking each new danger in his stride, she thought – in fact he seemed to be revelling in it. He and the few other children left in Dover seemed to spend all their time roaming the cliffs and watching the dogfights over the Channel. She only wished she could be as carefree, but the constant noise was fraying at her nerves. And she knew that if the Germans did break through, it wouldn't be long until they reached the market square and God knew what would become of them all then.

Would Alfie be one of the soldiers tasked with trying to repel them? she wondered. Since her fiancé had left a few weeks before, she'd received one drawing: a picture of him and her brothers, Bert and Jimmy, with their fingers to their lips. They were all grinning and Alfie was winking at her. Underneath, the caption had read cryptically, 'Mum's the wurd'. It was frustrating. If he were more confident in writing, would he have told her more? She doubted he'd have been allowed to, so she supposed she'd just have to be content with what she had. Her mother thought they'd been sent on some secret mission, which Marianne didn't like the sound of. Secret missions usually meant more danger, and she knew that Jimmy, in his grief at losing his best friend Colin, would be the first to put himself in the line of fire.

It felt like they'd been sitting in the basement for hours, but it was probably no more than an hour, when suddenly the basement door burst open and Jasper stumbled in, his face black with soot and his helmet tilting at an angle on his bushy head.

Nellie jumped up. 'Jasper, oh thank God! What's going on out there? It sounds like all hell's been let loose.'

'Surprise attack,' he gasped, starting to choke.

Nellie hurriedly poured him a cup of tea from the large brown pot on the table and handed it to him.

He took a gulp, and cleared his throat. 'Eastern dock's on fire,' he said finally. 'Ships destroyed. Fire engines—' He started to cough again. 'Sent home,' he gasped. 'Bloody lungs.' He thumped his chest. 'Never recovered from that gas attack.' Finally, he stopped coughing for long enough to say, 'Luftwaffe gone.'

'What about people? Any dead?' Nellie asked urgently.

Jasper nodded solemnly. 'Planes in the sea. Windows smashed around East Cliff and Athol. No civilians dead. But the sailors . . .' He shook his head. 'Black with tar and burned to a crisp.'

'God have mercy on their souls!' Gladys exclaimed as she made the sign of a cross over her chest.

'Bastard buggering Hitler!' Nellie cried.

Polly let out an indignant squawk, 'Bloody man!'

Nellie turned on her. 'And you can keep your mouth shut and all.' She glared at the parrot. 'Blinking thing. It's going to drive me mad. I've half a mind to let it fly off.'

'Gran!' Donny gasped. 'You can't do that.'

'What can we do?' Nellie asked Jasper, ignoring her grandson. 'Should we go down there to help?'

'No!' Jasper coughed again. 'It's too dangerous. The firemen are tryin' to put out the fires on the ships.' He shook his head. 'They came out of nowhere! Not even a warning. Bloody incredible, the RAF were. Ducking and diving, shooting those buggers down. Plenty of our boys went down too. Poor bastards.' He slumped into a seat at the table. 'Got any sugar for the tea, love?' he asked Nellie. 'Me nerves are shot.'

Nellie's eyes flew to the back of the basement where the wall sloped downwards. She glanced over at Marianne, who shook her head.

Nodding imperceptibly, Nellie reached into her apron pocket. 'I got one lump, Jasper. And cos it's you, I'll let you have it. Otherwise, you should know better than to ask for sugar.' She dropped the small lump into Jasper's cup.

'Your last sugar lump, eh, Nellie. Always knew it was love.' Lou Carter winked at her as she rose from her seat.

Nellie glowered back. 'I'd 'ave given it to you if you'd come in lookin' like you'd been done over by the entire Waffa.' Nellie had somehow never mastered the word 'Luftwaffe'.

The woman chuckled. 'Course you would, love. Well, seeing as the planes have gawn, I'm back to the whelks. Plenty will be hungry after that lot.'

The all-clear sounded just then, and everyone started to gather their bags. Donny raced to the door. 'I'm going to have a look, Mum. Maybe me an' Fred can help.'

'Donny, no! You can't—'

But it was too late; the boy was already racing out of the door.

Edie Castle emerged from the tunnels beneath the castle where she had taken shelter when the raid had started, and went to stand at the edge of the cliff, staring down at the thick pall of black smoke that hid the harbour from view. Every so often, the wind gusted the cloud away and she could see two ships on fire, bright orange and yellow flames leaping into the air, while figures raced around the docks spraying them with water from long hoses, but they may as well have been using thimbles for all the good it was doing. Mr Pearson, her boss at the garage where she was training to be a mechanic, walked up and stood beside her, sucking on his pipe.

'What a farce. Not a breath of a warning and then there they were.' He shook his head sadly. 'I can only thank God that me nephew Bill wasn't one of them poor buggers in the planes.'

His eyes strayed out over the sea where the tail of a Hurricane, its distinctive red, white and blue stripes standing out in contrast to the khaki paint on the body of the plane, poked out of the water like the fin of a great sea beast. The pilot had managed to eject, and was now floating some distance from his stricken plane, his white parachute looking like a giant jellyfish floating on the water. He wasn't the only one. Several pilots from both sides had been shot down and the rescue boats were desperately searching for survivors. Edie knew it was unlikely that all the men had survived and she silently agreed with Mr Pearson. Thank God Bill wasn't among them.

'Where is Bill now?' she asked. Edie and Bill had a patchy friendship, which had all but ended when he'd discovered that she'd been having an affair with a married man. He'd made his disapproval of her very clear and he'd left to start his pilot training before she'd had a chance to explain that she hadn't known the man was married. Not that she cared what he thought, she mused sulkily. It was none of his business what she did.

'He's taking his final exams now. Then he'll go where he's sent, I suppose.' Mr Pearson shook his head. 'Straight into this madness . . . God preserve him. His mum will be turning in her grave.'

'I imagine Lily will be busy up at the hospital,' Edie ruminated. 'I hope no one's died.'

Mr Pearson pointed his pipe down towards the flames rising up from the harbour. 'Don't look likely. I reckon there'll be more than a few hearts broken today.' He sighed and put the pipe back in his mouth, puffing silently as he blew smoke out of the corner of his mouth. 'Well, this isn't getting the cars fixed. I don't mind telling you, though, girl, every time there's a raid, I fear for the garage. Not the best spot to be in, sitting right beside the castle. We were lucky once, but I'm not sure we will be again.'

Edie shuddered. A Spitfire had almost crashed straight into the garage just a few months before, and she still had nightmares about it. Now, of course, those nightmares had become embellished by the sights she saw overhead each day, and the knowledge that at any moment her family could be ripped away from her.

Still, she'd see them all tonight, she thought, with a surge of anticipation. She'd been living up at the garage like a recluse for too long, and she was glad that Lily had persuaded her to go to the dance at the town hall. It felt like years since she'd had fun – or seen her family, come to that. She'd been avoiding the café for the last few weeks in an attempt to prove to her mother that she wouldn't be moving back. There was no way she'd give up her new-found independence to live under Nellie's thumb again.

And it wasn't just that. She still blamed herself for bringing Donny's father back into their lives. If it hadn't been for her, her nephew would be safe in Wales right now. But instead, he had been put through a terrible ordeal and, as a result, Marianne refused to evacuate him again. Her sister, she knew, thought Edie was staying away out of anger and resentment, but it wasn't that. It was shame. Pure and simple. But maybe now it was time to put that aside and start to live again.

'I'll be staying at home tonight after the dance,' she said. 'I won't make it back before curfew.'

'Good. You should do that more often.' Mr Pearson nodded approvingly. 'You've let that toerag destroy your family and it's time to put it back together.'

'It's not that bad!' she said indignantly. 'I saw them a few weeks ago.'

'And that ain't right. Young girl like you needs her family. I'm no substitute.'

Edie took his arm and gave it a squeeze. 'Oh, I don't know, Mr P. You do a pretty good job. Far better than my own father – well, from what I can remember of him.'

Mr Pearson gave her a small smile. 'That weren't your dad's fault, love.' He sighed. 'But there. You were just a tiny kid and weren't to know he couldn't help the way he was. He's not the only good man I know ruined by the last war.' He stared down at the smoking harbour. 'And there'll be a few more of 'em ruined by this one.'

They fell silent as they watched the rescue boat. The tail of the Hurricane had now disappeared beneath the water, but, to Edie's relief, she could see that they were pulling a limp form from the sea.

'Please, please, please . . .' she whispered, straining her eyes to see if there was any movement from the man. But, from this distance, it was impossible to tell whether he was dead or alive.

Mr Pearson patted her shoulder. 'Come on, girl. Reckon I've seen enough. If we get our skates on you can leave early and go pretty yourself up for the dance.' Since petrol rationing had been introduced Pearson's Garage worked almost exclusively for the services, and being within spitting distance of the castle, where both the army and navy were stationed, meant there was a never-ending stream of vehicles that needed their attention.

Edie nodded and turned to follow him, feeling her spirits rise slightly. With the terrible destruction she'd just witnessed, the thought of seeing her stalwart mother brought a smile to her face. Right now, she needed Nellie's strength and reassurance. In whatever form it might come.

Lily slumped into ⟨...⟩
of stew she was hol⟨...⟩
rubbing her temples. S⟨...⟩
that the other three woul⟨...⟩

The hospital was house⟨...⟩ ⟨...⟩se, and the walls still seemed to be s⟨...⟩ ⟨...⟩sery of the people who had lived there. Paint⟨...⟩ ⟨...⟩rey, the underground room had no windows, and ⟨...⟩ ⟨...⟩ bulbs that hung in a row across the ceiling were dim. The food wasn't much better, she reflected, as she stared at the watery brown stew on her plate, the only colour coming from a few slices of overcooked carrot. But then, she was spoiled living at the café, where food was always plentiful, and Marianne was acknowledged as being one of the best cooks in town.

The other tables were half-full and the atmosphere was muted after the difficult and traumatic morning. So far, dozens of seriously injured men had passed through the recovery room, where it was her job to wake them gently and help with any additional dressings that needed to be applied. But Lily knew there were still many more men – both enemy and allies – waiting to be treated.

...hours.

...dous burns,

...ng stomach, she had

...She'd managed to swallow

...me, but the weak groans of agony

...had emitted before he gave up his fight for

...ed in her mind.

...rubbed her eyes, wondering if she'd ever be able to ...ase the sight of the man's raw wounds and the stench of burning flesh. She'd been working with Sister Murphy and Sister MacDonald, and she'd noticed their slight impatience with her when they'd seen her pale face and shaky hands as she'd wrapped a man's badly burned legs with moist bandages.

'If this is too much for you, Nurse Castle,' Sister Murphy had said, 'please go and join your colleagues in cleaning the wards.' The woman had never spoken to her like that before and Lily had immediately taken a deep breath and straightened her back.

'I'm fine, thank you, Sister,' she'd said, managing to stop her hands shaking by sheer force of will.

At that moment, her grim thoughts were interrupted by Pauline, who slammed down her tray on the table beside her.

'I may as well just become a bloody skivvy and have done with it!' she fumed. 'If this is what nursing's all about then you can count me out.' She huffed as she plumped heavily down on to the chair.

Lily smiled at her. Pauline's grey dress was patched with damp and her hair, which had been so neat that morning, was slipping out of its pins and starting to fall around her face.

'If it's any consolation, bandaging a man whose skin's been burned off isn't any picnic either.'

Pauline wrinkled her nose. 'Maybe not, but at least it's nursing. All I've done is empty stinking bedpans, scrub the floor and dust the bloody tables. Again and again.'

At that moment, there was a slight stir as Dr Toland raced in. She'd taken off her hair covering and changed her white coat – which had been smeared with blood the last time Lily had seen it. Beside her limped Dr Ramsay and the two rushed over to another doctor Lily didn't recognise and sat down, talking intently for a few minutes before the three got up and ran out again.

Lily nudged Pauline. 'Look at her,' she said with admiration. 'That's what I'd like to be one day.'

Pauline gazed after the small, slim woman and grimaced. 'What, forty and with your hands deep in other people's insides day in and day out?' She shook her head. 'Why she can't leave it to the men, I don't know.'

Lily stared at her friend, indignant. 'What do you mean? Why should she leave it to the men when she's probably better than most of them? There should be more women like her. Wish I could train to be a doctor, but Mum wouldn't hear of it, even if she could afford it. Says I shouldn't get above my station.'

Pauline laughed. 'Come on, Lily! You! A doctor? You wouldn't look so pretty wearing a filthy white coat with blood smeared all over your face, would you? What chance would you have of finding a husband then?'

'I'm only eighteen! What would I do with a husband?'

'I could think of a few things.' Pauline winked lasciviously, making Lily laugh despite herself.

'Maybe one day,' she said. 'Though I draw the line at that one.' She nodded towards Dick Brown, who'd taken a seat at a table to their right with a few of the other porters. A cigarette was clamped between his lips and the man's beady brown eyes were glinting at them out of his sallow face. Whenever he was near, Lily could feel his eyes burning into her. She'd met men like that before, and she knew that if she got too close, his hands would find a reason to touch her. She shuddered as she thought of his nicotine-stained fingers and turned away from his smirking face.

Pauline looked over at the man, then quickly looked away. 'Too right. He's the sort to trap you against a wall soon as look at you. I won't be going into any supply cupboards when he's nearby.'

'Who's nearby?' Dot asked, as she joined them at the table.

'Dick Brown.'

Dot pulled a face. 'Dirty Dick, you mean. Rose – one of the nurses we're billeted with – told us that he pinched her bum the other day. Still, I don't tend to have much trouble from men like that.' She gestured to her face and wiry brown hair and grinned. 'Can't imagine why, given I'm such a beauty,' she said disparagingly. 'But if you have any

52

trouble, let me know.' She flexed a plump arm, showing a surprisingly large lump of muscle. 'I've got three older brothers and they taught me how to take care of myself.'

Lily laughed. 'I know what you mean. I've got three brothers as well. Not many can take advantage of me.'

They chatted amiably about their families for a moment before Vi joined them.

'So what was your *special* job?' she asked Lily abruptly. 'Me, Dot and Pauline have been cleaning all bloody day.' She held up her hands to show pink, wrinkled skin. 'I'll be needing to plaster these in cream this evening. My mum would have a fit if she saw 'em. "Vi," she'd say, "a woman's hands are a sign of her worth." And these are the hands of a char.' She looked at Lily's hands. 'Yours don't look so bad, though. Don't see why you should get out of the cleanin' when there's so much to do.'

'For your information, madam, Lily's been working at this hospital for the last two years and already knows more about nursing than all of us put together.'

Lily smiled at her friend, surprised she'd bothered to stick up for her. But then, Pauline would use any excuse for a fight.

'So? She's just started as a nurse like us, so she should do what we do.' Vi glared at Pauline.

'Girls, girls, no need to fall out. I expect I'll be back mopping with you tomorrow. Anyway, what about tonight, eh? What are you wearing to the dance?' Lily looked around eagerly. After today, she needed a night out to dance and laugh and flirt. 'You two are still coming, aren't you? Seeing as Pauline's staying with me now, she'll have to come.'

53

'Wouldn't matter where I was living; only death would keep me away,' Pauline said eagerly.

Vi sniffed. 'Bet it won't be a patch on the Palais.'

'Where's that then?' Pauline asked.

'Hammersmith, of course. Don't you know anything?'

'Not sure dancing's quite my thing,' Dot said. 'Not much call for it out in the Derbyshire countryside. And anyway, my mum always says I'm like a baby elephant. But I say we should go, Vi, and you can teach me. Maybe I can prove my mum wrong.' She grinned. 'Though I wouldn't put money on it.'

'Come on, Vi; it'll be fun. And thanks to working in my mum's café, I know half the soldiers hereabouts. Here, you two should come over to the café one day. My sister cooks the best food.' She held up a lump of gristly meat and wrinkled her nose. 'You'll not find this sort of stuff in her kitchen.'

'Ooh. Posh, aren't you. Café. Where I come from it's called a caff. And I bet you *do* know half the soldiers hereabouts. And not just from the caff, neither.' Vi gave Lily a disdainful look.

Lily rolled her eyes, refusing to be drawn into an argument. Pauline, however, had no such qualms.

'Don't put yourself out, Vi. Reckon we'll manage to have more fun without you and your mean mouth. Better still, why don't you just hop off back to Hammersmith if it's so bloody great.'

Vi stood abruptly, her stew unfinished. 'Oh, don't you worry, I'll not be staying here a minute longer than I have to.' She flounced out of the room, leaving her tray still on the table.

'Gawd, what the devil's wrong with her?' Pauline muttered.

'Don't be too hard on her,' Dot said. 'From what I can tell, she left home because of some trouble with her stepfather. And now her mum's not talking to her, so she's all alone and feeling scared.'

Lily felt a flash of sympathy for the girl, but Pauline just shrugged. 'Not our fault, is it. She should just get on with things like the rest of us.' She got up as well. 'Anyway, girls, there's floors to clean. Apparently the next ward will be the Nissen hut. Those prisoners better not try any of their Kraut nonsense or they'll wish they'd died like they should have when they got shot down.'

Lily looked at Dot, eyebrows raised and Dot grinned. 'Well, she has a point. My brothers are out there fighting and if anything happens to one of them I won't be accountable for my actions.'

Lily thought of the tall, handsome German she'd helped that morning, and the picture of his family, and found she just couldn't agree. Surely deep down they were all the same?

Sighing, she picked up her own tray and followed the others out of the canteen, aware again of Dick Brown's eyes following her. She just hoped he didn't turn up at the dance tonight. If he did, one thing she knew for sure: there'd be a few girls with bruised backsides in the morning.

Chapter 7

As Edie walked down Castle Hill later that afternoon, the air was still thick with smoke, and the stench of burning fuel made her nostrils sting. Throughout the day they had received various reports from soldiers about the number of men injured. Thankfully, though, Donny had appeared not long after she had got back to work to tell her the market square was undamaged and everyone was safe.

There had been no further raids that day, although the droning of aircraft had continued, punctuated by explosions as planes continued to fight over the Channel. It was a wonder either side had any left, she reflected.

Turning into Castle Street, the long row of tall Victorian terraced houses cast a shadow over the road, and she was delighted to see that everyone was carrying on their business as if nothing had happened. She stopped for a moment outside Jasper's forge halfway down the hill. As always the door was open, and she could see his grey, bushy head bent over the forge, hammering at a small metal object.

'All right, Jasper?' she called.

Jasper's head shot up and his soot-smudged face broke into a broad grin.

'Edie! Stay right there!' he ordered, as he carefully put down his tools and wiped his hands on his leather apron. 'Come for a cuppa? Or are you on your way to see your mum?'

'Going to the dance tonight. You all right after this morning?'

Jasper's expression sobered. 'That was a bad business. Choking on smoke we were, down there.'

She walked forward into the small space and instinctively waved her hand in front of her face as the heat hit her. Behind Jasper, an iron bar was fastened to the brick wall, and hanging from it was an assortment of tools, from tongs to hammers. At the far end hung a row of horseshoes, ready and waiting for when the dray horses came in needing to be shod.

Carefully skirting around the leather bucket of water by Jasper's feet, she put her hand on his arm and looked up at his face, concerned to see that his usually merry blue eyes were bloodshot and he looked pale and tired, with beads of sweat standing out on his forehead.

'Jasper, you don't look so good. Why don't you stop this and come and let Marianne feed you?'

Jasper wiped his brow with his sleeve and gave her a tired smile. 'You know, that sounds like the best idea you've had for a long while. But I can't right now.' He gestured at his workbench.

Edie looked quizzically at the bowl-shaped object that Jasper had been hammering at and noted that beside him, ranged along a wooden shelf, several other grey metal bowls with wide rims were cooling. 'What's this? The town run out of bowls or something?'

Jasper laughed and picked one of the objects up and plonked it on Edie's head. 'Someone complained they couldn't get helmets for love nor money the other day, cos the factory ones are all going to the military. So I thought I'd churn out a few for the rest of us, see if I couldn't make up the shortfall.'

Edie took the helmet off and stared at it in dismay. 'How's this going to help in an air raid?'

'Believe me, Edie, this could save your life. Keep that one. I'll be bringing more round for the rest of them. And here . . .' He picked a small helmet off a table nearby, and Edie saw that a Spitfire had been carefully painted on the front. 'This one's for Don and—' he picked up another adorned with a Hurricane '—this one's for Fred. You reckon they'll like them?'

Edie smiled and put her arm around Jasper's massive frame and gave him a squeeze. 'They'll love them.' He was quite simply the kindest man she knew; what he saw in her mother she'd never understand. But whatever it was, she thanked God for it, because Jasper had taught them all what it was to have a father.

Jasper's face creased into a pleased smile. 'I'll bring 'em round tomorrow then. I'll make one for Mr P and all.'

She stood on tiptoe and kissed the man's bristly cheek. 'All right. See you later.'

As she passed the Granada Cinema, she spotted her old school friend, Jo, smoking with some friends outside Hubbard's Umbrella Factory on the opposite side of the road. They were dressed in brightly coloured floral overalls with matching turbans, as Mr Hubbard liked his girls to look feminine, but to Edie they just looked like her mother on a particularly lurid day. She grinned; on second thoughts, that wasn't fair. At least they matched.

'Oy, Jo!'

The girl looked over in surprise, then stepped forward as Edie crossed the road towards her. 'Edie bloody Castle. Been ages, girl. Why ain't you never at the café no more? You still living up the garage?'

'Yup. And Mum is sulking cos I won't move home.'

Jo grinned. 'Can't say I blame you. Your mum can be a bit much. Never forget the time she chased me out of there for trying to nick a biscuit.' She cackled as she remembered. 'Snatched up a fork and poked me in the hand. 'Ere, how're your dishy brothers? Ain't seen them for ages neither.'

'Rodney's up at the castle, and Bert and Jim are God knows where.'

'Shame. Was hoping they were hereabouts to come to the dance for my farewell tonight. You coming?'

'You're leaving?'

'Yup. Joined the WAAFs, didn't I. Start me training next week somewhere up north.' She grinned. 'My chance to get out of this hole. If I never come back it'll be too soon.'

'I dunno. I like it here.' Edie looked up at the white building on the corner of Russell Street that housed the umbrella factory, then squinted up the hill, taking in the busy street. She loved the tall Victorian houses with their colourful signs advertising their various businesses. But she especially liked the fact that all she had to do was look up and there was the castle, rising majestically above the tree-covered hill. She couldn't imagine being anywhere else.

Jo snorted. 'All right for you. You've got your mum's café to run to if things go wrong. What have I got? A dad in prison and a mum drunk more than she's sober and living in a couple of dingy rooms up Connaught. Nope. I've had it with this place. Nothing for me here. Still, no point feeling sorry for myself. So what do you say? You coming?'

Edie smiled. Jo was right, she was lucky and she needed to start remembering that. 'I'm on my way to get changed with Lily.'

'Gawd no! Lily's not coming, is she? All the lads'll be after her, leaving us with the dregs.' Jo threw down her cigarette and crushed it under her toe. 'Anyway, I've got to be getting back to the umbrellas. See you later.'

Edie watched her disappear back into the factory, suddenly filled with remorse. It had been too long since she'd seen any of her friends. What was the point of hiding away at the garage, when at any moment they could all be killed? Still, at least she was taking the first step by going out tonight. The last time she'd been to a dance war had just been declared and she'd spent the evening wishing she was with that bastard Robert – or Henry, or whatever his name was.

This time, she'd make sure she enjoyed herself properly.

As she neared the bottom of the road, she caught sight of three familiar figures dressed in khaki crossing Castle Street towards the green gate that led to the backyard of the café. Two tall and dark-haired, and one a little shorter with light brown hair. For a moment her heart stopped. Surely, they couldn't be . . .

'Bert! Jim!' she screamed as she started to run.

One of the group turned and walked towards her, holding his arms out. Without slowing down, she ran straight into them, throwing her arms around his neck.

'What are you doing here?' she squealed, looking up into her brother's dancing blue eyes. He was grubby and soot-stained, but even so, Bert managed to be one of the most handsome men she had ever seen – and didn't he just know it. 'Jesus, Bert! You're filthy.'

Her brother grinned and looked around at the other men. 'We've been at the harbour. Thought we'd pop in and surprise Mum on our way back to barracks.'

'But . . . how come you're in Dover? Where are you stationed?'

Bert tapped his nose with his finger. 'That's for us to know and you to find out.' He winked. 'We've just been deployed and arrived in the middle of an air raid. Sent straight down to the harbour to help out.'

Jimmy walked up then, and although he was smiling, it wasn't his usual carefree grin. Edie stared at him uncertainly. She wanted to hug him, but he had folded his arms as if to stop her. The third man had no such qualms as he jogged up, sweeping his brown hair out of his eyes. 'All right, Edie?'

'Alfie! Does Marianne know you're here?'

He shook his head. 'Nope! It'll be a surprise.' He looked down at his blackened uniform. 'I was thinking the next time I saw her I'd spruce myself up a bit, you know? But . . .' He shrugged.

Edie grinned at him affectionately. Everyone loved Alfie, but the fact that he'd managed to bring Marianne out of her shell meant he'd always have a special place in her heart. 'She'll take you any way she can have you, as well you know. Come on, then. Mum'll be beside herself.'

She pushed open the back gate and stared briefly into the scullery window set in the brick wall immediately to the left of her. Gladys was standing at the sink, her hands deep in the sudsy water, singing 'Onward, Christian Soldiers' in a loud warbling voice. Holding her finger to her lips, Edie opened the back door and tiptoed past Gladys, gesturing for the others to follow.

The café had just closed and Nellie was walking into the kitchen holding a tray of dirty crockery, while Marianne was kneeling in front of the range, scrubbing

62

at the oven doors, her chestnut hair falling out of its bun and hanging down the back of her blue summer dress.

'Surprise!' Edie shouted as she leapt into the kitchen.

Nellie yelped and dropped the tray, the crockery tumbling to the floor with a crash, white shards scattering across the black-and-white tiles.

'Edie!' Nellie yelled. 'What the hell do you think you're playing at?' She stared down at the crockery. 'You'll be paying for this lot, girl!' She looked up at her daughter and spotted the three figures looming behind and put her hand to her chest.

'Jim! Bert! Alfie! Hell's bells, I always said you'd be the bleeding ruin of the café, and now look!' But her face was wreathed in smiles as Bert slipped past Edie and caught his mother up in a tight hug.

Alfie was staring down at Marianne, his head cocked to the side. 'All right, love?' he said sheepishly.

Marianne dropped the brush she was holding, stood up and, her face flushed and her hazel eyes swimming with tears, raised a hand to his cheek. 'Oh, Alfie, is it really you?' It had only been a few weeks since she'd last seen him, but it felt like a lifetime.

Alfie bent and kissed her parted lips tenderly, then he pulled her close and put his forehead against hers. 'In the flesh, my darling. And happier than you can ever know to see you.'

Marianne threw her arms around his broad shoulders, half sobbing and half laughing.

Jimmy was the only one who didn't move. Behind him, Gladys emerged from the scullery and pulled him round to face her. 'Oh Jimmy, Jimmy, Jimmy. It's good to see your face, lad.'

He forced a smile, and gave her a brief one-armed hug round the shoulders. He was behaving so unlike her once-effusive brother, who had always hugged them with abandon and made them laugh, Edie thought, concerned.

Nellie walked over to stand in front of him, staring at him intently. 'Well, Jimmy, my lad, You got a hug for your old mum?' Jim bent and put his arms briefly around her, before he let go. 'Hello, Mum. You're looking well.'

'Wish I could say the same for you. Look at you.' Ignoring his stand-offish manner, she put her arms around his waist, her head only reaching halfway up his chest, and squeezed. 'I can feel every bone in your body. What have you been doing to yourself?'

He shrugged. 'We've been training hard is all. Being turned into fighting machines.' His tone was bitter. 'If the Germans invade, it's our job to kill the buggers. And make no mistake, I'm more than ready to do it.'

There was a brief silence at his words, then Marianne stepped forward, her arms outstretched. 'Jim—'

His face softened as he caught his sister up in tight hug, and Edie breathed a sigh of relief. Marianne and Jimmy had always been especially close and it was good to see that at least that hadn't changed. But then Marianne whispered something into his ear and he released her quickly, his face losing all expression. 'I'm fine,' he said abruptly.

To cover the awkward moment, Alfie stepped forward and clapped Jimmy on the shoulder. 'You reckon you can rustle us all up a cup of tea, Marianne, while me and the boys show that we're not just good for fighting, and clean up this mess?' He gestured towards the scattered china on the floor. 'Think I can still remember where the broom is.'

'As if I'd let you do that. Edie, seeing as this is your fault, you can clean it up. And, Glad, give her a hand, love. Marianne, get the tea on and maybe some of that carrot cake. And you lot—' she shooed them out of the kitchen '—take the weight off. You look like you've been through it today.'

Bert stepped carefully over the crockery as he made his way to the door, where he stopped abruptly.

'What the—?' he exclaimed. Then he let out a guffaw. 'Don't tell me you've taken in Polly the parrot? Hey, Pol, how's Hitler getting on?'

'Bloody man!'

Alfie shoved past him and started to laugh. 'What is that?'

'That is Polly. Gerald Headley's place was damaged last night so the parrot needed somewhere to stay. Said he'd come and get her once repairs were done. And she's been good as gold. Even during that kerfuffle this morning while we were in the basement.'

Jimmy came through into the café and for the first time a genuine smile passed over his face as he went straight over to the bird and stuck his fingers through the cage. 'Hello there, old girl.'

Polly nipped his fingers before flapping her wings and squawking.

'Me and Colin used to visit the bird all the time, and when Col got himself a job at the barber's we became good friends. Didn't we, Pol?'

'Looks like she remembers you,' Nellie said softly.

'Do you, Polly? Remember me and Colin?'

'Colin.' The bird stamped her feet, her head on one side. 'Where's Colin?'

'Bloomin' heck, did she just—' Gladys was watching through the hatch. 'I thought she only knew two words!'

'Polly's cleverer than most humans, aren't you?' Jimmy tickled her feathers.

From the door, Edie saw her brother's beautiful, dark-lashed blue eyes mist over with tears. 'Col's gone, Polly,' he said. He swallowed and turning abruptly away from the bird, went to sit at a table.

Nellie had also noticed her son's expression and sat down beside him, putting her arm around his shoulder. 'He's only listed as missing. There's still hope, love.'

'How many times do I have to tell you, Mum,' he ground out. 'He's dead.' Jimmy shrugged her arm off. 'Reckon you should get rid of Polly as soon as you can. You can't have a parrot in the café.'

'Well, until I'm told otherwise, she can stay. Where are you now, anyway?' Nellie stared at Jimmy in consternation, and Edie knew how she felt. She had no idea how to talk to him either. It was as though he was surrounded by an invisible barrier, keeping them all at arm's length. He had more affection for a bird than he did his family.

'We're around. Ready for when we're needed,' Jimmy said vaguely.

'Do you really think we'll be invaded?' Edie breathed.

'Yes. And if this morning's anything to go by, it'll be sooner rather than later,' Jimmy said grimly.

Nellie sat back. 'Course we won't. The RAF'll see 'em off.'

'If it hasn't escaped your notice, Mum, the RAF are losing planes nineteen to the dozen. Doubt they'll have enough to finish the job.'

Nellie's eyes sparked with anger. 'Oh, I've noticed, thank you, Jim. Every bloody day we all notice. And let me tell you, this café will be burned to the ground before it serves a single Jerry soldier.' She got up. 'Anyway, I can see it's no use talking to you at the moment. Don't know why you bothered to come here if all you can do is spread doom and gloom.'

Jimmy stood. 'You're right. I don't know why I came. It was these two that wanted to.' He looked around the room and nodded. 'I'll be seeing you.' He threaded between the tables and opened the front door, the bell tinkling merrily as he walked out into the late afternoon sunshine.

'What did I say?' Nellie asked indignantly.

Bert sighed. 'Try not to mind, Mum. He's not been himself since Colin . . .' He waved his hand.

'And what's that got to do with me? Alfie lost his friend John, but I don't see him sitting around with a face like a slapped arse.' Her cheeks were flushed with anger, clashing with her purple scarf as she hurried to the door and wrenched it open. 'Oy, Jimmy! I expect to see you Sunday for lunch. And make sure you bring your manners, or don't bloody bother!'

Jimmy ignored her as he strode purposefully across the square and went into the Turners' shop. Nellie watched curiously, wondering why he was going there. A moment later, he came out again, Reenie beside him. He didn't even glance over to the café as he took Reenie's arm and they began to walk up Cowgate Hill. Nellie frowned. Since when had Jim and Reenie been such good friends that he'd rather go and speak to her than be with his own family? she wondered angrily.

'All right, Nell?' Lou Curtis shouted from behind the whelk stall, interrupting her thoughts. The market square was still bustling with shoppers and several of them had stopped to watch the altercation. 'What's Jim doin' here? Been chucked out of the army, has he?'

Nellie glared at her, hands on hips. 'I'd worry about your own son if I were you; he continues hawkin' illegal stuff, he'll soon come a cropper.'

'Ain't that a bit pot and kettle. I 'ear you've been up Houghton to see him once or twice yourself.' Lou grinned, revealing a missing incisor.

Nellie sniffed. 'Never go near the place – it's full of spivs and con artists. The apple didn't fall far from the tree when it came to your boy.'

Lou flushed and stalked towards her, the buttons on her beige overall straining over her large chest and stomach. 'I reckon Roger Humphries might be interested to hear about your little trip.'

The woman was several inches taller than Nellie – if not that much wider – but Nellie didn't budge an inch as she narrowed her eyes. 'You tell him then. He might also be interested to know about those ciggies you sell under the counter. Very foreign-sounding names apparently.'

Nellie turned and walked into the café, slamming the door behind her and turning the sign to 'Closed'.

Refusing to let Nellie have the last word, Lou banged on the window. 'You just wait, Nellie Castle. You'll get your comeuppance and I for one will be celebratin'.' Spittle sprayed the window as she glared through a gap in the tape on the glass.

Nellie walked over and made a rude gesture at the other woman. 'You better get a sponge and clean off that filth, Lou Carter.' Then she pulled the blackout curtains across with a snap, plunging the café into darkness, with only the light from the kitchen illuminating the astonished faces standing behind her.

'Right then.' Nellie rubbed her hands and turned towards the others with a grin, her hazel eyes sparkling; the argument seemed to have lightened her mood. 'Let's have that cup of tea, then. And someone stick the light on, for gawd's sake. It's dark as a tomb in here.'

Chapter 8

Lily spent the rest of the day in the recovery room with Sister Murphy. This time, though, she managed to keep going without fainting or vomiting.

'This'll be your last patient for the day, Nurse Castle,' Sister Murphy said, watching as Lily took the pulse of a German pilot who had been rescued from the sea. He had an oxygen mask over his face, and his torso was heavily bandaged. Looking at his face, Lily realised that he was no older than her, with only a wisp of moustache over his top lip, and smooth, hairless cheeks. His eyelids fluttered, and Lily's heart leapt with relief.

'He's coming round, Sister,' she said.

Sister Murphy came over and took his other wrist, nodding in satisfaction as the boy opened his eyes and blinked at them in confusion. 'Get a porter to wheel him to the hut, then tell the duty nurse there to administer morphine if needed. He should make it through.'

She turned briskly away, and Lily pushed open the door to go in search of someone to help her. Her heart sank as she saw Dick Brown exiting the lift pushing an empty trolley.

'Could you give me a hand?' she asked politely.

The man came towards her. 'For you, *Nurse Castle*, anything.'

Swallowing down her dislike, Lily gestured behind her. 'I need help taking a man to the hut.'

The man's eyes roamed from her feet to her face. 'Another Jerry bastard we're wasting our money on. Tell you what, come for a drink with me, and I'll think about it. Better yet, why don't you invite me to your mum's café for a free meal. I reckon you an' me might find we have quite a bit in common.'

Lily wrinkled her nose. 'As if,' she said shortly.

'Mr Brown.' Sister Murphy had come out of the recovery room. 'Kindly do as Nurse Castle has asked, and keep your suggestions to yourself.'

Immediately, the man's attitude changed and his expression turned obsequious as he nodded, pushing the empty trolley against the wall and stalking towards Lily. She heard him mutter, 'Stuck-up bitch,' as he passed her, before he disappeared into the recovery room and yanked the trolley out after him. There was a groan from the bed.

'For God's sake be careful. The man's just had an operation,' Lily snapped, seeing tears of pain leaking from the boy's eyes.

'Why should I care?'

He passed her in a waft of tobacco fumes and body odour and Lily tried not to breathe in as she followed him to the lift. She hesitated at the door and stared into the small space. With the trolley in place there wasn't much room left and the thought of being so close to that man made her skin crawl. 'I'll walk up.'

Dick reached out and grabbed her arm. 'Oh no you don't, missy. I'm not hanging around waitin' for you to stroll up the stairs. We go together.'

He slid the metal grille shut and pushed the button for the ground floor so Lily had no choice but to make herself as small as possible and pray he kept his hands to himself.

As the lift shuddered upwards, she felt his arm slip around her and quick as a flash his hand squeezed her breast.

'Get your filthy hands off me!' she cried, as she jabbed her elbow into his solar plexus. Like Dot, she knew a thing or two about defending herself.

He let out an 'oof' and the stink of his breath almost made her gag. He bent forward and whispered in her ear, 'You're a lively little bitch, ain'tcha.'

Without turning around or saying a word, Lily brought her heel down hard on his foot.

He grunted. 'Go on, girl, give it your best.' He bent closer. 'You might want to grab my balls while you're at it.'

Lily whipped her head around and glared at him. 'You touch me again, you disgusting little worm, I'll knock you to kingdom come.'

He chuckled. 'You just try it, girl, and you'll soon see who's in charge.'

Lily felt his hand start to wander over her backside, and tried to step closer to the grille. They were nearing the ground floor now, so she bit her lip and kept her mouth shut. At last the lift juddered to a stop and she yanked the doors apart and hurried out through the back into the grounds. With a nod to the two soldiers guarding the hut, she entered, noting quickly that twelve of the beds were now occupied, and most of the patients had come in that day.

She glanced towards Felix's bed. He looked pale and had a thermometer sticking out of his mouth while Pauline straightened his sheets.

Pauline gave her a cheeky grin. 'I'm on temperature duty. Must be my lucky day.' She nodded her head at the man in the bed. 'Best-looking bloke in the hospital. Shame he's a bloody Kraut.'

'For God's sake, Paul,' she hissed as she got closer.

'What? Not as if they can understand a word I say. Can you, you bastard?' She whipped the thermometer from his mouth then marked the temperature on a chart before shaking it carefully. The thermometers were fragile and if they broke one they'd be reported to Matron.

The bed beside the man was empty, so Lily pulled down the sheets and gestured to Dick. He wheeled the trolley over, giving Pauline a long, considering stare. Pauline rolled her eyes and grimaced at Lily.

A howl of agony brought Lily's attention back to her patient, as Dick Brown dropped the boy onto the bed.

'Careful.' She hurried over and smoothed the boy's hair back from his face and arranged the blankets over him.

'Oh yeah. Forgot we had a Jerry-lover in our midst,' Dick Brown said loudly. 'You checked on your boyfriend tonight?' He nodded towards Felix, who was watching them, his expression blank.

'That's enough, Mr Brown. Kindly leave now.' The ward sister's voice rang out as she strode across to them. 'Nurse Elliott, you have precisely five minutes to get those temperatures read, and yourself out of this hospital.'

'Sorry, Sister.' Pauline turned to Lily. 'Meet me out front?'

Lily nodded. 'Should only be a few more minutes.' She turned back to her patient, who was still groaning. 'Shall I get him some painkillers?' she asked the sister.

'I'll deal with it,' the nurse said, giving Lily a narrow-eyed stare. 'And a word of warning: don't get too friendly with any of this lot. They're prisoners and you won't go far if you're found to be fraternising with the enemy.'

Lily flushed to the roots of her hair, feeling her stomach fizz with anger. 'But I wasn't—'

The sister raised her hands. 'That's all I'm going to say about it. Now off you go.'

Lily looked around her, feeling humiliated, but most of the men seemed to be either sleeping or sunk in their own misery. Not surprising, she supposed, given that they were now prisoners. Her gaze fell on Felix again, and their eyes met. Lily felt her cheeks redden as she turned quickly and left.

After collecting her cloak and bag, Lily found Pauline standing outside the front door sharing a cigarette with Dot and Vi.

'At last!' Pauline dropped the cigarette to the floor and crushed it under her heel. 'We better get our skates on if we want to look our best tonight.' She looked at Lily's face closely. 'What's up?'

'What's up?!' Lily couldn't hold in her anger a moment longer. 'Bloody Dick Brown accused me of being a Jerry-lover, all because I told him off for throwing that poor boy onto the bed. And then the ward sister warned me against getting too friendly with the enemy!'

'The bloomin' cheek of her. As for that Dick Brown . . .' Pauline shuddered. 'Why does he *stare* like that?'

'And to top it off, the bastard felt me up in the lift!'

'Blimey!' Dot said. 'You should report the bugger.'

Vi merely raised her eyebrows at Lily. 'Well, if you will swan around like you're God's gift, then it's your own fault if men think you're coming on to them.'

'Coming on to them!? I wouldn't touch that dirty creep if he was the last man on earth!'

'As for the rest,' Vi continued as if Lily hadn't spoken. 'You did look a bit cosy with that Kraut when you came down with him earlier. His hands were all over you. Didn't see you protesting then.'

'Leave it out, Vi. She was just helping the bloke, that hardly makes her a German spy.' Dot looked at Lily sympathetically. 'You gonna be all right? Maybe it'd be for the best if you steered clear of the hut for a while. Tell you what, if you get told to clean it, I'll swap with you.'

Lily tried to calm her breathing. 'Thanks, Dot. I might just take you up on that.' She took a few deep breaths. 'Anyway, like you said, Pauline, we better get a move on. See you at the dance later?'

The other girls nodded, and catching Pauline's arm, Lily pulled her along the drive.

'I don't know why that man has it in for me,' she said, as they walked down Union Road.

'I know what you mean; he's the same with me. Still, I've got just the thing to help us relax and forget about the likes of Dirty Dick.' She reached into an old leather satchel that was slung over her shoulder and pulled out a hip flask. After twisting off the lid, she took a large gulp, then offered it to Lily.

Lily took it and gave it a sniff, before handing it back. 'Blimey, Paul. You'll be two sheets to the wind before we get home if you drink any more of that. What is it?'

'Dad's whisky. Figured I shouldn't let it go to waste.'

'Won't he be annoyed?'

Polly shrugged and took another slug of the drink. 'So what if he is? If they want to go off and leave me, then what do they expect?'

'What, they've gone for good? I thought it was just a few weeks?'

'Who knows? Dad don't share his plans with the likes of me and Mum.'

Lily wasn't sure what to say to that; she'd always thought Pauline had a happy home life, but maybe that wasn't the case. They continued on in silence for some way until they turned into London Road. Lily looked around her appreciatively. Having been underground for most of the day dealing with horribly injured men, she was glad to see that everything looked so normal. The evening sun was casting long shadows between the tall Victorian buildings, and to make the most of the rays, the girls walked in the middle of the road, Lily balancing on the old tramlines.

'What I wouldn't give to see a tram trundling down here now; buses are all well and good, but it's just not the same,' Lily said, her shoulders drooping with exhaustion. Her blue cloak was hung over one arm, the red lining showing up vividly against her grey dress, and her blonde hair, now minus its cap, straggled round her face.

Pauline nodded, and they nattered amiably about the evening ahead. A group of sailors standing outside the King's Hall on Biggin Street wolf-whistled as the girls walked past. Pauline turned and made a rude gesture and they laughed.

'See you at the town hall, girls? First dance is mine,' one of them shouted.

Lily rolled her eyes at Pauline. 'Well, at least we know who to steer clear of. Why did they have to stick a load of randy sailors in there? That place is cursed, if you ask me. Remember when it burned down?'

'How could I forget? Dad were livid. He'd managed to get tickets to the grand cinema opening on account of the fact he'd laid the carpet. Then just a few days before, *poof*, the place went up in flames. And now the town is going the same way,' Pauline said with a catch in her voice.

Lily took Pauline's arm and gave it a squeeze. 'But they rebuilt it, didn't they? Just like we'll rebuild once the war is over.'

Pauline took another sip of her whisky and shrugged. 'If we live long enough to see it.'

Lily fell silent at that as they past Woolworths, its windows empty and covered with brown paper, and the Guthries' bakery, now shuttered and quiet. So much had changed in such a short space of time, and there was going to be much more change ahead. She sighed and nudged Pauline. 'Think I need a drink after all.'

Pauline handed her the flask and Lily took a tentative sip, choking as the fiery liquid made its way down her throat. 'On second thoughts,' she said, eyes watering as she handed it back, 'I'll stick to cordial or a port and lemon.'

They reached the market square and Lily noted with surprise that the blackout curtains were already drawn in the café, despite the fact it was still light. 'Let's go round the side,' she said. 'Looks like Mum's closed up for the night.'

Pauline hesitated. 'You reckon we've got time for a quick butcher's down the front,' she said, glancing out at the sea. In the gap between the buildings on New Bridge, they could see a convoy of ships making its way over the horizon, a couple of planes hovering protectively over it.

Lily glanced at her watch. 'Don't see why not. Come on.'

They crossed the road and turned left along Marine Parade, stopping at the barricade that had been erected to prevent people getting too close to the eastern harbour, and stared in horror at the damage from the morning raid. Alongside the jetty they could see the smoking remains of two ships, both listing to one side. A thick black plume of smoke still rose from one of them, and the air was heavy with the pungent smell of burning fuel.

'Jesus bloody Christ; no wonder so many died. I was speaking to one of the firemen at the hospital and he said they went in and out of that ship dozens of times to try to rescue the men,' Pauline said.

Lily shuddered and turned away. The sight vividly brought back the memory of the poor burnt seaman who had died in agony in front of her. She stared over towards France where the coastline stood out, bathed in the rosy glow of the setting sun. It looked like a fairyland, but she knew how false that was; thousands had died there just a few short weeks ago and no doubt there were many more still dying as the RAF bombed the coast relentlessly.

Suddenly, she was desperate to get back home. 'I can't look at this any more. Come on.'

They trailed back along Marine Parade. To their left, the sea sparkled and danced in the gentle breeze and scores of people were strolling up and down Marine Parade, enjoying the balmy evening. If it hadn't been for the smoking ruins beneath the white cliffs and the small crowd of people who stood by the railings, binoculars in hand, watching the convoy move steadily across the water, it would have been an idyllic seaside evening.

A sharp burst of gunfire drew their gazes back to the sea. It seemed the watchers would get their wish as, like a small swarm of gnats, black shapes had suddenly appeared in the sky above the French coast. 'I don't want to watch, Pauline. Let's go!'

But Pauline couldn't take her eyes from the scene, and she went and joined the crowd, pulling a reluctant Lily with her. They watched plumes of water burst around the ships, as the Hurricanes hovering above broke their formation, ready to fight off the enemy attack.

Dropping her gaze, Lily noticed a couple of small figures standing in front of her. She clapped her hands over one of the boys' eyes, laughing as he let out a yell and spun round.

'Auntie Lily, did you see? That Hurricane just *blasted* the Messerschmitt out of the sky! Like, *Kapow, crash*.' His hands came up expressively as he mimicked the noise of an explosion.

'Isn't it time you got home for dinner, Don? And you, Fred? Your gran'll be wondering where you are. Come on.' Freddie lived with his grandparents and father, Wilf, above Perkins Fish opposite the café.

Reluctantly, the boys cast a last look at the planes standing out in sharp contrast to the rose-pink sky. Suddenly, one of the planes dropped, smoke trailing from its tail, and plunged into the sea. The boys cheered. But a man beside Donny cursed. 'That was one of ours, boy! What you cheering for?'

'Hey, all right,' Lily said to the man, squeezing Donny's shoulder protectively. 'It was just a mistake. No need for that tone.'

Donny dropped his arm dejectedly. 'Still, we got one of theirs too,' he said sulkily, kicking at the ground.

'I think you've both seen enough for one day. Let's go see what your mum's got to eat.' Lily grabbed both boys by the napes of their necks and turned them in the direction of home.

The market square was quiet when they arrived, aside from the distant explosions and aircraft noise, and Phyllis Perkins, Freddie's grandmother, was sluicing water onto the ground outside the large open door of the fish shop.

'Just found this little plane spotter down by the sea-front,' Lily called over to her.

Mrs Perkins turned round. She was a slim woman of medium height, her hair still blonde with only a few streaks of grey, despite being well into her fifties. She wiped her hands down her apron as Freddie dashed over. 'Did you see the planes, Gran? They must have shot down at least a hundred!'

Mrs Perkins laughed affectionately. 'Not as if I can miss them, is it? Swarming over night and day. I swear my head's not stopped aching since Dunkirk. Get in with you, Fred. There's sandwiches in the kitchen.' She turned to Lily and nodded towards the café. 'Been a bit of upset this evening. Your mum and Lou Carter at it hammer and tongs about something to do with your brother and her no-good son Terence.'

'Which brother?' Lily asked in surprise.

'Your Jimmy. Him, Bert and Alfie arrived this afternoon.'

Donny started to jump up and down in excitement. 'Alfie's here?' He spun round and ran across the square, eager to see the man who would one day soon be his stepfather.

Lily was equally excited to see her brothers. 'Is that why the curtains are drawn already?'

'No. That was something to do with Lou. You know I love your mum dearly, but sometimes it might help if she kept her mouth shut. You couldn't tell her that from me, could you, love?'

'I tell her that all the time! But you know Mum. Only people that can shut her up are ...' She paused, then laughed. 'You know what, no one can shut her up. See you later, Mrs Perkins. Me, Pauline and Edie are off to the dance at the town hall.'

Mrs Perkins shook her head. 'I don't know how you have the energy. Reenie said she's going and all. And Marge'll be down for the night. You young girls these days: working all day, dancing all night . . . just the thought makes me bones ache.' She rubbed her back. 'Then again, I dare say you deserve some fun.'

With a brief wave, the girls hurried across the square and through the back gate. Lily shoved open the door and hurried inside. 'Oy oy!' she shouted. 'Any brothers here to say hello to the ministering angel!'

Bert came through into the kitchen and Lily squealed with excitement, throwing herself into his arms. 'Albert Castle! Bloody hell, what are you doing here?' She drew back. 'You might have washed before you came visiting,' she said, taking in the soot-blackened uniform.

'Yeah, there was the small matter of a few burning ships to deal with today.'

'You were there? Smoke's still rising, covering East Cliff.' She looked over his shoulder, expecting to see Jimmy, but instead saw Alfie, Donny hanging off his arm.

'Where's Jim?'

Bert shrugged. 'Bit of a row with Mum. Apparently he's gone off with Reenie.'

'Reenie Turner?' Lily said, surprised.

Bert nodded. 'Those two have been scribbling letters to each other like no tomorrow since we went back to the regiment. She sent him a card to say sorry about Colin, and it started from there, apparently.'

Before she could comment on this strange turn of events, Bert nodded at Pauline who was standing quietly beside her. 'And who have we here?' he said with a smarmy smile.

'You remember my mate, Pauline, don't you? She's come to stay for a few weeks.'

Bert grinned. 'Pauline Elliott! Well I never, ain't you grown?' His eyes ran over her appreciatively and Pauline blushed.

Lily smacked him on the arm. 'Don't be a creep. We're just stopping to eat and get changed and then we're off to the dance at the town hall. Can you come?'

'It just so happens we can. Alfie's hoping to persuade them to let him play his trumpet.'

'Well, that'll be a sight better than old man Filbert and his wife.' Lily laughed. Mrs Filbert had a terrible voice, but she stood gamely on the stage every week singing her heart out, while her husband accompanied her on the piano.

Lily walked through into the café where Edie was finishing a plate of food. 'Hey, Edie, you remember Pauline, don't you?'

Edie frowned slightly. 'Hello, Pauline,' she said coolly.

Pauline smiled uncertainly. 'Good to see you, Edie. Been a while.'

'It's good you're coming tonight,' Edie said. 'Was just talking to my mate, Jo. She's off to join the WAAF so it's her farewell dance. You remember Jo, don't you?'

Pauline reddened. 'Course I do.'

'I'm sure she'll be happy to see you.' Edie turned away dismissively.

'You're late,' Nellie said before Lily could query Edie's less than warm welcome.

'Yeah, me and Pauline took a quick look down the front. Found Donny and Fred watching the action as usual.'

Nellie looked at Pauline. 'Hello, Pauline, love. Been a while since we've seen you. Last time was when you went off for a walk up the Citadel.' She started to chuckle and Lily turned to Pauline, eyebrows raised.

Her friend looked furious. 'For your information—' Pauline started indignantly.

Lily, who had no idea what her mother was talking about, nudged her friend in the side and shot her a meaningful look. The last thing she needed was for Pauline to get off on the wrong foot with her mother.

Pauline took the hint and smiled weakly. 'Yeah,' she said. 'Me and Kath enjoyed the walk in the rain.'

Nellie laughed harder. 'You might not have guessed it but you girls used to cheer me up no end. Anyway, water under the bridge now. How's your mum, love? Lily tells me her and your dad have gone away for a bit.'

Pauline shuffled her feet. 'Mum's all right, thanks, Mrs C. And thanks for letting me stay.'

'You're always welcome. And when your mum gets back, you tell her she can always come and stay if she needs as well.' She nodded at her meaningfully, while Lily stared between them, wondering what her mum was getting at.

'Oh, no, she wouldn't want to do that. And I'll go home soon as they get back.'

A squawk from behind reminded Lily of their other guest. 'Here, Pauline, you remember Polly from the barber's?'

Her friend smiled and went over to greet the bird. 'All right, Polly. How's tricks?'

The bird flapped its wings and stamped its feet.

'I always thought that bird was a girl,' Bert said. 'But maybe he's a bloke, judging by his reaction to you, Pauline. Looks like he likes you. Can't say as I blame him.' He came over to tickle the bird's grey feathers.

Lily threw Bert a glare, very aware that Pauline looked ill at ease. She'd never seen her friend so shy.

'That's enough, Bert.' Nellie glanced at Pauline. 'Don't want to have to send the poor girl to the Citadel again.' She cackled wickedly, then winked at Pauline. 'Sorry, love. Only joking. It's Bert I need to send away these days.'

Pauline shot a glance at Bert and then looked away, her face puce, but from anger or embarrassment, Lily couldn't tell. Pauline's next words answered her question.

'I think we need to get a move on,' she said shortly.

A sudden screeching from the basement made everyone jump.

Marianne groaned. 'Looks like Donny's got poor Alfie giving him a trumpet lesson again.' She stood up. 'I better go and rescue him, then we can all go and get ready.'

'*You're* coming?' Lily said in astonishment. It took a lot to get Marianne to a dance.

She blushed. 'Well, if Alf's playing, I don't want to miss it. And Reenie and Marge'll be there, so it'll be nice to catch up with them.'

Lily clapped her hands. 'The Castle sisters out on the town! Come on then. But before we do, what's there to eat?'

'There's some potato salad and a cheese and onion pie in the kitchen.'

Edie stood up. 'Bert, hadn't you and Alf better get back and clean yourselves up?'

Bert looked at his watch. 'You're right. See you later, girls.' He winked at Pauline, who blushed again.

In the kitchen, Bert opened the basement door and yelled down. 'Oy! Alf! Time to go and let the ladies get ready.'

The noise stopped and soon Alfie and Donny appeared, Alfie carrying a large black leather case. 'Can't wait to give the old lady an airing,' he said with a grin, holding the case up.

Bert slapped him on the arm. 'Hey, that's no way to talk about my sister, mate!' He laughed heartily at his own joke, and Marianne flapped her hands at them.

'Get out, both of you.' But she was laughing, her eyes sparkling and her cheeks flushed as she stood on tiptoe to give Alfie a kiss. 'See you later, love.'

He grabbed her waist and kissed her soundly on the lips. 'I can't wait.'

Donny had been watching intently. 'Yuck! Just cos you're going to be married, doesn't mean you can do all that soppy stuff!'

'Don, mate, if you want me for your dad, soppy stuff is part of the bargain, all right?' Alfie said.

Donny wrinkled his nose and sighed. 'Oh, all right. But not in front of me, please.' He grinned cheekily as they all laughed.

Bert turned to Pauline. 'And you, young lady, are to save the first dance for me.'

Pauline stuck her nose in the air. 'All depends what else is on offer,' she said haughtily.

'Quite right too, Paul. And I doubt you'll have much trouble finding someone better either. Go on up; I'll just grab us a couple of plates of food and we can eat while we get changed.'

Edie loitered in the kitchen as the others left.

'You sure you should be hanging out with her?' she whispered, as Pauline followed Marianne up the stairs.

'Pauline? Why not? I've known her for years and we work together,' Lily said as she cut a large slice of pie.

'Well, just watch yourself, won't you? My mate Jo had a run in with her over a boy a couple of years back, and she spread some evil rumours around town to put him off her.'

Lily raised her eyebrows. 'And how do you know that was Pauline? I mean she's got a bit of a temper, but she's not sly.'

'Just don't say I didn't warn you,' Edie said as she went to the door at the bottom of the stairs.

Lily stared after her. She did remember a rumour that Jo had been sleeping around with half the soldiers at the barracks. And now she came to think of it, Pauline was the one who'd told her. But that didn't mean she was the one who had started it.

Shaking her head, she dismissed the thought from her mind as she picked up the plates and hurried after her sister. There wasn't much time to get ready and she wanted to squeeze as much fun out of the evening as she could before curfew forced them all back home again.

Chapter 9

Marianne was grabbing a clean skirt and blouse out of the large dark wood armoire when Lily entered the room.

'I'm moving into the boys' room while Pauline stays,' Marianne explained, smiling at Pauline, who was perched on the bed sipping from her hip flask. 'Give us all a bit of space.'

'You're not wearing those!' Lily set down the plates on the dressing table and pointed disdainfully at the blue skirt and white blouse dotted with small pink flowers that Marianne was holding.

'What's wrong with them?'

Lily stomped over to the wardrobe and pulled out a lilac chiffon dress. 'Remember this? Wasn't this what you wore to the last dance you were at with Alfie?'

'But that's for best!' Marianne exclaimed. 'Anyway, I'm only going to watch Alfie play and catch up with the girls; not as if I'll be dancing or anything.'

Lily sighed. 'Suit yourself,' she said. 'But you haven't seen your fiancé for weeks, don't you want to look your best?'

Marianne wrinkled her brow and looked down at herself. 'He's just seen me looking like a bag lady, can't see that he'd care. Or do you think he would?' She looked uncertain and Lily felt guilty. Marianne's confidence had grown in leaps and bounds since Alfie had come into her life, so sometimes she forgot how shy and worried her sister had been after Donny's birth. None of them, including Marianne herself, had even been aware she was pregnant when her waters had broken in the café as she served a customer. The scandal had rocked the community and Marianne, ashamed and hurt by some people's harsh words, had hardly ventured out of the café since. But then her brothers had brought Alfie home with them on leave, and he'd fallen for her hook, line and sinker. With the help of Alfie's love, it seemed to Lily that Marianne was finally breaking free of the shame that had crippled her for so many years.

She smiled. 'You're right. You could wear a flour sack and he'd still think you were the bee's knees.'

Marianne coloured and hastily left the room as Lily went to the wardrobe, grabbing a white blouse and a red pleated skirt that she loved to dance in because it flew up around her when she twirled, revealing her garters. Then she pulled out the green cotton dress with white polka dots that she'd promised Pauline she could borrow. It had a tight bodice and a full skirt, with a white belt clasped around the waist. She threw it over to her friend and sighed when she saw she was taking yet another sip from the flask.

'Haven't you had enough?'

Pauline held it up to her, and Lily shook her head.

'I haven't had that much. And anyway, it makes me feel more relaxed.'

'Well, just as long as I don't end up having to look after you for the whole night.'

Pauline scowled and screwed the lid back on, before going over to the dressing table to cut herself a piece of cheese and onion pie.

'Mmm.' She closed her eyes. 'Your Marianne is a whiz in the kitchen. I've been wondering what a man like Alfie could see in her, but maybe it's this. They say the way to a man's heart is through his stomach, after all.'

Lily bristled. 'There's plenty to see in Marianne. If you hadn't noticed, she's beautiful and probably the kindest woman in the world.'

'Sorry I spoke,' Pauline muttered. 'I didn't mean anything by it.'

Lily was too annoyed to reply. She knew that deep down Marianne often wondered what Alfie saw in her and she hated the fact that others might wonder the same.

The two girls ate in silence, then, once finished, they quickly got changed. 'Sit down, Paul, and I'll do your hair,' Lily suggested. She didn't want an atmosphere between them tonight. Pauline smiled with delight and obediently sat on the stool at the dressing table.

'What did Mum mean about the Citadel?' Lily asked, running a brush through Pauline's thick brown hair.

Pauline shook her head. 'Nothing. Well, nothing much. Just me and Kath were a bit foolish a few years back and your mum made sure we knew it.'

Lily smiled ruefully. 'Don't worry about it. If I had a penny for every time Mum made sure I knew I was being stupid, then I'd be rich.'

Pauline stared at Lily's reflection in the mirror. 'You're lucky living here.' She looked wistful. 'I always wanted brothers and sisters, but it's just me. And here you are with loads of them.'

'Yeah well, it's not all it's cracked up to be,' Lily said through a mouthful of hairgrips. 'Edie can be a right pain and Bert always manages to wind me up. I was always jealous of you having a proper dad.'

Pauline looked away. 'Well, dads aren't all they're cracked up to be either. I don't think I ever saw your dad. What was he like?'

Lily stared at the paisley pattern on the curtains – purple, green and red, her mother's choice, of course – her mind going back to the days when her father used to sit in the sitting room day in and day out; sometimes he wouldn't talk for days, and others he'd rage and shout. 'My dad . . . He didn't talk much. And he hardly ever left the house. Anyway, Jasper's always been more a dad to us than my real dad ever was.'

'What's the deal between Jasper and your mum, then? You reckon they'll ever get married?'

'God knows! I've always wanted them to, but Mum seems dead set against it.' She shrugged.

'Love, eh?' Pauline said sympathetically. 'Never what you expect. Not sure it's for me anyway.'

'I thought you wanted to marry a pilot or doctor?'

'I never mentioned love, did I? I just want some handsome man to keep me in comfort for the rest of my life.'

'Handsome like that German pilot?'

'Yup. Handsome like the German. Only English. Don't want no Kraut babies running about.'

'Aren't babies just babies?'

'I suppose . . . Unless they're Kraut ones.'

Lily laughed as she patted Pauline's hair, smoothing back a stray strand from her face. 'Funny old day, eh? What with Kraut pilots, sleazy porters and all that.'

'I reckon you should watch that pilot. I saw the way he was looking at you. I don't trust him.'

'What's he gonna do? Dr Ramsay reckons he's got stomach cancer, so I think I could outrun him if he tried anything. Unlike that bugger, Dick.' Lily shuddered at the memory of his hands on her. 'Half a mind to report him to Matron.'

'Yeah, he's a nasty piece of work. Always staring and smirking.'

Lily stuck a final hairpin into the victory roll and stepped back. 'There. What do you think?'

Pauline patted her brown hair and grinned. 'I reckon if you wanted to give up nursing you could get a job down the hairdresser. Now sit down and I'll do yours, though I can't promise it'll look as good as mine. Still, don't think it'll matter. You'd have half the blokes slavering after you, even if I chopped it all off.'

'Don't talk rot, Paul.' Lily sat down and watched in the mirror as Pauline got to work, a look of fierce concentration on her face, as she did her best to put Lily's hair up into a victory roll.

'You still haven't told me what happened with Mum,' she said.

Pauline sighed heavily. 'Do you remember years ago when me and Kath had a crush on your brothers? Kath liked Jim, and I liked Bert. We'd come and sit in the café just so we could see them and try to get them to ask us out.'

Lily grinned. 'I'd forgotten that. Mum used to moan about all the girls who'd come and sit over a cup of tea for hours just to moon over the boys. So what happened?'

'Your mum happened.'

Lily raised an eyebrow as Pauline continued. 'One day she came over and gave us a note from Jim and Bert that said to meet them at the top of the Citadel in half an hour. So we rushed out and ran all the way. It was cold and raining when we got up there so we found a sheltered spot and waited. And waited. Then, when it started to get dark, we went home. Poor Kath couldn't stop crying, and I never forgave your brothers. It was only later I realised we hadn't been stood up and the note actually came from your mum. She just wanted us out of the café for good. And it worked. I've not set foot in there since. Well, until today that is.'

Lily laughed. 'You never told me that! I just thought you didn't like Mum.'

Pauline shook her head. 'I was too embarrassed. I really liked your brother, you know. And what she did was humiliating.'

'I'd just forget about it, if I were you. Anyway, if you want my advice, I'd stay away from Bert. He might be pretty, but he's the love 'em and leave 'em type and he'd only break your heart.'

'I don't want to marry the bloke, Lil. Can't a girl have a bit of fun without everyone talking weddings? Like I said, when I marry, it'll be to a man who can look after me. I mean it. I'm not skivvying up at the hospital for the rest of my life.' She gave Lily's hair one last pat and stepped back. 'That'll do.' She took the hip flask from her pocket and took a sip. 'Now, come on. Let's go and have a laugh!'

Lily looked at Pauline's flushed cheeks; she seemed half-cut already. Bert ought to watch out – with the amount of Dutch courage Pauline was putting away, she'd be all over him like a rash.

∽

'Get a move on, you two!' Marianne shouted up the stairs. She could hardly wait to leave. It had been the best surprise of her life when she saw Alfie walk in through the kitchen door. She smiled to herself. And it had been even better when they'd been able to sneak down to the basement for a quick cuddle. She longed to be married to him and have a little house of their own, and maybe a brother or sister for Donny. Obviously, she'd have to stay at the café for now, but she couldn't remember a time when she'd felt so happy. Although she worried constantly about Donny and his future, now that she had Alfie at her side, she felt confident that she could overcome anything.

'Don't think I've ever known you so eager to go dancing,' Nellie commented as she took a sip of sherry. 'It does my heart good to see it. About time you started to behave like a young girl. Although, you're hardly a spring chicken, are you? Still, better late than never.'

'Thanks very much, Mum!' Marianne said indignantly.

'You *are* old, though, Mum,' Donny piped up. He was sitting in the chair opposite Nellie reading a comic. 'Though not as old as Gran.'

Nellie reached over and gave him a gentle cuff around the head. 'Less of your cheek, young man,' she said, smiling.

Edie rolled her eyes at her mother. 'Why is it that you can't just give a straight compliment, Mum?'

Nellie eyed her contemplatively. 'I only speak the truth, love. And while we're on the subject, it's high time you found yourself a suitable young man. A pretty girl like you shouldn't have any trouble. Plenty of men around who won't know about your indiscretion. Though they might be put off by the overalls and grease.'

'There you go again. Pretty, but smelly and with a bad reputation.'

'Ah, now I didn't say smelly *or* bad reputation, did I? No one gives a fig for that. We've all got too much else on our minds, so if you don't want to be left on the shelf, then you'd best get your skates on.'

'I'm only twenty, for God's sake!'

'By the time I was twenty I had Rodney and Marianne.'

'Yeah, but that was back in the Dark Ages. Things are different now.'

From the radio, the bongs indicating the news was about to start rang out across the room as Lily and Pauline walked in, interrupting the argument.

As the girls collected their jackets and gas masks, Nellie let out an exclamation. 'I don't know which attack they're talking about,' she said to no one in particular.

The girls looked at her blankly.

'According to the news, the RAF fought off the Waffa's attack and there was minimal damage.' She sighed. 'I don't know, girls. I listen to the news and don't know whether I'm coming or going sometimes, when my eyes tell me a different story.'

'Not much we can do about it, though, Mum. I mean, if anyone speaks out about the lies, they'll have us locked up in a jiffy. Anyway, I'm sure they have their reasons,' Edie said.

'You put too much faith in the government, girl. I've seen it all before. The lies they tell to keep us on track.' She drained her glass and held it out to Marianne. 'Pour us another before you leave, love. You know, girls, I don't think this town'll ever be the same if today's anything to go by. All those bastards have to do is hop across the Channel to drop their bombs. There can't be enough planes in the world to stop 'em. Before you know it, we'll have bloody Hans and Karl demanding strudel in the café.'

Her speech was met with dead silence. Finally, Lily shook her head. 'In which case we best be off to enjoy our last few days of freedom.'

'Yes, cheers, Mrs C.' Pauline saluted Nellie mockingly with her hip flask and took a swig.

'Are you drunk?' Nellie demanded sharply. 'I warn you, if you puke anywhere in this house, then you better clean it up before I see it, or you and I will fall out. Now go on and enjoy yourselves. Me and Don will hold the fort.'

They needed no further urging as they rushed down the stairs. 'Blimey, your mum's a barrel of laughs, ain't she?' Pauline huffed as they walked out of the back gate and turned left into Castle Street.

'She just speaks her mind, that's all. And if you don't like it, you shouldn't stay here,' Edie snapped, then she grabbed Marianne by the arm and pointedly marched as far ahead of Lily and Pauline as she could.

'Sorry, I spoke,' Pauline grumped.

'Don't mind her. Let's just go and dance and forget the horrible war even exists.' Lily was determined to enjoy herself. After the day they'd had, they deserved a bit of fun.

Chapter 10

They weren't the only ones making their way to the Gothic, flint-covered building on Maison Dieu Road. The weekly dance was always well attended, and they soon joined a rowdy group of sailors who had clearly spent the early part of the evening in the pub as they sang, 'They'll Always Be an England' at the tops of their voices all the way down the road.

Ahead of them, Lily saw Marianne and Edie stop to chat to a tall woman in Wren's uniform. Beside her stood a smaller girl with blonde curly hair. 'There's Marge and Reenie.' She pointed. 'Doesn't look like Marge has managed to persuade Rodney down, though.'

'Ooh, Rodney.' Pauline gave a little shiver. 'If he's here I might give up on Bert. Rod's always struck me as the type a girl can rely on. All those dark, brooding good looks.'

Lily laughed. 'Yeah, if you like the sort with a stick up his arse. Anyway, he won't come. He never does. He prefers to brood up at the castle. All right, Marge, Reenie,' Lily shouted, as she sped up to join the group.

The women turned and Marge gave a wolf whistle. 'Looks like someone's out for some fun,' she said, pointing her cigarette at Lily.

Lily gave a little twirl. 'No harm in trying to look your best. I learnt that from a certain red-headed Wren.' She gave Marge an arch look and Marge grinned at her in return. 'Don't suppose you've managed to drag Rodney down from his bunk?'

Marge raised her eyebrows. 'And why would I do that? The man wouldn't know fun if it jumped up and bit him on the bum.' She gave a loud throaty laugh.

'Well, I just want to dance,' Reenie interjected. 'Last thing I need is a man. I've got enough to do with the allotments and the Dig for Victory committee.' Despite obviously making an effort, Reenie still managed to look like a gardener, even when wearing a skirt and blouse. Both were wrinkled and, as always, she wore a sensible pair of lace-ups. Although, her clear skin, curly blonde hair and sparkling blue eyes made her look almost pretty, Lily thought. If she could get her hands on Reenie for just an hour, she reckoned she could make her look like a princess.

'If you say so, Reens.' Lily wasn't sure she believed her. For a start, there was the curious news Bert had told her about Reenie and Jim, and on top of that she could have sworn she'd spotted Reenie and Wilf Perkins sneaking off together just the other morning. Still, it was no business of hers.

They moved with the crowd up the steps, and once through the blackout curtains, they handed over their money and headed to the arched entrance that led into the magnificent galleried hall. Marianne gave a little squeal of excitement as the sound of a trumpet drifted out of the door.

Inside, the wooden floor was crowded with couples dancing, and around the gallery, men and women were standing drinking and smoking beneath the beautiful vaulted ceiling, watching the dancers below. Lily knew that somewhere around here were the remains of an old medieval building, and she wondered fancifully whether there were ghosts watching, and what they made of this crowd of merrymakers in the midst of war.

At the far end of the long room on a large stage, an old man with grey hair and a pipe clenched in the corner of his mouth was gamely trying to keep up with Alfie and his trumpet, while a woman of uncertain age with dyed blonde hair and wearing a long black satin dress stretched tightly over her corseted middle, sang a slightly out-of-tune version of 'Begin the Beguine'. It would have been funny, Lily thought, if it didn't make her think of the last time she'd seen Alfie perform. On that occasion, Alfie's best friend and band partner, John, had been playing up a storm on the piano. It was probably the last time they'd ever played together, she thought sadly, as she remembered the cheeky kiss she and John had shared, and now they never would again. But if Alfie was feeling sad, he didn't show it as he stood swaying to the music, the lights bringing out copper tints in his brown hair.

Marianne went to stand directly in front of the stage and waved up at her fiancé. As soon as he spotted her, Alfie stopped playing and walked to the front of the stage, holding his hand down to her. With no trumpet to guide him, the piano player faltered and the singer trailed away. A groan went up from the crowd of dancers.

Alfie stood up. 'Sorry, folks. Slight change of plan,' he called out. 'Hands up all you girls who love a soldier?'

A cheer went up as a disgruntled sailor stepped forward. 'Or a sailor,' he bellowed.

Alfie ignored the heckle. 'This one's for all you soldiers out there and the girls who love you!'

He swiftly consulted with Mr Filbert and then had a word with Mrs Filbert, who looked distinctly put out. Then, raising his trumpet to his lips, he started to play, 'The Girl Who Loves a Soldier', his eyes never leaving Marianne. She blushed, before moving over to the side of the room and sitting down at a table.

'Now that's true love,' Edie said wistfully to Lily.

'God, that man!' Marge said dreamily. 'Don't you just love him? Lucky, lucky Marianne.'

Pauline, meanwhile, had lost interest in the events on the stage and was searching the room. 'There's Bert,' she said eagerly, spotting him standing near the bar. She grinned at Lily. 'See you later.'

'Oh dear,' Edie said gleefully, as she watched Pauline push her way over to her brother and pull him on to the dance floor. 'This will be fun.'

Lily shot her a look. 'Don't be mean.'

'As far as I'm concerned she deserves him,' Edie said dismissively, then spotting Jo standing with some other people she used to be at school with on the other side of the room, Edie went over to join them.

Lily looked around to see if she could see Dot and Vi, then cringed in dismay as a familiar figure caught her eye. Dick Brown – that was all she needed. Just then a dashing man in air force blue asked her to dance, so she took his hand gratefully and melted into the crowd, hoping the porter hadn't seen her. Soon, she was laughing as she was twirled around in the melee, her red skirt flying up, her frilly garters on show, and the day's trials disappearing like mist being blown off the sea.

∞

Marianne's cheeks were still burning with pleasure and embarrassment as she watched Alfie. How had she got so lucky? she wondered. After all those years feeling worthless, Alfie always managed to make her feel special. She smiled as she watched him doing what he loved best and marvelled at the fact that this funny, handsome, talented man was all hers.

Her eyes turned to the dance floor and she spotted Bert's tall figure twirling Pauline around. As Pauline spun back into his arms, she took hold of his lapels and pulled him close, reaching her face up as she tried to kiss him. Bert avoided her mouth, and his eyes met Marianne's over the crowd. He raised his eyebrows at her and mouthed, 'Help.' Marianne laughed and shook her head. Bert was more than capable of looking after himself.

She saw Lily had noticed her brother's dilemma and, as Pauline tried to kiss him again, her sister rushed over and, grabbing Bert by the arm, pulled him away, throwing a laughing remark at her friend over her shoulder. Marianne wasn't sure who she was trying to protect, but she suspected it was Pauline. It didn't look like her friend was grateful, though, but Lily's partner gamely stepped in and took over, while Bert gave Lily a swift kiss of gratitude before they set off in an energetic foxtrot.

'I see Bert's in demand.' A voice beside her made her jump and she looked up at a tall, handsome man wearing khaki, his dark hair swept back from his face.

'My brother usually is when it comes to the girls,' she said with a smile. 'How do you know him?'

'Just met him today, actually. And that man up there.' He nodded towards Alfie.

'He's my fiancé,' she said proudly.

The man examined her. 'So you must be the famous Marianne who cooks like an angel. I only met Alf tonight as we walked down to the dance, but all he could talk about was you.' He held his hand out to her. 'Charlie Alexander, Royal Medical Corps and responsible for the health of that lot up at the barracks.'

Marianne shyly took his hand, unsure what more to say. She looked around the hall. The stained-glass windows had been removed and boarded over, but even so it was impressive.

'This is a beautiful room, isn't it?' Her eyes scanned the crowded gallery above them, then returned to the dancers, and with a jolt she saw Jimmy dancing with Reenie. Unlike most of the dancers, the two of them were very close, holding on to each other and swaying as they talked intently. What did those two have to talk about? she wondered. Of course, they'd known each other most of their lives, but even so, until today, she hadn't been aware they'd ever been good friends. Her mind went back to the last dance she'd been to and a picture of Reenie and Jim laughing and dancing as she and Colin watched on suddenly came to her mind. Maybe they'd been closer than she'd realised, she thought with a pang of grief at the thought of Colin. Because after the argument with her mother, and Jimmy's obvious unhappiness, she hadn't expected to see him here, but clearly Reenie had managed to persuade him otherwise. Still, she was sure it was no more than friendship; there was no way Jim would be romantically interested in her friend.

Charlie Alexander followed her gaze. 'And that's your other brother, isn't it? Quiet chap.'

'Mm,' Marianne answered vaguely.

The trumpet stopped suddenly, so she looked over to the stage as Mr Filbert started to play 'Kiss Me Goodnight, Sergeant Major'. A loud cheer went up from the dancers as the portly Mrs Filbert started to warble, marching comically on the spot.

Marianne half stood as she saw that Alfie had jumped down and was making his way towards her. She really hoped he wasn't expecting her to dance. To her relief, Lily grabbed him before he could reach her, and wound her hands round his neck, pouting her lips at him as she sang. Marianne sat back down just as, out of the corner of her eye, she noticed Jimmy and Reenie slip out of the hall hand in hand. Brow furrowed, she glanced over at Alfie, wondering if he'd noticed, but he was swinging Lily around.

She knew she shouldn't, but she had to see what was going on. Jimmy had confessed to her when he got back from Dunkirk that he thought Colin's death was God's punishment on him for being 'unnatural' and that from then on, he was going to try to change. But surely he wouldn't use Reenie, of all people, to try to prove he was 'normal', as he put it? Reenie was one of her best friends, and several years older than him to boot. She thought back to the desperate grief in his eyes, the way he had closed in on himself and refused to speak to anyone. Yes, she thought. He definitely would. Reenie was gentle, older and one of the sweetest women she knew; who could be better as far as Jim was concerned?

She turned to the man, who was watching Alfie and Lily through narrowed eyes. 'I-I have to go. So nice to have met you,' she said hastily, before pushing her way through the crowds, praying that her suspicions were wrong.

Lily saw Alfie frown and followed his gaze, watching as Marianne ran out of the hall. 'Do you want to go after her?'

Alfie hesitated. 'Do you mind?

'Course not! I shouldn't have waylaid you like that. Go on.' She let go of his hand and gave him a push in the direction of the door. Alfie didn't need telling twice, as he made his way towards the exit.

As she walked off the dance floor, Lily collided with a hard chest. Unusually for Lily, the man was at least six inches taller than her. Taller even than her brothers. 'Beg your pardon,' she said merrily, looking up into a tanned, weathered face. Her heart skipped a beat. He seemed familiar, but maybe that was because he looked a bit like Cary Grant. Then she remembered where she'd seen him before: it was the man from the hospital that morning who'd made that annoying remark about her setting her sights higher than a prisoner of war. She felt her cheeks flush with annoyance as she opened her mouth to give him a piece of her mind. But he spoke before she had a chance to say anything.

'Looks like you've been abandoned,' he said sardonically. 'Allow me to take his place.' He caught her round the waist, and Lily scowled up at him, trying to pull away.

'No, thank you. I don't want to dance with you.' The man was gorgeous, but his disapproving expression and the memory of their previous meeting dispelled any attraction she might have felt.

'Really? I'm hurt. But then, I suppose as I'm neither a prisoner of war nor an engaged man, you wouldn't have any interest in me. I just hope you haven't done any permanent damage by flirting with that poor girl's fiancé. Although by the look on her face when she left, I don't hold out much hope.'

She stared back at him in bemusement. 'Do you mean Marianne? Why's she upset?'

'Oh, so you know her? Which means you must know that she's engaged to Alfie. The man you were hanging off like a limpet.'

'We were only dancing.'

'From where I was sitting, it looked a bit more than dancing.' He raised an eyebrow. 'Bert not enough for you?'

Lily felt her temper rise. 'Bert's hardly my type.'

'Really? He seems to be most women's type.'

'Well, I'm not most women.'

'Clearly. If this morning's little display was anything to go by. Let alone your performance with poor, hapless Alfie just now.'

She glared back at him angrily. 'Look, mister! I don't know who you are, but—'

'Perhaps this gentleman would prefer to dance with me.' Pauline's voice interrupted her and the smile she gave Lily told her that she'd not forgiven her for taking Bert away. Presumably this was her way of getting her own back. Well, she was welcome to him.

'Perhaps he would.' Lily smiled sweetly at him. 'Pauline, this is . . .?'

'Charlie Alexander,' the man said. 'And I'd be delighted to dance with you. I feel you're owed a dance.' He looked pointedly at Lily.

Lily folded her arms across her chest and stared at him challengingly. 'Careful, Charlie boy. It'll hurt when you fall down from that high horse.' Then, seething, she left them to go in search of some familiar faces.

Spotting Edie sitting at a table chatting to Jo, she went over and plopped down in a seat beside them.

'That man all but accused me of being some sort of floozy!' she said indignantly, waving her arm towards the crowded dance floor.

'Which man?' Edie asked.

'That one over there, dancing with Pauline. Thankfully she took him off me. Think she's cross I stole Bert away from her.'

'Huh! She's been on the sauce almost all night. If he's not careful, she'll have him up against a wall,' Jo said, her freckled face screwed up in disgust as she watched Pauline being manoeuvred around the floor. 'But can't say as I blame her with that one. He's a looker, ain't he?'

'Can't say I noticed,' Lily said airily. She wasn't about to admit she agreed.

'All right, Lil?' Dot's cheerful voice made her stand up with delight. 'Dot! Where've you been?'

'Who's that dish with Pauline?' Vi said. With her blonde hair down and clipped behind her ears, and her slanted eyes highlighted with eyeshadow, Lily had to admit she looked pretty. She wished she could say the same for Dot, but the girl's hair was standing out from her head, the heat and humidity having caused it to frizz even more than usual. Her face was make-up free, and her skirt and blouse made her look dumpy around the middle.

'Apparently, he's someone who doesn't like our Lily,' Edie said. 'Which makes a nice change.'

Lily nudged her. 'You attract your share.'

Edie grinned. 'I did have a bit of a dance with a yummy Polish pilot. Couldn't understand a word he said, so we had to resort to the language of love.' She giggled. 'He was a good kisser too. But then someone tapped him on the shoulder and he ran off.' She shrugged. 'I noticed a few RAF boys leaving. They've probably been pulled back to base.'

Jo was still watching Pauline narrowly. 'If that man prefers her to you,' she said to Lily, 'then he not only needs his eyes testing, but his head and all.'

Vi's eyes sharpened with interest. 'Don't you like Pauline?'

Lily hastily intervened before Jo could spread her gossip. 'Edie, Jo, these are my fellow trainees up the hospital, Vi and Dot.'

Out of the corner of her eye, she noticed a man come up to Charlie Alexander and say a few words. He nodded, then murmured something to Pauline before hurrying out of the door, leaving Pauline fuming in the middle of the dance floor, until a familiar figure in civilian dress took his place.

'Hey! Isn't that Dirty Dick?' Vi said, shuddering. 'What the hell is he doing here?'

'I saw her drinking with him over at the bar earlier. Downing them like they were going out of fashion, she was,' Jo observed.

Lily stared over at Pauline. Dick wasn't a lot taller than her and he was whispering in her ear. Finally, Pauline stood back and shook her head, stumbling away from him and going to sit down at a table, head in her hands.

Dot had noted the scene too. 'Maybe I'll just go over to make sure she's all right.'

Lily followed her. 'What was all that about, Paul?' she asked when they reached the girl.

Pauline sat up and hastily wiped her eyes. Her lipstick was smudged and the carefully pinned victory roll was looking more like a bird's nest. 'What?' she said with a false smile.

'You and Dirty Dick over there.'

'Oh, nothing. He was just being his usual dirty self.' She grabbed her bag and took out her hip flask, taking another healthy glug.

'Haven't you had enough?' Lily asked with concern.

Pauline glared up at her. 'It's none of your business. And if you don't think I'm good enough for your brother, then at least have the guts to say so.'

Lily frowned.

'What? You think you can just pull your brother away when me and him are having a fine old time and I wouldn't say anything?' She stood up, wobbling slightly. 'Well, thanks a bunch.' She stumbled off in the direction of the toilets.

Lily made to follow but Dot caught her arm. 'Don't. You'll only make things worse. I'll go.'

Lily smiled gratefully at her. Dot was probably right, but if she was going to be sharing a room with Pauline for the foreseeable, she didn't want to fall out with her.

Chapter 11

Marianne ran out of the entrance and down the steps, turning her head to see if she could spot her brother. But with no street lights, it was impossible to see anything. She walked a few steps along the road, listening carefully, and finally she was rewarded with a low hum of conversation coming from around the corner of the town hall. She pressed up against the flint wall and inched along carefully, then stopped as she heard a voice.

'Thank you for today, Reenie,' Jimmy was saying. 'I was ready to kill Mum this afternoon before I spoke to you. In fact, thank you for everything. You've no idea how much your letters have helped me.'

So Bert had been right; they *had* been corresponding. But why hadn't Reenie ever mentioned it to her?

'Glad I could help. I don't know why you let your mum rile you like that.'

'Let's forget about her. I wanted to say something to you . . .' There was a pause.

'What is it?' Reenie whispered.

'I've known you a long time. But I've never really *seen* you. Do you know what I mean?'

Reenie laughed. 'Not really.'

'You've always been my sister's friend. But . . . Well, I feel we've grown close over the past weeks, and this afternoon I realised how much I like being in your company.'

'And I like being in yours. But . . . Hang on, you're not trying to tell me—'

'I'd like to get to know you even better.'

'Come on, Jim. I'm what, five years older than you? You're like my kid brother or something.'

There was silence for a moment. Then Jimmy's voice came again. 'Is that something a kid brother would do?'

Marianne held her breath as she waited for Reenie's reply. What the hell was her brother playing at? How could he lead Reenie on like this?

'N-no . . .'

'And did you feel like I was your kid brother when I kissed you.'

Reenie giggled. 'I haven't been kissed in so long, who knows?'

'What's wrong with the men around here? I think you're quite irresistible.'

There was silence again, and Marianne peeped round the corner, aghast as she saw the two shadowy figures kissing. She bobbed her head back. She should go; she shouldn't spy on them like this. But . . . she couldn't let this happen.

'Do you mean this, Jim?' Reenie said after a moment. 'I mean, you're a handsome man, everyone says so. But look at me. I'm hardly Mae West.'

'I don't want Mae West. I want a real woman. A woman who knows me, understands me. And as for age . . . I want someone mature.'

Reenie snorted. 'Well, that makes me feel even better than when Mum calls me an old maid.'

'You are nothing like an old maid. You are kind, pretty and easy to talk to . . .'

The conversation stopped and she could hear the sounds of more kissing. Feeling sick, Marianne turned round and walked back to the entrance. Alfie came out as she reached the door.

'What's going on?' He caught hold of her hands.

'Jimmy's sweet-talking Reenie and it's just not right! You have to stop him!'

'Hang on there! A man doesn't get involved in another bloke's romancing.'

'But it's not romancing, is it? It's Jim trying to be someone he's not. And Reenie doesn't deserve that. He's only picked her cos he knows her and knows she's never had a boyfriend. It's . . . it's . . .' Words failed her for a moment. 'It's dishonest!'

Alfie sighed and pulled her into a hug. 'Maybe he really does like her.'

'Of course he doesn't. He loves Colin.'

'Some people find they love both sexes. It's all about the person.'

Marianne pulled away from him. 'How you know so much about this stuff makes me wonder about you.'

'I've just been around the block a bit. Seen a few things. And maybe that's what's happening with Jimmy.'

'No! He's trying to prove he's like everyone else, so he's decided to woo Reenie. Someone he feels safe with, someone gentle and kind. *That's* what this is about. He's *using* her.' She pulled away and started to pace. 'I *know* my brother, Alf. He's told me everything about himself. And I know for sure he feels nothing but friendship for Reenie. *My* friend, for God's sake! I mean, if he was going to do this why couldn't he have picked someone I didn't know!'

'I just don't think you should interfere.' He put his arm around her shoulders. 'Jimmy and Reenie are grown-ups; they can make their own decisions. Come back inside and mind your own business.'

Reluctantly, she went with him. But the first moment she could she was going to have stern words with Jimmy.

∞

Lily watched anxiously for Dot and Pauline's return. It felt like they'd been gone for hours and she hoped Pauline hadn't passed out in the loos. 'I'm not surprised she's in a state, the amount she's been drinking. She started the minute we left the hospital,' she said to Edie.

Someone touched Lily's shoulder. 'Fancy a dance?'

Lily spun round then recoiled as she saw Dick Brown. 'No, thank you,' she said coolly. 'As you can see, I'm talking to my sister.'

Dick looked at Edie and smiled coldly. 'Your sister, eh?' He took her hand. 'You don't look alike.' He planted a wet kiss on the back of Edie's hand. 'But always a pleasure to meet another Castle.'

Edie grimaced and pulled her hand away, wiping it on her skirt.

'Look, just go away, will you, Dick,' Lily snapped.

Dick grabbed her round the waist. 'Aww, don't be like that, Lily. I've been waiting years for a girl like you.'

Enough was enough. The man had tormented her all day, and she wasn't going to allow him to ruin her evening. Reaching up her hand, she slapped his face hard. 'I said,' she gritted out, 'leave us alone.'

Bert appeared at her shoulder. 'You got a problem, sis?' he asked.

'Yes. This man is hassling me and Edie.'

Bert took Dick's arm. 'Perhaps it's time you left, mate.'

Dick looked up at Bert, assessing his chances, but it was clear who'd be the winner. Bert was tall and well muscled and Dick barely reached his chin.

'Another Castle? Well, well. You lot breed like rabbits, don't you? Or should I say rats?'

Bert tugged him away. 'That's it. Out!'

Jimmy came up then, Reenie hovering behind him. 'Need a hand, Bert?'

Dick stared at Jimmy. 'And another one? Seems tonight is a bit of a family reunion, eh? Very cosy.' He shook his arm free. 'I can see meself out. As for you, Lily, I'll be

116

seein' you tomorrow.' He gave her a wink, then turned on his heel and disappeared.

'Bloomin' heck,' Reenie said. 'What was that all about?'

Edie shuddered. 'Ugh. I can see why Pauline was so upset. What a creep.'

Vi nodded. 'Dirty Dick we call him. And we all try to stay out of his reach.'

Reenie took Jimmy's arm. 'Lucky you were here, Jim. What a hero.'

Lily nudged Edie, eyebrows raised, while Bert stared pointedly at his brother. 'Hello,' he said suggestively. 'What's all this then?'

'Mind your own business,' Jim said, smiling slightly.

Well, Lily thought, if Reenie could restore Jimmy's good humour, then she was happy for the two of them.

On stage, Alfie started to play 'Horsey Horsey', always a signal for the end of the evening, so Edie jumped on to Bert's back, while Jim turned to Reenie. 'You want me to carry you out?'

Reenie hesitated. 'Only if you're sure? I'm no lightweight.' She laughed nervously.

He turned, holding his arms out behind him so she could jump on to his back. Reenie looked delighted as Jimmy jogged towards the exit with her.

Marge and Marianne came to stand by Lily. 'What have I missed?' Marge exclaimed, watching Jimmy and Reenie, her pencil-thin eyebrows raised so high they had practically disappeared into her hair.

117

Lily shook her head. 'I honestly have no idea. Jimmy and Reenie . . .? She's miles older than him!'

'Not *that* much older, if you don't mind,' Marge said. 'Even so, I wouldn't have predicted that in a month of Sundays. Reenie's always been so besotted with Wilf Perkins that she's never looked at another man. What do you reckon, Marianne?'

'They're only having fun. It's hardly marriage, is it?' Marianne's tone was short, but as the music ended at that moment, and the main lights came on, Lily didn't get a chance to comment. But it was odd, she thought. She had the distinct feeling that Marianne wasn't happy about Jimmy flirting with Reenie, and she couldn't understand why. If they wanted to have a bit of fun, then why not? And Reenie was a sweetheart, so surely no harm could come from it.

∽

Out in the vestibule, crowds of people were standing around shouting to each other. Lily looked around for Dot and Pauline and was relieved to see them emerge from the loos, Dot's arm around Pauline's waist. As they approached, Lily could see that her friend was swaying, her eyes glassy.

'Uh-oh. Lucky you're coming home with us, Paul. Not sure you'd make the walk back on your own.'

Bert came over and Pauline grabbed his arm, hugging it to her cheek. 'Bertie, Bertie, lovely Bert. You'll take a poor girl home, won't you?' She blinked up at him, attempting to look pleading, but her lipstick was smudged and she seemed as if she was about to collapse. She grabbed his lapels. 'And maybe we can take a little walk, eh? Down by the sea? Find a quiet spot and—'

'God's sake, Pauline!' Lily burst out before she could embarrass herself any more. 'Leave it out, will you.'

'What do you care?'

Bert held his hand up. 'No need to worry about me, Lily. And who am I to argue if a pretty girl wants to take me for a walk by the sea?' He grinned down at Pauline.

Pauline gave Lily a triumphant look. 'At least your brother knows how to treat a woman.'

'How you getting back to the castle, Marge? I can see you back, if you like?' Bert said.

Pauline moaned, her arm going possessively round Bert's waist. 'She'll be fine. I want it to be just you an' me.'

'Thanks, Pauline,' Marge said drily. 'But you don't need to bother, Bert. I've already arranged to walk back with some of the girls.' She looked around. 'And as it seems that Reenie's gone off with your brother, I'll love you and leave you.' She gave Marianne a kiss then strolled over to a group of Wrens who were waiting for her by the door.

'Right, so who am I walking home?' Bert said.

'You go ahead,' Marianne said. 'I'm waiting for Alfie.'

'That's code for get lost, I want to walk home with my fiancé by myself,' Edie said drily.

'Dunno how someone like you managed to nab a man like that,' Pauline slurred. 'He's lovely. Almost as lovely as you, Bert.'

Marianne looked as if she'd been slapped, and Bert swung Pauline up and over his shoulder. 'That's enough from you, young lady. Let's get you home.' He strode briskly to the door, Pauline's hands hitting him on the backside as she giggled drunkenly.

Lily shook her head. 'Take no notice, Marianne. The girl's drunk as a skunk.'

'Like I said, Lil. She's trouble. You need to watch your back with her,' Edie cautioned.

Lily shook her head. 'She's just had too much to drink, that's all. She'll have a head on her at work tomorrow that's for sure.'

Alfie emerged and grabbed Marianne around the waist. 'Ready to go, love?'

Marianne laughed, her doubts swept aside by his effusive greeting. 'Sooner the better.' She planted a kiss on his lips and leant back to look up at him.

'God, you're lovely,' he murmured, as he pulled her back in for another kiss.

Lily coughed exaggeratedly and Alfie let Marianne go. 'Sorry. But how can anyone resist your sister?' He tucked Marianne's hand through his arm. 'Come on then, you lovely ladies. Let's get you home for some beauty sleep. Did you all enjoy yourselves?'

'It was grand. All except Dick bloody Brown and that bloke who thought I was trying to steal you from Marianne.' Lily had almost forgotten about him after the drama of Pauline and Dick.

Marianne's brow wrinkled. 'What bloke?'

'Tall, dark hair, brown eyes. Looks a bit like Cary Grant. Said his name was Charlie Alexander.'

Alfie laughed. 'Well, you certainly examined him carefully, eh? Dr Charlie's setting up a hospital at the barracks. He seems like a good bloke.'

'He was nice,' Marianne added. 'But now I come to think of it, he was staring at you a bit strangely, Lily. Maybe he was less worried about me and more jealous of Alfie,' she said archly.

Lily hit her on the arm. 'Think I preferred it when you stayed in the kitchen and never said a word.' They walked through the blackout curtains and down the steps. Around them, people were shouting and singing as they hurried to get home before curfew, and Lily and Edie walked ahead, allowing Alfie and Marianne to have some privacy. As they reached Castle Street, Edie turned and shouted into the dark. 'Hey, you two, me and Lil were just wondering when the wedding's going to be.'

There was a pause as the two shadows stopped and seemed to stand staring at each other. Then Alfie shouted back, 'We thought next month.'

Lily grinned with delight. 'Looks like we better warn Mum we've got a wedding to prepare for!'

As the girls approached the café's back gate, they could hear Pauline drunkenly singing, 'Show Me the Way to go Home' and Bert's exasperated voice floated towards them in the darkness. 'For God's sake, shut up, Pauline.'

Lily giggled. 'Having fun?' she asked Bert as Edie pushed the gate open for him.

'No, I'm bloody not!' he growled. 'My bum's black and blue from her pinching it, and she's been singing loud enough to bring out the Luftwaffe. On top of which, I'm terrified she'll be sick down my back.'

Laughing, Lily and Edie hurried into the kitchen, Bert stumbling in behind them, with Pauline still singing at the top of her lungs.

Bert lowered her to the kitchen floor and she promptly collapsed, giggling, onto the black-and-white tiles.

'Bertie!' she cooed, looking up at him through a tangle of hair. 'Come and join me, Bertie Bertie, Bert.'

He leant down to help her up, at which point she grabbed his tie and pulled him down on top of her. 'There, that's better,' she sighed as she wrapped her arms tightly around him, while he struggled to release himself.

The door at the bottom of the stairs crashed open and Nellie, wearing her bright pink dressing gown with a yellow scarf tied over her curlers, stalked in. 'Will you lot—' she began, then stopped as she took in the scene. 'Albert Castle! Get up this instant!' she exclaimed.

Bert scrambled up, shamefaced. 'It wasn't my—'

Nellie held her hand up. 'I don't want to know. As for you, young lady—' she pointed at Pauline '—you better get to bed now. Lily, get her a couple of aspirin and plenty of water. And take a bowl up; don't want her being sick over the sheets – they've just been laundered.'

Pauline squinted up at her and grinned. 'Good evenin', Mrs C. Why have you got a c'nary on your head?' She went off into peals of laughter as Nellie shook her head and stomped back upstairs, slamming the door shut behind her, leaving her three youngest children snorting with helpless laughter.

Once they'd calmed down, it was clear there was no way Pauline could walk up two flights of stairs, so Bert carried her up to the bedroom and dumped her unceremoniously on the bed.

'That's the last time I offer to take a girl home,' he said, beating a hasty retreat.

Edie watched from the bedroom door, a wide grin on her face as Lily hovered by the bed, a bowl in her hand. 'I'll leave her to you then,' Edie said. 'Sleep well.'

Lily stared after her enviously, but she was soon distracted as a moan from the bed warned her that Pauline was about to be sick. She got the bowl in place just in time and held her friend's hair back from her face as she was violently ill.

Afterwards, Pauline lay back on the pillows, her arm over her eyes.

'Blinking heck, Pauline,' Lily snapped. 'All that bloody whisky – I'm not surprised you're sick.'

Pauline let out a sudden sob, and Lily sighed and sat down beside her on the bed. 'Hey, come on! It's all right.'

'It's not,' Pauline wailed. 'He'll kill—' She got no further before starting to sob again.

'It's all right, love,' Lily said comfortingly. 'No one'll kill anyone.'

'You don't understaaand,' she wailed. 'He will. He'll kill her.'

'What are you talking about?'

Pauline just shook her head and buried her face in the pillow. Lily watched helplessly as her friend's body shook until finally the sobs became whimpers and she fell asleep.

Wearily, Lily got undressed and lay down on the other bed with a groan. What a night. She'd never seen Pauline like this before. She hoped her drinking tonight was a one-off, because if this became a regular thing, her mum wouldn't stand for it. And what did she mean by *He'll kill her*? Sighing, she turned over; it was probably just drunk talk.

She thought back over the rest of the evening, and grinned as she remembered Jimmy and Reenie; she couldn't see that lasting two minutes, but still, good luck to them. Her thoughts darkened, though, as she remembered Dick Brown and his insults. She didn't like to admit it, but the man was starting to scare her. Was that who Pauline was talking about? Had he threatened her in some way? They'd just have to steer clear of him as much as they could. Luckily, she wouldn't have any trouble avoiding that Charlie Alexander. A picture of his face came into her mind: brown hair, brown eyes, tanned skin and deep dimples that carved lines down his cheeks when he smiled. Although he hadn't smiled at her; just at Pauline. Ah well, she thought, you win some, you lose some. And he was clearly arrogant and opinionated, so it was probably for the best.

Chapter 12

The alarm went off at five thirty the next morning, and Lily groaned as she turned it off and switched on the bedside lamp. Pauline was snoring loudly in the bed next to her, a tangle of brown hair spread across the pillow.

Lily reached over and poked her. 'Wakey-wakey, sleepyhead.' When there was no response, she threw back her blankets, climbed out of bed and sat down heavily beside Pauline, giving the eiderdown a firm slap. 'Pauline! Wake up.'

Pauline let out a moan as she turned over and peered up at Lily through red-rimmed eyes. 'Go away,' she said. 'Can't you see I'm ill?'

'You will be if you don't get up. Matron'll have your guts for garters. Come on.'

Pauline sat up and swung her legs to the floor, noting that she was still wearing Lily's dress from the night before. Suddenly, she put her head in her hands. 'Please tell me Bert didn't carry me home.'

'Bert didn't carry you home,' Lily said obediently.

'And I didn't pinch his bum or drag him down to the floor.'

'Nope. None of that happened either.'

Pauline looked up at her hopefully. 'Really?'

Lily laughed. 'No. Not really! And you told Mum she had a canary on her head.'

Pauline threw herself back on the bed and squeezed her eyes shut. 'Please just let me die.'

'No! Up!'

Reluctantly, Pauline got up and stumbled from the room, leaving Lily chuckling to herself.

By the time they had made their way downstairs, Marianne was already clattering about in the kitchen, humming as she added fresh coals to the range. A loaf of her home-made bread and some margarine and jam sat waiting for them on the small table at the side of the kitchen, as well as a pot of tea.

Lily ate hungrily standing up, while Pauline sat down at the table and pushed the bread away from her, but drank the tea down thirstily.

'I feel I should apologise to your mum,' Pauline said sheepishly. 'I made a fool of meself.'

'Best not do it now. She'll still be asleep and she's like an angry bear if you wake her,' Lily said through a mouthful of bread as she picked up her gas mask and cloak.

'Later then.'

Marianne turned to her. 'Don't worry, Pauline. We all make mistakes. Especially Mum.'

126

With a grateful smile, Pauline took a last swig of tea and followed Lily out of the back door.

❧

'Jesus Christ, Pauline. How much did you put away last night?' Vi's words rang out across the canteen as the girls joined her and Dot at their usual table for a quick cup of tea before starting work. 'The way you were slobbering over Bert at the end was embarrassing,' she said disapprovingly.

Pauline dropped into a chair, laying her head on the table. 'Don't remind me.'

Lily laughed. 'Never mind. Bert's used to women throwing themselves at him. He'll just think it's funny. At least it wasn't that Charlie bloke; the one with the stick up his bum.'

Pauline looked up. 'Charlie Alexander! I'd forgotten about him. Dreamy velvety-brown eyes. Wouldn't mind seeing him again.'

'I thought you liked my brother?'

Pauline winced and put her hand to her head. 'No chance of that now! He won't speak to me again.'

'Oh well, plenty more fish in the sea.' Lily stood up. 'You reckon your stomach can handle emptying chamber pots, Paul?'

'If you value your life, don't even mention those words to me.'

'Stick with me,' Dot said kindly. 'You can mop and I'll do the sluicing, and soon you'll feel better. Best thing for you is to bring it all back up, get it out of your system.'

'If I'd been at home, I would have tried to.'

Lily wrinkled her nose. 'That's disgusting.'

'Best thing for you when you've overdone it.'

Lily wondered how often her friend overdid it; it seemed it wasn't unusual for her.

Pauline stood up reluctantly. 'Anyway, I hear one more word about last night, you're dead. I mean it!'

Even Vi laughed at this as they made their way out of the canteen. As they got through the door, Sister Murphy appeared and caught Lily's arm. 'Matron wants a word with you, Nurse Castle. Now, if you don't mind,' she said. 'You three, come along with me.'

The others looked at her curiously, but Lily just shrugged. She had no idea what she could have done to warrant a visit to Matron's office and her stomach clenched with nerves.

Hurrying up the stairs, she tapped tentatively on the wooden door that stood beside the hospital's main entrance.

'Enter,' Matron's voice rang out.

Lily stepped inside, relieved to see that Matron was smiling at her. 'Ah, Nurse Castle, please come in and take a seat.'

She perched nervously on one of the straight-backed wooden chairs opposite Matron's desk and watched the woman shuffling papers about. Finally, she found what she needed and looked up. 'I've had a request,' she said, holding the piece of paper out towards her. 'And as we can't spare any of our more experienced nurses, you seem to be the next best thing.'

Lily read the official-looking letter curiously. It was from a Colonel Partridge asking for a nurse to help out at the barracks at Drop Redoubt. She looked up. Did Matron mean to send her up there? She felt a little buzz of excitement at the thought of being let off cleaning duties for the day.

'What do you think?' Matron asked.

'I'd be more than happy to help,' Lily said.

'Good.' The woman smiled at Lily approvingly. 'I've had good reports about your work in the recovery room yesterday, so I think this might be very beneficial. The doctor up there is on his own, so no doubt he'll need help with all sorts of things you wouldn't get to do here. If you do well today, it might become a regular thing – if we can spare you, that is. So collect your things and get going. The doctor's outside waiting to take you up there.' She gestured to the window, and Lily saw a khaki-coloured van with a canvas roof stretched tightly over the back sitting in the driveway.

Lily stood up. 'Thank you, Matron.'

Once she'd collected her cloak and bag, Lily hurried outside, excited to be off on a new adventure.

'Oh!' she exclaimed as she rounded the truck and saw a tall, dark-haired figure leaning against the vehicle smoking a cigarette. Her spirits sank; this was all she needed. Still, at least it cleared up one mystery. If Charlie Alexander was the doctor at Drop Redoubt, that must be where her brothers were as well, which was interesting. As far as she'd been aware the place had been empty for years.

'Dr Alexander?'

He looked round at the sound of her voice. '*You're* Nurse Castle?' he said, raising his eyes to the sky. 'Of all the nurses in the hospital, I get you. You don't look old enough to have left school, let alone be a trained nurse. Don't tell me you offered so you could see Bert again!' He paused suddenly as if he'd just realised something. 'Oh. Your surname's Castle,' he said.

Lily fluttered her eyelashes and put her hand to her chest. 'Gosh. Thank you so much for reminding me, Dr Alexander; I'd clean forgotten.'

'Which means . . .'

Lily gave him a smug smile. 'That's right; Bert is my brother and Marianne is my sister. Which makes Alfie my soon-to-be brother-in-law.' She folded her arms and raised an eyebrow challengingly. 'Perhaps you have something you'd like to say to me?' She tapped her foot with mock impatience.

Charlie sighed. 'You're right; it seems I owe you an apology. I jumped to all sorts of silly conclusions last night. I think that scene at the hospital yesterday morning didn't help. I'm sorry.'

Lily nodded. 'Doesn't mean you had the right to talk to me like that,' she said angrily. 'Or make insinuations about my behaviour with the prisoners. Do you know how much trouble I'd get into if people really believed I was having a relationship with a prisoner?'

His cheeks coloured slightly and he looked away, shamefaced. 'I really am sorry. I don't know why I said that to you yesterday. Especially as there was nothing to base my assumption on.' He took off his hat and held it to his chest, his brown eyes staring sincerely into hers.

'And do you swear never to jump to stupid conclusions again?' she asked.

'Scout's honour.' His dimples appeared as he smiled and, in spite of herself, Lily found she was smiling back. 'But that doesn't alter the fact that I was expecting someone older and with a bit more experience.' He threw the cigarette onto the ground. 'But I suppose beggars can't be choosers,' he grumbled as he opened the door for her.

Lily pursed her lips and climbed in. Couldn't the man just stick with an apology? she thought angrily. It wasn't her fault she'd not been training long. Still, at least spending the day up at Drop Redoubt meant that she'd be able to steer clear of Dick Brown, so she should be grateful for small mercies.

They sped through the town in an uneasy silence and as Charlie drove the truck swiftly up Military Road, Lily stared out of the window. She had lived in Dover all her life, but had never fully explored this part of Western Heights because it was said to be haunted by the ghosts of soldiers from the Napoleonic wars. She knew that Drop Redoubt was linked to the Citadel somehow and as far as she was concerned each structure looked as sinister as the other. She craned her neck out of the window as they approached the fortification, gazing up at the tall brick walls rising on either side of them. The top of the building, she knew, was covered with grass to camouflage it from the air.

Charlie slowed the truck as they approached a wooden bridge where sentries stood barring the way. After their identity cards were checked, they were waved on and soon they drew to a stop in front of an arched entrance. Charlie jumped out and came round to open the door for her. 'Come on,' he said shortly, turning to stride towards the entrance.

Lily stuck her tongue out at his back, then slammed the door and hurried after him through the arched doorway that led into a long passageway with a curved roof. Doors leading to smaller tunnels were dotted along the walls and dim electric lights ran the length of the ceiling, throwing long shadows on to the bricks. She shivered. 'I wouldn't like to be here on a dark night.' Despite herself, Lily moved closer to Charlie's tall figure.

'It's not so bad. Though—' he stopped and pointed to a flight of steps that presumably led up to the top of the fortification '—I often see a soldier wearing a red jacket and holding a musket right here. Friendly chap,' he said casually. 'I always tip my hat.'

'Are you joking?!' Lily breathed. 'There really are ghosts here?'

'Yup. But he seems a nice enough fellow. Look! There he is!' Charlie said suddenly.

'Where?' she squeaked, as she jumped closer to him, grabbing his arm as she strained her eyes to see what he was looking at. She saw nothing but the cold, dank brick wall.

Charlie chuckled, his dimples deepening as his eyes sparkled, and, just for a moment, Lily wished they hadn't got off to such a bad start, because when he laughed like that, he was much too handsome for her liking.

'Only joking. You can hold my hand, if you like.' Charlie held his palm out to her.

'I'm quite all right, thank you.' Lily walked past him with her nose in the air, ignoring the proffered hand.

'Wooooh.' The ghostly sound echoing off the brick walls made Lily jump again.

She whirled round as Charlie came towards her, his arms raised and fingers clawed.

Lily folded her arms angrily. 'Can you stop that! I know I was being stupid. But seriously, I don't like this place.'

Charlie relented. 'I'm sorry. Come on. Not much further. And maybe we can start again? I really do apologise for the misunderstanding last night, and for what I said yesterday morning. If we're going to work together, we should at least be able to be civil.'

Lily sighed and held out her hand. 'All right, let's shake on it. And from now on, don't jump to conclusions about me. For example, just because I've only just started my training, doesn't mean I have no experience. The reason Matron sent *me* is that I've helped out at the hospital for around two years now. So I'm not completely ignorant.'

Charlie smiled. 'You're right; I was being rude.' He took her hand and stared into her eyes earnestly. 'I really am sorry.'

Lily smiled. 'Good. You should be.' His palm was soft and warm and he was standing so close to her that Lily could smell his cologne. She inhaled. It was delicious. Woodsy and earthy; it suited him. Suddenly embarrassed, she quickly pulled her hand away.

'Shame,' he said. 'I meant what I said about holding my hand if you're scared.'

'I'm fine, thank you,' Lily huffed as they continued down the passage. Although, despite her words, she kept a careful eye out for any ghostly soldiers. Finally, he opened a door to the left, entering a large, domed room. Five beds lined the walls, two of which were occupied, though there was space for many more. Other than that, there were none of the usual comforts that patients enjoyed at the Casualty Hospital, such as a chair or a bedside dresser. In the centre of the room, a large table was piled with dressings and bandages, but not much else.

Lily raised her eyebrows. 'Where are the beds?'

'Good question. We've been running around Dover trying to source some, but it seems most spares have been taken to the caves and the rest have been snapped up by the hospital at the castle.'

'My mate Pauline's dad – you met her at the dance – works at Turpenny's furniture shop. I could ask her?'

Charlie grinned. 'You'll be worth your weight if you could find me some beds. Anyway, just so you know, the dark-haired chap at the end needs the most care. The orderlies have been doing their best, but they're not trained and if what you told me is true then you won't have too much trouble.'

'You do know I might not be able to come very often? You better hope that on the other days you don't need a nurse.'

'I'm hoping you can teach the rudiments to my orderlies. The rest, I can cope with. But it's not all bad. Look at this.' At the end of the room, Charlie opened another door, and switched on the light. It illuminated a bright, clean space, with an operating table in the centre, and metal shelves containing surgical equipment ranged around the walls. There were also trolleys with trays of scalpels and other tools standing ready, and a stainless steel autoclave for sterilising equipment plugged into a socket in the wall.

'Impressive!' Lily said. 'So,' she said, taking off her cloak, 'where do you want me to start?'

'The dark-haired lad I pointed out earlier needs his dressings changed every two hours. Nasty shrapnel wounds to his legs that need sluicing constantly. The other one should be fine and I'll probably send him back to the barracks today. And, when you're not doing that, we could do with some help cleaning out this room, which I'd like to use for critically ill patients.' He opened another door. In comparison to the ward and the operating theatre, this one needed to be thoroughly scrubbed.

'On my own?' she squeaked.

'We'll all muck in. But a nurse's eye would be useful.'

She sighed. 'All right. Show me to your supplies and I'll get started.'

Charlie clapped his hands together. 'Good. And by way of an apology, would you have lunch with me later?'

Lily's heart began to beat a little faster as she stared into his sincere brown eyes. He really was quite distractingly attractive. Finally, she smiled. 'All right then. Seeing as you ask so nicely.'

'Good!' Charlie said, brisk again. 'Everything you need for Private Daley is on the table. I've got paperwork to get on with. But if you need me, I'm just across the tunnel in the room opposite.'

Lily got to work, smiling to herself. She was beginning to think that maybe Dr Alexander wasn't so bad after all.

The day passed quickly, as, together with two order-lies, she swept, scrubbed and organised the side ward, and in between times she had to wash her hands and change her apron to go and check on Private Daley, who lay groaning while she changed his dressings. Both legs were covered in angry, seeping wounds, and she could understand why Charlie was being so careful about cleaning them.

She had just finished rebandaging the man's legs for the second time that day when Charlie came in yawning, his dark hair mussed from where he'd been running his fingers through it. 'I'm sorry I'm late for lunch,' he tutted. 'I've been wrangling with bureaucracy again. Come on, I've got a pile of sandwiches and the weather looks lovely. Let's eat outside.'

He led her up one of the many staircases and they emerged on to the grassy roof of the building that looked out over the Western Docks, the two arms of the jetty stretching out into the sea. There were fewer ships docked than usual, she noticed. After the terrible attacks both harbours had suffered, the navy seemed to be moving some of them out.

Lily ate the meat paste sandwiches hungrily. 'This beats the hospital canteen in the workhouse basement,' she said finally, wiping her fingers on the grass and lying back to stare up at the sky, hands behind her head. 'It's so quiet,' she said. 'Where are all the planes?'

'No idea. It is oddly quiet. I've got used to the constant drone and crash-bang-wallop noises that come with living here.'

'Maybe they've given up,' she said hopefully.

'Ha! More like they're preparing for something big.'

She sighed. 'Do you think they'll succeed?'

'Not if the RAF have anything to do with it. Those pilots are a plucky lot and they won't give in.'

She put her arm over her eyes to shade them from the sun, feeling relaxed in his company, their earlier tension now completely dissipated. 'Tell me something about yourself, Charlie Alexander. Are your mum and dad still alive?'

'Far as I know,' he said cheerfully. 'Dad's a butcher in Cambridge. I have him to thank for my fascination with cutting up bodies.' He grinned down at her and she wrinkled her nose.

'You know, I always fancied being a doctor. But ... well, Mum just couldn't afford to pay for the training and I'm not sure I'm clever enough anyway. How did you manage it?'

'Scholarship. Worked and worked and managed to get in to Cambridge. You should go for it. I think you'd make a fabulous doctor.'

She smiled. 'Not as if you know enough to be any judge.'

'Well, your matron seems to think highly of you. And I can see that you're intelligent and you have compassion by the way you've been treating Private Daley. Pretty much all you need.'

She stared up at his face and again felt a flutter in her stomach. She wasn't lying when she said she'd like to study medicine, but she'd never seriously thought it would happen for a girl like her from the market square in Dover. Somehow, though, this man was making her believe she could.

'Tell you what. Why don't I get Mum and Dad to send me some of my medical books. Plus, it'll give me a good reason to come back and see you.'

'Would you really?' she asked eagerly.

'I really would. They might take a month or so to arrive, but when they do I can run them down to you.'

She sat up and touched his hand. 'Thank you, Charlie. That means a lot to me. Could you drop them at Castle's Café in the market square?'

He grinned at her. 'If only I'd known this is all it would take to get you to be nice, I'd have done it last night.'

She huffed out a laugh. 'You were too busy insulting me.'

He held her gaze. 'I know. I was an ass. Truth is, though, I was just a tiny bit jealous of Bert and Alfie. The reason I spoke to you yesterday morning was because I wanted you to notice me. But I made a complete hash of it. Then when I saw you again, I wanted you to be dancing with *me*. If I'd known all I needed to do was give you a medical book to grab your attention, I'd have brought some with me and dumped them at your feet.'

She laughed. 'Oh, stop it. I've already forgiven you; you don't have to flatter me to get in my good books.'

'I mean it, Lily.' He held her gaze, his eyes serious. 'I seem to have taken a bit of a shine to you. What do you say you and I go out one evening? Maybe to the cinema?' He asked casually, but his fingers were tearing nervously at the grass.

Lily's stomach swooped. He was asking her out! She smiled, delighted. 'I'd say yes. After medical books, the pictures are my favourite thing.'

'Monday?' he asked hopefully.

'Yes, let's. It'll be fun.' She glanced at her watch. 'But right now, I better get back to work, or my boss'll send me back to the big bad hospital up the road.'

Charlie stood up and stretched his arms above his head. 'I promise you he won't. I wish I could have you here every day.'

She gave him an arch look.

'Just in a professional capacity!' He held his hands up.

'Shame,' she said cheekily. 'Because—'

Her words were cut off by a terrific crash over to the right of them and they both dived to the ground, lying prone, their heads up, eyes searching the sky for planes. But there weren't any.

'What was that?' Lily said, sitting up and staring around.

Charlie squinted out over the sea. 'I have no ide—' Another crash made them both drop again. This time, below them, near the trees, something exploded and great gouts of earth shot into the sky.

'Jesus Christ,' Charlie breathed in alarm. 'Keep low!' he shouted as, catching Lily's arm, he hauled her over to the stairs, shoving her down in front of him, as somewhere down below in the town, another loud explosion sent Lily's heartbeat into overdrive.

Chapter 13

It was a busy lunchtime in the café when an explosion echoed down the hill and in through the open door. Every head went up, as the customers looked around in bemusement. There had been no siren and the sky had been uncharacteristically quiet that day.

Gladys squeaked in shock as she dumped a plate in front of a group of soldiers and scrambled to the door to join the crowd in the market square who, as one, had stopped to stare up into the clear blue sky.

Jasper was sitting at his usual table by the kitchen door, tucking into Marianne's tasty rabbit stew and mash, and he rose immediately, rushing through the tables to join Gladys.

Nellie stared around the room. 'What the hell was that?' she exclaimed as Donny thundered down the stairs from the apartment above.

'Mum, we're being attacked!' he yelled, running into the café.

Some of the soldiers stood, putting their steel helmets on in readiness. 'This is it,' one of them said grimly. 'The invasion has started.'

'You can't be serious?' Nellie said, as her stomach swooped with nerves.

Jasper returned. 'Everyone get down to the basement NOW!' he shouted, as another boom shook the windows.

Nellie shoved Donny into the kitchen. 'Get downstairs, lad, and try not to worry.' She turned back. 'But what *is* it, Jasper?'

Jasper was jamming his helmet onto his head. 'I don't know, Nel, but I don't like it. A bomb's dropped near Snargate, I think. Whatever it is, you need to get this lot to safety!' He ran for the door, knocking into Gladys, who was coming back in, her face pale with shock.

'Don't go, Jasper! It's too dangerous.' Nellie's voice was shrill as she grabbed the birdcage, in which Polly was squawking and flapping her wings, and clutched it to her chest.

Jasper turned and flexed his arm at her. 'Don't worry about me, love! It'll take more than the Nazis to bring me down.' He winked and ran out.

Nellie watched him leave, her heart in her mouth. She was always worried about him during the air raids, but at least she understood the dangers then. But this? This could be anything. And if the soldier was right and the invasion had started, then they'd be sitting ducks, waiting for the Nazis to come and gun them all down while they cowered in the dark.

'Come on, Mum.' Marianne took her arm. 'Do as he says. He'll be fine.'

Nellie swallowed, trying to bring her fear under control as she allowed Marianne to lead her to the basement. She wasn't used to having someone take charge of her, but just this once she felt paralysed by uncertainty and fear – fear for the community she loved and for the foolish old man who'd run out into certain danger as though a strong arm and a tin helmet would be enough to protect him from whatever had just landed on their town.

∽

When the all-clear sounded, everyone in the basement at Castle's Café breathed a sigh of relief. They'd sat for the past hour in tense silence, listening to the muffled crashes and explosions, and straining to hear the telltale drone of a plane. But there'd been nothing.

As they emerged, Nellie made her way out of the back gate and into the market square. Dust and smoke were swirling in the air, and around her people were venturing out, looking puzzled and shocked.

'You got any idea what that was?' she called over to Phyllis Perkins, who was standing outside the fishmonger, hands on her hips and a bemused expression on her face.

Ethel Turner came out of the grocery store and the three women met in the centre of the square, staring down to the seafront, where a cloud of dust could be seen rising up into the sky.

'Not a clue, Nel. All I know is that it's scared the wits out of me.' Phyllis shuddered. 'One minute we're serving fish, the next *Boom!* But no planes.' She looked up again at the empty sky.

By this time, several more people had congregated in the square.

'It's started.' Gladys was standing in the doorway of the café. 'Saints preserve us, we need to leave now!'

'Oh, stop being so daft,' Nellie exclaimed. 'I don't see Nazi soldiers, do you?'

'They're sly ones, though,' Lou Carter growled. 'They could have been here all along, just waiting for the signal.' She pointed towards the sea, glinting blue under the bright sun. 'Any moment now, they'll be comin' up the beach, and I for one won't go down without a fight!' She marched over to her stall, and after fishing around under the counter, she came out brandishing a pistol. 'Who's joinin' me?' She looked around at the few men in the group, most of whom had fought in the last war. 'You've still got your pistols. They might need a bit of oilin' but they'll do!'

'Oh, I feel much better now,' Nellie said sarcastically. 'Lou Carter and a group of old men with guns running around the place sounds more dangerous than Hitler himself walking in to order a piece of pie. No, if it were an invasion, then we'd be hearing guns going off all around.'

Jasper puffed up then. 'Shells!' he called. 'Bloody shells from France! That's what the word is.' He removed his helmet and rubbed at his bushy grey-blond hair. 'One landed down on the front, and there's more damage up on Western Heights.' He shook his head. 'They keep on like this, the whole town'll be rubble before we know it.'

'There could be more at any moment. Quick, back to the shelters!' Gladys ran over and grabbed Nellie's arm, trying to pull her back inside.

'For the love of God, stop your wailing, Gladys. We start panicking now, we'll be dead by tomorrow for sure.'

'She's right, though, Nell. It was already bad enough, but if this keeps on, we might all have no choice but to leave,' Phyllis Perkins said.

'You can do whatever you please, but I'm going nowhere,' Nellie said staunchly, but then she sighed as she looked around her beloved Market Square, imagining the havoc the shells could wreak on it without warning. 'How are we supposed to carry on when they just keep finding more stuff to chuck at us?'

Jasper put his arm around her. 'Hey, Nell, we'll find a way, right? We can't let those buggers chase us out of our homes!'

Nellie leant her head against his shoulder briefly, then stood up straighter. 'Come on, everyone, back to work. Like Jasper says, we can't let the buggers beat us. And if anyone needs a bit of help, send 'em my way. Castle's will do what we can to make sure folk don't go hungry.'

'You're one in a million Nellie Castle.' Jasper patted her shoulder fondly.

Nellie looked up at him. 'Yeah, and so's Hitler,' she said sardonically. 'Anyway, let's get back to it before the next bloody siren goes. Anyone fancy a cuppa?'

'Love to, but best get on. The queue was a mile long before this all started.' Ethel Turner grabbed her husband by the arm. 'Come on, old-timer. Let's make sure people can at least get some dinner tonight.' They trotted across the square and disappeared under the red and white awning above their shop.

There was a general murmur of assent as people started to disperse, most of them returning to the queues they'd been forced to leave, but despite this pretence at normality, everyone was tense, staring around fearfully, wondering if this was the beginning of the end they'd all been dreading.

'Let me get you a cuppa at least, Jasper.'

'Can't stop now, love. Gotta go and make my report.' Suddenly, there was a whistling sound above them and, a few seconds later, a crash came from the direction of Snargate Street. As one, the people in the square hunched down, hands over their heads while Jasper started to run down King Street, shouting at people to take cover.

'Another one!' Gladys screamed as she ran back inside. 'This is it! We're all going to die!'

Nellie hurried after her and put her arm around her friend's shoulders, pulling her tight against her side. 'Stop this, Glad! You're not helping. Get back downstairs and calm down.' Despite her brave words, though, Nellie's hands were shaking as she stood by the café door and called out. 'There's room in the basement for any that needs it.'

Then she stood aside as people rushed past and through to the kitchen where Marianne and Donny were holding the basement door open.

Chapter 14

'I think we should go and see what's going on?' Lily said as she and Charlie stood listening to the distant sounds of explosions. 'People might need our help.'

Above them, they could hear the ack-ack guns going into overdrive, causing the room to shake. But what was the point, Lily wondered, if there were no planes to shoot down?

Charlie nodded. 'You're right.' He grabbed a black bag from under his desk and a torch from the drawer, which he handed to her. 'Come on. The quickest way is through the tunnels. It'll bring us straight out onto Snargate.' With his free hand he grasped her arm and hustled her out of the room and towards some spiral stairs that led down into the hillside. Lily kept the torch's beam on the ground so they wouldn't trip over any unexpected rubble, and they clattered down the steep steps. After winding round three flights, Lily was starting to feel dizzy and she breathed a sigh of relief when they finally emerged into a large cavern. She stared around in amazement. Seating had been cut into the chalk walls, and people were sitting or standing in groups, talking anxiously about this new development. Against one wall, a stainless-steel urn sat on a large trestle table, cups and saucers laid out beside it. It seemed, though, that the urn was empty as people were ignoring it.

Charlie urged her on through a wide tunnel towards the entrance and emerged at the end of Snargate Street by the Masonic Hall. Lily paused briefly and looked up the steep hillside that rose behind the street, astonished that they had managed to come down from the top of Drop Redoubt right to the town, but she didn't have time to ponder for long. Beside her, Charlie was swearing roundly, and she followed his gaze. Snargate Street was clouded with dust and smoke, and, halfway down, a couple of buildings seemed to have collapsed. She followed him, stepping carefully over the smashed glass and rubble, as he made his way towards the damage, pausing beside a woman sitting on the pavement. Her face was grey with dust and she was holding on to a small boy who was screaming as blood poured down his face.

Further along, Lily could see a group of people digging in the rubble of the buildings. She spotted Jasper standing on the pile of bricks, handing what looked like a door back to the man behind him. 'Jasper,' she called, running towards him, while Charlie knelt beside the woman.

'Lily! That girl needs treatment. Can you help?' He gestured with his head at a slight figure lying in the road, while beside her a middle-aged woman screamed frantically, 'Doris! Wake up!'

Lily ran towards them and took the screaming woman gently by the arm. 'Let me have a look at her for you,' she said.

'Tell me she's not dead!' The woman started to sob.

148

Someone led her away while Lily knelt beside the figure and gasped. It was a girl she used to be at school with, she realised. Doris had left when she was fourteen to work in her family's newsagent's, and they'd not had a lot of contact since. She looked at the remains of the shop. The glass from the windows lay sparkling on the road like diamonds, and the doorway had been completely blown away. The poor girl must have been serving behind the counter when the shell hit.

Gently she put her fingers to Doris's neck, finding a faint pulse, but she had no idea what she could do for her. Scrambling up, she ran to Charlie who was cleaning the cut on the little boy's head.

'I'll do that. That girl needs you more.' She pointed behind her. Charlie nodded and ran towards the inert figure.

'It came out of nowhere,' the little boy's mother was muttering. 'One minute we was walkin' down the road. Next, wham!' She shook her head and, clasping her hands around her knees, started to rock backwards and forwards.

'All right, love,' Lily soothed as she cleaned the boy's cut and started to wrap a bandage around his head. 'You're safe now, and your boy's going to be fine.'

'But what was it?' she wailed.

'I don't know. But it's stopped now, so try to keep calm for your little one. You're scaring him.' The boy's screams had faded into whimpers now and he had stuck his thumb in his mouth. Finishing the job, she picked him up and held him out to the woman, who grasped his small body tight to her as she struggled to hold back her sobs. 'I'm sorry.

It's just the shock of it. I'll be right as rain in a jiffy,' she said bravely. 'Long as my little Peter's all right then we'll get through.' She kissed the top of her son's dusty head.

Hearing the welcome sound of an ambulance, Lily patted the woman on the shoulder and walked over to Jasper who was still with the group clearing the rubble of the collapsed buildings.

'Anything I can do, Jasper?' she called.

'Get back!' he replied urgently as he backed away from the building. 'Everyone! Get back! The whole lot's gonna come down.'

The crowd scrambled back as, with a groan, the building folded in on itself.

Lily stood with her hand over her mouth, her eyes stinging as a cloud of dust engulfed them. Charlie came to stand beside her and she gave him a questioning look.

He shook his head. 'There was nothing I could do,' he said sadly.

Lily glanced behind him and saw that Doris's mother had laid her coat over her daughter's face and was now lying, her head on the girl's chest, sobbing broken-heartedly. She tried to recall their time at school. Doris had always been in trouble, she remembered, and when she'd left, she'd burned her school skirt in the playground, and run off with her group of friends cackling. Lily smiled slightly at the memory. She'd been so full of life and mischief. Why hadn't she seen more of her once she'd left? Lily wondered. It was too late now. Her eyes filled with tears and she wiped her hand across her face.

Charlie put his arm around her shoulders. 'Can you do more? Can you go and check that man over there?'

Lily straightened up and nodded. 'Yes. Yes, of course.'

Gently, Charlie led her over to a middle-aged man who was sitting in a doorway, his eyes glazed with shock as he stared sightlessly ahead, before leaving her to help somebody else.

Jasper came over to her. 'What are you doing here? And who's that?' He nodded towards Charlie, who was talking earnestly to an ambulance driver.

'That's Dr Alexander. Runs the barracks hospital up Drop Redoubt. I was sent to help him today.'

Jasper took in her pale face and tear-stained cheeks and laid a gentle hand on her shoulder. 'Why don't you get off, love? There's plenty here to help.'

She shook her head. 'No. This is what I do now, Jasper. I can't crumble at the first challenge, can I?'

'That's the spirit. You're a chip off the old block, aren't you?' He smiled approvingly at her.

'Seems so.' Lily tried to smile back, but found her face was too stiff from trying to hold back the tears. 'Not sure whether that's good or bad.'

'Oh, I think it's good, love. Definitely good.' He patted her cheek affectionately.

Lily nodded gratefully. Jasper's words had given her the strength she needed to keep going, and she knelt down beside the injured man, speaking softly to him as she took his elbow, and with Jasper on his other side, they helped him to the ambulance.

Chapter 15

Once the all-clear sounded, news reached the café of the devastation in Snargate Street. Immediately, Nellie hauled out a large wicker basket from the pantry, and between them, she and Marianne filled it with the food that Marianne had prepared for distribution to any who needed it. It was becoming a well-oiled routine now, and within ten minutes, the basket was loaded onto the small trailer on the back of the bike, and Nellie was cycling down King Street.

As she turned into Snargate Street, she stopped, panting and squinting through the dust that still swirled in the air. After taking a flask from the voluminous pocket of her apron, she took a slug of tea and grimaced; no sugar. She wasn't sure she'd ever get used to drinking it without her usual three spoons.

She rubbed her backside. She was getting better at this cycling lark, after making half a dozen trips up to Houghton Without, but she didn't like it. Not one bit. She was trying out a new supplier tonight; someone much closer to home. The only problem was she wasn't sure she could trust them. Maybe she'd talk to Jasper about it. He was disapproving of the risks she was taking in buying extra food on the black market, but he understood her reasons. Marianne, of course, wanted her to stop altogether, so there was no point speaking to her. Not a risk-taker, her Marianne.

Her gaze was drawn towards the end of the street where two of the buildings had collapsed into each other. People were swarming around the ruins like ants, and when the crowd parted slightly, she saw Jasper's familiar figure. He had his arm around a girl in nurse's uniform, the blonde hair that was escaping from her cap gleaming in the sunlight. Lily! she realised in astonishment. What was she doing here? At that moment, Jasper stroked her daughter's cheek and smiled, his bushy head bending close to Lily's. Nellie's breath caught as she thought about how different her life could have been. She shook her head impatiently. 'You are a foolish old woman, Nellie Castle,' she said to herself as she got back on the bike and set off again, taking care to avoid the worst of the rubble.

Lily had just settled the man into the ambulance when she heard a familiar voice echo down the street.

'Jasper!'

Both she and Jasper turned and the sight that greeted them managed to bring a small smile to Lily's lips as she watched her mother wobbling towards them on the old café bicycle. Suddenly, the trailer bumping behind her tipped over and the basket spilled into the road.

'Hell's bells and buckets of stinking bloody gore!' Nellie's loud curses floated towards the group digging through the rubble and, as one, they turned to gape at her.

Jasper let out a loud guffaw and Lily heard several others join in. Today Nellie was wearing a bright orange summer dress, dotted with yellow daisies, and a yellow overall with pink, red and purple flowers. On her head was the tin hat Jasper had made for her, to which she'd attached a length of pink ribbon. Nellie's love of bright colours was frequently eye-watering, but in this scene of destruction, it provided a welcome distraction as people cheered. The arrival of Nellie Castle could only mean one thing: food.

'Bloody thing!' she cursed. 'And who put all those bricks in the way?'

'Nellie, love! Why didn't you send Donny?' Jasper called.

'Because I'm not a fool. That boy would have eaten half the food before he'd got down King Street, that's why.'

'All right, Mrs C. Least we can rely on you. Was hoping to see Mrs Palmer with the WVS van, but she ain't arrived yet!' A man holding a shovel over his shoulder mopped the sweat from his face with a dust-covered sleeve.

'That's right, Jack, you can always count on me! Spotted Mrs Palmer on the way as it happens. She's busy chatting to a journalist from the *Gazette*.' She pointed back up the road. 'A photographer's takin' photos while she pours tea and grins like a maniac.' She rolled her eyes. 'Only Nosy Palmer could make the shelling of Dover all about her. Come and get it then!'

Lily went to help her mother as she opened the basket to reveal several old biscuit tins.

'Here you go, folks,' Nellie called out, as people started to crowd around her. 'Marianne's sausage rolls, some sarnies and . . .' She opened the final tin with a flourish. 'Jam tarts. No tea, though, I'm afraid. Unless the leccy's still on and someone can boil up a kettle.'

'Thanks, Mrs C. Just what the doctor ordered,' said a man in a filthy white shirt and grey trousers held up with braces, as he grabbed one of the sausage rolls with one hand and reached for a tart with the other.

Nellie smacked it away. 'Oy! Don't be greedy, Cecil Dyson.'

'Mum,' Lily hissed at her, 'where did you get the supplies for all this? Sausage rolls? You said the sausage meat was only for use in the café when Donny asked for some the other day. If you keep insisting on feeding everyone we'll go out of business.'

'Oh hush, Lily. We're doing fine.'

'Girl's got a point, Nel. You seem to be feeding half the town.' Jasper raised his bushy eyebrows in query.

Nellie avoided their eyes by holding out a tin to a young woman with a baby on her hip. 'And one for the nipper as well, love. That's it,' she said in approval, as the toddler stuffed a tart into her mouth. 'Listen to the pair of you. We all have to make sacrifices, and if it means a little less for us, at least we're not leaving people to starve.'

Charlie ambled over and Nellie held out one of the tins to him. He took a sausage roll with a nod of thanks. 'Lily, it might be a good idea if you go back to the hospital in the ambulance. I think you may be needed there more than here with me.'

Nellie raised her eyebrows at Lily. 'Who's this?'

'This is Dr Charlie Alexander. I was sent to help him up at Drop Redoubt today. Charlie, this is my mother, Nellie Castle.'

Nellie examined him from the top of his dark head to his dusty black boots. When she raised her eyes back to his face, Charlie was smiling at her. 'Very pleased to meet you, Mrs Castle. I've heard a lot about you from your sons.'

Nellie smiled charmingly. 'You know my boys, do you? Don't believe a word they say.' She thrust the tin she was holding under his nose again. 'Here. Have a tart.'

Charlie took one gratefully. 'Mmm. Please pass on my compliments to Marianne. Alfie didn't exaggerate when he said she cooks like an angel.'

'Well, Dr Alexander, if you'd like to try some more of her food, you must join us for lunch on Sunday.'

Lily elbowed her mother in the side, but Nellie ignored her. Poor Charlie barely knew her and Castle lunches could be hit-and-miss affairs. The last thing he needed was to sit at a table full of her squabbling family.

Charlie shot Lily a questioning glance and she shook her head at him. He hesitated for a moment before turning back to Nellie. 'I'd be delighted,' he said, then grinned at Lily, who frowned back. 'But in the mean-time, I need to steal your very clever and capable daughter away.'

Nellie waved her hand. 'You get on, Lily, love. And I'll look forward to seeing *you* on Sunday, Dr Alexander.'

'Likewise,' Charlie shot back over his shoulder, as he took Lily's arm and hustled her towards the ambulance.

'You don't have to come, you know. It might be better if you didn't. It can be a bit . . . Well, just a bit.'

'In that case, I can't wait. I could do with some proper grub. Now get going, and I'll see you on Sunday.'

Lily sighed as she sat between the two stretchers, one containing a boy of about twelve, who was sobbing as he held his injured arm, and the other, the silently staring man she'd helped earlier. She turned her attention to the young boy and tried her best to make him comfortable as Charlie saluted her and shut the doors.

∽

'Well,' Nellie said to Jasper. 'He seems nice.'

'Didn't look like Lily was too keen on him coming on Sunday.'

Nellie sniffed. 'Sometimes people need a little push in the right direction.'

'You can't be serious? The girl's eighteen. She's got her whole life ahead of her. Don't you think you liking him will be more likely to turn her off?'

'Man like that? You underestimate the power of attraction, Jasper.'

Jasper grinned down at her. 'Oh, I don't think I do, Nel. It's you that does that.' He stared at her meaningfully.

Nellie blushed and turned away from him, collecting up the empty tins and depositing them back in the basket. 'I best be off.'

'Give me a sec and I'll walk back with you,' Jasper said, holding the handlebars of the bike as Nellie lifted her leg over the seat.

'Don't be silly. I can manage and it looks like you've still got plenty to do here. Oh, and Cecil,' she called over to the crowd of people who were once again attempting to clear the road of rubble, 'if I see Mrs Palmer, I'll send her your way, shall I?'

The man looked round and grinned. 'You do that. Don't think I don't appreciate your grub, but I could do with a cuppa right now.'

Nellie sniffed in annoyance. It grieved her that Mrs Palmer and the Women's Voluntary Service would always have one up on her, no matter how many tarts and sausage rolls Marianne made.

As she wobbled uncertainly back the way she had come, a green van turned into the road and trundled slowly towards her. With Cecil's words still stinging, Nellie stopped, got off the bike, and stood in the middle of the road. The woman at the wheel slowed and sounded the horn, gesturing for her to get out of the way.

Nellie went up to the open window. 'You wouldn't have a spare cuppa for an old woman who's been handing out food to the poor afflicted people of our town, would you?' She grinned at the woman smugly.

Mrs Palmer, her brown hair piled into a topknot and wearing a spotless white apron, stared down her nose at Nellie. 'As far as I can make out Market Square remains untouched, Mrs Castle. And I doubt very much you *ever* go short of tea. Now, if you'll just get out of the way I can get on with my work.'

'Down there, you mean? Them that have had their houses and businesses shelled to pieces and now have no food and no shelter? Don't you worry about them. I've made sure they've all had a bite to eat. Maybe if you weren't so busy posing for photographs, I might not have been needed. Still, no harm done, eh, Mrs P? S'long as they get help, that's the main thing.' She peered into the van. "Ere, you haven't got a biscuit and all? I'm famished after cycling here with a trailer full of food . . .'

Mrs Palmer sighed impatiently. 'I wasn't posing for photographs.'

'Really? That weren't you pouring tea at the counter while that gent told you to hold the cup higher and smile more? I'm sick of all these journalists poking their noses in our business. Hundreds of them every day standing on the cliffs watching men die. And then they go back to the Grand for a meal and a pint of beer. I had one in the café the other day with his hat and his camera and his smarmy grin.'

'I was publicising the services offered by the WVS,' Mrs Palmer replied primly. 'And if my face reminds people we're here to help, then who am I to say no to the journalists? But that's by the by. I've been meaning to come and talk to you. Last time we had the pleasure of a conversation you promised to help me in any way you could. And I have just the thing. I'll pop in one day soon and we can discuss it.'

Nellie's face coloured at the memory. 'When I promised that I was under extreme pressure. And if you so much as whisper what you learnt that day, you'll be sorry.' The last thing Marianne needed, Nellie thought, was for this woman to start blabbing about who Donny's real father was. He came from a prominent and well-known Folkestone family and if people discovered the truth it would bring unwelcome attention to Marianne and Donny, especially considering the number of journalists that were hanging around.

Mrs Palmer smiled innocently. 'You know I'm not one to gossip. But if people ask . . . Well, I'm not one to lie either.' She shrugged expressively and Nellie took a step towards her.

'You breathe one word, just one word of what you know, then I won't be keeping quiet about the skeleton in your brother's closet. There's a certain brothel madam in Folkestone who has some tales to tell about him.'

Mrs Palmer blinked. 'What are you talking about?'

Nellie smiled grimly. She and Marianne had found Donny being cared for in a brothel, and you could have knocked her down with a feather when she'd realised the madam was one of her childhood friends who she'd not seen for years. It seemed she'd left Dover after falling pregnant by Mrs Palmer's odious brother, Horace Smith, and had had to resort to prostitution in order to support herself and her baby.

'Your brother might be bashing the Bible hard now, but it weren't always that way, was it? Remember Hester Erskine?'

The other woman started the engine. 'I'd rather not know,' she said. 'As far as I'm concerned Horace can sort his own messes out. But you can expect a visit from me soon. Like it or not, if the past weeks have been anything to go by, then there's no point us being at loggerheads when we all need to pull together to help our community.'

Nellie nodded reluctantly and moved out of the road. 'Maybe you're right.'

'Good.' Mrs Palmer started to drive off, waving cheerily out of the window, leaving Nellie staring after her, a mulish expression on her face.

'That sounds like one nil to Mrs Palmer.' Jasper laughed as he walked towards her, having watched the exchange.

Nellie sniffed. 'We'll see about that. Still, she's got a point. We shouldn't be arguing with each other when we've got a bigger enemy to worry about.'

They were nearing the market square when the air raid sirens went off again. Nellie had been vaguely aware of the planes flying towards the Channel, but it was so commonplace that she'd not taken much notice. Now, though, as the familiar wail echoed around she stopped and looked up at the sky.

'Damn and blast the bloody Waffa and that bloody siren,' Nellie exclaimed. 'I expect you need to be off, love.'

Jasper nodded. 'That I do. So hurry to the shelter now, and I'll see you later.' He knocked his knuckles on Nellie's tin hat. 'Glad to see you're wearing this.'

'Suits me, don't you think?' Nellie grinned. 'Especially with the ribbon.' She swung her leg over the saddle. 'See you later,' she called, waving a hand in the air as she wobbled across King Street, the pink ribbon streaming out behind her like a banner.

Jasper shook his head as he watched her. That woman would be the death of him, he was sure. But he wouldn't have it any other way.

Chapter 16

Lily hopped down from the ambulance as soon as the driver opened the doors and hurried inside the hospital, leaving a couple of orderlies to help the patients.

As soon as she entered the basement, Sister Mackenzie called her over. 'What are you doing here?'

'Dr Alexander told me to come back with a couple of the injured from Snargate. Said he thought I'd be needed here more.'

Sister Mackenzie rubbed the back of her neck and sighed tiredly. 'Noah's Ark Road's been hit as well.' She nodded towards a man in an ambulance driver's uniform who was sitting on a hard-backed chair by the wall, his head in his hands as his shoulders shook with silent sobs. 'Poor love,' the sister said quietly. 'Sent out to Noah's Ark to help, only to find his house had been destroyed with his wife inside.'

Lily gasped. 'Is she . . .?'

The other woman nodded sadly. 'I'm afraid so. Could you find the pastor and ask him to come and comfort him? Then get yourself a cup of tea. You look as if you could do with one. The others are on their break at the moment.'

Lily nodded and raced off to do as she was told.

'What a day!' Lily slumped down into a chair in the canteen a few minutes later.

'Oh, so you're back then,' Vi said. 'Have fun with the dishy doctor, did you?'

'How did you know where I—'

Vi shrugged. 'Had to help unload an ambulance. Spotted you getting into the van with him. Honestly, I don't know why you keep getting the best jobs. Just cos you've done a bit of bandaging in your spare time doesn't make you a nurse.'

'Leave it, Vi. I'm not in the mood,' Lily sighed.

'We heard about the shelling. Terrible it is. Got a few injured in already. Did you see any of it?' Dot asked sympathetically.

Lily nodded and turned to Pauline. 'I was at Snargate. Do you remember Doris Massey?'

Pauline grinned. 'How could I forget her? Me and her got done stealing from the sweet shop one day.' She looked reflective. 'Dad were furious and banned me from seeing her again, but course I ignored him. Works down her dad's newsagent's on Snargate . . .' She trailed off as she noticed Lily's expression. 'Oh no. Not Doris.' Tears came to her eyes as Lily nodded.

Pauline stared sightlessly ahead of her. 'Poor little cow,' she whispered. 'Oh, the poor, poor cow.'

Dot put her arm around Pauline's shoulders. 'Hey. I'm sorry about your friend. Why don't you sit here for a bit longer? Me, Vi and Lily can cover for you.'

'Haven't we got enough to do?' Vi said. 'We've been covering for her hangover all day; she'll just have to get on with it like the rest of us.'

Pauline stood up. 'You're right, Vi. I do need to get on with it. No point sitting around moping when there's work to be done.'

Lily watched as her friend walked out of the canteen, her shoulders slumped. She was waylaid at the door by Dick Brown, who said something to her. Lily frowned. Last night he had reduced Pauline to tears, and now she watched as Pauline shook her head and pushed past him. The man stared after her, a slight smirk on his face, and when he turned and saw Lily watching them, he grinned maliciously at her. Lily shivered involuntarily.

She jumped as Dot clapped her on the shoulder. 'Come on, Lily. Time to get back.'

Lily took a last gulp of her tea and rose. She'd speak to Pauline about Dick later. Something was going on, and she wanted to know what it was.

With a stream of casualties coming in from the shelling, it wasn't until they were walking home that Lily got the chance to speak to Pauline. 'What did Dick say to you today?' she asked as they walked under the railway bridge at the end of Union Road. Tonight, the mood was very different from the previous evening when they'd both been looking forward to the dance. But it wasn't just them; it seemed as if everyone in Dover was moving more

165

carefully, looking warily about them, wondering what else might hit the town. She noticed, too, that, without exception, people had started to wear their helmets. She'd have to remember to wear hers tomorrow as well. She'd laughed when Jasper had brought them round, but he was right. They could save lives.

Pauline shrugged. 'Dick's full of it, that's all. You know what he's like.'

Lily looked at her friend sharply. Pauline was lying, she was certain of it. If it had just been him being his usual creepy self, it would never have upset her that way. Lily linked her arm through her friend's. 'Promise you'll tell me if he gives you any trouble,' she asked.

'I can handle him,' Pauline said staunchly, her jaw tense.

'I know you can. But still . . . Promise?'

Pauline softened slightly and squeezed Lily's arm. 'But what if it's something you don't want to hear?'

'What do you mean?'

'Nothing. Just asking.'

Lily didn't answer. Pauline was lying again. But what could Dick have to say that would upset her so much?

They walked the rest of the way in silence, but as they came to the market square, Pauline pointed to the steps of the covered market. 'Here, isn't that your Jimmy?'

Lily looked over. Two figures were standing behind one of the pillars; the man was tall with dark hair and wearing a corporal's cap. She watched in astonishment as he bent forward and kissed the woman he was with.

166

It was Reenie, she realised, noting the trousers and curly blonde hair. So it hadn't just been a little bit of flirting last night, she thought wonderingly. He really was interested in Marianne's friend.

Pauline whistled. 'I wouldn't have put them two together in a million.'

'Nor me. But it's none of our business. Come on, I don't want to spy.'

Nellie had the wireless on and was listening to the news as they walked in.

'Here she is,' she said. 'The angel of Snargate. You did good today, girl. Jasper was tellin' me how you helped.'

'I just did what I could, Mum. Like everyone else.'

'Still, you made me proud, love. Go and wash your hands and we'll have dinner.'

∽

'So,' Nellie said once they were all seated, 'tell me about this Dr Alexander.'

Lily groaned. 'Oh God, I forgot you invited him to lunch.'

Marianne started at that. 'You didn't, did you, Mum? And Rodney's bringing Marge ... How can I make one chicken stretch between—' she counted on her fingers '— eleven of us.'

'Oh hush. We've got plenty. And anyway, we got Pauline's rations now as well.'

'Reckon it'll be twelve,' Pauline said with some relish. 'We just saw Jim and Reenie canoodling on the steps by the market hall.'

Marianne gasped. 'What?'

'Yeah. Right cosy they looked, didn't they, Lil?'

'What? Uncle Jim and Auntie Reenie? Really? Are they getting married?' said Donny excitedly.

'No, they're not!' Marianne said sharply.

The others looked at her in surprise and she blushed. 'I mean, well, I'm just surprised, is all.'

'I'd have thought you'd be happy,' Nellie said. 'Almost as much as if Rod and Marge ever manage to get it together.' She waved her fork around. 'Which is why I got Donny to make sure Marge was invited on Sunday. Rodney's always needed a poke in the ribs to show him what's right beneath his nose.' She took a mouthful of corned beef.

'Are you saying *you* invited her?' Marianne said.

'Well, Rodney wouldn't do it off his own bat, would he? It's stuck too far up his arse.' She cackled at her own joke while Donny let out a snort of laughter.

'Gran, that's rude!'

'Ah, but it's the truth. Although I can't deny Jim and Reenie's a bit of a surprise.'

'Well, people go for all sorts, don't they, Mrs C?'

Lily was surprised by Pauline's tone; as if she was angry with Nellie about something.

'They do. I mean, look at your mum and dad. Odd couple if ever I saw one. Your mum was always the life and soul back in the day, and pretty as a picture. But your dad was a bad-tempered so-and-so—' She stopped abruptly, suddenly aware that she was talking

168

to the man's daughter. 'Sorry, love. Didn't mean anything by it.'

Pauline shrugged. 'It's no secret that he's got a temper. But at least he never hides who he really is.'

'What do you mean by that, Pauline?' Marianne asked.

'Just that some people aren't honest, that's all. They can trick you into believing they're one thing, then it turns out it was all a lie.'

'You're not wrong there,' Nellie said. 'Some of the stuff I know about folk round here would make your hair stand on end. But I'm not one to gossip.' She chortled.

'I just bet it would, Mrs C, I just bet it would,' Pauline said.

Nellie glanced up at her sharply. 'If you've got something to say, madam, then come out and say it.'

Pauline blushed and shook her head.

'Good. And I've not forgotten your behaviour last night, neither.'

'I'm sorry about that. It won't happen again.' Pauline seemed genuinely contrite.

Nellie patted her hand. 'Don't worry any more about it. We all make mistakes, after all. Important thing is we don't repeat them.'

'I won't touch another drop. Scout's honour.' She held up three fingers and Nellie nodded.

'Then we'll say no more about it.'

Marianne pushed her plate back and stood up. 'Right, well, I'm going down to make some bread and to see how

I can scrape together enough for a Sunday roast for twelve people. Don, you're on washing-up duty.'

'But, Mum, I'm going out to see Freddie.'

'No, you're not. You're washing up and then you're going to bed.'

Everyone stared after Marianne as she walked out of the room. Donny's eyes were round with shock. His mother was rarely cross with him, and he hadn't even done anything wrong this time. 'I don't have to, do I, Gran? I can go out?'

'You do as your mum says,' Nellie said. 'Although I can't imagine what's got into the girl. You know what the matter is, Lily?'

Lily shook her head. 'She seems annoyed about Reenie and Jim for some reason.'

Pauline laughed. 'Seems to me that I hit a nerve with what I said. Maybe Marianne's not as sweet and kind as you all think.'

'That's not true!' Donny said fiercely, jumping up from the table.

Nellie sat back in her chair and eyed Pauline narrowly. 'And here was me thinking you were genuinely sorry about yesterday. I don't know what your problem is, girl. But whatever's on your mind, don't go taking it out on those that don't deserve it. Especially when you're a guest in this house.'

Pauline looked down away. 'You're right. I'm sorry, Mrs C. It's just been a long, difficult day, what with the shelling and my friend Doris Massey dying.'

Nellie tutted sympathetically. 'I were right sorry about that, love. I didn't realise she was your friend.' She pushed her chair back and stood up. 'Now, let's see what they have to say about today's goings on in Dover, shall we?'

She went and sat in her armchair, clicking on the radio just as the bongs of Big Ben were played.

Lily stared at her friend, bemused. She knew Pauline was upset about Doris, but it was more than that. Something else was eating at her. And as for Marianne, she couldn't work out why she seemed so upset by the idea of Jim and Reenie being together. Personally, she thought it was sweet, and if Reenie could bring back the happy, cheerful brother she loved, then she was all for it.

Chapter 17

That night, once everyone had gone to bed, Nellie stayed on in the sitting room with a cup of cocoa listening to some big band music on the radio. She laid her head against the lace antimacassar and closed her eyes. It really had been a hell of a day, and Marianne was right; they didn't have enough to keep making the food drops and then there was the wedding to cater. Still, everyone would bring a little something for that, and hopefully she'd be able to get a few bits and pieces to help them out tonight.

'Mum, we need to talk.'

Nellie opened her eyes to see Marianne standing in front of her in her dressing gown. She sighed. 'Now? I've got to go out in a bit.' She knew very well what her daughter wanted to talk about and she wasn't in the mood to justify her actions.

'That's what we need to talk about. I'm worried about you doing this. Lou Carter already threatened to tell Roger and . . . well, I think you should stop.'

Nellie raised an eyebrow. 'I see. And I should just stand by while people are struggling, should I? As long as we're all right, then I shouldn't worry, is that what you're saying?'

'But they won't starve, will they? Mrs Palmer and the WVS always make sure people have something, and she gets her food legit. You can't save everyone.'

'I'm not trying to *save* anyone. I'm trying to *feed* them. Like I've always done.'

Marianne sighed and knelt in front of her mother, taking hold of her hands. 'And I love you for that, Mum, I really do. But it's dangerous. What would we do if anything happened to you?'

Nellie patted Marianne's cheek affectionately. 'Oh, I think you'd manage, love. You're stronger than you think. And now you've got Alfie, I don't have to worry about you as much as I used to. Oh, it's gonna be a wonderful wedding. I'm gettin' a bit of extra sugar and butter and whatnot and I'm going to make you the best wedding cake that's ever been. Won't *look* as good as your concoctions, but it'll taste better.'

'Don't you dare! It's one thing for you to be getting food to give away, but don't risk it for me. Especially considering how you wound up Lou Carter the other day. Please don't go up Houghton today.'

Nellie snorted. 'Don't worry about Lou. She wouldn't dare do anything. She dobs me in, then I'll dob her. And in any case, I only do this to help out. But that one's in it to line her own pockets. As for her Terence – bent as a nine-bob note, that one. Always has been. Did I ever tell you about the time I caught him sneaking into the kitchen and trying to nick some pots and pans to sell as scrap?'

'Yes, Mum, you did. But that's beside the point. Doesn't matter why you're doing it; it's illegal. The law won't care whether you eat the food yourself or not. Wouldn't it be better to use the café food? We can just put a few extra customers down on the forms to justify the extra supplies.'

Nellie looked outraged. 'But that'd be fraud!' she said. 'Anyway, you shouldn't worry; the law'll have to catch me first. And I've found another supplier.' Nellie tapped her nose. 'Closer to home as well, thank gawd.'

'And that's another thing. You're going to have to start being nicer to Roger.'

Nellie's eyebrows almost disappeared into her tightly curled hair. 'Marianne, I am listening to what you're saying, but I'm not comprehending. Be nice to Roger – the man who's been sniffing around you like a dog on heat for years? The man who, when he asked you to marry him, told you it was on condition you gave up Donny? No, I won't be nice to him. Anyway, he'd get more suspicious if I was nice. I mean, doesn't matter what I say, he's still here every day, watching you. Your wedding can't come soon enough. Then at least he'll have to give up.'

Marianne huffed. How could she make her mother see the danger she was putting herself in? She loved being able to help people, but not at the expense of her mother's freedom and reputation.

'While we're on the subject, I had a quick word with Mrs Palmer today, and she wants us to join forces. I'm thinking she'll ask me to help set up a tea stand in the caves, so we're gonna need more tea and all, as well as the rest.'

'For God's sake, leave it to the WVS! You can't feed the whole of Dover.'

'Maybe not. But I can give it a good go!'

'But how can we afford it?'

'We're turning a healthy profit, what with all the extra custom. It's only fair we give a bit back.' Nellie leant her head back and closed her eyes. 'You couldn't get me a glass, could you, love? I could do with a bit of a pick-me-up before I go out.' She held up the bottle of sherry that stood on the table beside her.

Marianne crossed the narrow corridor to the tiny galley kitchen at the top of the stairs. It contained only a free-standing gas stove and hob with a rack above it for the plates, and a dresser that Jasper had made, where they kept the crockery and glasses. Nellie had painted it bright yellow to match the wallpaper. Standing on tip-toe, Marianne took down one of the glasses.

'Promise you'll be careful, Mum,' she said as she handed it to her. 'And I don't mean just when you go off and get the stuff. I mean in what you say to people. Especially Lou Carter.'

Nellie sniffed in disgust. 'I've said it before and I'll say it again, the problem with you young people is that you've got no gumption. If Lou Carter wants a battle she can have one. The woman's got the brain of a gnat, so let her do her worst.'

Nellie started as she heard a creak from the stairs. She looked at Marianne, her finger to her lips as they both sat quietly and listened. When no further sound came, Nellie turned up the volume on the radio.

'It was probably just Lily,' Marianne said.

'Let's hope so.' Nellie took a sip of her sherry.

'There's nothing I can do to persuade you not to go, is there?'

'Course there isn't. So why don't you tell me what you need, and I'll see what I can do.'

Marianne shook her head, but she went to the table and opened a folder of papers, flicking through the recipes she'd cut from various magazines, calculating the supplies she had and what she could make to keep the family fed and still have enough left over to make extra for anyone who needed it. But if today was anything to go by, then even with the goods her mother was sourcing from God knew where, she wasn't sure how she'd be able to stretch them to supply a tea stand in the caves.

'So, what do you need?' Nellie pulled Marianne from her thoughts.

'Everything: sugar, flour, butter, tea . . . And it would be good to get a side of bacon. Something I can put in little cheese and bacon pies. But the most important thing is tea.'

'Right you are.' Nellie stood up. 'I'll be off to see a man about a dog, then. Don't wait up!' She winked at Marianne as she left the room.

Marianne shook her head. Her mother seemed to relish this cloak and dagger business, but if she continued to make people angry, it wouldn't be long before someone decided to take their revenge on her.

∽

The searchlights danced across the night sky as Nellie cycled down Leyburn Road, wincing as the trailer rattled behind her. At least now she'd found a new source, she didn't have to cycle all the way to Houghton Without, but even so, this was always the most nerve-wracking part of her journey. With the town under a permanent curfew, any patrolling policeman or soldier would stop her, so she kept an eye out. Not that she could see much. If she hadn't known the streets like the back of her hand she'd have come a cropper for sure. Still, it had been a fruitful journey. She'd got everything Marianne needed, and if they were careful it could last another couple of weeks. She'd need to get it down to the basement and out of sight tout suite, though. And maybe they'd have to find a way of disguising the boxes better. After the way the girl had spoken tonight, she wasn't sure she could trust Pauline. And it seemed she was a drinker. And drink loosened lips. The memory of Pauline and Bert on the kitchen floor the night before made her lips twitch. Canary on her head indeed, cheeky little madam.

She was chuckling as she turned on to Tadwell Street, but suddenly her heart stopped as she saw a faint torch-light ahead of her. She got off the bike and wheeled it to the side of the road, melting into the shadows, and waited, heart in mouth. It was black as pitch aside from the searchlights, but at least the sky was quiet, and there'd been nothing from the ack-acks, so she'd lay good money that no raid was imminent. She squinted into the blackness, watching as the small beam of light moved in the opposite direction. She counted to two hundred, then took hold of the handlebars and turned on to Maison Dieu.

'Who goes there?' The loud voice almost made her fall drop the bike, and Nellie came to an abrupt stop as a figure emerged from the darkness.

She breathed a sigh of relief. 'Jasper!' she whispered. 'You nearly gave me a heart attack.'

Jasper shone the torch at her face, but as the lamp was covered with brown tape aside from a small strip in the middle, it didn't blind her as it once might have done. 'For the love of God, Nellie! What the devil do you think you're doing out at this time?'

He moved the torch and the thin light moved slowly over the bike and the trailer piled with boxes that had been tied down with string. He brought the beam back to her face and shook his head.

'Nellie, love, I know you're doing this for all the right reasons, but I don't like you being out in the dead of night. It's too risky. You should have let me do this when I offered.' He put the torch in his pocket, then took the bike's handles from her and started to walk it down the street. 'I can move around at night, no questions asked, when I'm on patrol.'

'And I said then that I didn't want you involved. My decision, my risk. No one else's.'

Jasper sighed. 'You're a stubborn old woman.'

'That I am. So next time, it'll be me going out again. Can't have your good name ruined in the town.'

Jasper laughed. 'And what about yours?'

Nellie snorted. 'My names been mud for years.'

'People'd understand if they knew why you did it.'

'Well, I prefer to keep my business to myself. I don't want no rewards. I just want to help folks keep body and soul together for as long as this mess is going on.'

'So you're saying you'll be cycling round in the dead of night, risking arrest and worse for the rest of your days, is that it? Cos the way things are going, either we're going to end up speaking German, or we'll be living on our nerves for the next few years.'

'Whatever it takes, Jasper. Whatever it takes.'

They had reached the gate on Church Street now and Nellie held it open so Jasper could wheel the bike in.

'What have you got this time?' Jasper whispered as they unloaded the boxes.

Nellie put a finger to her mouth, and put her shoulder to the back door, placing a box in front of it to prop it open, before going back out to help with the remaining packages.

One by one, they took the boxes quietly down to the basement where they stacked them onto the hidden shelves Jasper had built under the sloping roof. When they'd finished, she stood back and mentally ticked off what she'd bought: bacon in the icebox, plenty of tea, and enough marge, flour and sugar to make more bread and pies for any that needed them, and a little bit extra – no matter what Marianne said, she was going to make sure her daughter had the best wedding cake possible. It went against her rules to buy something for her own use, but this was a special occasion, and Marianne deserved it. She wondered briefly where her contact managed to get the goods; she had a suspicion he was skimming off the army supplies and for a moment she felt guilty, but then, she figured, it was all for a good cause, and the army wouldn't starve.

She took a cloth and draped it over the shelves, disguising them from view. Now Pauline was living here, she wondered whether she should find a better place to hide the food, but for now this would have to do.

They climbed back up the stairs and Nellie filled the kettle. 'Quick cuppa?'

'Go on then. And I want you to tell me where you go, who you see, and when you next intend to top up your supplies.'

Nellie placed the kettle on the hob and tapped her nose. 'You can want as much as you like. Doesn't mean I'm going to tell you.'

'For God's sake, woman, can't you see sense? The more you do this, the more likely you are to be caught. And what then? What if you find yourself in a cell for your trouble?'

Nellie grinned. 'Then I'll expect you to break me out.' She sat down opposite Jasper and put her hand over his. 'Don't worry about me, love. I'm tough as old boots and a quick talker. I'll be all right.'

Jasper looked sceptical. 'Let's hope you're right, but I think we should have a practice run.' He stood up and cleared his throat. 'Mrs Castle,' he said in a fair imitation of Roger Humphries, 'I see you're out in the dead of night with a trailer full of black market goods. Explain yourself or it's straight to the nick with you.'

'Officer Humphries,' Nellie said, getting into the scene, 'if you'd care to check the trailer, you'll find I've done nothing wrong. That's it. Bend right over and look in that box.' She stood up and lifted her foot, kicking the imaginary policeman's imaginary backside. Then she cackled. 'See? Nothing to it.'

The kettle whistled and she went over and lifted it off the heat, then put it down on the side. 'On second thoughts, I need a stiff drink.' She went into the pantry and, moving aside some bags of flour, found the bottle of brandy she kept for emergencies. As she came out, she heard a creak and her eyes flew to the door at the bottom of the stairs. She cursed under her breath. It was wide open. Why hadn't she closed it when she'd gone out? It can't have been a coincidence that she'd heard someone lurking twice tonight. Whoever was there had probably heard every word she and Jasper had said, and unless it was Marianne checking she'd got back safely . . . but she would come down to say hello.

She went to the door and looked upstairs; it was too dark to see anything, but she could have sworn she heard muffled steps.

Jasper joined her. 'Who do you reckon that was?' he whispered.

Nellie shrugged. 'Someone was listening to me and Marianne earlier as well.' She frowned. 'Could have been Donny, I suppose, but my money's on Pauline. She was behaving strangely towards me earlier.'

Jasper frowned. 'In which case, I think it's best I take the stuff tonight. Just to be on the safe side.'

Nellie hesitated then shook her head. 'Nah. It's fine. These old buildings are prone to creaking, and the girl wouldn't hurt us. Not when she's so fond of Lily and Bert.' She told Jasper about the incident the night before as she poured brandy into two teacups.

Jasper's shoulders shook with laughter as he raised his cup. 'Canary, eh? She's got a point.' They clinked cups briefly, then each threw back their drinks and slammed them back on to the table.

Nellie grinned. 'Nothing like a sniff of danger and a spot of brandy to get the heart pumping.'

He shook his head. 'I'm finding that shells and bombs are more than enough danger for me. Speaking of, I best get on with my rounds.' He put on his helmet, gave her a swift kiss on the cheek, and made his way to the back door. Nellie followed and stood on the doorstep, straining to make him out in the darkness. He paused at the gate.

'And don't think you've heard the last of this,' he whispered into the dark.

She smiled as the gate shut, and after washing up the teacups, made her way to bed. If Pauline had been listening, then so be it. She wasn't about to apologise for her illegal dealings. She had absolutely nothing to be ashamed of.

Chapter 18

Marianne rose early on Sunday morning, her mind full of the preparations for lunch. She couldn't wait to see Alfie, but she was dreading having to sit across the table from Reenie and Jim. She was furious with her brother for leading her friend on like this. She knew Jim was in terrible pain after losing Colin, the man he'd told her was the love of his life, but using sweet, unconfident Reenie to try to prove a point to himself was unfair. To both of them. He could never be happy living a lie, and if he continued with this sham romance, he'd break Reenie's tender heart. Maybe the boys would be sent away soon, she thought hopefully. But then, that meant Alfie would go too, and she couldn't bear that.

Throwing on her oldest jersey and a pleated skirt, she hastily put her hair into a bun then ran down the stairs and out into the market square. At this hour on a Sunday, all was quiet, and she paused for a moment, relishing the peace. This morning, even the planes were quiet; she just hoped it would last. She didn't want lunch ruined by an air raid – or worse, shells. Skipping across the cobbles, she went up Cowgate Hill, walking swiftly between the overgrown trees and hedges, enjoying the sound of the birdsong that they heard so rarely now; even the gulls' cries were drowned out by the constant drone of aircraft and explosions that they were subjected to at every hour of the day.

As she'd expected, she spotted Reenie kneeling beside a neat row of cabbages, pulling out weeds and throwing them into a wheelbarrow by her side. As always, her hair was tied up with a red polka-dot scarf, blonde wisps escaping around her face, and she was wearing a pair of dirty overalls.

'Reens!' Marianne called from the fence.

Reenie looked up and smiled as she took off her gardening gloves and rose to walk over to Marianne.

'All right, Marianne. I've got your spuds over in the shed. I've also saved you some carrots and a lovely cabbage.'

Marianne followed her into a large shed, where Reenie picked up a bulging sack. 'Veg is on the top. I've added a few extra potatoes as my contribution. And I'll bring some beer.'

Marianne smiled weakly. 'So you're still coming then?'

Reenie looked surprised. 'Why wouldn't I? I was chuffed when Jimmy asked me. What are you cooking?'

'Mum managed to get us a chicken. Lucky we have so many spuds, though, cos the chicken won't stretch to twelve. And then I'll make marmalade pudding for after. So . . . this thing with Jimmy, it's a bit sudden, isn't it?' Marianne probed.

Reenie shrugged. 'I've known him all his life; hardly sudden. I wrote him a letter to say how sorry I was about Colin. I didn't expect a reply, but he wrote back and we've been writing regular since. Funny, really. He's always been around, but I never realised what a truly lovely bloke he is till now. Who would have thought, eh?' She chortled. 'Wilf disapproves, of course.'

'Why? What did he say?'

'Told me Jimmy is too young. I'm too old. I'm making a fool of myself—' She turned round and marched out of the shed. 'Though what it's got to do with him, I don't know.'

'I always thought that one day you and Wilf might—'

'Might what? Stroll off into the sunset together with Freddie?' She snorted. 'The man's my dead sister's husband, for God's sake.'

'But before he married her . . . What happened, Reenie? How did June end up with him and not you?'

'Nothing happened. He just preferred June. Most people did.' She laughed shortly. 'She made sure of it. Anyway, that's ancient history. And now I might have a fella, he's suddenly looking down his nose at me. Do you think I'm making a fool of myself? I mean, Jim's . . . Jim's special, isn't he? Loads of girls fancy him. So what would he see in an old maid like me?'

This was her chance to discourage Reenie, Marianne realised. But her friend looked so vulnerable that she didn't have the heart. And what could she say anyway? 'Well . . . it's not serious, is it? I mean, it's not like you're about to get married, or anything?'

'Of course not. But he's sad, Marianne. Sad about Colin and the war, and worried about what'll happen. Says he finds it easy to talk to me . . . And if I can cheer him up, then that's got to be good. He certainly cheers me up. And he's made me feel . . . attractive; given me hope that I won't just be an old maid digging up cabbages for the rest of my life.' She noticed Marianne's guarded expression. 'You don't think he's just playing with me, do you? To get his end away, I mean. But why would he? He could have any girl he wanted, so why pick me if he's not serious? It's not as if I'm much of a catch.' She gestured towards her muddy overalls.

'Far as I'm concerned you *are* a catch. But as for Jim, I don't know, Reens. It's not like I know much about men. But just . . . don't rush into anything. For all we know he'll be gone tomorrow, so protect your heart, all right?'

Reenie regarded Marianne narrowly then whistled. 'Oh, I see how it is. You don't think I'm good enough for him. You agree with Wilf, don't you?'

'No! Of course I don't. If anything I think *he's* not got enough for *you*, and I just don't want to see you hurt.'

Reenie blew a lock of hair away from her face. 'I'm a big girl; I can look out for myself. Why does everyone think I'm stupid? Just cos I've never had a bloke before doesn't mean I can't sniff out the wrong 'uns.'

'I know that. I just want you to be happy. I want you to be sure that he's the right man.'

'Like you said, we're not getting married.' Reenie's tone was fractious.

It was so rare for her to get angry that Marianne's heart sank. It looked like her friend was already falling for her brother. She'd have to try a different tack. If she

187

could persuade Jimmy to back off now, hopefully Reenie wouldn't be too badly hurt. And maybe, just maybe, Jim's interest in Reenie would finally bring Wilf to his senses and he'd realise that Reenie was much more to him that just his dead wife's sister.

Marianne patted her arm. 'Hey, I'm sorry. I didn't mean to upset you.' She heaved the sack of veg onto her shoulder, deciding it would be best to leave now before she said any more; Reenie had been a truly loyal friend and she'd hate to fall out with her. 'I'll see you later. It'll be wonderful to have everyone back together. And Mum's even invited that doctor bloke from the dance. Lily's been working with him up Drop Redoubt.'

Reenie grinned at that. 'And no doubt he's after Lily. Well, good luck to her. I wonder, though, whether you'll be giving her the same talk you just gave me.' She raised her eyebrows, and when Marianne didn't answer, she nodded. 'No, I didn't think you would.' Angrily, she pulled on her gloves and went back to her weeding without another word.

With a resigned sigh, Marianne made her way back to the café. Maybe she shouldn't interfere; after all, like Reenie said, she was a big girl and, frankly, she had better things to worry about. Like her wedding dress. She'd been looking through some magazines and had found just the thing. It wasn't quite what she'd envisaged when she was a young girl, but with the clothing shortages, she didn't want to make things too difficult for her friend Daisy, who had offered to make her a dress. When Daisy had run the second-hand clothes stall in the market, everyone had gone to her if they needed a special outfit. But after the birth of her daughter a couple of months before, she and her husband, Stan – who had been badly injured at Dunkirk – had moved to the country. Marianne missed her desperately, and the thought of seeing her and her baby again soon lifted her spirits.

Feeling more cheerful, she made her way into the café and dumped the vegetables on the table, then rolling up her sleeves she got stuck into peeling the potatoes as she hummed the 'Wedding March'.

∾

Lunch was ready well before time, and while Lily laid the table in the café, Marianne ran upstairs to change; today she wanted to look pretty for Alfie.

She was just pulling a blue-striped cotton dress over her head when there was a knock on the door and Alfie walked in.

'Alfie!' Shocked, she pulled the skirt down over her thighs and turned her back as she did up the buttons at the front of the dress.

She jumped as his arms snaked round her waist. 'Don't do them up on my account,' he whispered into her ear, making the hairs on the back of her neck stand on end.

She smiled and turned, putting her arms around his neck.

'God, Marianne. Can we marry sooner? How about tomorrow? The end of September is too far away for my liking.'

She giggled. 'It's only a few weeks. You'll just have to be patient. Anyway, Daisy hasn't had time to make the dress yet, and I want to look my best for you on our wedding day.'

'I don't care about any of that; I just want you to be my wife. And then I can start proceedings to adopt Donny.'

Marianne leant her head on his chest. 'But I care. And as far as me and Don are concerned, you're already his dad.'

He sighed and dropped his arms. 'All right. I'll wait. But it won't be easy.'

She nodded. 'For me either. I want to be your wife more than anything.'

He picked her up and twirled her around. 'And in the meantime, I'll see about getting you a proper engagement ring.' He put her down. 'Although I'll never find anything to outshine you.'

'Oh, I don't know, I reckon Jasper might have some old tin lying around the forge that he could fashion into something.'

Alfie frowned and tipped her chin up. 'Stop that. I don't want to hear you put yourself down again. Even if I dug out diamonds from the mountains of Africa, they wouldn't be able to outshine you.'

She laughed. 'Alfie, I love you – I couldn't love you more – but now you're being stupid.' She grabbed his hand. 'Come on. I've got lunch to finish and I think there's a small boy in the basement waiting for you to help him with his trumpet practice.'

Chapter 19

Lily was putting the finishing touches to the table when Pauline walked in, teetering on a pair of high, wedged sandals and wearing a tight khaki-coloured cotton dress with shoulder pads and buttons down the front.

Nellie, who was reading the paper at her favourite spot behind the counter, cackled at the sight of her. 'Where you goin' then? Sunday lunch down the Grand?'

Pauline patted her brown hair, which Lily had once again curled into a victory roll. 'I just thought I'd make an effort.' She eyed Nellie's outfit of a red dress and green cardigan. 'And you look . . . er, very nice, Mrs C.'

Nellie smiled. She'd not forgotten the creaks on the stairs, but nothing had happened in the few days since that night, so she was giving Pauline the benefit of the doubt. 'Don't think I can't tell you're lying, love. But then, each to their own. You wouldn't catch me dead wearing khaki. Seen enough of that colour to last a lifetime.'

Pauline looked at Lily uncertainly. 'I think you look lovely, Paul.' She'd made an effort herself, putting on lipstick and paying special attention to her hair, which she'd washed the night before so it fell in shining waves down her back. She didn't want to admit it to anyone, but she was excited at the prospect of seeing Charlie again. Since the day of the shelling she hadn't been able to stop thinking about him, and she hoped he felt the same way.

The café door opened and Bert walked in, looking handsome as always in his uniform. He whistled at the sight of Pauline. 'Ain't you a sight for sore eyes, Paul.'

Pauline blushed. 'You don't look so bad yourself.'

'Tell you what, once lunch is done, why don't you and me go for that walk along the seafront you promised me the other night?'

'Well, that all depends . . .' Pauline said flirtatiously.

'On what? Whether you can walk anywhere in those?' He pointed at her feet.

Lily rolled her eyes. 'I'll tell you what, Bert, instead of flirting with my friend, why don't you go and fetch the glasses. Where's Jim?'

Bert nodded towards the window. 'Over at the Turners'.' He winked. 'Seems love is in the air, eh? Oh, all except for you, Lil. Charlie said to tell you he's sorry he can't make it. Some sort of emergency. Asked me to give you this.'

He handed her an envelope and, swallowing down her disappointment, she tore it open.

Dear Lily,

Sorry I can't make lunch today. We've got a disgruntled colonel in the hospital who seems to think I'm here to be his personal lackey. But I haven't forgotten that you promised to go to the pictures with me tomorrow. Gone with the Wind's on at the Granada, and a little bird told me it's your favourite film. Let Bert know whether you can make it, and if you can, I'll be waiting outside the cinema for you.

Love Charlie

Bert was watching her closely. 'So what does he say?'

'He says the thought of sitting at a table with you makes him sick, so he's staying away. And when you get back tell him yes.' Lily smiled smugly as she slipped the note into her pocket.

Bert whistled. 'He's asked you out, hasn't he? Well, no accounting for taste, eh? And seeing as he was asking me questions about what you like, I reckon I know where you'll be going.' He turned to Pauline. 'Fancy the pictures tomorrow, Paul?'

Pauline's eyes sparkled. 'I wouldn't say no.'

'That's a date, then. Can't let my baby sis go out unattended.' He winked at Lily who frowned back at him.

'I actually hate you right now, Albert Castle.'

Nellie laughed. 'Might ask Jasper if he fancies a trip and all.'

'Don't you dare, Mum. Anyway, you hate the pictures.'

'I do not. Just haven't had the chance to go for a while. But you're all right. I've got a council meeting tomorrow.'

Jim and Reenie came in then.

'Here are the lovebirds,' Bert said. 'Finished canoodling, have you?'

Marianne poked her head through the hatch and frowned. 'Jim, come here, will you? I want a word.'

'Give us a chance. I've only just walked in the door.'

'Now, Jim.'

Sighing, he turned to Reenie. 'Won't be long, love.'

Lily noticed Reenie shoot a glare at her sister, and wondered what the problem was.

Reenie took off her cardigan and went to lean on the counter in front of Nellie, keeping one eye on the hatch as she asked Nellie. 'What's the news, Mrs C?'

Nellie shook out the paper. 'The news is bad. As usual. But let me see . . . The invasion could happen any day, and Dover is now known as Hellfire Corner.' She chortled. 'Quite right too. Cos we give the Waffa hell every time they show up. Oh, and they're not going to reopen the schools. Too dangerous, what with shells as well as bombs dropping on us at all hours.' She sighed. 'Bloody papers are now calling the kids here "dead-end kids". Flipping cheek. Our kids have more courage in their little fingers than that bunch of no-goods down the Grand have in their whole bodies.'

But Reenie wasn't listening, Lily noticed. She was watching Jimmy and Marianne who were standing close together carrying out a whispered conversation. Curious, she walked over and crept into the kitchen.

'You're not being fair,' Marianne hissed.

'It's none of your business.' Jimmy was standing with his arms folded across his chest, his expression deadpan.

'Of course it is. She's one of my best friends—' Marianne broke off as she noticed Lily at the door. 'What do you want?'

Startled by her sister's harsh tone, Lily was saved from answering as the back door opened and the final guests arrived. Marge, looking glamorous in her Wren's uniform, was holding a cigarette as always, Rodney close behind, smiling at something she'd said, while Edie and Jasper brought up the rear.

'Now this is what I like to see.' Jasper rubbed his hands together. 'All the family back together and with a few extras added in.' He sniffed appreciatively. 'And good grub to boot.'

'About time,' Nellie said. 'Thought you lot were never gonna get here. Come on then, grab a pew and let's eat.'

When they each had a plate full of potatoes and veg and a sliver of roast chicken, Nellie clapped her hands. 'Before we eat, I just want to say a few words.' Everyone around the table groaned and Nellie eyed them sternly. 'Just a few. I'm thankful to have my boys with me today. Few people have that luxury these days. I'm thinking especially of the Guthries as they continue to wait for news of Colin.' She looked at Jimmy, who refused to meet her gaze, while Reenie put her hand over his in comfort. 'And I also want us to remember Alfie's friend John and all the others that were lost at Dunkirk. And to all our brave pilots fighting night and day to keep the enemy from our shores. But it's not just them.

There are those as lost their lives here in Dover just going about their normal business. To Doris Massey—' she looked at Pauline and Lily '—your old classmate, and to poor Pat Stafford, who was just doin' the ironin' when a dirty great shell landed on her house. May they all rest in peace.'

There was silence round the table as people's thoughts went back over the last few difficult weeks. Finally, Reenie held up her glass. 'To the fallen,' she said. 'But we hold out hope that Colin will come home safe to us.' She looked at Jimmy, who shook his head, his lips in a firm line and his eyes downcast as he fiddled with his glass.

To dispel the awkwardness, Alfie cleared his throat. 'If I can just try to lighten the mood with a bit of good news. Me and Marianne have an announcement. We've set a date. All being well, on the twenty-first of September, Marianne will become Mrs Lomax.'

Donny let out a cheer at that.

Nellie raised her glass. 'Let's just hope the dress'll be ready and we have enough food, eh?'

'We don't care about any of that.' Alfie took Marianne's hand. 'We just want to make things official as soon as possible while the regiment's still in Dover.'

The table broke out into excited chatter, but Lily kept her eyes on Jim. He looked pale and tense, and she wondered what he and Marianne had been arguing about. Or was it Reenie suggesting that Colin might still be alive that had upset him? There was no knowing with Jim these days.

'Jasper, you'll give me away, won't you?' Marianne asked.

196

Jasper beamed. 'I'd be honoured, love. Truly.'

'And you two will be bridesmaids,' Marianne continued happily, nodding at Edie and Lily.

'What about us?' Marge asked. 'Can't we be your bridesmaids too?'

'Oh. I just thought you might . . .' Marianne blushed.

'Don't tell me you thought we were too old?' Marge rolled her eyes. 'I reckon me and Reenie would do you proud, what do you say, Reens?'

'No way! I was bridesmaid at my sister's wedding and she made me wear a pink dress with ruffles all down the front and a skirt that stuck straight out. I looked like a blinking sugarplum fairy.'

Marge broke out into laughter. 'You still got that dress? We could get Edie to wear it.'

Edie pulled a face. 'I'd rather wear my overalls. In fact, seeing as clothes are scarce, I might have to.'

'I will play the "Wedding March" when Mum walks in,' Donny piped in. 'Alfie's teaching me.'

'That'll be . . . nice, Don.' Marge's expression set the table rocking with laughter and the earlier solemn mood was dispelled.

By the time Marianne brought out the marmalade pudding, everyone had relaxed. 'So Rodney,' Bert said, 'when are you and Marge going to get it together?'

Marge snorted. 'Shall we say never? You know I'm not the sort to be tied down.'

'Ah, but if it's the right man, Marge,' Bert teased.

'I'm sure Marge will know when it *is* the right man,' Rodney said, visibly annoyed. 'And it won't be me, so stop stirring and concentrate on your own life.'

Bert laughed. 'Oh, don't worry about me. I've got my sights set on a certain little lady.'

Pauline, who had been hanging on Bert's every word throughout lunch, smiled at that.

'Any woman who falls for you should have their head examined,' Lily said.

'Oh, this one definitely doesn't need her head examined. And I have it on good authority from the manager of the Hippodrome that she'll be here at Christmas to raise the spirits of the troops.'

Pauline sat back, deflated.

'What are you gabbling about? Last I heard, the best the Hippodrome could come up with was a woman with a couple of raggedy snakes,' Nellie said. 'And what she did with them is not for the ears of children.' She nodded towards Donny.

Bert tapped his nose. 'It's hush-hush so keep it under your hat, but they've only managed to get a promise from Vera Lynn.'

There was a gasp around the table. 'You're not serious,' Alfie said excitedly. 'Do you think she'll need a trumpeter to accompany her? I was on the bill with her once, a couple of years back. She might remember me.'

'You'll have to sort that out with the Hippodrome, mate. But I'm ready to welcome her with open arms and show her the sights of Dover.'

'It'll do you good,' Nellie said. 'Cos I bet that girl wouldn't look at you twice. About time you got taken down a peg or two.'

Bert put his hand to his chest. 'How could you, Mum?'

Nellie pointed her knife at him. 'Your trouble is you're too much like your dad. You need a strong woman to tame you.'

'You saying I need a woman like you?'

'That's exactly what I'm saying.'

Bert held up his hands. 'That's me never getting married then. What about Jim and Rodney? What sort of women should they have?'

Nellie stared at her other two sons reflectively. 'Jim needs someone kind. Someone soft with a happy nature.' She winked at Reenie, who blushed. 'As for Rod. He needs a woman who'll stand up to him. Someone who can show him he's not always right and can't control everything.'

Rodney frowned. 'I don't think I'm always right.'

'Course you do, Rod,' Marge scoffed. 'It's what makes you so good at your job and so bad at having fun.'

Nellie smiled smugly. 'There you go. Right in front of your nose.'

'Not on your Nellie, Nellie.' Marge laughed.

'And while I'm on the subject, Edie, you need a man that can put up with your temper and not let you walk all over him.'

'Flamin' cheek!' Edie gasped. 'There's nothing wrong with my temper.' She slammed her spoon into her bowl to a chorus of jeers from all except Rodney who was sitting opposite the large front window, and stiffened suddenly. 'Who the hell . . .?'

Everyone turned to look and Lily gasped, her eyes shooting to Pauline in surprise.

As soon as Pauline saw who it was, her face paled and she dropped her spoon in shock. Because standing with his nose pressed flat against the window and a grin on his face was Dick Brown. Lily half rose, ready to tell him to bugger off, but Pauline beat her to it. She pushed her chair back with a clatter and ran out of the door, wobbling on her high sandals. As soon as she reached the man, she grabbed his arm and pulled him round the corner onto Castle Street.

'Who's that? And why's he pulling stupid faces through the window?' Donny asked curiously.

'He works up the hospital,' Lily said. 'Nasty piece of work.'

'That's the man from the dance!' Bert suddenly realised. 'Cheeky sod. What's he doing here?'

Lily got up. 'I don't know, but I'm going to check Pauline's all right.' She hurried into the backyard and, inching open the gate, peered out to the right towards the market square. Pauline and Dick were standing very close on the corner, Dick holding Pauline by the arms. Lily couldn't hear what he was saying, but her friend looked distressed and was shaking her head. Lily was about to tell him to take his hands off Pauline when Dick shoved her slightly against the wall and raised his voice.

200

'You better think about it soon, Paul. Otherwise you know what will happen.'

He turned and walked away, whistling tunelessly, his hands in his pockets.

Lily rushed up to Pauline, who was slumped against the wall holding her stomach.

'What was that about?' she asked urgently. 'Did he hurt you?'

Pauline shook her head. 'Nothing. It was nothing. He just wants me to . . .' She waved her hand around.

'To what?'

'Have a drink with him.'

Lily's eyes widened. 'So he came here and stuck his nose against the window just so's he could ask you out?' she said disbelievingly.

Pauline nodded. 'But then we always knew he was a queer one.' She reached her hand into the pocket of her dress and pulled out her hip flask.

'Paul!' Lily was shocked as she watched Pauline take a swig.

'I just need something to calm me nerves,' she said.

Lily clamped her mouth shut; it was obvious Pauline wasn't going to tell her what the conversation with Dick had been about, and she'd be even less likely to if she had a go at her about her drinking, so she took her arm and led her back into the café. 'You can tell me later, all right?'

Pauline didn't answer, but once back inside, her demeanour changed. 'It's all right, folks,' she said cheerily.

'I sent him off with a flea in his ear. Bloomin' cheek of him. The man can't leave me alone.' She grinned at Bert. 'But I have bigger fish to fry. You fancy that walk now?' she asked.

Bert looked surprised. 'Now?'

She put her hand on her hip and cocked her head. 'No time like the present, eh?'

Bert grinned. 'Never a truer word spoken. Excuse us, Mum. And thanks for the grub, Marianne. I'll see the rest of you around. Come on then, you.' He took Pauline's arm, and together they walked out of the door while the rest of the group watched them go in amazement.

'Well,' Nellie huffed indignantly. 'The little floozie. Right in front of his mum's nose and all.'

'They're only going for a walk, Mum,' Marianne said.

Jimmy sniggered. 'Yes. Just a *walk*.'

Alfie stood up suddenly. 'I think that's a very good idea. Marianne?' He held his hand out to her.

She immediately took it. 'Sorry, Mum. Don't suppose I can leave the clearing up to you lot?'

Nellie sighed. 'Go on then. At least you two are engaged.' She watched them leave then heaved herself up from the table. 'Well, looks like the party's over. Jasper, come and have a tipple with me upstairs. As for the rest of you—' she gestured at the table '—sort this lot out, will you?'

Lily folded her arms and frowned. Bloody typical. She was left with the clearing as per. And as for Pauline . . . Whatever was going on with Dick Brown, it was driving her friend to drink. And jumping straight into Bert's arms was only going to make matters worse for her.

∞

Lily was already in bed when Pauline returned much later that night, flushed and rumpled. As she walked in, Lily sat up and looked at her enquiringly, but Pauline refused to meet her eyes as she got ready for bed.

'So? Are you going to tell me what that was all about?' she asked eventually when Pauline had finally snuggled under the covers.

'Me and Bert had a walk then went for a few drinks in the Oak. That's all.' Pauline's speech was slurred as she turned her back on Lily and let out a loud yawn.

'That's not what I'm talking about and you know it.'

'Shut up, Lil. I'm tired. And we got work and the pictures tomorrow.' She pulled the blankets over her head.

Lily lay back with a sigh; she wouldn't be getting any more information out of her tonight. Still, at least she had tomorrow night to look forward to.

Chapter 20

It was four in the morning when the air raid siren went off and Lily groaned, pulling the pillow over her head.

Marianne opened the door and shouted, 'Get up! Air raid!'

'I've only just gone to bed,' Pauline moaned.

But Marianne was already running down the stairs. She bashed on her mother's door, before gently opening Donny's.

'Come on, Don. We need to get downstairs.'

Donny burrowed further under his covers. 'Can't I stay here this time, Mum?'

'No, love. Come on.' She pulled back his blankets and he rolled out of bed straight onto the floor. Marianne bent over to tickle the bare flesh that showed between his waistband and stripy pyjama top. He giggled and jumped up, his hair sticking up around his head, making him look a little like Polly.

The noise of the planes was louder now, and Nellie came out of her room, pulling her pink quilted dressing gown around her, her hair in curlers under a yellow scarf.

'Lily! Get a move on!' she shouted as she went into the sitting room to collect the birdcage.

Lily and Pauline appeared and together they trooped downstairs, their pace increasing as a loud crash told them that this was no false alarm.

The air was chilly in the basement and Marianne covered Donny with a patchwork blanket as he lay on some cushions, his eyes shut, while the others sat around the table, blankets wrapped around themselves.

'You got this place set up nice,' Pauline said, looking around in the dim light. As well as the rag rugs and cushions, Nellie had hung some of the more colourful pictures the local children had drawn at the Christmas party the previous year on the walls, and despite the damp chill, the place looked inviting bathed in the warm glow of the hurricane lamp.

Nellie watched Pauline closely as the girl got up to explore the basement, going towards the back and bending down to get a better look at the shelves.

'What's this?' she asked, moving aside a sheet and exposing the set of shelves on which several cardboard boxes had been arranged.

'Leave that. It's just old stuff we've not thrown out. Come back and play cards with us,' Nellie said.

'You want to play cards, Gran?' Donny said sleepily. 'You never let me play cards in night raids cos you say I should sleep. But I know it's cos you just don't want to.'

'It's practically morning, Don. And I can't think of a better way to start the day than a good game of rummy, can you?'

Pauline walked over to the table. 'Sorry, Mrs C. My mum always said my nosiness would be the death of me.'

'You're all right, love. It's just junk,' Nellie said.

'It didn't look like junk,' Pauline said archly.

'Well it is! And I'd prefer it if you didn't poke around, or it's back to the Citadel with you! Although, judging by the time you got back tonight, that ship's already sailed.' She gave Pauline a disapproving look. 'You do know Bert's not serious about you, don't you?'

Pauline folded her arms. 'How would you know?'

'Because I've lost count of the number of girls who've had their hearts broken by him. If all you want is a bit of fun, then Bert's your man. But if you've set your sights on anything else, you're going to be disappointed.'

'I don't think you know your son as well as you think you do.'

'I forgot to tell you, Mum,' Lily said hastily before her mother could reply, 'me and Paul have our first night duty starting next week.'

'That should keep both of you out of trouble then. 'Ere, did you see this?' She held up a newspaper. 'There's an article about them four pillars.'

'Who?' Lily asked, bemused by the swift change in subject.

'English people who support the Nazis and are secretly helping them here. The lot of them need to be rounded up and shot if you ask me.'

'I think you mean Fifth Columnists. I read that and all,' Pauline said.

'Did yer? When did you find the time between drinking and flirting with my son?'

'Leave it out, Mum,' Lily said, shooting an apologetic glance at her friend. 'Tell me more about these people. You reckon there are any here in Dover?'

'Bound to be. Hey, what if Mrs Palmer's one? Or her no-good brother, Horace Smith?' She chortled. 'To be fair, Mrs P's all right when all's said and done. But I'd pay good money to see Horace get his comeuppance.'

Horace Smith had always made his contempt for Marianne very plain, and had done his best to stop his own son, Davey, from playing with Donny.

'I hate Mr Smith,' Donny said. 'But I think that might not be nice for Davey, Gran.'

Nellie looked at her grandson in surprise. 'Donald Castle, you put me to shame. Given the man has tried to stop you and Davey being friends all these years, he don't deserve your consideration. Anyways, I reckon it'd be a good outcome for Davey. The man's a horror.'

Marianne couldn't disagree. He'd denounced her loudly to any who'd listen ever since she'd had Donny. And all because she wasn't married. She wondered if the man would change his attitude once she was Mrs Lomax. Somehow she doubted it.

Another loud explosion rocked the building and all conversation stopped as they held their breath and waited.

Finally, Nellie huffed and picked up the cards. 'Come on then, Don. Let's play. Anything to keep our minds off what's going on out there.'

Lily yawned. 'If you're not using the cushions, Donny, think I might try to grab forty winks.' She lay down and wrapped her blanket tightly around her and within minutes she was asleep.

∞

Lily was woken by Marianne gently shaking her shoulder. 'Lil, it's over.'

Nellie rose stiffly to her feet. 'Gordon Bennett, I could do with another few hours in bed.'

Lily checked her watch. 'Barely worth going back to bed for half an hour.'

Marianne yawned. 'Not for me either. I'm going to get started on some bread.'

'And I might take myself up to the Citadel,' Pauline said pointedly. 'Watch the sun rise before work.'

Nellie rolled her eyes. 'Seems like you could teach Hitler a thing or two about bearing a grudge,' she said. From under the cloth in the corner came a soft squawk from Polly, and Nellie shook the cage in annoyance. 'And you can shut up and all.'

Lily sighed. It seemed her mother and Pauline were not destined to be the best of friends. And if Bert carried on with Pauline, she knew it would end in tears.

∞

When they got to the hospital early that morning, Lily and Pauline stopped in the canteen as usual before their shift started. They had just sat down at their regular table when a voice came from behind them.

'Morning, girls.'

Lily wrinkled her nose. Dick Brown; just who she didn't want to see.

Lily pointedly ignored him, but Pauline took a breath, before turning round. 'All right, Dick?'

'Looked like you lot had fun yesterday.' He grinned.

'It was all right. Though we could have done without the interruption,' Pauline said sharply.

'How're your mum and dad?' he asked her.

'They were fine last I heard.'

'Due back soon, are they?'

'That's none of your business,' Pauline snapped.

'Keep your knickers on, girl. I was just bein' friendly. How about we have a chat later?'

Without waiting for an answer, he walked away, leaving Pauline staring after him, her face pale.

'I thought you had a chat yesterday,' Lily said. 'Come on, Paul, what's going on? He wasn't really asking you out yesterday, was he?'

Pauline shrugged.

'What were you arguing about?'

She shrugged again. 'I was just having a go at him for staring in the window like that. It was rude.'

Before Lily could reply, Dot and Vi joined them at the table. 'Good morning,' Dot said cheerfully. 'Hope

209

you managed to get some sleep last night. Bloomin' siren never seems to shut up. Still, our last day shift, eh? Don't know about you, but I'm looking forward to night duty. Bit of a break from routine. And I'm used to staying up all night with lambing and whatnot on the farm.'

'I'm not looking forward to it,' Vi said sulkily. 'Only time I like to stay up all night is when I'm having fun. Still, I expect I'll manage. Not sure about you, though, Pauline.'

'What do you mean?'

'You keep swigging from your flask, chances are you'll pass out on duty.'

Pauline flushed. 'I don't know what you're talking about.'

Vi raised an eyebrow. 'Don't ya? You think no one can smell it on you? You can eat as many mints as you like, but if you're not careful Matron'll sniff it out and you'll be out on your ear.'

'You're a spiteful bitch, Vi Williams. And if I like a drink now and then, what's it to you?'

'Just sayin', Paul. You ought to be careful. My nan was a right one for the sauce, and she ended up yellow as a daffodil and dead by fifty.'

Without a word, Pauline stood up and stalked away.

Lily watched her go with a concerned frown. Vi was right; Pauline's flask was always with her at the moment. Last night when she'd returned from her walk with Bert, she'd stunk of booze, but Lily hadn't thought anything of it, because she'd been in the pub with Bert. But now she thought about it, there was always the faint aroma of alcohol around her. And she did eat a lot of mints. But surely she wouldn't be stupid enough to drink on duty?

After Pauline's bad-tempered departure, the other three quickly finished their tea. But as Lily was hurrying to the supply cupboard to fetch the mop and bucket, she stopped short as she saw Pauline and Dick deep in conversation again. Those two really did seem to have a lot to say to each other, but she couldn't begin to imagine what. She marched up to them. 'Come on, Paul. No time for a chat, we've got to get on.' She shot a glare at Dick. 'And what were you doing round mine yesterday?'

Dick smiled. 'I was just taking a stroll. You lot looked very cosy. And all that lovely grub. Give my regards to your ma when you get back. On second thoughts, I might pop in there myself later. Can't deny your sister's a good little cook. Catch you later, Pauline.'

'Urgh,' Lily said as she turned to Pauline, whose face was paper-white. 'Hey, what's up, love? Did he try to feel you up or something?'

'No! No, he didn't. I just don't like him, is all.' She turned the handle of the cupboard and went in, causing a racket as she kicked over one of the metal buckets before reaching in to her pocket to pull out her flask.

Lily grabbed it from her before she could open it. 'For God's sake, Pauline! Vi's right. You'll be chucked out if they catch you. And Bert won't be happy if you turn up to your date drunk.'

Pauline's shoulders sagged as she sighed. 'You're right. I'm sorry. Take it away and hide it from me till later.'

211

'But why do you drink so much?'

'It just . . . helps me. When I'm nervous or worried or something.'

'What are you worried about?'

Pauline hesitated, and Lily briefly wondered if she was going to confide in her. But then Pauline waved her hand vaguely in the air. 'Well, it's nerve-racking, ain't it? Bombs, shells, bloody planes. I can't hear myself think for the noise. The wonder is we're not all drinking.' She picked up the mop and bucket and left without another word.

Chapter 21

Nellie groaned as the bell above the door rang and the tall, thin figure of Muriel Palmer, clad in a smart blue dress and a tin hat, strode in. Instead of taking a seat, she marched up to the counter and held out a hand. Nellie looked at it for a moment before raising her eyes to the other woman's.

'To what do I owe the honour, Mrs Palmer?' she asked.

Mrs Palmer withdrew her hand with a frown, blinking as she took in Nellie's outfit. Today, she was wearing the bright pink apron covered in yellow flowers over her red summer dress. The effect was startling. 'As promised, I have come to talk to you about how we can join forces.' She glanced to her right and her eyebrows rose at the sight of Polly watching her from the cage, her head cocked to one side. 'Is that a parrot?'

'No. It's a German spy,' Nellie said sarcastically. 'So be careful what you say around her.'

Mrs Palmer sighed. 'I had hoped we could have a civilised conversation. But perhaps I need to speak to someone else about my cave task force.'

Nellie relented. 'All right. Let's take a seat. Glad, bring us a couple of teas, would you?' she said, as she came around the counter and sat down at Jasper's usual table, gesturing for the other woman to take the seat opposite.

Mrs Palmer perched primly on the edge of the chair, her handbag on her lap, and nodded her thanks as Gladys placed a cup of tea in front of her.

Gladys threw a perplexed look at Nellie, who just shrugged. The last time Mrs Palmer had been in, she'd galvanised them all to help the evacuated soldiers, and, Nellie thought grudgingly, she'd done a pretty decent job of that so the least she could do was hear her out.

'Like I said the other day,' Mrs Palmer began, taking a sip of tea, 'now that Dover seems to be in sight of the German guns as well as the German planes, the caves are starting to be utilised more and more by the townsfolk. The WVS has been tasked with providing refreshments to families who take shelter, and when I considered who best to help me with this endeavour, only one name came to mind.'

Nellie was flattered in spite of herself. 'Funnily enough me and Marianne have been talking about that very thing. We reckon we could provide soup, tea and sandwiches. Just need something to keep it warm. They've got electrics down there, haven't they?'

'They have. And there's talk of arranging proper sanitary facilities. I anticipate that with the caves being as big as they are, we could all move there.'

'Not on your life,' Nellie asserted. 'Shells or no shells, I'm not budging. But that don't mean we can't help out.'

Mrs Palmer smiled. 'I must say, Mrs Castle, you are far more receptive than I anticipated. Now ... What I suggest is—'

Her words were cut off by a commotion at the door as Roger Humphries strode in purposefully, his expression grim as he looked around the room.

'Constable Humphries! I wasn't expecting to see your ugly mug again today,' Nellie called to him.

He walked directly up to her. 'I'm here in an official capacity, Mrs Castle,' he said pompously, as the customers looked on curiously. 'Perhaps you and I could go into the kitchen for a little chat?'

Nellie stiffened and crossed her arms. 'Why?'

Roger glanced around, then bent closer to Nellie. 'We've had some disturbing reports from a concerned member of the public and I've been instructed to verify them.'

Nellie stood up then, her face paling. 'What are you talking about?'

'If you could step into the kitchen with me, Mrs Castle. I need to speak to Marianne as well.'

Around them, the customers had gone silent as they waited for the latest drama to unfold, and at a table by the window, Nellie noted a scruffy-looking man wearing a checked shirt, his tin hat sitting beside him on the table. She frowned. The journalist had been coming in almost every day, sitting at the table, listening to the conversations around him and scribbling busily in his notebook.

With a sinking heart, Nellie led Roger into the kitchen where Marianne was frying rissoles for lunch.

'What seems to be the problem, Roger?' she asked, turning to look at them in surprise.

'The problem, Marianne, is that we've had reports of contraband goods being stored in the café. Which leads us to believe that *someone* here—' he looked at Nellie '—has been procuring goods illegally.'

Marianne felt her stomach clench as she shot a look at her mother, who, though pale, looked composed. 'And who told you that?' she asked.

'It doesn't matter who. I'm here to verify the reports, and if I find there has been any wrongdoing, then I have no alternative but to report the matter to the highest authority.'

'My, Roger. Here's me thinking you was just a humble copper, but all the time you have a direct line to God,' Nellie sneered.

Roger flushed. 'This is not a joking matter. If the reports are true, then there will be serious consequences for you and the café.'

There was a knock at the back door and when Marianne went to answer it she found two more policemen waiting there. Without a word, she stepped back and let them in.

Gladys poked her head through the hatch. 'People are still ordering food, Nellie. Shall I tell them to leave?'

'Don't you dare. Marianne, get on with your work. As for you lot, wasting your time harassing innocent people, you should be ashamed of yourselves. But if you must, you must.

Go on then. Search away. And if you find anything send it my way. We're a bit short of quite a few things as it happens. Now, if you don't mind, I need to get back to my meeting.'

Nellie marched back into the café and sat down at the table. 'Where were we, Mrs P?'

Mrs Palmer stared through the kitchen door curiously. 'What's that all about?'

'It appears someone's gone and told the police we've got black market goods here. But he won't find anything.'

'Won't he?' Mrs Palmer took a sip of tea and replaced the cup very precisely on the saucer then looked at Nellie carefully.

Nellie held her gaze for a moment, then looked away. 'He might.'

'You don't seem too concerned.'

Nellie shrugged. 'My conscience is clear. Anything he finds has been bought solely for the purpose of helping people.'

Mrs Palmer was silent for a few moments. Finally, she gave a slight smile. 'That's very altruistic of you, Mrs Castle. I suppose under those very special circumstances, getting a little extra can be excused.'

Nellie smiled back. '*Alitistic*, eh? Whatever that is, that sounds about right.'

'So you're saying they *might* find something?'

Nellie sat back. 'What if they did? You still want my help?'

'Oh yes. I still want your help. And I might have to confess to the good constable that you have very kindly

217

allowed the WVS to store a few bits and pieces here since our storeroom got damaged by the shells the other day.'

Nellie stared at her in shock. 'You'd do that?'

'If, as you say, the goods are for local use, then just this once – and I mean, *just* this once – I will see what I can do.'

'Well, well, well. Maybe you an' me have more in common than I thought.'

'Maybe we do. Now, do you want me to talk to the man?'

Nellie gestured towards the kitchen door. 'Be my guest.'

Mrs Palmer stood up and swept into the kitchen. 'Mrs Castle,' she said loudly, 'we'll be sending a van around later to pick up the goods you've so kindly stored for us now that we've found a new place.' She stopped short as she caught sight of Roger emerging from the basement carrying a bag of sugar. 'Oh, how very kind of you, Constable Humphries. But the van won't be here till this afternoon, so if you come back then, you can help us load.'

Roger stared at the woman. 'What do you mean? I am here investigating a very serious allegation, and it appears I've caught you red-handed, Mrs Castle. There's bags of stuff down there.'

'Well, of course there are, Constable. I put many of them there myself,' Mrs Palmer said haughtily.

Roger's mouth dropped open. 'Are you telling me that *you* have been buying black market goods.'

Mrs Palmer drew herself up to her full height. 'How dare you. The very thought!'

'I-I mean, this bag of sugar . . . and the flour. Are you telling me it's yours?'

'Of course it's mine. Well, not mine, exactly. These are goods assigned to us by the mayor himself for the relief of the townspeople. You didn't really think that Mrs Castle would be trading on the black market, did you?' She gave a tinkling laugh. 'Can you imagine? A woman of her character. Why, there would be an uproar.'

'I-I . . .'

Nellie was watching the scene with growing admiration. Who'd have thought Muriel Palmer would be saving her bacon – literally! 'It's a scandal, that's what it is. The police are harassin' me. What I'd like to know, Rog, is who had the gall to imply that *I* would do such a thing? Marianne, take that sugar from the constable, will you? Stick it back where it belongs, nice and safe, so Mrs P can collect it later.'

'I-I most heartily apologise for the misunderstanding, Mrs Palmer; I'm sure we're all very grateful for your efforts.' He held the bag out to Marianne, who was standing by the stove fiddling nervously with a tea towel. 'Of course, you must put it back, Marianne. And apologies for interrupting your work.'

Nellie tapped her foot. 'And me, Roger? You got anything to say to me?'

Roger stared down at his feet for a moment, but finally he cleared his throat. 'I am sorry for the inconvenience, Mrs Castle. Let me gather the other officers from upstairs, and we'll be out of your hair.'

Nellie followed him to the bottom of the stairs. 'And if I find any of your buffoons have nicked my drawers there'll be hell to pay,' she shouted. 'I know what you lot are like – any excuse to wear a woman's knickers.'

Laughing uproariously, she winked at Mrs Palmer, whose lips were twitching. 'I don't mind admitting, Mrs P,' she whispered, 'I'm not often lost for words but that little performance was worthy of the Hippodrome.'

Mrs Palmer inclined her head. 'Like I said, Mrs Castle, just this once.'

'Understood. And I'd be delighted to give you a hand. How about we pop down the caves now and you can show me what's what?' She darted into the pantry and returned holding up her large wicker basket. 'Marianne's taken to doing a batch of baking each morning to hand out in the basement, but we may as well take it to the caves now. Then maybe later you can bring your battle bus round to Church Street and we can load up. What do you say?'

'You want to go now? But what about—?' She nodded towards the stairs.

'Marianne and Glad can see them out.' She took down her tin hat from the hook and made her way through the café, Mrs Palmer following along behind.

At the door, Nellie paused and stared at the journalist. 'You get all that, did you, Ron Hames? I don't know why you spend your days loitering in here. Why aren't you on the cliffs with the other ghouls, watching those young men's lives get shot down in flames, or propping up the bar at the Grand?'

The man shook his head. 'There's enough of them there. I'm interested in the people's war, Mrs C. And I'm especially interested to hear about the policemen wearing your drawers.' He held up his notepad and pen.

Nellie rolled her eyes. 'You've been here all day eavesdropping on conversations. You could be a German spy for all I know. So go on, git! Give us a bit of privacy. And if I see one word printed about any of this, you'll not be welcome in here again.'

The man grinned at Nellie and stood up. 'I'll leave for now. There's enough material in this café and the market square to keep my editor happy for weeks.' Chuckling, he slammed his helmet onto his head and walked out into the square where he was swiftly swallowed up by the crowds of people.

Outside, Nellie paused as she stared at Lou Carter, who was serving some servicemen at the whelks stall. It was only a few days since the woman had threatened to report her, and she felt her anger swell. Pushing a couple of people aside, she marched up to the counter.

'Reckon you should get rid of those cigs soon as, Lou. Wouldn't want our friendly local bobby sniffin' around your stall, would you?'

Lou frowned. ''Scuse us a mo, love,' she said to the waiting soldier. 'What are you on about, Nellie?'

'As if you didn't know. Just had a visit from Roger Humphries. No harm done, given as I've done nothing wrong, but I don't need the hassle.'

'And you think *I* dobbed you in?'

221

'Last I remember, you said you would, and seems for once you were as good as your word.'

Lou narrowed her eyes. 'I might shout me mouth off now and again, but you know me well enough to realise I got no time for the boys in blue.' She stared through the windows of the café, then frowned. 'I think you should be lookin' closer to home.' She nodded towards the window. 'I seen that young man before.'

Nellie followed her gaze and for the first time noticed the young man sitting in the corner by the window. He had his cap pulled low over his face, but she recognised him all the same. It was the same man who'd watched them at lunch through the window the day before. The same young man that Pauline had rushed out to see.

'Who is he?'

Lou shrugged. 'No idea. He buys a tub of jellied eels from me now and gain. Always very interested in your place. Askin' questions.'

'Like what?'

'Stuff about you and the kids.' She hesitated. 'I feel like I've seen him before . . . he has the look of someone . . . I just can't quite bring it to mind . . . So I'd start my questions there, if I were you. You and me have our differences, but I'm no grass.'

Nellie stared thoughtfully through the window. Lou was right. The Carters had always skirted on the wrong side of the law, and she couldn't see the woman reporting her, no matter what her grievance. So who had? And why was this man so interested in her and her family?

She nodded. 'I'll believe you this time. But if those rozzers are back at my door, then you and your Terence need to watch out, cos I might not be so forgiving next time.'

Lou folded her arms across her ample chest. 'I'm tellin' you, Nell, if you're havin' trouble, then it's nothing to do with me. If I want to have a go I'll do it to your face.'

Nellie nodded reluctantly. 'Fair enough. But do us a favour. Let me know if that one comes back, and if you see him and that Pauline together. He were round here yesterday and the minute she saw him she were off like a whippet.'

Nellie joined Mrs Palmer, who'd been watching the exchange from a few feet away. The woman shook her head. 'My my, I never realised what a hotbed of scandal it was here. What with police raids, journalists and conspiracies over the whelks, it's a wonder Mrs Christie doesn't come here for inspiration.'

'Who?' Nellie asked.

'You know, Miss Marple – *Murder at the Vicarage*?'

At Nellie's blank look, Mrs Palmer sighed. 'Oh, never mind. Hopefully, there'll be no murders here, at any rate. Though judging by the look of Mrs Carter, I have my doubts.'

Chapter 22

As Nellie and Mrs Palmer bustled down King Street, a loud whistling overhead made them duck instinctively as they clutched each other by the arm. Moments later, an explosion rumbled through the town, and the windows around them rattled. They stared at each other in alarm as, late as always, the air raid siren started to ring out.

'We should keep going,' Mrs Palmer panted. 'It's not far now.'

They began to trot down the street, Nellie slightly behind as she struggled to run and carry the basket, before skidding right into Snargate Street. A loud crash sent some roof tiles toppling to the ground and Mrs Palmer grabbed Nellie's arm to pull her to safety, but not before one of the tiles glanced off Nellie's helmet with a loud clang, knocking it off her head and sending it flying into the middle of the road. Before she could retrieve it, Mrs Palmer dragged her into a shop doorway, where the two women stood, watching the hat's pink ribbon fluttering slightly in the dust.

'Cor, close shave, Mrs C,' a man standing in a doorway on the opposite side of the road shouted across at them.

Nellie grinned. 'Jasper always said he'd be the saving of me. Looks like he might have been right.' She rubbed at her greying curls, the sound of the tile clanging on her helmet still ringing in her ears. 'You all right, Mrs P?' She looked at the woman's pale face with concern.

'I'm fine, thank you. And now that we're allies, I think it's time you started calling me Muriel.'

Nellie laughed. 'Only you would think of social niceties in the middle of a shell attack.' She glanced down the road. ''Ere, you reckon we should make a dash for it?' She stared enviously at the people she could see further down the road disappearing into the entrance of Barwick's Caves. 'The sight of Massey's over there makes me nervous to stand in a doorway. Snargate seems to be in the direct line of fire.'

Lined with tall buildings on both sides, the street was usually in the shade, but now, with the jagged hole in the terrace standing out like a missing tooth, there was a puddle of sunshine on the road, glinting off Nellie's helmet.

'I'm not sure. We might—' Mrs Palmer's words were cut short as an explosion from the seafront made their ears ring.

'That's it! I'm not waiting here any longer. Help me with this basket and let's go!' Nellie shouted. The two women, the basket bumping between them, broke cover, pausing briefly so Nellie could scoop up her helmet; she gave it a swift kiss, plonked it on her head and they set off again. Soon, they ducked inside the entrance of the cave where they dropped the basket and stood panting for a moment.

'Hell's bells!' Nellie exclaimed finally as she looked around. 'It's a whole other world down here.' The white, rough-hewn walls rose to a curved ceiling, along which ran some electric lights. A group standing at the entrance made way for them, and they ventured further in.

The tunnel widened and Nellie noted the bunk beds and home comforts along each side. Armchairs were dotted here and there and someone had even hung a painting of the white cliffs on the wall and laid a colourful rag rug on the floor. Soon they came to a larger space with a dome-like ceiling where several people were perched on the seats carved into the chalk walls, nattering and sipping tea almost as if they were in the café, Nellie thought. Along one wall, a queue of people stood patiently waiting to be served by a couple of middle-aged women, who stood behind a table pouring tea from a large urn.

'Looks like you don't need me after all. This place is set up nice already,' Nellie said.

'On the contrary; we do need you. Supplies are tight and volunteers, though plentiful, don't necessarily have your resources. I think you and I can do a lot of good here.'

Nellie turned on the spot, taking in every detail. 'Impressive place. Lily said she came down here from Drop Redoubt the other day. But where do all these other tunnels lead?' she asked, gesturing around her.

'Everything joins up. That one there runs to Shake-speare Cliff, and that one runs under the town all the way to Pencester.'

Nellie whistled. 'I knew they were here. We used them last time round, but we never ventured that far in. And now it's a proper home from home.'

'Well, it could be. Just needs a bit of thought, and we might even set up a small school in here. What do you think? Seeing as the council aren't going to reopen the schools.'

'Sign our Don up,' Nellie said. 'He could do with a bit of schooling in something other than planes and bombs.'

'Mrs Palmer, a moment if you please,' a familiar voice echoed across the chamber.

Nellie groaned. 'You can't be serious. Shouldn't you be off looking for criminals instead of following me around?'

Roger Humphries pointedly ignored her. 'I've just been telling people to take their furniture away. There are explicit rules for cave use. One of those is that it is absolutely forbidden to stake a claim by leaving furnishings or bedding of any kind. And yet I see that's exactly what people have done. Aside from taking up room, it's a health risk.'

'Constable Humphries,' Mrs Palmer said in her poshest voice, 'the more time people are forced to spend here, the more they'll need some home comforts. Dear Mayor Tilbury agrees, and he is fully aware that people are bringing things here to help make this difficult situation a little more bearable. Now, I know how hard you work, so I should imagine you could do with some refreshment, and maybe one of Marianne Castle's delicious pies. She made them especially for people taking shelter.' She picked up

227

the basket and took it to the table, gesturing to one of the women behind it to pour a cup of tea.

Roger stared at the pies greedily, before finally taking one and biting into it. 'Mmm. Bacon,' he mumbled appreciatively as he chewed. Then he stiffened, and stared at Nellie. 'Four ounces of bacon a week and you make—' he checked the tin '—at least thirty cheese and bacon pies, Mrs Castle? Would you care to explain how?'

Nellie snatched the pie from his hand. 'No one said you have to eat one. There's plenty here who'd thank me for it.'

He snatched it back. 'I didn't say I didn't want it, did I? I was just asking where you got so much bacon. Mrs Palmer explained the supplies in your basement, but far as I was aware that was a one-off. So, where did all this come from?'

'There are five of us in the house. And we all donate our ration.'

'You *all* donated your ration?'

'Is that a crime?'

'As long as that's all you used.'

'Any extra supplies are made up by the WVS, Constable Humphries. All legal and above board, I assure you.'

Roger gave an obsequious smile. 'Of course, Mrs Palmer. Of course. Now, if you could assist me in encouraging people to take their belongings home, I know the chief constable would be most grateful.'

'I'll do my best, Constable. In the meantime, why don't you move along, there's others who need a cup of tea.'

Roger almost bowed. 'Thank you for your cooperation, Mrs Palmer. We really are most grateful.'

'Are you grateful to me for the pie, Roger?'

'Naturally, Mrs Castle. Please pass on my compliments to Marianne.'

As he turned and left, Nellie grinned at Mrs Palmer. 'You really could teach me a thing or two about handlin' the constabulary. Flattery and condescension. I should try that next time.' She paused. 'On second thoughts, I won't.'

'For the good of the town only, Mrs Castle. Otherwise you know I'd have to report you,' the other woman said sternly.

'I wouldn't expect anything else.' Nellie grinned suddenly. 'Who'd have thought, you and me working together, eh, Muriel? Well, now I've seen the place, I can see what a job it's going to be. You'll need more than one stand, in my view.'

Mrs Palmer nodded. 'We will. And there are other caves over in East Cliff and more up near Crabble Hill. But I'll find other people to help there. I'd like you to concentrate your efforts here. But please be discreet about any—' she waved her hand vaguely '—dealings. I have my reputation to think of.'

'You're not the only one. Folk see me cosying up with you and the WVS they'll think I've lost my bite.'

'So we have an agreement?' Mrs Palmer held out her hand.

'For now.' Nellie shook the proffered hand. 'But like you said; for the good of the town only.'

They were startled as somebody started to laugh. 'Well, this is a sight I never thought I'd see! But between the two of you, you might just help pull us through. Anyway, if that lot's quietened down outside, think I'll get back before the next emergency hits. Told Derek I was only popping out to get a few bits, then got caught out by the siren. Lucky for me and all, or I'd have missed the sight of Nellie Castle and Muriel Palmer being civil to each other.'

Nellie beamed. 'Mavis, me and Mrs P— *Muriel* – was just discussing trying to set up more refreshments stands and you could be just the person to help us. You're only down the road and you got a nice big kitchen. You been in the Royal Oak, Muriel? Good grub, and better company.'

Mrs Palmer smiled primly. 'Hello, Mrs Woodbridge. Actually, I was going to try to enlist your help.'

'There you are then. I done the job for you.'

Mavis sighed. 'All right, pop in any time.' She cocked her head. 'But now I need to get back.'

'It's advisable to wait an hour before venturing out after a shelling, I've been told,' Mrs Palmer informed them.

'Huh! And what if the hour's nearly up and another one drops? Then you're stuck waiting another hour. No, I'll take my chances. What about you, Nell, you coming?'

Nellie put her helmet back on. 'Definitely. This place is better than I thought, but it still gives me the heebie-jeebies. I'll send Don to collect the basket later, Muriel.' She held out her hand to the woman. 'And no offence, but here's hopin' that you and I don't have to work together for too long.'

Mrs Palmer took her hand and smiled. 'None taken, Nellie. And remember what I said: *just the once*, so please be a little more circumspect.'

Nellie grinned. 'Course I will, Muriel, love. You know me, circumcision is my middle name.'

Mrs Palmer's eyes widened for a moment, then she shook her head, as though at a naughty child.

Nellie laughed uproariously as she took Mavis's arm and they made their way back to the entrance.

Once the two women were out in the open again, Nellie breathed a sigh of relief. 'I don't mind telling you, Mavis, if it's between being buried in a collapsed tunnel or beneath my own house, I know which one I'd choose.'

'Too right. I'll just keep taking my chances in the basement at the pub. Advantage being there's a bar down there. It gets busy during night raids, I can tell you. Those pilots don't half know how to put it away.' She paused and looked up to the sky. 'You know, back in June there were around a dozen that came in regular. Only six of 'em left now. Lovely young lads. Brave as lions.'

'Bastard buggering Waffa,' Nellie said. 'One hour in a room with that Hitler, I'd sort him out.'

Mavis smiled sadly. 'If only it were that simple. You an' me would see 'im off.'

Nellie grunted. 'By the way, Mave,' she said as they came to the junction with New Bridge. 'Marianne and Alfie have set the date for the twenty-first next month and I was wondering whether I could buy some beer and bubbles off you for the wedding party?'

Mavis beamed. 'Oh, that's wonderful news! And as if I'd make you pay. Me and Derek'll be happy to give it as a wedding present. Oh, and I bet Daisy and Stan'll come back with little Maggie!' Mavis looked delighted at the prospect of seeing her granddaughter again. 'Just think, Nell, this time last year you never thought you'd see your Marianne wed. And after all those years of trying, I never thought my Stan and his Daisy would give me a grand-child. Yet here we are. It just goes to show, don't it, that there's always a ray of light, no matter how dark the times.'

Nellie nodded. 'You're right there, love. The world's gone stark staring mad, but there's still joy to be had in the little things.'

Chapter 23

As Pauline and Lily hurried home at the end of their shift, Pauline, who had persuaded Lily to give her back the hip flask, took a long drink.

'Do you reckon Bert's serious about me?' Pauline asked, wiping her mouth.

Lily sighed. 'You'll have to ask him, but if you want the truth, I'd say no.'

Pauline huffed and took another swig while Lily eyed her warily. She couldn't wait to see Charlie again, but if Pauline went on at this rate, she'd have to spend another night looking after her. Actually, she thought, bloody Bert could look after her – he'd invited her, after all.

'Here, Paul, no offence, but would you mind if I met Charlie on my own? I mean, you and Bert don't want to sit with us at the cinema, do you?'

'Don't worry about that. Last thing I want is to watch you two canoodling when I've got my own bloke to see to. Anyway, me and Bert are meeting for fish and chips before it starts.'

Lily breathed a sigh of relief. 'Although I won't be canoodling. I've only just met the bloke.'

Pauline snorted a laugh. 'What's that got to do with the price of tea in China?'

Lily giggled. 'You're right. Absolutely nothing.'

Spurred on by the thought of the evening ahead, the girls quickened their pace and were soon clattering up the stairs towards the bedroom.

'Oy!' Nellie called out as they ran past the sitting room door. 'Before you get changed I want a word with the both of you.'

'What's up?' Lily said, leaning on the door frame and shooting a questioning glance at Marianne, who grimaced in reply.

'*Someone* got the police round here looking for black market goods.'

Lily's eyebrows rose. 'You've been buying illegal stuff?'

'Never you mind about that; what I want to know is *who* told them to come here.' She stared hard at Pauline, who flushed a deep red.

'You think *I* did it?'

'Did you?'

'No! Of course I didn't.'

Nellie gave her a searching look. 'If I find out any different, then I'll have to ask you to go. And while we're on the subject, I want you to tell me about that bloke who turned up here yesterday. He were in the café when Roger and his gang came round today. Why did you run out to speak to him like that?'

'Cos I thought he was out of order. He had no business staring at us like that. I don't like him.'

234

'Mum, you can't seriously believe . . . ?'

'All I know is the other night, when Jasper and me were in the kitchen downstairs, someone was listening to us.'

'When was Jasper here the other night?' Lily asked.

'Oh, he popped in for a nightcap a few of nights ago,' Nellie said airily.

Lily raised her eyebrows at Marianne, who shrugged.

'Was that you, girl?'

'I don't know what you're talking about. Honest, Mrs C, I'd never bring trouble to you. Especially given that me and Bert is going out.'

Nellie looked sceptical at that. 'I'm willing to give you the benefit of the doubt for now. And I'm sorry to upset you. But if it weren't for Mrs Palmer, things could have gone badly for me.'

'Blimey! Are you telling me old Nosy Palmer helped you out?'

Nellie pointed at Lily. 'Don't you go being disrespectful about Muriel. She's doing her best for this community, and I can name a few that might take a leaf out of her book. Now, Pauline, go and get me a glass. I need a drink.' Nellie held up her bottle of sherry.

Pauline looked relieved to be dismissed and crossed to the little kitchen.

'Mum,' Lily whispered, 'how could you accuse her like that?'

Nellie shrugged. 'I was just asking the question.'

Before they could say any more, Pauline bounded back in holding a couple of glasses.

'I brought two. Hope you don't mind if I have a little tipple too?'

Nellie's lips tightened in annoyance as Pauline poured a small measure of sherry into each glass.

'I don't think you've got time,' Lily said hastily as Pauline took the glass.

'Just a quick one. Then I'll get changed.' She threw the drink back.

Nellie cackled. 'When I sent you to the Citadel all them years ago, I thought I was protecting *you* from *Bert*. But you carry on like that and I might have to start protecting him.' She drained her drink, then pointedly poured more sherry into her own glass, ignoring the fact that Pauline was holding hers out for more.

'I have to hand it to you, though; in my day we weren't so forward. Do you reckon you can keep your hands to yourself tonight? Or will I have to pull him away from you again?'

'I didn't hear Bert complaining,' Pauline snapped. 'Anyway, I better get on. You coming, Lily?'

'I'll be up in a minute.' As soon as she heard the bedroom door closing upstairs, Lily rounded on her mother.

'Mum,' Lily hissed, 'what are you playing at? Pauline's my friend and she wouldn't do that to me.'

'You sure about that? I'm not saying she did do it, but all the same, keep an eye on her. Edie told me what she done to her friend, so she's got form.'

'But this is different—'

'Like I said, keep an eye on her. That's all I've got to say on the matter.' With that, Nellie switched on the wireless and turned her head away.

In the bedroom, Lily found Pauline pulling up the zip of a red dress that she'd been planning to wear, then she picked up Lily's brush and began to pull it violently through her dark hair. 'The cheek of your mum, thinking I'd dob *anyone* in to the police.'

Ignoring the comment, Lily stared pointedly at Pauline's hairbrush on the dresser, then looked back at her. 'Something wrong with your brush?'

'I prefer yours, is all,' she said. 'Why, you think I've got nits or something?'

'It's not just the brush.' Lily began to undress, her movements jerky with annoyance. 'It's the dress. I was going to wear that tonight. You could at least have asked.'

Pauline threw the brush onto the bed and forcefully pulled the zip of the dress down, tugging it off to reveal Lily's best brassiere underneath.

'For God's sake, Pauline! I'm happy to share, but my brassiere too!'

Pauline undid the clips at the front and threw the garment at her.

'Fine! Take it.' She pulled her liberty bodice from the bed and put it on. 'Now I look like my bleeding mother.' She stalked to the wardrobe and gazed inside. Finally, she sighed deeply and pulled out the green dress she'd worn to the dance. 'Looks like I'll have to wear this again then. That's if it's all right with your ladyship,' she sneered.

'I don't mind you borrowing my clothes, but just ask next time,' Lily said through gritted teeth.

'What's it to you? You've got plenty of stuff. Café must be doing well, eh? Can't see why your mum would start dealing on the black market the amount she's raking in.'

'She's not dealing on the black market!'

'Seems someone thinks she is,' Pauline said, tugging the dress over her head. 'Charming, isn't it? I spend all day slaving away up at the hospital, doing my bit, and this is the thanks I get.'

'You don't have to stay here, you know.'

Suddenly the fire went out of Pauline. 'Do you want me to leave?' she asked in a small voice. 'I know I'm not always the easiest, but I'm not a snitch, and I didn't go to the police. For God's sake, I didn't even know about it! And I'm sorry for taking your clothes.' She sniffed. 'It's just ... I like living here. I always wanted a sister, and being here with you, it feels like I finally have one.'

At her friend's dejected expression, Lily felt a pang of guilt and stood up to pull Pauline into a hug. 'Hey, I'm sorry. I like having you here too. Let's just go and enjoy ourselves tonight with two of the handsomest men in Dover.'

Pauline pulled away and grinned, her mood changing abruptly again. 'Bert is gorgeous, ain't he?'

'I suppose. If you like that kind of thing. Personally, I prefer Charlie.'

'I should hope so and all. You'd be a right perv if you didn't.' Pauline laughed as she brushed out her hair again and hastily applied some lipstick. 'Right, that's me done. See you later.' Snatching up her bag, she raced to the door.

Lily sighed. She'd lied when she said she liked Pauline living at the café; in fact, she was beginning to regret inviting her. The more she thought about it, the more strange things were beginning to feel. What with Dick and his odd behaviour, and the fact that Pauline was clearly scared of him. And now this latest incident with the police coming round ... But right now, she didn't have time to think about any of that if she wanted to look her best, so she pushed thoughts of Pauline out of her head and pictured Charlie instead. Was it possible she'd only known him for a couple of weeks? It felt like longer, even though they'd only really spent time together that once.

Suddenly, she felt nervous. He was older and more sophisticated than her; he'd studied medicine, worked in a field hospital, and in terms of experience, he was so far ahead of her that, for the first time in her life, she felt a little out of her depth with a man. She stared critically at herself in the mirror. She wasn't vain, but she knew she was pretty and the red dress looked good on her. But it wasn't her looks she was feeling uncertain about; it was everything else. Could she ever be enough for a man like Charlie? Rubbing her finger into the remains of her lipstick, she spread it over her lips then took the pins out of her hair; there was no time to style it as she had wanted, so she brushed it and clipped it behind her ears, threw a cream-coloured cardigan over her shoulders, slipped on her sandals and raced down the stairs and out of the back door.

Chapter 24

Lily poked her head around the back gate, peering up the road towards the Granada Cinema; she didn't want to get there before Charlie and end up standing around on her own. And what if he didn't turn up? He hadn't come to lunch yesterday after all.

There was a crowd milling around outside the cinema, and she strained her eyes in the dim light, trying to spot Charlie. Before the war, the huge arched window above the entrance used to light up the street, but now it was in darkness. Then she saw his tall figure leaning against the white wall of the cinema, staring down towards the market square. Her heart skipped a beat as she watched a couple of girls glancing back at him. At well over six foot, he was an impressive sight, and tonight he was all hers. There was no telling what the future held for either of them, so she shouldn't waste her time with silly insecurities. Anyway, she was only eighteen and there was so much more she wanted to do with her life; a serious boyfriend just wasn't in her plan at the moment, so for now she would enjoy the time she had with him and let the future take care of itself.

After smoothing down the red cotton skirt over her hips, she opened her compact and checked there was no lipstick on her teeth, then she stepped out of the gate. She'd show those girls what sort of woman Charlie deserved, she thought, as she sauntered casually across the road – and she would enjoy every single second.

Charlie's face lit up when he saw her and he rushed forward to kiss her cheek. 'Look at you!' he said. 'I already knew you scrubbed up well, but tonight . . .' He put his hands on her shoulders and held her away from him. 'You are beautiful, Lily Castle. Has anyone ever told you that?'

Lily grinned cheekily. 'They might have. And you don't look so bad yourself. I've been watching those girls ogling you.'

'They can ogle all they like. I only have eyes for you.'

'Flatterer. Come on.' She took his hand and led him to the entrance of the cinema. 'I love this place. It always makes me feel a bit like that French queen. The one who got her head chopped off.'

Charlie whistled as they entered through the blackout curtain. 'I see what you mean,' he said, gazing around. With a black-and-white tiled floor and duck-egg blue walls with gold cornicing, the foyer was impressive. From the lobby a marble staircase with an ornate gold balustrade led up towards a landing beneath the arched window. Here, the staircase split into two, rising towards the high, domed ceiling where, before the war, a large ornate glass chandelier used to hang.

They walked through the door on the ground floor into the auditorium. On the stage at the front, a man in tails and a bow tie sat at an organ playing the *Gone with the Wind* theme tune. Lily clasped her hands and shivered. 'Oh, this music gives me goosebumps every time I hear it.'

Charlie grunted non-committally. 'How many times have you seen it?'

'Only about ten times.' Lily grinned. 'It's my absolute favourite.'

They sat down on the red velvet seats and Charlie took a small paper bag out of his pocket and presented it to her with a flourish.

'For Madame,' he said. 'A present fit for a French queen or a Southern belle.'

Lily clapped her hands with delight. 'Toffees! For little old me.' She fluttered her eyelashes at him, before fishing out a sweet and popping it in her mouth. She took another and held it up to Charlie's lips. He took it quickly, managing to kiss her fingers as he did so, staring at her intently. To Lily, his expression was part challenge and part invitation, and she was more than happy to accept both, so she licked her fingers provocatively, then laughed and flicked his sleeve.

He smiled back and took her hand as the organist finished playing and the small platform he was sitting on sunk beneath the stage. The screen came down and the Pathé newsreel began. To her surprise, it showed planes fighting over the Channel, the white cliffs clear in the background, while the voiceover talked about houses being bombed.

242

'Is that really how people round the country see Dover? Hellfire corner?' She laughed. 'Mum hates it when anyone says that. It's not *that* bad.'

Charlie raised an eyebrow at her sceptically. 'People are living in caves and being shot at and shelled every day. You sure it's not *that* bad.'

Lily shrugged. 'We're getting by, aren't we?'

Someone behind her tutted disapprovingly and Lily turned around and stuck her tongue out at them.

Charlie put his arm around her shoulder, pulling her against him tightly. 'I can see I'm going to have to keep you in check,' he whispered into her ear, causing a shiver to race down her spine.

'You can try,' Lily whispered back. 'But don't get your hopes up.'

The newsreel finished then, and with a sigh of satisfaction she sat back to enjoy the film.

Charlie kept hold of Lily's hand throughout, but she was barely aware of it as she became immersed in the story. At one point, as Scarlett O'Hara dug in the earth looking for food, she gripped his hand tighter, mouthing the line she knew was coming. 'As God is my witness . . .' But just as Vivien Leigh raised her hands to the sky and opened her mouth, the ear-splitting wail of the air raid siren drowned out the words and the reel came to a juddering halt as a wobbly sign flashed onto the screen: 'Air Raid in Progress'.

'Oy! Turn it back on!' someone behind them shouted.

A voice came over the loudspeaker. 'Ladies and gentlemen, please make your way to the nearest shelter.'

243

Lily craned her neck and saw a woman stand up and wave her fist towards the projectionist. 'As God is my witness, I will never leave this cinema again!' she shouted.

The audience erupted into laughter, as Lily groaned, 'It's Pauline. She's bloody drunk again!'

Lily shouldn't have worried though as several other women in the audience jumped up and started to chant the words along with her.

Finally, the defeated voice of the announcer came over the loudspeaker again. 'On your own head be it,' he said, and the film juddered back into life.

Charlie leant over and whispered, 'Don't you think we should leave?'

She gave him a sharp look and hissed, 'What a white-livered little coward you are!' and turned back to the screen.

Charlie chuckled and handed her another toffee. 'Well, at least let me make sure you never go hungry again.'

She took the toffee absently, her eyes never leaving the screen.

By the time the film finished, Lily felt exhausted with the emotion of it all. Outside, the all-clear was just sounding, and as they emerged on to the street a bright red glow in the sky made the dark silhouette of the castle stand out in vivid contrast. The murmur of the emerging crowd was silenced as people stopped to stare at the scene. 'It's as if we've stepped into our very own film set,' Lily whispered. 'It looks like St Margaret's has taken a beating.'

244

Just then, Pauline bounded over to them, clutching on to Bert's arm. 'Did you hear me? I got everyone chanting,' she said excitedly. Her eyes were glassy and her speech was a little slurred.

Lily glanced at Bert who rolled his eyes.

'The whole cinema heard you, love,' Bert said. 'And now I think I need to be getting you home before you fall over. As for me, I should get back to barracks, make sure I'm not needed.'

'Nooo!' Pauline protested. 'It's not fair. We've hardly had any time together. Can we do it again soon?'

'Course we can,' Bert said placatingly. 'You coming, Charlie?'

Charlie shook his head. 'Seeing as it's not near the barracks, think I'll stay out of this one.'

Lily took his arm. 'Good. Tell you what, let's pop to the Royal Oak for a quick drink. My mum's friend Mavis runs it, and you should get to know her if you're going to be around for any length of time.'

They walked swiftly away, Lily feeling slightly guilty that she'd left Bert to deal with Pauline's disappointment. But then, he'd brought all of this on himself, so she didn't feel *that* bad.

She led Charlie across the market square to Cambridge Road, where the pub was situated. Once inside, she held tightly to his hand as he pushed his way through the crowd of servicemen and women towards the bar.

'All right, Mavis?' Lily said when they finally got to the front.

'Hello, Lily, love.' She eyed Charlie. 'Who's this?'

Charlie held out his hand and smiled charmingly. 'Dr Charlie Alexander. Delighted to meet you.'

A slow smile spread across Mavis's face. 'Well, you're a handsome fella, ain't ya? But I give you fair warning, Doctor, a handsome face is all well and good, but can you deal with the Castle family?'

Charlie grinned at her. 'Oh, I think I'm up to the challenge.'

'You better be, lad. If you've not heard already, bad things happen around them.' She cackled. 'Just joking. Oh, and Lily, tell your mum me and Derek are putting a barrel of beer aside for your Marianne and Alfie's wedding party, and we've got some bubbles as well. And it's all legit, so no danger of the law takin' it away.' She went off into peals of laughter while Lily smiled weakly.

'What was all that about?'

'Buy me a drink and I'll tell you.'

They sat in the snug with their drinks and Lily filled him in on what had happened at the café that day.

When she'd finished, Charlie laughed. 'Who needs *Gone with the Wind* when you've got that much drama going on? Seems to me what you need, Miss Castle, is a nice relaxing walk along the seafront.' He stood up and held his hand out to her.

Lily smiled at him. 'I think you might be right, Doctor.' She stood and took his hand, and they made their way down to the front, stopping at the railings to gaze out at the rippling sea, the water shining in the light from the full moon.

'I can't remember when I've had this much fun,' Charlie said quietly. 'I hope you want to see me again, Lily?'

She turned to him. 'Really? You're not put off by my drunk friend, Mum's illegal dealings and visits from the police?'

Charlie paused and in the darkness Lily couldn't see the expression on his face. Finally, he said, 'You know, if I had to list the things I wanted in a woman, those are the exact qualities I'd choose. I've no interest in anyone whose family isn't in trouble with the law.' He pulled her close and brushed his lips over hers. Lily put her arms around his neck, returning his kiss with fervour. For the first time in her life, Lily thought, she could actually feel the electricity she'd read about in romantic novels. In fact, she could have sworn she'd even seen sparks. As their kiss deepened, a loud explosion made them jump apart.

'What was—'

'Shells!' Charlie shouted, grabbing her hand and pulling her towards the pile of sandbags around the bandstand in Granville Gardens. He pushed her down behind them and they sat, panting, as the ack-ack guns exploded into life, firing futilely into the sky.

Despite the rush of fear that had gripped her, Lily started to giggle. 'I thought the kiss had really made me see sparks! But it was the flash of the shells firing,' she gasped out.

Charlie laughed, the searchlights arcing across the sky illuminating the whites of his eyes. A loud crash from the cliffs to the west made the ground tremble and he tightened his arm around her shoulder. 'I can honestly say that you are the first girl who's literally made the earth move for me.'

Lily's giggle turned into a guffaw and, as another flash of red reflected over the sea and the air raid siren started to wail, Charlie wrapped his body more tightly around hers .

'We can't stay here,' he yelled into her ear. 'Where's the nearest shelter?'

'Pub basement's our best bet, but I want to get home!'

She scrambled up, and hand in hand they flew up Bench Street, dashed across Townwall Street and Chapel Lane to King Street, before finally skidding round the corner into Church Street. Thrusting open the back gate, Lily dashed inside and ran straight down to the basement, Charlie close on her heels.

At the bottom of the stairs, he stopped and tipped his hat politely. 'Good evening, everyone,' he said casually. 'Mrs Castle, I am delivering your daughter back safe and sound.' He gazed around the room and smiled at Pauline, who had sat up hastily when they'd come in, her hair a tangled mess, her lipstick smudged. 'I'm glad to see you got home safely,' he said. 'It's so lovely to see you again, Marianne. And you must be Donny.' He ruffled the boy's dark hair. 'Alfie's told me such a lot about you. Just to reassure you both, I spotted him on the parade ground this morning, and he looked fit as a fiddle. Sorry I can't stay to talk more, but I think I'd better go.'

'You're leaving now?' Lily squeaked.

'That shell was too close to the barracks for comfort. See you later this week?'

She shook her head. 'I'm on nights for a week.'

He bent to kiss her firmly on the lips. 'Don't think for a minute that that's going to stop me seeing you. I'll find a way,' he murmured.

'Promise?' Lily wound her arms around his neck, oblivious to the others watching them.

He smiled against her lips. 'Wild horses wouldn't stop me.' Then with a brief wave, he turned and bounded up the stairs.

'Be careful,' Lily called after him, but the door had already shut so she didn't know whether he heard her or not.

'Well,' Nellie said with a gleam in her eye, 'you've done well for yourself there, girl. An officer *and* a doctor. And he'd have given your dad a run for his money in the looks department.'

Lily shrugged, trying to appear casual. 'He's all right, I suppose.'

'You don't fool me. I ain't never seen those stars in your eyes before. You've got the look of Marianne after she's just seen Alfie. Might be we have another big event to plan for soon?' she said archly.

'Mum! I'm not marrying the man. We've only had one date. Anyway, did Pauline tell you what happened at the cinema? It was a right laugh.'

She looked over to Pauline, who was sitting huddled on the cushions clutching a blanket around herself. To Lily's surprise, there were tears pouring down her cheeks.

'Hey, Paul.' Lily sat down beside her and put an arm around her shoulders. 'What's wrong?'

'He seems so lovely,' she wailed. 'And he really likes you, I can tell. And . . . and . . . Bert just dumped me at the back gate like a sack of spuds and ran off. He didn't even kiss me.'

'Maybe if you weren't half-cut then he'd have stuck around a bit.' Nellie levelled a disapproving glare at Pauline.

'I only had a couple.' Pauline sniffed. 'Same as Bert. But he don't think I'm good enough for him, I can tell.' She turned her head into Lily's shoulder. 'My dad's right, no one's ever gonna love me.' She started to sob in earnest.

Lily shot a bemused look at her mother. 'What did you say to her?'

'Nothing. The girl stumbled down here, stinking of booze, and hasn't uttered a word till now. I thought she'd passed out.'

'It was bad of Bert to leave her like that. State she's in,' Marianne interjected. 'I'll be giving him a piece of my mind next time I see him.'

'Are you *drunk*, Pauline?' Donny asked gleefully.

'Donny!' Marianne reprimanded. 'Apologise to Pauline immediately.'

'But that's what Gran said.' At his mother's hard stare, Donny looked down. 'I'm sorry if I was rude, Pauline.'

Pauline didn't respond, and Lily felt the shoulder of her dress grow wet as her friend sobbed helplessly against her. 'Lily,' Pauline whispered quietly. 'Lily, I don't know what to do.'

'What do you mean, love?'

'He'll kill her,' she mumbled.

Lily moved away and gently helped her friend lie down on the cushions. Pauline had said this before, but she had no idea what she was talking about. 'Who'll kill who?' she whispered.

'Mum,' she said vaguely. 'Mum.' Her body relaxed then and she started to snore.

'What's she yabbering about?' Nellie asked.

Lily shrugged. 'She keeps saying, "he'll kill her", but I don't know what she's going on about.'

Nellie stood up and came to kneel beside them, groaning as her knees cracked. 'Pauline, love,' she said loudly. 'Who's going to kill who?'

Pauline groaned. 'Go away. Too loud.'

Nellie shook her. 'Pauline! Tell me now. What do you mean?'

Pauline opened bleary eyes and stared up at Nellie for a moment, then she shut them again, her head falling limply to the side.

'We'll not get anything out of her now, Mum. Last time she was this bad she said the same thing. I don't know . . .'

Nellie stood up and wrapped her dressing gown more tightly around herself. 'That's the trouble with drunks. They talk so much bloody nonsense you don't know what's true and what's not. I tell you, Lily, she don't clean up her act, she's got to go.'

'You can't throw her out! Not until her mum and dad get back. If she lives on her own she'll drink herself into a stupor every night.'

Nellie pondered this for a moment. 'I'll have a chat with her,' she said finally. 'And I'm going to have a word with that son of mine and all. How could he get a girl into

251

this state?' She shook her head. 'Like my mum always said, "Handsome is as handsome does", so what does that make Bert?' She sighed deeply as she poured herself a cup of tea and flicked open the newspaper.

Lily smoothed the blanket over her friend then went to sit down beside her sister.

'You all right, Lil?' Marianne asked gently.

'Yeah. Just . . . I don't know. I wish I could help Pauline; something's really scaring her and I don't think a chat with Mum will help.'

'Do you want me to have a word?'

'Would you?' Marianne's gentleness had soothed them all when they were growing up, so maybe she could do the same for Pauline.

'Course I will.'

Lily gave her sister a kiss on the cheek. 'Alfie is the luckiest man alive.'

Marianne laughed softly. 'I don't know about that, but I am definitely the luckiest woman. Your Charlie seems lovely too.'

Lily yawned and put her head on Marianne's shoulder, rubbing her face against the soft quilting of the dressing gown. 'He really is.' She closed her eyes, her mind full of Charlie's sparkling dark eyes and the kiss they had shared. She smiled at the memory. The more she thought about it, the more she was certain that the sparks she'd seen when he'd kissed her had nothing to do with the shells being fired across the Channel.

Chapter 25

It was just as well they were on nights, Lily thought the next morning, because there was no way Pauline was in any state to work. It had been a job to get her upstairs once the all-clear had sounded the night before, but somehow between the three of them they had managed to half-carry her to bed.

By three o'clock, Pauline was still asleep and Lily, who'd spent the afternoon thoroughly cleaning the apartment and Polly's cage, took her a cup of tea and a plate of sandwiches.

'Pauline!' she shouted as she plumped down on the bed. 'We've got lessons.'

'Shh,' Pauline mumbled from beneath the blankets.

'Eat this and you'll feel better. Then you can tell me why you were muttering about someone killing someone else.'

Pauline sat up and grabbed the plate of sandwiches. 'Wha?' she said after she'd taken her first mouthful.

'Last night. You said, "He'll kill her," and that's the second time you've said that when you've been drunk.'

Pauline swallowed her food and stared at Lily bemused. 'I said that?'

'Yes. And while we're on the subject, where's your flask? I'm throwing it away.' She stood up and started searching through Pauline's bag.

Pauline set the plate aside and snatched the bag from Lily. 'Gerroff! That's my private property.'

'You can't keep drinking, Paul. You never used to be like this.'

'Well, that was before the war, weren't it? And don't worry. I'll not take it to work. Will that satisfy you, little Miss Prissy?'

'I suppose. But promise you won't? You'll get sacked if you're not careful.'

Pauline shrugged. 'Course I won't. You worry too much. Anyway, it was fun last night at the pictures, wasn't it?'

Lily smiled in spite of herself. 'It was.'

'Reckon you, me, Bert and Charlie can do a proper foursome one night?'

Lily hesitated. She doubted Bert would want to, but how could she tell her friend that? 'Course,' she said vaguely. 'But once you've eaten, get up and get dressed or we'll be late for lessons.'

The girls' lectures had been delayed thanks to the constant state of emergency at the hospital, but now they were on night duty they were due to have lessons every afternoon before their shift started.

Pauline flopped back onto the bed. 'My brain aches just thinking about it. But still, least we won't be running into Dick Brown while we're on nights, eh?'

'Good point. And no cleaning!'

∞

If the girls thought night duty would be more relaxing, they were soon disabused as they spent their shift either mending sheets by the dim light of a hurricane lamp, or soothing patients who, in the dead of the night, found the nightmare of war returning full throttle.

Lily was assigned to the Nissen hut with Sister MacKenzie, and she found it unsettling to be there at night. These patients were the enemy, and even though there were two soldiers posted outside to guard them, it was eerie being with men destined to spend the rest of the war as prisoners. It was worse when there was an air raid, as they had to find a way to get the men to the basement in the dark, and as Lily helped Felix, the prisoner with stomach cancer, over the grass one night, she shivered at the thought that he could turn on her at any moment.

To make matters worse, Charlie hadn't come to see her as he'd promised. Had he had second thoughts? Lily wondered, as she and Pauline wearily made their way back home from the hospital nearly a week later. They only had one more night duty left, and she was tempted to go up to Drop Redoubt to speak to him, but would that seem desperate? She'd never felt like this about a man before, and she had no idea what to do. The boys she'd gone out with in the past had always hung around like bad smells until she was forced to tell them to do one.

Her thoughts were interrupted by the air raid siren and, as the noise overhead increased, the girls ducked into a doorway. A burst of gunfire made them jump, and peeking out round the wall they gasped as the barrage balloon that floated over Granville Gardens burst into flames. The plane responsible continued on its path, roaring over them, so close they could almost see the pilot's face.

'It's got the bleeding balloon attached!' Pauline screamed.

The girls watched in horror as the balloon was dragged up New Bridge, setting fire to an empty bus parked by the market hall before it finally detached itself and fell in a ball of flames into the market square.

'It's hit Lou Carter's stall!' Lily shouted, starting to run, Pauline close on her heels. It was too early for the stall to be open, but had she been there setting up?

To their relief, they saw the woman coming down the steps of the market hall carrying a box. She dropped it in disbelief as she stared at the scene.

'Me fish!' she shouted. 'They've bloody blown up me whelks and eels!' Lou ran towards her stall, trying desperately to grab a barrel from the flames. But as she did so, the flames leapt up her arm and she let out a cry of agony as she fell back.

Lily and Pauline increased their pace and as soon as they reached her, Lily dragged off her cloak and threw it over Lou's arm, wrapping it round as best she could and patting at it in an effort to put out the flames.

Suddenly, a deluge of cold water made her cry out and she looked up to find Jasper standing above her, a bucket in his hand, his expression frantic.

'Lily, love, are you all right?' He reached down and pulled her up, wrapping his arms around her and dropping kisses onto her hair.

'I'm fine, Jasper,' she half laughed. 'Least I was til you nearly drowned me then crushed me half to death.'

Jasper loosened his hold, but refused to let her go. 'Never, ever, ever go rushing in to danger like that again!' he said fiercely.

Lily pulled back. 'Says the man who does it every day!' She looked down at the sobbing woman lying on the cobbles. Pauline was beside her, attempting to unwrap the cape from her arm, but the woman was screaming blue murder and wouldn't let her touch it. 'Now let me do my job, for gawd's sake!'

Jasper released her and she knelt down. 'All right, Lou. Let's get you inside and have a look at the damage,' she said gently.

Nellie rushed towards them. 'Jesus Christ, Lou! It's a bit of burnt fish and a scalded arm. Stop bawlin' like a baby, you're scaring the kids.'

It was only then that Lily noticed that Donny, Freddie and a few other children had appeared. They didn't look scared though; if anything they looked excited.

257

Nellie's words did the job the bucket of cold water hadn't managed, and Lou stopped screaming and opened her eyes to glare at Nellie. 'Me arm's just been burnt to a crisp. If you were me you'd be hollerin' as well.'

Nellie raised an eyebrow. 'You want a cup of tea, Lou? With a tot of brandy for the shock?'

Lou sat up, clutching her arm, and Jasper bent down to help her stand. 'You wouldn't be able to spare a bit of egg and sausage and all, would yer?' she said hopefully.

Nellie chuckled as she put her arm around the woman's ample waist. 'Let's see what we can do. And I'll get Don to run for the doctor.'

'No need, Mrs Castle,' a voice said, and Lily jumped as Charlie suddenly appeared through the thick black smoke that had enveloped the square, a large canvas bag over his shoulder. 'I'll take a look.' He grinned at Lily. 'Like I said, always a drama around here, isn't there? You trying to recreate the burning of Tara?' He nodded at the barrage balloon, jumping back as Ethel Turner, her hair still in curlers beneath a scarf, threw a bucket of water over the flames. She was swiftly followed by Reenie and several other residents of the square.

Lily grinned sheepishly as she pushed her sodden hair off her face. 'Worth a try, don't you think?'

'Definitely. Fancy breakfast?'

'I wouldn't say no. I'm starving.' She looked down at herself and grimaced. 'But first, I need to change.'

As they entered the café, he pulled her round and looked down at her. 'If it weren't for the risk of you catching your

258

death, I'd disagree. You've never looked lovelier to me.' He put his hand on her cheek. 'God, you scared me when I saw you dash towards the flames!'

'You saw that?'

'I was walking down Cowgate. I've never run faster in my life. Don't do that again, Lily.'

She laughed. 'Funny. That's what Jasper said. But when you live on the front line, you've got no choice but to do what you have to.'

He sighed and shook his head. 'I suppose you're right, but I'd prefer not to see it in the future. Anyway, before I forget.' He took the bag from his shoulder and handed it to her.

Lily staggered slightly under the weight and peered inside curiously. 'You remembered,' she exclaimed, pulling out a large hardback book embossed with gold. '*Gray's Anatomy*,' she said reverently.

'Not the latest edition, I'm afraid.'

She hugged it to her chest. 'It doesn't matter. Thank you, Charlie,' she said with a tremulous smile, ignoring Pauline's derisive snort beside her. 'This is the best present you could have given me.'

His eyebrows rose. 'I really hope I can do better than that one day. But I'm glad you like them.' He gave her a little shove towards the stairs. 'Now go and get changed before you catch your death, while I take a look at that woman's arm.'

Gladys came up and put an arm around Lily, giving her a swift kiss on the cheek. 'Well done, love,' she whispered.

Then she turned to Charlie. 'Nell's taken Lou upstairs. Go on up and I'll bring some tea with a tot of brandy. You too, Pauline. Reckon you could use a little pick-me-up and all.'

Lily opened her mouth to refuse the brandy. Pauline hadn't had a drink all week and she didn't want to set her off again. But seeing her friend's pale face, she shut her mouth. Gladys was right; they could all do with it.

∞

Later, Lily and Charlie sat at a table by the window watching the clean-up operation in the square as the fire brigade attempted to remove the balloon. The cobbles where it had landed were blackened and the smell of burning rubber was still in the air, but aside from having to skirt around the firemen, life had returned to its normal bustling routine in the market square.

Nellie came over and placed two plates of sausage, egg and fried bread in front of them, then returned with the teapot to refill their cups. 'Now, if you want anything else, you just ask,' she said. Lily stifled a grin. If it had been anyone else, she'd say her mother was fawning. She stared at Charlie over the rim of her teacup. He had a smudge of soot down one side of his face and he looked tired, as if he, too, had been up all night. But the way he was looking at her, as though she had done something miraculous, made her feel warm and tingly inside, even though as far as she was concerned she really hadn't been in much danger.

Luckily, Lou wasn't badly injured, and Charlie had wrapped her arm in wet bandages and told her to take some aspirin for the pain and get some rest. Lou had scoffed at that. 'What? With my stall destroyed? I've got stuff to do if I'm to get back up and running. But thanks, Doc. And if you ever need anything – cigs, chocolate, booze – you come to me and I'll sort you out.'

The woman was now sitting at another table devouring her free breakfast and loudly telling everyone about her brush with death.

'So . . .' Charlie said. 'I'm sorry I couldn't come sooner. It's been a bit . . . hairy.'

Lily raised her eyebrows. 'What do you mean?'

He shook his head. 'I can't say. But, well, we've all been on high alert. Just in case.'

Lily felt her stomach swoop at that. 'Just in case of what?'

He didn't answer, but she knew very well what he meant. Had the invasion nearly happened without any of them realising it? 'And now?' she asked carefully.

'Now, it looks like the RAF have managed to buy us a bit more time.'

She nodded, knowing he could say no more.

'So tell me how you've found your first week of nights,' he said, moving the conversation on to safer ground.

As they chatted, the café filled up around them and soon all anyone could talk about was the barrage balloons. Every balloon in Dover had been shot down, apparently. And several had landed on houses, so they'd been lucky in the square not to have more damage. But all of Lily's attention was on Charlie, and as far as she was concerned, they were the only two people in the room.

'Hey.' Nellie's loud voice rang across the room. She was standing at her usual post at the counter reading the newspaper. 'Did any of you see what Churchill said about the pilots? That stuff about so much being owed by so many to so few? I reckon he's right and all. You lot have been doing us proud.' She nodded to a group of pilots sitting at a table by the wall. Without exception, they looked exhausted, their eyes red-rimmed and their faces unshaven.

'He'll be referring to our liquor bill from last night,' one of them said, to loud guffaws from the rest of the customers.

Nellie chuckled. 'You could be right, love. My friend Mavis at the Oak says you lot drink more than your body weight. But then, I'd say you deserve it. Just so you know, there's no slate here, so if you're hoping to do the same, you can hop it.'

Charlie laughed. 'I like your mum,' he said. 'She's not as bad as Jim's been making out.'

'Jimmy has? Why?'

Charlie shrugged. 'I dunno. I don't speak to him much, but he seems angry with her about something.'

Lily sighed. 'Jimmy's been angry since Dunkirk. He didn't used to be like that. But I hoped now he's got Reenie he'd maybe start to feel a bit better.'

'Reenie's your friend at the allotment?'

She nodded.

'Mm. Yes. I've spied them walking round the Heights once or twice.'

'Really?' It seemed while she'd been looking the other way, Jim and Reenie's relationship had been deepening. 'Maybe I'll find out more at Marianne and Alfie's wedding in a couple of weeks.'

'It's that soon?'

'Yes.' She hesitated a moment. 'Would you like to come?'

'Shouldn't the bride or groom do the inviting?'

'They won't mind. We're having a party here afterwards, and everyone round here'll be coming. Mum's been collecting contributions for the food, and been feeding an enormous cake with brandy for the past two weeks. And before you ask, I'd rather not know where she got the ingredients.'

Charlie grinned. 'In that case, I'll do my best. It all depends on . . .' He waved his hand around vaguely. 'But I'd like to see you before then. I didn't just come down here this morning to give you the books and have breakfast, you know. I wanted to ask you . . .' He hesitated a moment. 'Would you have dinner at the Grand with me?'

Lily flushed with pleasure. 'No one's ever taken me to dinner before! Usually it's fish and chips on the seafront or the pictures. And I've never had dinner at the *Grand*.'

'So that's a yes?' He grinned, his dimples cutting deep lines down his cheeks.

'That's a yes,' Lily whispered, suddenly feeling shy.

'Then I'll pick you up at seven thirty tomorrow. But now I think you need to sleep. And so do I.'

Lily yawned widely as she stood and followed Charlie out of the café, suddenly realising how exhausted she was.

Charlie paused and contemplated the black cobbles for a moment. 'Promise me you won't get into any more trouble before then? I'm beginning to realise that Mavis was right about your family.'

She laughed. 'I'll do my best,' she said as he took her hand and bent to kiss her cheek.

'Tomorrow can't come soon enough,' he murmured.

She smiled softly at him then watched as he walked across the square and up Cowgate Hill, hugging her arms around herself with excitement at the prospect of the following evening. Then, yawning again, she turned and made her way upstairs, already counting the minutes until she'd be with him again.

Chapter 26

The ward was quiet as Lily sat beside one of the injured German pilots, attempting to get him to drink some water. The lamp above the bed cast a glow over the boy, emphasising his pallor. She put a hand on his forehead. It was cold and clammy, his lips cracked and dry. He shouldn't be this cold, she thought.

'Nurse Castle,' Sister Mackenzie called. 'I'm going to spend a penny. Corporal Stanmore is just outside, but I'll be back in a jiffy.'

'I need another blanket for the boy,' Lily said.

'Take one from the cupboard. I'll check him when I'm back.'

Lily went to the cupboard at the end of the ward where extra linen was stored, then returned to the bed and tucked the blanket she'd found securely around him. She felt his pulse. It was weak. Perhaps she shouldn't wait for the sister to return and should call the doctor now.

She stood by the bed, dithering about what to do before finally deciding to ask one of the soldiers on guard outside if they could go. Opening the door, she found only one man there, which was unusual. 'Can you call for the doctor?' she said. 'One of the patients has taken a turn for the worse and I'm not sure he'll make it.'

The man threw down his cigarette. 'You'll have to wait. I'm on my own at the moment.'

'I'm not sure he can wait,' she said. 'I think he's about to die.'

'I remember you,' the man said. 'Last time I saw you, you sat and shared a fag with one of them. And the answer's no. Not until I have cover.'

Lily huffed with annoyance. Although he did have a point, she supposed; he couldn't leave the hut unguarded. As she closed the door, the sound of retching made her sigh; Felix was being sick again. He was the enemy, but even so her heart went out to him. Dr Ramsay had been administering treatment, but he had told her privately that he thought it was only a matter of time before the cancer killed the man. She grabbed a bowl from the nurses' station and walked swiftly towards Felix's bed. But when she got to him, instead of leaning over the bowl as she had expected, the man's hand shot out and grabbed her wrist with surprising strength. She cried out in alarm as he pulled her arm behind her back and thrust her forward. 'Shut up,' he said, twisting his body and somehow managing to push her down onto the bed. Lily fell with a grunt, her heart hammering as she let out another muffled scream. He slapped a hand over her mouth. 'Silence,' he hissed, and Lily's breath caught in her throat when she felt the prick of a knife at her neck. 'You scream, I kill.' The hoarse voice sent shivers down her spine and she nodded. His grip loosened and she managed to turn her head to look up at him and was surprised to see a thick jersey poking out under his pyjamas. Where had he got that? The prisoners weren't allowed clothes, but someone must have given him the jumper. Then, to her horror, he raised his arm, his hand curled into a fist, and brought it crashing into her jaw. Pain exploded in her head and for a moment, Lily saw stars, then everything went black.

∽

Lily opened her eyes as pain lanced through her head. It was pitch black and she lay, trying to remember what had happened. Then it all came flooding back to her and she groaned. Had Felix really just knocked her out? The relentless throbbing in her jaw told her clearly that he had. Her hands tingled with pins and needles and, as she attempted to move, she realised they were bound securely behind her back. She struggled against the bonds, wincing as the rough rope cut into her wrists. How long had she been unconscious? she wondered. And, more importantly, where were Corporal Stanmore and Sister Mackenzie? Had Felix killed them? That terrifying thought galvanised her and she started to struggle against the ropes in earnest, her head shaking from side to side, her eyes wide open with panic. She felt as if she was suffocating, and her wrists were burning where the rope had rubbed the skin raw.

'Calm down, Lily,' she whispered to herself. 'Calm down, calm down, calm down!' Her voice had been rising in pitch as she repeated the mantra to herself, failing miserably to bring her fear under control. She inhaled deeply and forced herself to lie still, holding her breath for a moment before releasing it. It seemed to help and soon her mind cleared as she realised that though she was in a desperate situation, the man had left and she wasn't in immediate danger. Her best bet was to shout as soon as the door opened.

Time lost all meaning as she lay in the darkness, eyes staring and wrists burning. She closed her eyes and began deep breathing again. Soon they would come. Soon she would be released and all would be well.

The sound of the door opening and a scream brought her eyes wide open again. 'Nurse Castle! Nurse Castle!' Sister Mackenzie sounded on the verge of panic.

Lily let out a shout. 'I'm here!' She kicked her legs.

At last the blankets were pulled off and Nurse Mackenzie's pale, shocked face appeared above her. The woman looked as terrified as Lily felt. 'Jesus, Mary and Joseph!' she exclaimed. 'What's gone on here? Where's Muller?' She looked around the ward. 'Corporal Stanmore's been stabbed! If you're unharmed I need to get back to him.'

'Please can you—' But Sister Mackenzie was gone before Lily could ask her to cut the ropes, and once again she was left helpless, tears leaking out of her eyes. Corporal Stanmore had been right all along: you couldn't trust the prisoners as far as you could throw them.

Sister Mackenzie's screams had woken the other patients who were now sitting up, gazing at Lily in wonder and calling incomprehensibly to each other. One of the men limped over and stood looking down at her reflectively, making no attempt to undo the ropes. Finally, he let out a cackle of laughter as he limped back to bed. Cheeks flaming with anger and humiliation, Lily shouted, 'You bloody bastard! I hope you all bloody die.'

A commotion at the door made her turn her head as Corporal Stanmore's colleague arrived accompanied by several other soldiers and an officer. One of them ran up to the patient who'd laughed at Lily. 'Where is he?' he screamed in his face. But the man just shook his head. 'Fuck!' the officer shouted before running out again.

'Can someone please untie me!' Lily shouted. 'Help!'

The man stopped at the door and turned to stare at her before calling, 'Can one of you useless bastards release the bloody nurse! And don't let her go anywhere.'

A soldier came over to Lily and cut the ropes with a knife. 'What the hell happened?' he demanded.

Lily shook her head. 'I-I don't know. I thought the prisoner was being sick and I brought him a bowl—' she indicated the discarded tin bowl lying a few feet away '—and then he pulled me on to the bed and—' Lily put a hand to her throbbing jaw, wincing as her fingers brushed over a large lump.

'Why didn't you scream, for God's sake? Give the guys outside some warning.'

'I did! But then h-he held a knife to my throat and h-he said he'd kill me. Then he punched me and I blacked out.' Lily started to shake uncontrollably as the shock caught up with her. 'It was so quick. I didn't know what was happening.'

'Bloody useless woman,' he ground out. 'The prisoner was meant to be near death, for God's sake!' He looked at her narrowly. 'He obviously had inside help.'

Lily's eyes widened as his implication became clear. 'You think I—' She gulped, unable to finish the sentence.

'Did you?'

Nurse Mackenzie came up to them then. 'That's enough! I will not have you harassing one of my nurses. Can't you see she's in shock? This was *not* her fault; she was simply in the wrong place at the wrong time.'

The odious man turned his suspicious gaze on the sister. 'Whereas you, it seems, were in the right place at the right time. How could you leave a young girl like this in a room full of prisoners?'

Sister Mackenzie looked outraged. 'If you must know, I had to visit the necessary. What *I* want to know, is why you're trying to blame *my* nurse, when the fault is clearly on your inept soldiers!'

The room was getting crowded now as more military came in, followed by Matron and Dr Ramsay. 'What on earth is going on?' Dr Ramsay shouted. 'Nurse Castle,' he said, seeing her sitting on the bed. 'Are you all right?'

'I'll tell you what's going on! This man is accusing *our* nurse of helping a German prisoner escape!' Sister Mackenzie said indignantly.

Dr Ramsay's head whipped around and he stared at the man. 'How *dare* you! Our nurses deserve protection, not

270

accusations. Look at her! The poor girl's been punched in the face and is clearly in shock. She needs comfort, not the baseless accusations of a man who should know better!'

He took Lily's arm and helped her up. 'Come on, Nurse. Let's get you a hot, sweet cup of tea, and some ice for your jaw. Then you can tell me what happened.'

Grateful for Dr Ramsay's support and sympathy, Lily allowed him to lead her from the hut. His arm tight around her waist felt comforting, and if she was honest, her legs were so shaky, she would have fallen if he hadn't been holding her up.

He took her to his office, where he poured a small tot of brandy into a glass and handed it to her. 'What a bloody awful thing to have happened. Drink it all up, now,' he said, as she choked on her first sip. 'You'll feel better after. Then you can tell me all about it.' He perched on the edge of his desk.

Once again, Lily went through the events, while Dr Ramsay listened sympathetically.

'I thought he was near death,' she said eventually. 'But he was so strong.'

Dr Ramsay ran his hand through his dark hair. 'I just don't understand it. The man's been sick as a dog for weeks. I was so sure . . .' He shook his head. 'Now, much as I know you need to go home, I'm afraid after an incident like this, the police will need to be involved. They're on their way, but I'm sure you have nothing to be concerned about.'

Lily gasped in dismay. 'Why would I be concerned? I haven't done anything wrong!'

'Of course you haven't, but this is serious, so they'll need to ask you some questions. Just sit quietly and they'll be with you shortly. But if you don't mind, I need to go and talk to the sergeant.'

Lily nodded dumbly, staring into the amber liquid in her glass. Why was it moving like that? she wondered, holding it up. Then she realised her hands were shaking so much, it was a wonder she hadn't dropped the glass.

∞

Lily wasn't sure how long she waited but she was aware of frantic voices outside the door. She wondered if everyone knew what had happened. Did Pauline? Dot and Vi?

Her question was answered soon enough when the office door was thrust open and Pauline ran in followed by Dot and Vi.

'Lily! Are you all right?' Pauline stopped abruptly as she caught sight of Lily's face. 'Oh my God! Your face!' She rushed forward and put a comforting arm around her shoulder.

Tears gathered behind Lily's eyes as she leant in to her friend; there was a faint smell of alcohol coming off her, and she wondered briefly if Pauline had broken her promise about not drinking at work. But what did she care? She had far worse things to worry about right now.

'What happened, Lily?' Dot asked, kneeling in front of her and taking her hands in hers. 'Oh, you poor love, your hands are freezing.' She started to rub them, running her fingers briefly over the weals on Lily's wrists caused by the ropes.

'Blimey, Lily, the whole hospital's talking about how you helped a prisoner escape!' Vi exclaimed.

Lily's head shot up. 'What do you mean?'

'I heard it from Dick Brown. He said you tried to get the soldiers to leave their posts and the only reason you would have done that was to help the prisoner escape.'

Lily stared at her in horror. 'But—'

'Shut your mouth, Vi!' Pauline shouted. 'How could you believe anything that man says?'

Vi looked shamefaced. 'I didn't say I believed it.' She patted Lily's shoulder in an effort to comfort her. 'I just said that's what folk are saying.'

The door opened again and Dr Ramsay walked in with a couple of policemen who Lily didn't recognise, stopping short as he saw the other girls. 'What the hell are you all doing in here? Get out now, before I report you to Matron.'

At the door, Pauline looked back at Lily. 'Don't worry,' she mouthed.

But how could she not worry when the policemen were staring at her as if she was no better than dirt, and Vi had just suggested that everyone believed she'd helped Felix escape. Nausea swirled in her stomach as she waited for someone to say something. Finally, once the door was shut, one of the policemen stepped forward and, taking her by the arm, he pulled her forcibly to her feet.

'Lily Castle, we are arresting you on suspicion of aiding and abetting a prisoner of war.'

Lily was so shocked that though she tried to protest, she found she couldn't get a word out as the man hustled her to the door and into the corridor, where a crowd of people were standing, staring open-mouthed at the sight of her clutched between two policemen. She dropped her eyes to the floor, unable to look at her colleagues. Did they believe she'd done it? she wondered faintly.

Dimly, through the buzzing in her ears, she heard a voice shout. 'Hey!' Pauline was running up behind them. 'What do you think you're doing? She had nothing to do with any of this!'

'If you would kindly step away, miss,' one of the policemen said.

But Pauline ignored him as she followed, shouting admonishments.

Through the shock and humiliation, Lily couldn't make head or tail of what she was saying, but, as she was thrust into the back seat of a police car, she managed to turn and stare out of the back window. Through it she could see Pauline standing in the driveway staring after them, her mouth gaping open in shock. Dick Brown came up to her then and murmured something in her ear, and she turned, slapped him round the face and ran inside the hospital.

Chapter 27

'Two plates of egg on toast, four bacon sarnies, and a bowl of porridge. And make it snappy!' Nellie shouted at Marianne through the hatch.

She turned around and took a step back in shock as she noticed a tall pilot looming over her. His hair was light blond and his eyes were the brightest blue.

'Does Edith Castle live here, ma'am?' he said.

Nellie's eyebrows rose at his accent. 'Who's asking? And why?'

'Pilot Officer Greg Manning,' the man said. 'I have a letter to give to her.'

'Leave it with me and I'll see she gets it.'

The man shook his head. 'I'd rather give it to her myself. It's sort of personal.'

Nellie's nose was practically twitching with curiosity. 'Edie don't live here, love. You'll find her up at Pearson's Garage. Top of Castle Hill just by the castle, you can't miss it.'

He smiled his thanks and turned to leave.

'Hold on,' Nellie commanded – there was no way she was letting him leave without getting some answers first.

He stopped and turned. 'Sit, have breakfast. Any friend of Edie's is a friend of mine.'

The man smiled, his teeth bright against his tanned face. 'Well, that's an offer I can't refuse,' he said.

She led him to the table where Jasper was sitting finishing off his breakfast. 'This is . . .?'

'Greg Manning.' The man held out his hand to Jasper.

'Here to give Edie a letter.' Nellie's eyebrows rose suggestively. 'But wants to give it *personally*.' She winked at the man, who blushed.

'Really, ma'am, it's not like that.'

'You Canadian?' Jasper asked, his mouth full of toast.

'I am. How did you know? Usually people can't tell the difference between Canadian and American.'

Jasper nodded. 'There's a difference, all right. Difference being, you're here, and they're not. Pilot, are you?'

He looked down at his uniform. 'Looks that way.'

'So how do you know Edie?'

'Oh, I don't. It's just—' He stopped and looked at Jasper curiously. 'You her father?' he asked.

'As near as she's got. So?'

The man sighed. 'I have some sad news for her. A friend of ours was shot down yesterday, and before we fly we all write a letter. His was to her.'

'Really? I didn't know Edie was walking out with anyone. Not after—'

Before Nellie could say any more, Jasper intervened. 'And who can blame her for not telling you, way you run your mouth off sometimes, woman.'

Nellie shot him a look and held out her hand. 'Here, give it over and I'll make sure she gets it.' She tried again.

'Like I said, I need to deliver it myself. It's not that I don't trust you, but, you see, the man had no family to speak of and so . . . Well, I feel I need to be his family right now. And he spoke of her often, so I think the news would be better coming from someone who knew him.'

Ethel Turner, who'd been eavesdropping shamelessly, piped up then. 'Quite right, lad. If you handed it over, soon as you leave she'd be holding that over the kettle.'

'I would not.' Nellie blushed to the roots of her tightly curled hair.

Phyllis Perkins cackled. 'There ain't no secret Nellie won't try to ferret out of you, so if you and Edie are involved, then keep it close to your chest.'

'Oh, no. We're not . . . that is, I've never met her.'

'She tell you to say that, did she? She don't like me knowing stuff about her. Don't know why. Now, what can I get you? Sausage, eggs, fried bread, bacon?'

'That sounds perfect. And coffee?' he asked.

Nellie shook her head. 'We're out, and even if we weren't it's not much cop so you're better off with tea.'

She bustled away, leaving Greg looking after her, bemused. 'Don't worry, lad. You don't have to drink it,' Jasper said.

Jasper had just settled down to question the young man further, when the café door burst open and Pauline stumbled in, her face bright red from exertion, her tin hat hanging round her neck from the thin leather chin strap.

277

'You gotta come quick!' she shouted as the room went silent and all eyes turned to her. 'Lily's been arrested!'

Nellie, who had just turned from the hatch holding a plate full of food dropped the plate, oblivious to the mess and the hot splash of egg as it penetrated her stockings.

'What?'

'She's been arrested for helping a German prisoner escape,' Pauline panted.

'You can't be serious?' But she could see from the girl's expression that she'd meant every word. For a moment, Nellie stood speechless, unsure what to do next. All she knew was that this girl seemed to bring trouble wherever she went, and she was sick of it. 'How bloody dare you!' she screeched. 'How dare you come in here and accuse my daughter – *your* friend – of something like that in front of all our friends!'

A hubbub went up around the café. 'And you have the cheek to mouth off about my kids! Least mine aren't bloody traitors!' Lou Carter said loudly from where she was sitting at a table in the corner.

But Nellie barely heard her as she stepped over the broken crockery and food and went to collect her coat and helmet.

Jasper, who'd been staring at Pauline with his mouth open, pushed his chair back and jumped up as around him the tables started to empty, all except Phyllis and Ethel, who were sitting frozen with shock.

Donny, who'd been at the table in the kitchen having his breakfast, flew through the door, shoving Pauline hard in the stomach. 'You can't say that about my aunt! She never would help a German. Never never never!'

Jasper, his usually ruddy cheeks pale, pulled Donny away. 'That's enough, Don. Of course she wouldn't, but it's not Pauline's fault, is it? Sounds like there's just been a huge misunderstanding, so I'll go up to the police station with your mum and sort it out. Lily will be home before you know it.'

Donny had started to sob and Marianne put her arm around his shoulders, pulling him close and leading him upstairs.

'As for you, missy—' Jasper waved a plump finger under Pauline's nose '—next time you have private news, don't shout it out to the whole bloody market square.'

Pauline was sobbing. 'I didn't mean to. It was such a shock. And she's been smashed in the face. Honestly, I'd never hurt Lily. She's the only true friend I've ever had.' She collapsed into a chair and put her head on the table, her shoulders shaking as Gladys put an arm around her shoulders.

'That were unnecessary, Jasper. Can't you see the girl's just upset.'

But Jasper ignored her as Nellie came back into the café, shrugging on her coat, her tin hat already balanced on top of her head. 'Glad, you're in charge,' she said. 'Not that there's much to do right now.' She looked quickly at the empty tables, the breakfasts half-eaten, egg congealing on the plates.

279

Jasper took her hand and for a moment they stared at each other. Then he nodded slightly. 'I'll wait outside,' he said quietly.

Ethel Turner stood up and made her way over to Nellie, putting an arm around her shoulders, but Nellie barely noticed as she bent to pick up her large black handbag from behind the counter. She paused briefly and looked at the few people remaining – her true friends – and with a nod at each of them, she turned and went out of the back door.

Jasper was waiting for her in the yard. 'It's best if you don't come, Jasper. This is family business.'

'That's why I'm coming, Nell. And you can't stop me.'

Nellie put her hand on his arm. 'You can't, love.'

'This is different. That girl ... that girl means more than life to me. And she needs me.'

Nellie's face crumpled and she fell against Jasper's broad chest, inhaling the familiar scent of him. Then she pushed herself away and straightened her shoulders. 'I'm going alone.'

'For God's sake, woman. You've kept me from her all of her life and I won't let you do it any more.'

'Kept you from her? And how have I done that?'

'By not telling her. By not marrying me. By denying the truth every single day. Well, not any more, Nellie. Not any more.'

Nellie stared into Jasper's face. She knew every wrinkle, every bristle and every crevice of it by heart. She'd watched each one appear over the years. And she'd probably caused

280

a fair few of them. Her shoulders slumped and she raised her hand and rested it on his cheek. 'I'm sorry, Jasper. I'm so sorry.' Tears flooded her eyes and once again she buried her face in his chest. 'She wouldn't do this, would she, Jasper?' she whispered. Knowing the answer but desperate to have someone else say it too.

'Nellie, Nellie—' Jasper took her shoulders and stared down at her '—how can you even ask?' He pulled her in to him, wrapping his sturdy arms tightly around her. 'Not our girl, Nell. Not our girl,' he whispered into her hair.

Nellie sniffed and pushed away from him, wiping at her eyes. 'I'm just being foolish. Of course not our girl. She takes after her dad. Honest and loyal as the day is long.' She smiled slightly at him.

Tears sprang to Jasper's eyes and started to run down his bristled cheeks. 'Ah, Nell. All my life—' He pressed his forehead to Nellie's, then stood up straight. 'So many times I've wanted to take that girl and squeeze her. Tell her how much I love her. Tell her—'

'Stop it!' Nellie held up her hand. 'Don't say it. It wouldn't be right. We disrespected Donald in life, I won't disrespect him in death.'

Jasper swallowed and looked away. Then he stiffened suddenly.

'What do you think you're doing?' he shouted at Pauline, who was standing at the back door watching them.

Nellie whirled round and paled.

Pauline's face was expressionless. 'I wanted to see if I could help. And you're right, Mr Cane. Lily would never do something like this.' With that she turned and left.

Nellie and Jasper stared at each other, then Jasper sighed and put his arm around her. 'Let's cross that bridge if we ever get to it, love. We have more important things to consider right now.'

Nellie nodded and, putting her arm through his, they made their way to the police station.

Chapter 28

Edie pushed the starter button and turned the key in the ignition of the Bedford truck and listened intently to the spluttering of the engine, trying to identify where the problem might lie. In the rear-view mirror, she could see exhaust fumes rising in a thick black cloud, and the smell of burning petrol almost made her choke. She was about to try again when a man poked his head through the window, startling her.

'Excuse me, ma'am,' he said loudly.

She opened the door, forcing him to move aside, and jumped down.

'Hello there. Were you looking for Mr Pearson? He's out at the moment, but he won't be a—' She stopped, suddenly registering the man's RAF uniform. 'It's not Bill, is it?' she gasped. Mr Pearson's nephew was still in training, but that didn't mean he couldn't have had an accident.

The man shook his head and took his cap off, causing a lock of thick golden hair to fall onto his forehead. 'No, ma'am. Are you Edith Castle?' he asked.

She nodded uncertainly. 'Yes. How can I help you?'

283

'Would you mind if we went into the office?' He ran his eyes down her blue overalls, the front liberally smeared with oil. 'I'm afraid I have some bad news for you.'

She swallowed. 'For me? Is it my brothers?' Although why a pilot would come to tell her news of her brothers was beyond her.

In answer, the man walked towards the red door of the small, whitewashed office building next to the forecourt and held it open for her.

'If you don't mind, I think you should perhaps sit down.'

She followed after him and perched on one of the hard-backed chairs, staring at him expectantly.

'It's Pavel,' he said gently. 'He was shot down yesterday, and he left this letter for you. I thought it would be best if I delivered it myself.'

Edie's brow wrinkled. 'Pavel? I think you might have the wrong woman.'

'No. It's for you. He dictated the letter to me. He couldn't write English, you see.'

'But I don't know a Pavel . . .'

'That's not how he tells it.' The man thrust the letter into her hands.

Puzzled, she tore it open and removed the single sheet of paper.

Dear Edith,

If you are reading this, then it means I have perished somewhere in the sky above you. We have not known each other long, but I wanted you to know that you have

made my time in England special. My comrade Greg
has helped me to write this letter as my English is not so
good. He is a very good man and has been like a brother
to me. Perhaps you could befriend him as you did me.

Thank you for the good memories.

Much love,

Pavel

Edith stared at the letter in consternation, trying to remember when she might have met this man who seemed to remember her with such fondness. Her mind went back over the past few weeks, and the memory of the Polish pilot she'd spent time with at the dance came back to her. His name had been Pavel and she'd felt drawn to him because he seemed so shy and uncertain. And after being lied to and cheated by Henry, a man she thought she had loved, it had felt good to be in control. They'd danced and kissed and she'd been disappointed when he'd been called away so suddenly. After he'd gone, she'd realised she had no idea where he was stationed or what his second name was, so she'd never seen him again. Could it really only have been three weeks ago?

'How sad,' she said, folding the paper and holding it against her chest. 'I remember him now. I met him at a dance a few weeks ago, and he seemed very shy.'

'Is that all?' Greg asked.

'What do you mean?'

'I mean I've spent the last few weeks listening to him talk of nothing but Edith, and all you've got to say is "how sad"?'

'But—'

'I'd heard you Brits were cold, but this really takes the biscuit.'

'Hang on a minute!' Edie stood up and thrust the letter back at the pilot, but he didn't take it. 'I met him once at a dance. We shared a few kisses before he was suddenly called away. What do you expect me to say?'

'I expect,' he gritted out, 'for you to express grief, show that his life meant something to you. Jesus! The man gave his life for your country!'

'And I'm grateful. But why did he leave a letter for me and not his family?'

'His family were all killed by the Nazis! He told me he hoped to one day make a family with you.'

Edie stepped back in surprise. 'Me? But . . . Honestly, I met him once! I truly am sorry he's dead, but I can't pretend to be heartbroken when I'm not.' She unfolded the letter and read it again. 'But I *am* sorry. Very, very sorry that I was the only person he could think of to write his final letter to. That he was so lonely he created a fantasy life.' Her eyes really did fill with tears at that. She remembered how happy he'd been to dance, and how excited he'd been when they'd kissed. At the time, she hadn't given it a moment's thought, but now . . . Now she was glad she'd taken the time with him. Glad she'd made him happy, even if just for a moment. Happiness was so fleeting that the thought she'd inspired just a tiny bit in someone else made her feel warm inside.

'You honestly didn't know him?'

Edie shook her head.

The man slumped down in a seat with a deep sigh and looked up at her. He really did have the most incredible eyes, she thought distractedly.

'I'm sorry for getting angry with you. What he says is true. He and I became close; I suppose I felt responsible for him as he always seemed like a lost soul. He was so shy. Even amongst his fellow countrymen, he was more inclined to sit and listen rather than join in.' He paused for a moment, then held out his hand. 'Pilot Officer Greg Manning. Apologies for not introducing myself earlier.'

She shook his hand. 'That's all right. I'm very sorry that you've lost your friend.'

Greg nodded. 'And not just him,' he said. 'Too many of us.' He shrugged. 'But what can we do? It's that, or let this little island be invaded.'

'Would you like a cup of tea?' she asked. 'It might help.'

Greg laughed shortly. 'Not another damn cup of tea!' He stopped then, as if a realisation had just come to him. 'Say, your mom runs Castle's Café. Is your sister called Lily, by any chance?'

'Yes. Why, do you want an introduction? Most men do.' She smiled wryly. Of course Greg would prefer Lily.

He shook his head. 'From the sounds of it, I really don't want to know Lily. I was in the café when some nurse ran in and said she'd been arrested.'

'What?'

'Something about helping a prisoner escape.' Greg raised his eyebrows enquiringly.

'But . . . but that's ludicrous!'

Greg told her the little he knew and Edie sat back in shock. 'I just don't believe it!' She stood up and went over to the desk where she hastily scribbled two notes: one for Rodney and one for Mr Pearson.

Then she raced out of the door and deposited Rodney's note with the sentry on Constables Road, before starting to jog down Castle Hill.

Chapter 29

The journey from the hospital to the police station on Park Street, just off Maison Dieu Road, took barely ten minutes, but to Lily it felt like a lifetime. She stared out of the window as the familiar buildings flashing by, but she didn't really see any of them. Her mind was blank from the shock and all she was aware of was the feeling of nausea in her stomach and the fast, heavy thud of her heart.

As the car screeched to a stop outside the large red-brick building, the walls piled high with sandbags, she prayed that she wouldn't see anyone she knew. It was a futile hope, because the first person she saw as she was escorted into the building was Roger Humphries standing behind the desk. For a moment he looked shocked, but then he shook his head. 'Well, well, well. It seems I'm seeing a lot of your family at the moment. Although I was betting on it being your mother in here instead of you.' He smiled nastily at her, his small moustache bristling. 'The interview room's ready for you, Sergeant Trotter,' he said to the plumper of the two officers.

Lily barely registered his words as she was led through a door beside the reception where a long, grey-painted corridor stretched towards the back of the building. One of the policemen opened the first door on the right and thrust her down onto a chair in front of a rickety wooden table, the surface pockmarked with cigarette burns. She looked around at the drab, grey walls and the high, barred window, and wondered if this was what her life was going to be like from now on.

'Go and tell Inspector Forrest that the suspect is here,' Sergeant Trotter told his colleague as he sat down opposite Lily. He was a portly, middle-aged man, with small eyes and round, florid cheeks. The buttons of his jacket strained over his stomach as he took out his notebook and pencil from one pocket and a cigarette from the other. He lit it, inhaled and then blew smoke in her face.

She grimaced and waved a hand in front of her while he regarded her with a contemptuous expression.

'If it was up to me, you'd be straight in front of a firing squad, no questions asked. That's how we should deal with traitors in this country.'

Lily stared back at him, noting the broken blood vessels on his cheek and the bulbous nose of a man who drank too much, and for the first time since this nightmare had begun felt stirrings of anger. She was not going to let this man accuse her of something she hadn't done.

Drawing on all her courage, she glared at him. 'If it was up to me, you'd be called up and sent to a battlefield far far away. Might help you lose a bit of weight,' she said, folding her arms across her chest.

The policeman narrowed his eyes. 'I've heard all about you Castles from Constable Humphries. You think you're better than everyone else. Well, we've got a few questions for you, and after that, I expect the army will want a word as well. Doubt you'll be so high and mighty after that.'

Lily looked away, her bravado dissipating as the feeling of nausea returned, and she clapped her hand over her mouth. 'I'm going to be sick!' she squeaked.

Sergeant Trotter lumbered to his feet and managed to thrust a metal bin at her just in time as she threw up what little there was in her stomach. As she spat into the bin, the tears she'd been holding back flooded her eyes and she began to shake with fear and anxiety.

The policeman said nothing, merely sat back down and watched her as he smoked his cigarette.

Eventually, the door to the small interview room was thrust open.

'Lily Castle?'

Lily sat up straight and wiped her eyes on her apron, surprised to realise she was still in uniform.

'You should be crying. You are in deep, deep trouble. I don't need to tell you what happens to traitors in this country, do I?' the policeman said as he sat down at the table.

Lily stared mutely back at him. This was an altogether different kind of man to Sergeant Trotter. He looked to be in his fifties and although not tall, he was broad-shouldered, his grey hair was neatly combed and his blue eyes looked sharp and observant behind round, gold-rimmed spectacles.

'You have some explaining to do, young lady.'

'But I haven't done anything wrong!'

The man peered at her sceptically over the rim of his glasses. 'That's not how it appears to me.'

'That prisoner knocked me out! How could I have helped him?'

'Yes, you do have a nasty bruise on your face. Bet that hurts.' He smiled unsympathetically. 'Still, I'm sure he didn't hit you as hard as he could have.'

'What do you mean?'

'Just a tap to make it look like you had nothing to do with the escape, perhaps. But tell me this—' he sat forward '—where did he get the clothes he was wearing? Where did he get the rope he used to tie you up? Where did he get the knife? But, more importantly, why did you try to get the soldier outside the hut to leave his post in the middle of the night?' He sat back and crossed his arms over his chest.

'I thought . . . I thought one of the patients was dying. He's been so ill, and he needed a doctor. I would have gone, but Sister Mackenzie had left and I—' She stopped, knowing what his next question was going to be, and realising that waiting until the sister was out of the room to ask for a doctor did indeed look slightly suspicious in the circumstances.

'And you couldn't wait for your colleague to return? The *senior* nurse, who no doubt would normally take these kinds of decisions.'

Lily stayed silent, her stomach sinking.

'Do you want to know what else we've discovered?' the policeman went on.

Again Lily stayed silent.

'It seems this Felix Muller was a bit of a clever bloke. He knew that escaping from the POW camp would be harder than making a break from the hospital, so he found a way to be kept at the hospital until he was fit enough to make a run for it.' The man reached into his pocket and pulled out a small clear-glass bottle with a cork in the top.

'Do you know what this is?'

She shook her head.

He handed it to her. 'Take a sniff.'

She took the bottle. It smelled vaguely sweet and stirred a memory, but her mind was racing and she couldn't identify it. She handed it back and shook her head. 'I have no idea.'

'And you're training to be a nurse?' he mocked. 'This—' he placed the bottle carefully back on the table '—is Ipecac Syrup. I assume you know what that is?'

'Of course. It's used to make you sick if you've eaten anything—' She stopped. Was this why Felix was always being sick? Was he fooling them all into thinking he was about to die, when all along he was just biding his time until he could escape?

Inspector Forrest nodded knowingly. 'Precisely. And do you know where we found it?'

Lily shook her head.

'Under the escaped prisoner's pillow.'

'And you think *I* gave it to him?'

293

'Did you?'

'No! You can buy it in any pharmacy; anyone could have given it to him!'

'Which is why we will be carrying out fingerprint tests on that bottle.'

Lily's breath caught in her throat. 'But you just made me hold it!' She swallowed as she felt a trap closing around her.

'Did I? I don't remember that, do you, Sergeant Trotter?' He looked at the other man who'd been watching the interview in silence as he scribbled notes.

'Not a thing, Inspector,' he said deadpan, not looking at Lily.

Lily searched desperately for something to say. People went in and out of that hut all the time – nurses, doctors, orderlies, porters. She gasped. Of course. Porters. She wouldn't put it past Dick to do something like this. No doubt he'd been paid well for his trouble.

'The porter, Dick Brown. He could have done it. He was always in and out of the prisoners' ward.'

Inspector Forrest sat back with a satisfied nod. 'Funny you should mention him. He's been most helpful in our inquiries. Said you were on very friendly terms with the prisoner.'

'But I wasn't! I only saw him when I was working in the hut, and I was never alone with him.'

'According to you. What's going on between the two of you?'

'What?! Nothing!'

'Corporal Stanmore told us that he witnessed you sitting beside the prisoner's bed sharing a cigarette, cosy as you like.'

'But . . . that was only because I had to try to get him to leave the hut during an air raid. At Corporal Stanmore's request!'

She was suddenly aware of a commotion outside the door.

'Where's my daughter? How dare you accuse her of aidin' and abetting the Germans. What's got into you, Roger Humphries?'

Never had her mother's voice sounded sweeter. Just the knowledge that she was there, with all her bluster and determination, instantly gave Lily strength. A man's voice followed Nellie's, and though she couldn't make out the words, she knew it was Jasper. Between Nellie and Jasper she was certain they would find a way to get her out of this mess.

Inspector Forrest got up and left the room.

'You'll get what's coming to you,' Sergeant Trotter said, staring at her thoughtfully, and Lily noticed that the sun coming through the high window made the red veins on his nose stand out in stark contrast to his pasty skin.

Lily folded her arms and sat back in the chair, glaring at him defiantly. 'And what's that then? A full apology and an announcement of my wrongful arrest in the *Dover Gazette*?' Her mother's voice had given her the strength she needed to stand up for herself.

The policeman gave a short bark of laughter. 'It'll be a cold day in hell before that happens. No, my thoughts are a nice cosy cell, where you can spend the rest of the war. That is, if they don't hang you.'

The image this brought to her mind was so awful, Lily felt herself break out in a cold sweat as she instinctively put her hand to her throat, which already felt as if a noose was being tightened around it.

They sat in silence after this, as Lily tried to fight down the rising panic. She thought about Charlie Alexander. There'd be no dinner at the Grand tonight. In fact, he might never want to see her again. He'd been sanguine about all the other drama in her life, but this was something else. He could never be seen to be friendly with someone accused of treason. And if she was found guilty, what troubles would this bring down on her family? Would Rodney have to leave the navy? Would Bert and Jimmy be ostracised? As for the café, would people stop going there? It seemed the consequences of her simple act of kindness in helping the German prisoner just a few weeks before were unimaginable. If she'd known then what she knew now, she would have avoided that Nissen hut like the plague, no matter what orders she was given.

Finally, the door opened and Inspector Forrest returned looking flushed. 'Your mother seems to have got you a lawyer. I wonder why. Maybe this plan was cooked up between the two of you, eh?'

'I don't need a lawyer. I'm innocent. And you can't prove I had anything to do with that man escaping.'

'I pray you're right, Miss Castle.' A small, rotund, grey-haired man entered carrying a briefcase, which he put on the table. He held out his hand. 'Mr Wainwright. Your mother has asked if I can be of assistance. You may not know this but I had some dealings with your sister recently.'

'Did you?' He must be the solicitor who helped Marianne when that no-good Henry Fanshaw had turned up threatening to take Donny away. 'Oh yes, I remember. Thank you.' She managed a small, tight smile.

'Inspector Forrest has apprised me of the evidence against you, but now I'd like to hear your side of the story.'

'I swear this has nothing to do with me.'

Mr Wainwright turned to address the inspector. 'I need to speak to my client alone.'

The policeman nodded reluctantly, collecting the bottle of syrup from the table and gesturing for the other man to follow him.

Once the door had closed, Lily leant forward, elbows on the table. 'None of this has anything to do with me. I promise,' she said earnestly, then went on to recount everything the policeman had told her.

Mr Wainwright nodded thoughtfully. 'Deary me, the evidence is very flimsy indeed. Although, I must confess it's a shame that policeman got you to pick up the bottle like that; that's what's called tampering with evidence, and it's a crime.' He tutted softly. 'But there, it's done now. Do you have any idea who might have helped the prisoner escape?'

297

Lily's head was thumping as the thoughts swirled round and round her mind. 'I honestly don't know. But there's a man at the hospital, Dick Brown. He's always in and out of that Nissen hut. Maybe . . .'

Mr Wainwright regarded her steadily. 'Miss Castle, are you suggesting him because you don't like him, or because you have a genuine suspicion?'

Lily blushed and looked away. 'He's horrible,' she whispered. 'But he *does* have the run of the hospital.'

'As do hundreds of other members of staff, so set aside personal likes and dislikes and just focus on facts. Is there anyone at the hospital that you suspect of being a German sympathiser?'

Lily shook her head.

'I want you to think very carefully about that. Tell me about the prisoner's illness.'

'I don't know much about it. Dr Ramsay has been treating him for cancer. But that only came out after he was caught. He crashed his plane and was brought in with a broken ankle, although it wasn't seriously broken, I don't think.'

'And when did he exhibit signs of cancer?'

Lily shrugged. 'Honestly, I don't know. I didn't have anything to do with him and his treatment. I'm just a trainee, and with a serious illness like that, the more experienced nurses help the doctors.'

'And do you think he was faking it?'

'It looks like it, doesn't it? But how did he fool Dr Ramsay into believing he had cancer? Mind you,' she said reflectively, 'it's not as if it's an illness you can see, so I suppose it would be easy enough.'

Mr Wainwright nodded. 'No, indeed. Hmm.' He sat deep in thought for a moment, then jumped up. 'Right, let's see what I can do to get you out of here.' He tutted again. 'It really was unwise of you to pick up that bottle . . .' He sighed. 'But never fear, I have a few tricks up my sleeve.'

He went to the door and called the inspector back in. 'You have no proof that my client had anything to do with the prisoner's escape. So, until you have something concrete, I demand you release her.'

Inspector Forrest smiled grimly. 'I'm afraid that won't be possible. This girl has been implicated not only by a member of staff, but also by one of the guards.'

'And that's proof enough for you, is it?'

'Not yet. But we will be fingerprinting the bottle.'

'But my fingerprints are only on it because you made me pick it up!' Lily protested.

'I don't remember doing that.' The inspector smiled smugly.

'But you did!' Lily shouted. 'You gave it to me. So now it will have my fingerprints on it.'

'I trust you will be fingerprinting everyone else at the hospital as well?' Mr Wainwright asked the policeman.

'I don't see why we would have to.'

'I think I'll need to insist on it. Or I shall report you to the chief constable for your sloppy investigations.'

The inspector frowned. 'Very well. If you insist. But it'll be a waste of time.'

'Nevertheless.'

Inspector Forrest gave a brusque nod. 'I'll ask my constables to get on to it.'

'And that will include this Richard Brown and every other porter or orderly who's been into the hut? And every doctor and nurse who's treated the prisoners?' Lily had to hand it to Mr Wainwright, he was like a dog with a bone.

'Their behaviour towards the prisoners has never been in question . . .'

Mr Wainwright's eyebrows rose further. 'I see. And in your experience, criminals never cover their tracks or behave in ways to detract suspicion?'

Inspector Forrest looked away.

'Precisely. So, you have had Miss Castle in custody for the past—' he checked his watch '—three hours. I'd say that's quite long enough to establish what she knows. Shall we move this along and allow Miss Castle to go home?'

'Our investigations are incomplete.'

'I quite agree, Inspector. It seems there are many more people for you to question. They're waiting in another room, are they?'

'And Colonel Stokes will want to interview her.'

'Then Colonel Stokes can go through the proper channels. In the meantime, I am happy to vouch for Miss Castle not leaving town. So, if you've quite finished, we will take our leave.' He gestured to Lily, who had been watching the exchange with growing admiration. Mr Wainwright might look unprepossessing, but he was running rings around the odious inspector.

She stood up and smiled at him. 'Good day, Inspector. I hope I won't have to speak to you again.' And raising her chin, she walked through the door that Mr Wainwright was holding open for her.

The minute Lily emerged into the lobby, Nellie let out a cry and ran to envelop her in a hug. 'Oh, thank God!' She squeezed her tightly, whispering into her neck.

Jasper came over and put his arms around both of them, resting his cheek on Lily's head. 'Oh, my girl. You haven't half given us a scare.'

Mr Wainwright cleared his throat. 'If you please, I think it's best we leave.' He held his arms out and herded them through the door as quickly as he could.

'What's the hurry?' Nellie demanded. 'Other than getting her out of this place, of course.'

'I fear I rather bamboozled the inspector. He had refused to let her go, and I'm worried that he might drag her back in. So move along now.'

As they turned on to Maison Dieu Road, Lily stopped and threw her arms around the lawyer. She was several inches taller than him, so she planted a hearty kiss on his head. 'Thank you so much!' she cried.

Mr Wainwright blushed and stepped away from her. 'We're not clear of this yet, Miss Castle. My advice to you is to go home and lie low. Word will have spread and there might be a backlash against you. All of you.' He looked at Nellie, who nodded and put her arm around her daughter.

'Don't worry. I'll look after her. Anyone utters one word against my Lily, they'll have me to deal with.'

Mr Wainwright smiled. 'I don't doubt that, Mrs Castle. But even so, lie low. Keep quiet. And I will do what I can to make sure the police investigate the case properly. It's my opinion that they needed a quick arrest. And if only they'd look in the obvious place, I have no doubt they could get one.' He slapped his tin hat on his head and nodded at them. 'I'll be in touch.'

Then he waddled off in the other direction.

Jasper gazed after him in admiration. 'What a man. He don't look much, but, by heck, he's got the courage of a lion. And what place do you think he means to look, Lily? You got suspicions?'

'I have no idea.' Lily was mystified. Mr Wainwright seemed to have it all worked out in his mind, and now she'd seen him in action, she was confident he'd have her off the hook in no time.

'Well, let's get you home. I have a feeling this is when we discover who our true friends are,' Jasper said.

Nellie snorted. 'I don't think it'll take much guessing. And a hundred quid says there's a crowd gathered round Lou Carter's new stall. If I could have seen into the future yesterday I'd have told you to leave her to burn, Lily!' Then, with her arm protectively around her daughter's waist, she urged her along the pavement.

But her mother's words had brought the feeling of nausea back to Lily's stomach, and now the imminent threat of jail had been removed, her jaw was once again throbbing and she leant her head on Jasper's shoulder. As they walked home, she kept her face pressed tightly into his sleeve, hoping that no one would see her. It felt like she was living in a nightmare, and she still couldn't quite believe what had happened. But now the shock and humiliation were giving way to anger. If she could, she would hunt down whoever had framed her and feed them with a gallon of the bloody Ipecac that had caused so much trouble.

Chapter 30

Outside the back gate to the café, Edie paused to catch her breath and compose herself before going in to face the family. Footsteps behind her made her jump as Greg Manning jogged up to her. 'You're quick for a girl.' He grinned.

'What are you doing here?' She'd forgotten all about him in her mad dash home.

'I wanted to make sure you got here safely. You left in such a hurry that I was worried you might not be looking where you were going.'

The noise of aircraft overhead distracted her momentarily and she gazed up at the formation of Hurricanes. 'Don't you have a plane to fly or something?' she asked rudely.

'My rig needs a new propeller, but the factory in Southampton's been bombed so . . .' He shrugged. 'For now, I'm just hanging around waiting for a plane to become free.'

'Hadn't you better go back and do just that then? You can't come in with me.'

He held his hands up. 'Don't worry. I wasn't about to intrude on your family drama. I just needed to know you were safe. If only for Pavel's sake.'

'So now you have,' she said, pushing open the gate. Then she stopped, feeling guilty. This man was risking his life for her country, he'd just lost his friend, and he'd run all the way down the hill to make sure she was safe. She looked back over her shoulder. 'But thank you. It was very nice of you to see me home.' The sound of gunfire floated towards them from the sea and she took a deep breath. 'Take care of yourself, won't you?'

Greg grinned at her. 'I'll do my best. Can't promise anything though.' He held out his hand. 'Good to meet you, Edith Castle. Maybe we'll run into each other again.'

She took his hand. 'Maybe we will. And if we do, my name's Edie. No one calls me Edith, except my mother.'

He lifted her hand to his lips and kissed it, making her suddenly conscious of her filthy nails and the grease smeared across her palm. She tried to pull it away, but he held on tighter, turning it over and giving it a sniff. 'Ahh. The scent of motor oil. Reminds me of home.' Then he tipped his hat and walked towards the square.

She stared after Greg for just a moment, but then dismissed him from her mind as she raced into the kitchen.

The usually busy atmosphere of the kitchen was entirely missing as she walked in. Normally, Marianne would be bustling around the kitchen, while the café would be buzzing with chatter and laughter. But the kitchen was empty, and from the silence, it seemed the café was too.

'Hello?' she called.

From upstairs, she heard muffled voices and when she reached the sitting room she found Gladys and

Marianne sitting morosely at the table, each nursing a cup of tea.

As soon as she saw Edie, Marianne jumped up and came over to give her a hug. 'Is it true? Has Lily been arrested for helping a prisoner escape?' Edie asked urgently.

Marianne nodded. 'The arrested bit is true,' she whispered. 'But there's no way Lily would have done that,' she added fiercely.

'But how? When?'

Gladys shook her head. 'We don't know. Your mum and Jasper've gone to the police station.'

Edie slumped into a chair at the table. 'I was told that a nurse had burst in here and shouted it to practically the whole town. I presume that was Pauline?'

Gladys sighed and nodded. 'And a load of them left. Folk don't look too kindly on a traitor.'

'Where's Pauline now?' Edie asked. 'Perhaps she can shed some light.'

Marianne shook her head. 'She's asleep. I've just been up there and she was flat out. And the room reeked of alcohol. I tried to wake her but she just mumbled a load of nonsense.'

'She's drunk at ten o'clock in the morning!' Edie exclaimed.

'I know. The girl has a problem. And she got upset after Jasper shouted at her.'

'*Jasper* was shouting?' Edie said, surprised. 'Was what she did *that* bad?'

'Isn't shouting out that Lily's been arrested for helping a prisoner escape bad enough?' Gladys slapped her hand on the table in an uncharacteristic fit of temper.

Edie got up and began to pace around the small room. 'Everyone would have found out eventually anyway, and Jasper's usually so calm. There must be more to it. But how did the prisoner escape? And when? And where was Lily when it all happened? And why do they think it has anything to do with her?'

Marianne explained what she knew, which wasn't much.

'Right, I can't sit here doing nothing. I'm off to the police station to find Mum. I want to know *everything*.'

The thunder of footsteps on the stairs had them all turning and relief flooded through Edie as Rodney rushed in, closely followed by Marge.

Marianne leapt up and ran into Rodney's arms. 'Rod! Thank God you're here. Maybe you can make sense of all this.'

Though she felt a tiny bit resentful at Marianne's words, Edie had to acknowledge that if anyone could dig them out of this hole it was Rodney. With his clever mind and status as an officer in the navy, everyone respected him.

'You didn't have to come, Marge,' Edie said.

'Course I did. I wanted to show my support. Anyway, I saw Rod racing down here and my shift had just finished so . . .' She shrugged. 'But bleeding heck! There's a crowd out in the market square and they seem restless. Me and Rod only just avoided being lynched!'

Edie moved over to the window and looked down on the square. 'Hell's bells! And no surprises who's at the centre of the mob! Lou Carter mouthing off as usual. I thought her stall burnt down yesterday.'

'Didn't take her long to find another one. And more fish. Her Terence, no doubt. Fingers in all sorts of pies, that one. None of them good.' Gladys sniffed.

Rodney joined her at the window and swore roundly. 'Bloody gossipmongers, the lot of them. Well, I won't have it.'

He turned and stormed down the stairs. Edie and Marianne looked at each other and a silent agreement passed between them; if Rodney was going out to face their neighbours, he wouldn't go alone.

They raced after him and stood tensely as he threw open the door.

'You lot should be ashamed of yourselves!' he shouted.

The murmuring stopped as everyone turned to stare at him.

'You've known Lily all your lives, and yet you're ready to believe a load of lies about her!'

'The police don't seem to think they're lies, otherwise why would they have arrested her?' Lou Carter shouted.

Rodney levelled a hard stare at her. 'Just yesterday, Lily saved your life. And this is how you repay her?'

Lou reddened. 'It weren't that bad,' she said, rubbing her bandaged arm sheepishly.

Rodney ignored her. 'How many times has Mum helped you all in the past?' He stared around. 'You, Paddy

Arnold!' He pointed at an old man who worked in the pharmacy on Biggin Street. 'When your wife had pneumonia, who brought her chicken soup?' The man had the grace to look ashamed. 'And you, Miss Frost.' A thin woman with wispy white hair and a long, pointed nose narrowed her eyes at him. 'Have you forgotten when you broke your ankle a couple of years ago? Who came in to cook for you and clean your house?'

'Your mum paid Lily well to help me out. And I wouldn't have let her in the door if I'd known what sort of girl she was!' the woman retorted.

'That's right, my mum used her own money to make sure you were looked after and yet when *she* needs support, you look the other way.'

The woman shuffled her feet uncomfortably.

'You should think very carefully before you throw your accusations around,' he ground out. 'And another thing: how many of you have sheltered down Barwick Caves recently? Or in our basement? Had a nice cup of tea and a bun and chatted to your friends safe and sound while the shells fell, did you?'

'What of it?' Lou Carter shouted. 'Ain't a crime, is it?'

'Do you have any idea—' Rodney was truly enraged now '—who pays for that tea and food? My mother and sister scrimp around trying to find ways to make sure you're all comfortable and yet here you are looking down on us as if *we're* criminals! How could you *ever* think a single member of this family would help the enemy, even as the town is being bombed and shelled into oblivion!'

'No one's accusing you, are they, Rodney?' Miss Frost said. 'It's your sister we have an issue with.'

'When you slander my sister, you slander me.' He looked around at Marianne and Edie. 'And you slander them. And you slander my mother and my brothers who are doing their bit to keep this country safe.'

'And me!' Donny shouted indignantly. But Rodney didn't hear him, instead his angry gaze fell on the journalist in the shabby brown suit, who was scribbling frantically in his notebook. 'As for you, you can put your pen down. If you print one false word then you'll be out of a job. I know for a fact you're on your last warning after you slipped in a weather forecast last month. My commander was all for having you arrested.'

'Hey, I only print what I see,' he blustered. 'And if your sister has betrayed this country, then folk need to know.'

Rodney stepped forward, fists clenched, more than ready to punch the man's lights out. But a shout from across the square stopped him and he looked up as Ethel Turner, wearing a flowered overall, her hair covered with a blue scarf, pushed through the crowd, Phyllis Perkins and Reenie by her side.

'Rod's right!' Ethel Turner shouted, coming to stand beside him. 'You should all be ashamed of yourselves. Lily Castle is as honest as the day is long and you all know it! We've all seen her grow from a nipper. And weren't it your little 'un—' she pointed at a woman wearing a loose summer dress and holding a wriggling toddler by the hand '—what nearly died of the flu last winter? And who was it sat by his bedside at the hospital till the fever left him?' The woman looked away. 'Lily, that's who. And it weren't even her job. She was doing it out of the goodness of her heart.'

'I'd have done the same,' the woman muttered.

'Would you?' Rodney fumed. 'I remember you from school, Prue Jackson. You were in the same class as Marianne.' He glanced at his sister, who despite her shyness was standing with her head up as she stared unflinchingly at the crowd. These people were meant to be their friends and neighbours, but Marianne knew very well how it felt to be shunned by them. 'I don't remember seeing so much of you when our Donny came along. No, you scurried off like the rat you are. Like the rats you all are!' He paused. 'But seeing as we're neighbours, I'll give you one more chance to do the right thing.' He gestured at Phyllis, Ethel and Reenie. 'Anyone else want to join us?'

'I will!' A high-pitched squeak cut through the murmuring of the crowd as Freddie pushed through and came to put his arm around Donny's shoulder. Brian Turner and Reg Perkins also walked over to stand with their wives.

Nobody else moved and Rodney nodded his head jerkily. 'As the saying goes: "If you're not with us, you're against us." So you lot better be ready to grovel when the truth comes out!'

He shook Reg and Brian's hands, and smiled briefly at the women, before turning to go back inside, Edie, Marianne and Donny close on his heels.

311

Marge had been standing by the window watching the action and listening to his words through the open door. She clapped as he came in. 'Bravo, Rod! That was some speech.'

He smiled grimly. 'Much good it did us.'

Gladys was sitting at a table towards the back of the room. 'Your mum would be proud of you, Rodney. But where are they? They've been gone for ages!'

'I'm sure it won't be long. Let's have some more tea while we wait.' Marianne hurried into the kitchen to put the kettle on while the others sat down.

'What if they keep her in prison?' Gladys asked querulously.

'They won't,' Rodney said forcefully. 'Or they'll have me to deal with, and I'm more than ready to take the lot of them on. Do Bert and Jim know?' he asked.

'I can go and tell them,' Donny said eagerly.

Rodney nodded. 'If they can get away, I think Mum and Lily are going to need all our support today.'

In the kitchen, Marianne stood by the range contemplating the pans full of congealed eggs and bacon that she'd abandoned when Pauline had run into the café. What a waste, she thought. She'd be able to use the sausages and bacon, but the eggs were inedible now and the porridge would have to be thrown away. Suddenly, the shock of it all hit her, and she leant against the range, taking comfort from the heat radiating from it. Footsteps made her swiftly wipe her eyes as she turned to see Donny.

'Don't worry, Mum,' he said comfortingly. 'I'm going to get Alfie; he'll make everything right again.'

She smiled and dropped a kiss on his head, then took him by the shoulders so she could look into his face. 'Are you all right, love?'

Donny's usual cheerful expression was absent and he looked tired. 'I just don't think it's fair that they're blaming Auntie Lily when she's the nicest nurse in the whole hospital,' he said fiercely. 'But now Uncle Rodney's here, he'll make sure she comes home.' He wiped his sleeve across his nose. 'And so will Alfie,' he said decisively. 'He'll tell them what's what.'

She pulled him into a hug. 'Go on then. Go and see if your uncles can make it back. We're all counting on you.'

He nodded against her chest, then marched purposefully to the back door while Marianne set about making the tea.

'Are you all right, Marianne?' Reenie's voice made her jump as she was laying out cups and saucers on a tray.

'Just about.' She smiled shakily. 'And thank you for standing by Rod just now.'

'Where else would I be?' she asked simply.

Marianne nodded as tears gathered in her eyes.

'We've always stood together, haven't we? And that's not going to change. Even if—' She stopped and shook her head.

'Even if?'

Reenie sighed. 'Even if you don't approve of me and Jim going out.'

'Oh, Reens. It's not that I don't approve; it's just . . . Do you love him?'

Reenie hesitated. 'It's early days. I can't say what I feel. All I know is that since we started walking out, I've felt happier than I have for years. And I want you to be happy for me too.'

Marianne held her friend's gaze for a long while, then finally looked away. To be honest, right now she no longer cared. They were both adults, and if Jim wanted to live a lie, then let him. 'Then I am happy for you, love.' She rubbed her friend's arm. 'Why don't you come and join us for tea?'

The group around the table were sitting in silence when Marianne and Reenie came through. Edie was staring at the clock on the wall, as though willing the hands to move faster, while Gladys had collected her knitting and had made a start on a pair of socks, the needles flying as she sniffed back tears.

Marge and Rodney, meanwhile, were staring out at the square, though Marge's hand was resting on Rodney's arm in a comforting gesture.

Silently, Marianne started to pour the tea while Reenie handed round the cups. 'Do you think we should try to wake Pauline again?' she asked.

Edie shook her head. 'I went to check on her. She's still passed out from whatever she's been drinking. I don't blame her, though. I've half a mind to crack Mum's brandy open myself.'

'Hardly the answer, is it?' Rodney said, taking a sip of his tea.

Edie rolled her eyes. 'I didn't say I was going to, did I? God, Rod, I mean, I love what you did just now, but sometimes . . .' She shook her head.

'No need to snipe, Edie,' Marge snapped. 'If it weren't for Rod, here, then that lot would probably have stormed the café by now.'

'Hey,' Marianne said. 'The last thing we need is to be arguing between ourselves. What happened to standing together?'

Edie huffed and folded her arms, staring broodingly at her brother. 'Sorry,' she said begrudgingly.

Rodney nodded briefly. 'And Marge, you don't have to stick up for me. This is family stuff, you can go if you want.'

Marge looked as if he'd slapped her and Marianne put her hand over her friend's. 'Please stay, Marge,' she said gently. 'I need you.'

Marge gave her a weak smile and reached for a cigarette. 'Just for you, then, Marianne. And for Lily.' She lit the cigarette and puffed out a long plume of smoke while the room once more descended into silence.

Chapter 31

Nearly an hour later, Lily, Jasper and Nellie finally stumbled in, and Marianne immediately ran through into the kitchen, pulling Lily into a hug.

'Oh, love. My poor Lily,' she soothed as Lily began to sob into her shoulder. 'It's all right now,' she said, as though she was comforting Donny. 'We're all with you and we know you did nothing wrong.' She held Lily away from her and gasped as she looked at her face. 'You're hurt!'

Lily put her hand to her cheek self-consciously. 'Does it look very bad?' she asked. 'I may have to cancel my date with Charlie at the Grand tonight.' It was a weak joke and made her feel even worse. She wouldn't be going anywhere with Charlie any time soon, she realised; there was no way he'd be allowed to associate with a woman under suspicion of helping German prisoners. She wiped her eyes. 'Thank you,' she whispered. 'I don't know what I'd do if you thought I was somehow to blame.'

'As if we would.' Rodney leant against the kitchen doorway, gazing at his sister with a gentle expression.

Extricating herself from Marianne, Lily threw herself into his arms, clinging to him tightly. To have Rod's calm, steady presence here now brought her more reassurance than her mother's blustering and Jasper's emotional concern.

'I didn't know you'd be here.' She gazed up at him. Unusually for him, he looked slightly dishevelled; his hair not as immaculate as it usually was, his jacket unbuttoned.

'Oh, he's done more than just be here,' Marge said, coming up behind them. 'He's been out there giving everyone what for. And very impressive it was too.'

Nellie went to give her son a hug. 'And I bet they felt about an inch tall. You have a way of putting people in their place that even I've never mastered.'

Rodney sighed. 'It was no trouble, really, Mum,' he said sarcastically. 'All in a day's work for a pompous know-all like me.'

'God, Mum, why are you such a cow to him? You should have seen him out in the square, sticking up for you and Lily. He was a hero. And here you go, moaning about him again,' Edie snarled through the hatch.

Jasper put his hand on Nellie's arm as he saw her open her mouth to snap back, and gave her a warning look. She hesitated for a moment. 'I'm sorry, Rod,' she said. 'You know I love you. You've always been the very best person to have around in a crisis,' Nellie said.

'It's all right, Mum. I know you can't help yourself,' Rodney replied with a slight smile.

Nellie nodded and walked through to the café, where she slumped into a seat, her shoulders sagging. 'So, Lily, why don't you fill them in on everything,' she said, as

Gladys patted her shoulder comfortingly and Marianne placed a cup of tea in front of her.

'Nellie, Lily needs to lie down,' Jasper said.

Lily smiled gratefully at him. She really did feel as though she was about to collapse; her head was spinning and the room was coming in and out of focus; she was certain that she had a concussion.

Nellie jumped up. 'What was I thinking? Come on, I'll help you up the stairs. And I bet there's a bit of hot water if you want a bath.'

The thought of a bath was heavenly, but right now all she wanted was her bed. 'Just sleep, Mum. That's all I need.'

'I'll bring you some tea and aspirin up.' Nellie followed her through to the kitchen.

The back door opened just as Lily was staring at the flight of stairs, wondering how she'd manage to drag herself up them, and Bert ran in. Seeing her slumped against the door frame, he scooped her up, holding her securely against his chest. 'Jesus Christ, Lily. What mischief have you got into this time?'

She shook her head against his shoulder, relieved to no longer have to stay upright. 'Can you carry me up, Bert? I don't think I can walk that far,' she murmured, closing her eyes.

'Course I will.' He dropped a kiss on her head, and settled her weight more securely in his arms before starting to climb the stairs.

As they made their way up, Lily opened her eyes and whispered, 'Do Jim and Alfie know?'

'Not yet. They were out on duty when Don arrived. I left a note for them.'

'And Charlie? Does he know?'

Bert hesitated for just a moment, before nodding reluctantly. 'I paid a visit to the hospital before I left.'

'What did he say? Will he be coming to see me?'

Bert avoided her eyes. 'I don't know, Lil. It's hard for him. He was in the middle of something, and ... Well, you're not his family so he couldn't just leave.'

Lily's heart sank. For once in his life, Bert was trying to be diplomatic, but she could read between the lines. She closed her eyes again and sighed. What did it matter, anyway? She'd always known there was no real future for them. A man like Charlie and a girl like her didn't belong together.

Bert said no more until he opened the door to the bedroom, where he stopped, sniffing the air suspiciously. 'Bloody hell, it smells like the Oak at closing time on a Friday night!' His eyes drifted to Pauline, who was sprawled on the bed fully clothed, her hip flask lying open on the bed beside her, the eiderdown soaked with liquid. He shook his head. 'I know it's been a tough night and she's had a shock, but Pauline's got a problem with the booze. It's a shame cos she's a great girl, but she's going to get herself into real trouble if she don't get that under control.'

Lily yawned against his chest. She didn't care about Pauline's problems any more. She could drink herself to death for all she cared right now. But later, when she

319

felt stronger, she was going to ask her what Dick Brown had said to her outside the hospital. Because she couldn't shake the feeling that he was at the bottom of everything that was going wrong in their lives at the moment. As for Charlie, well, at least she knew where she stood.

Chapter 32

'So, are you going to tell us what happened?' Rodney asked his mother after Lily and Bert had disappeared up the stairs.

Nellie sighed deeply. 'Mr Wainwright got her released. Said they have no evidence, and when he left he muttered something about putting this right.'

'What right?'

'If you ask me, he's got suspicions as to who is really responsible. It's shameful; arresting a girl who's been punched in the face, tied up and left unconscious. She was just doing her job! But apparently one of the soldiers and that weird bloke who came round that lunchtime told the police she was on friendly terms with the German.'

Jasper slammed his fist on the table, making everyone jump. 'It's a bloody pack of lies! Our Lily would NEVER—'

'Jasper!' Nellie said sharply.

Jasper flicked a glance at her, and sat back down, head on his chest and arms folded. 'Well, it's a scandal, that's what it is. Blaming an innocent young girl for something she had no part in.'

Nellie stared at him stonily. 'I appreciate the help you've given me today, Jasper, but like I said earlier, this is family business. *Castle* family business, so maybe you should go.'

Jasper went still, his face paling, then he got up and left without another word.

There was stunned silence for a moment, broken by Donny, who had been so quiet everyone had almost forgotten he was there.

'Gran,' he whispered, tears in his eyes, 'that wasn't very nice.'

'How could you, Mum? Jasper's stuck by you through thick and thin. Whatever you do or say, he's always ready to back you up.' Marianne put her arm around her son. 'And you've upset your grandson. I don't know which is worse.'

'Marianne's right.' Edie got up. 'Every time I think you're not so bad, you go and show me that you're actually worse. I don't care what you say, Mum, but Jasper *is* family. And if it came down to a choice between the two of you, then I know who I'd go for. I don't know why he sticks around. I'm going to check he's all right. You coming Marianne? Donny?'

Without looking at her mother, Marianne stood up, and with her arm still round her son, they followed Edie out through the kitchen.

Marge and Reenie stared at each other uncomfortably for a moment, then Marge got to her feet. 'We'll be off and all, Mrs C,' she said with false cheeriness. 'You know where we are if you need us.'

After they'd left, Rodney sighed. 'Well done, Mum. We can always rely on you to make a bad situation worse. Anyway, now Lily's back safe and sound, I've got to get back to work before I get court martialled for going AWOL. Send Donny if you need me.'

Nellie didn't move or show any emotion until the door had shut behind Rodney, then she put her head in her hands.

Gladys, who had remained silent throughout, put an arm around her friend's shoulder. 'I don't know why I stick with you sometimes. All the good you do, all the help you give, and then things like this . . . I'd give my eye teeth for everything you have – a family, a man that loves you . . . Honestly, Nell, how could you treat Jasper like that?'

Nellie raised her head and wiped her eyes. 'I never mean it, Glad. Sometimes it's like a red mist descends and I can't seem to stop meself.'

Gladys rolled her eyes. 'You're forty-nine years old! Don't you think you should have learnt to by now? Even your Don's better at controlling himself than you. Look what happened here the other day, with the police getting tipped off. Seems someone's got it in for you and if you ask me, you probably deserve it.'

Nellie's shoulders sagged. 'I don't care about that. I know I rub people up the wrong way sometimes. But it's not that . . .' She looked up at her friend, tears pooling again in her hazel eyes.

'What? What is it, Nell? Short of one of them being killed what could be worse than what happened today?'

Nellie swallowed and shook her head. 'I . . .' She twisted her fingers together on the table, as though trying to decide what to say. 'You remember my Donald, don't you, Glad?'

Gladys's brow wrinkled. 'Of course I remember him. I'm not likely to forget, am I?'

'I mean, how he was?'

Gladys nodded. 'You both suffered, Nellie. God forgive me, but after my Godfrey got killed in the war and you took me in . . .' She paused and swallowed. 'All those years I lived here, there was envy in my heart and sometimes I *hated* you. You had a husband, kids, the business. And I had nothing. But then when Donald came back . . . As handsome as ever on the outside, but destroyed and ugly on the inside, I thought—' she crossed herself, but her expression was hard '—I thought, I was glad Godfrey was dead rather than having to see him turn into a . . . a *monster* like your Donald.'

Nellie's head came up at her vehemence, and Gladys took a deep breath, before continuing in a softer tone. 'It's far worse to feel your love die, to watch your husband become a broken, twisted man.' She put her hand on Nellie's. 'And yet, despite that, you kept going. You're stronger than me, love. Stronger than most women. But your temper'll be your undoing if you're not careful.' She paused for a moment. 'But how has he got anything to do with what happened just now?'

Nellie shook her head. 'Donald . . . Do you remember when he nearly strangled me? Thought I was the enemy coming to kill him?'

Gladys nodded. 'I remember. The doctor drugged him and I sat with him and the kids while Jasper took you to the hospital. Then when you came back, Donald moved in with Jasper for a bit to give you a break. God knows where you'd be without that man. Edie was right, your behaviour were shocking just now.'

Nellie stared at Gladys, desperate to unburden herself, but aware that her friend's strong faith might mean she'd hate her. Finally, she licked her lips. 'I'll tell you where I'd be. I'd be a mother of five. That's where I'd be.'

Gladys looked confused. 'Eh?'

'I'd have three boys and two girls. That's where I'd be without Jasper. Cos that night . . .' Nellie swallowed then continued in a whisper, 'That night, I didn't go to the hospital. I stayed at Jasper's.'

Gladys's mind went back to that time. Edie had been just one, little more than a baby. She used to sit and rock her, pretending that she was her own sweet girl. And some months after the incident, there'd been another baby for her to love . . . She sat back in shock as the realisation hit. 'Are you telling me that . . . Lily . . . ?'

At Nellie's nod, Gladys stood up and began to pace in agitation. 'Then what you said to him just now was even worse than I thought. And how come you never married him?'

'How could I? How could I when I'd betrayed my own husband when he needed me the most? How could I then leap into the next available bed, as if he'd never existed?'

'But that's not—'

'It is! And now Pauline knows that Lily's his daughter. She heard me and Jasper talking.'

Gladys shook her head. 'I know he were ill and it weren't his fault, but what he did . . . Donald didn't deserve your loyalty,' she said harshly. 'And what do you expect me to say to you? You've not just been lying to the kids, but you've been lying to everyone else as well. And what of Jasper? He loves you. He loves your children. He could have shown them what it was like to have a father, a decent man to learn from, but you refused to let him be a proper part of the family because of your stubborn pride?' She stopped as a thought came to her. 'Did Donald know?'

Nellie nodded miserably. 'He never forgave us. Either of us. And he never spoke a word to Lily. Not one word. Thank God she never noticed he treated her differently. Thought it was just the way he was.'

Gladys gathered up her bag and went to get her jacket and helmet. 'You are a stupid, stubborn old fool. You've had a good man pining for you, and you sit around feeling sorry for yourself. And what of Lily? How's she going to feel when the truth comes out? Which it will now that drunken madam knows. Pauline's resented you since your stupid games when she was nothing but a girl and she'll use this against you. Like I said, it's time you grew up and realised that your actions have consequences. And right now, the consequences are that you just might lose your daughter. I'm off before I say something I might regret. But you find a way to clean up this mess, or you'll not only be looking for a new assistant. You'll be looking for a new friend.' With that, she stalked through to the kitchen. 'And don't expect me back until you've sorted all this out,' she called through the hatch. Then she left, slamming the back door behind her.

Nellie sat staring straight ahead, afraid to move an inch in case it made her break down completely. Behind her, the parrot stirred in her cage. She'd sat in silence through most of the drama, as though sensing the tension in the air. But now she squawked gently, almost sympathetically. Finally, the dam broke and Nellie dropped her head onto the table and wept. For her children, who might never forgive her; for the love she'd been taking for granted that might now be lost; and for the girl she used to be: so full of joy and hope, never guessing that she would have to live through two world wars and watch her husband destroyed by his own mind.

Soon, though, the tears stopped and she sat up and took a deep breath. Gladys was right. She needed to sort this out, and she was going to start with Jasper.

'Finished feeling sorry for yourself, have you, Mum?'

She stood up and whirled round. Bert was standing in the doorway, arms folded, his expression inscrutable.

'How long have you been there?' she asked, her voice quivering with nerves.

'Long enough,' he said tonelessly.

'You heard me talking to Glad?'

He nodded slowly. 'Every word. But don't worry, I won't be telling Lily; poor love's got enough to deal with right now. But, Jesus, Mum . . . You have your faults, but one thing I've always thought I could rely on is your honesty. No matter whether I wanted the truth or not, I knew you'd give it to me. But now . . .' He shrugged. 'I finally realise that you're nothing but a grubby little liar. And worst of all, you've forced one of the best men I know to live a lie right along with you.' He shook his head. 'You should be ashamed of yourself.'

Nellie stood stock-still and watched through the window as her youngest son walked across the square. For a moment, her tears blurred her vision and she could have sworn it was Donald, restored to his youthful glory, walking away from her, his back rigid with fury at her betrayal.

Chapter 33

Before she left to find Jasper, Nellie went upstairs to check on her daughter. Opening the bedroom door, she wrinkled her nose at the smell, casting a brief glance at Pauline, who was lying on her back, limbs spread out like a starfish, snoring. Maybe she should speak to the girl, try to find out what she intended to do with the information. She knew, though, that any promise of silence she managed to extract from her would be worthless; it'd only take a few drinks and she'd be spouting her mouth off. But then, maybe it was time for the truth to come out. She'd hoped it would stay buried forever, but maybe that was wrong. And Lily didn't deserve to hear the truth from a girl in her cups.

She sat down gingerly on Lily's bed, careful not to wake her. She was lying curled in the foetal position, her glorious blonde hair covering the bruise on her face. Gently, Nellie stroked it away. She was so beautiful, her little girl. So clever and spirited; she couldn't be prouder of her. Her eyes filled with tears. Lily was the best of her and Jasper; her own fiery nature tempered with Jasper's kindness. But the brains . . . well, she wasn't sure where she'd got her brains from. The girl could be anything she wanted. She should have found a way, she thought, to let Lily study to be a doctor. Why hadn't she? They'd have managed it somehow and Jasper would have helped; he'd offered enough times. But she'd refused because she was worried that Lily would ask questions. She sighed. Everything led back to her stupid pride and the secret that had sat like a stone in her stomach since that terrible night. She shook her head. No, she needed to be honest; Donald's actions had been terrifying, but over the years, the memory that remained was of Jasper. His gentleness, how he had restored her faith, made her feel cherished and worthy. And given her this most precious gift. Why had she rejected him for all these years?

Carefully, she ran her fingers over the bruise on Lily's jaw. Her poor baby. What she had suffered today. She would fight tooth and nail to make sure no further harm came to her. The question was, which side of Lily's nature would win out when she finally told her the truth? Her mother's impulsive temper or Jasper's warm understanding? Only time would tell.

Quietly, she got up and tiptoed out of the room. It was time to speak to Jasper. She'd hurt him deeply; she only hoped he could forgive her.

∞

Marianne and Edie were in the kitchen with Donny, clearing away the remains of the breakfast service, when Nellie came downstairs. She couldn't even contemplate opening the café today; especially not after what she'd learnt about her neighbours' reactions to Lily's arrest. She felt deeply

330

betrayed by their willingness to believe that her daughter could have been involved in helping a prisoner to escape.

'I'm going to talk to Jasper,' she said. 'How is he?'

'How do you think?' Edie replied, clattering a pan on to the range.

'He's very sad, Gran. And you need to apologise,' Donny said from his chair at the small kitchen table where he was eating a sandwich.

Nellie stroked his hair. 'That's exactly what I intend to do, love. And while I'm gone and the café is closed, I want you to mop the floor and wash the dishes in the pantry.'

Donny groaned. 'Do I have to?'

'You do. Edie'll no doubt be getting back to the garage soon and your mum can't do everything on her own.'

'I'll be staying here for a bit, actually,' Edie said. 'To make sure Lily's all right.'

'Even so, Don is going to have to pull his weight now Gladys won't be here.'

'Where's she gone?' Marianne looked up at her mother sharply.

'She just needs a bit of a break, so she might not be in tomorrow either.'

'So you've managed to upset her and all, have you?' Edie said derisively. 'Why am I not surprised?'

Nellie shook her head. 'It's not like that. She just needs a break.' She stared at the pans of bacon and sausages. 'Marianne, why don't you make some pies with that lot and I'll take 'em over to the caves later. May as well make meself useful.'

'I intended to.' Marianne's response was short and toneless, and she didn't look up from her task.

Nellie waited a beat, to see if her daughter would say any more, or even look at her, but she didn't. Edie's bad temper she could take – that was nothing new – but for Marianne to be angry ... It was so unlike her. Nellie was used to being able to rely on her eldest daughter's sweet nature to smooth over her own rough edges. But it looked like she was well and truly on her own today.

Without another word, she made her way out of the back door, and turned left up Castle Street. She paused for a moment, astonished to see that life seemed to be going on as normal, while her own had been turned upside down. Staring up past the Granada, she could see Jasper's forge. The shutters were down, and a few people milled about outside, presumably waiting for it to open. Taking a deep breath she walked towards them.

'All right, Nellie,' an elderly man leaning on the door said. 'Heard your Lily's in a spot of bother. And now Jasper's not opened up, and I need to buy some more helmets. Never known him not to open, even when he's been up all night with air raids. What's up with him?' He looked at her curiously.

'He's not feeling too good is all,' Nellie said. 'Come back tomorrow.'

The man shrugged. 'Might pop down and get myself a cup of tea while I'm here then. Heard there's a bunch of people refusing to go into Castle's on account of your girl, but you can't blame the mother for the sins of the daughter in my book.'

Nellie bristled, feeling a welcome return of anger. 'My daughter hasn't got a bad bone in her body, Ted. And for your information, the café's shut today and all.'

'Sorry I spoke, missus. But if you're shut and Jasper's shut, and your Lily's been arrested, you can't blame a man for thinking it's all connected.'

'You can think what you like. Now if you don't mind, I need to check on Jasper.' She went up to the door and banged hard. As expected, there was no answer.

'Maybe he don't want to talk to yer,' he said. 'Finally had enough of yer bad temper and sharp tongue.' Ted snorted with laughter.

Nellie's head whipped round. 'If I were you, I'd get out of my sight before I knock your block off that scrawny little neck.' Digging in the pocket of her bright-pink cardigan, Nellie drew out a large key and fitted it into the lock. Jasper had insisted she have one after the night Donald had attacked her. As security, he said. In case she needed a place to shelter and he wasn't there; he needed to know she and the kids would always have a safe place to come. Her heart contracted a little at that. She'd taken this safe place for granted, and now it might be gone forever.

Opening the door, she stepped into the large space. As always, the forge was throwing out heat, and she skirted round it to the door at the back of the shop that led to the stairs. Unlike the café, Jasper's apartment was small and cramped, with only two bedrooms, a tiny kitchen, bathroom and sitting room. Since his wife Clara had died over twenty years before, he'd never redecorated, and the place, though clean, was drab. The brown flowered wallpaper was peeling, and the two armchairs, sitting either side of the brown-tiled fireplace, which had once been upholstered in plush green velvet, now had patchy spots of beige on the arms and headrests where the material had worn through. But despite this, on the dark-wood table by the window at which a couple of wooden chairs sat, was a jug of bright-blue love-in-a-mist. He'd have picked those from the fields up near the castle, she thought with a smile. It was typical of him. In the midst of darkness, Jasper would always find a way to bring colour.

But her smile faded as she looked at Jasper, who was sitting slumped in one of the armchairs, a glass of whisky in his hand.

'I didn't answer the door, cos I didn't want to see you,' he said, taking a gulp of his drink. 'I don't want to see anyone, which is why I sent the others away.'

'But I want to see you,' Nellie said uncertainly.

'It's not always about what you want, though, is it, Nell?' He let out a derisive snort. 'Though you'd not think it.'

She went over to him and sat down in the armchair opposite his, the bright pink of her cardigan and the light blue of her dress contrasting sharply with the drab green. 'I'm sorry,' she said simply.

He regarded her through tired, bloodshot eyes. His hair was even more unkempt than usual and his cheeks were pale beneath the growth of grey bristles. He shook his head. 'It's not enough, Nell.'

Nellie looked down at her hands, clutched tightly on her lap. 'Is there anything I can say?'

'I want my daughter to know who I am,' he said simply. 'I'm tired of being on the sidelines of her life. I'm tired of waiting for you to find the right moment. I want her . . .' He swallowed and closed his eyes. 'I want her to call me Dad,' he whispered finally. 'But you'll never give me that, will you?'

Nellie sat quietly, feeling the weight of his sorrow. So unlike Jasper, who to her was always light and safety. Solid and dependable as a rock.

'Do you know why I married Clara?' he asked suddenly.

'Because you loved her?'

He smiled slightly. 'I did. I loved her because she was sweet and gentle. But mostly I loved her cos she loved *me*. Big, bumbling Jasper Cane with hands like spades.' He spread out his hands, scarred and blackened from his work. 'She loved *me* and my bristly hair and my bristly moustache.'

'Loads of girls liked you, Jasper.'

He nodded. 'I've always been everyone's friend.' His voice was scornful. 'But when it came to romance . . . well, I were never a looker like your Donald, was I?' He laughed shortly. 'I don't know why I was friends with him sometimes. He took all the girls I liked one way or another. He didn't mean to, it was just the way it was. And then there was you. Not the prettiest, but you drew boys to you like moths to a flame. The two of you together, you were always at the centre of things, weren't you?'

Nellie smiled sadly. 'That were a long time ago, Jasper. I wasn't so lucky to have him in the end, was I?'

'I'd had my eye on you for years, Nell. Donald knew that. You made me laugh, you challenged me. You were so full of *life*! I never thought I stood a chance. Then Donald stepped in and I knew I'd have to forget about my dreams. Cos you only ever had eyes for him.'

Nellie's eyes flooded with tears. 'What are you saying?'

'You were always the one for me, Nell. But I accepted that I wasn't the one for you. Donald was my friend; I loved him like a brother. And so you became my sister. But you were never that in my heart.'

Nellie felt her cheeks burn with anger and guilt. She wished he hadn't told her that. It threw everything she'd thought about their friendship until that fateful night into a whole new light. 'So all those years you helped me with the kids, with Donald, it weren't for me. It was just so you could finally get one over on him, was it?'

Jasper regarded her through eyes swimming with tears. 'You know me better than that,' he whispered. 'Didn't you hear what I just said? I did it cos I loved you. And I loved him.'

She looked away, ashamed of herself, cursing her quick temper.

'But it's all gone now, Nellie. Those feelings have gone. You've finally shaken me off. All I want from you now is my girl. She's all I've got left. And if you don't tell her, then I will.'

'What about the wedding? Will you still give Marianne away?' she asked in a small voice.

'I would *never* let down one of the kids. I'll *always* be there for them. Always. But just not for you any more, Nell.'

Nellie felt the tears start to rise but fought them back. 'I never meant to hurt you,' she said.

He slammed his glass down on the table, making her jump. 'You've hurt me every day, Nellie! Every damn day since that girl was born! I understood when Donald were alive. What else could we do but hide the truth? I were ashamed as well. Ashamed that I'd taken advantage of the situation. Of you. But since he died, I've tried to show you how I feel. And you've thrown it back in me face every time. And I can't take it no more. Now, are you going to tell her, or am I?'

Nellie stood up. 'I'll tell her. But not till after the wedding. I don't want anything spoiling it for Marianne, and I don't know how Lily will react.'

He sighed deeply and nodded. 'Two weeks won't make much difference, but I'm only waiting for Marianne's sake, Nell. Not yours.'

She inclined her head, then walked carefully out of the room, her shoulders stiff with the effort not to cry. She should have told him that she loved him too, how much he'd come to mean to her. How she'd been denying her feelings all these years out of guilt for what they'd done. But it was too late now. She'd lost him and it was no more than she deserved.

Chapter 34

Lily opened her eyes and lay still for a moment, her head throbbing as the events of the past few hours came flooding back in a series of nightmare images. If she was lucky, Mr Wainwright would be able to get her out of this; if she wasn't . . . She didn't like to think about that. But surely they wouldn't have let her go if they'd truly believed she was guilty? They'd have locked her up and thrown away the key.

'You all right, Lil?' A hand pulled back the covers and Pauline's face hovered above her, her brow furrowed with concern.

'What do you think?'

Pauline sighed and plumped down on the side of the bed next to her. 'It'll all blow over. Then you can get back to your life and forget this ever happened.'

'But will everyone else forget, or will they always think of me as the girl who got away with it?' Lily tried to sit up, but the movement made her head feel as if it was being split open so she gave up and lay still.

'I brought you these.' Pauline held out her palm to show two aspirin. 'And some tea. I figured your head

338

would hurt.' She stared at the bruise that had spread up Lily's cheek. 'You're lucky he didn't break your jaw.'

Lily sat up, took the pills and swallowed them down with a mouthful of tea before lying back down. 'What time is it?'

'Four o'clock.'

She nodded. 'So Mum must be down there. I want to speak to her.'

'Café's closed and your mum's shut herself in her room. She asked me to let her know when you were awake, so I'll pop down and tell her.'

Lily raised her eyebrows. 'The café's shut? It's never shut! Even when Dad died, Gladys kept things running.'

'Well, she ain't here today. She's gawn and your mum's refusing to talk to anyone. I don't know what's happened.'

The faint smell of alcohol on her friend's breath reminded Lily. 'What was that between you and Dick Brown outside the hospital earlier? I saw you slap his face as the police drove me off.'

Pauline looked away. 'He's disgusting.'

At Lily's enquiring look she sighed. 'He said that's what came to girls as opened their legs to the Germans.'

Lily gasped. 'But I didn't! Is that what he's telling people?'

Pauline nodded slowly. 'Don't worry, no one believes him. And if they do, me, Dot and Vi'll make sure they hear the truth.'

Lily closed her eyes. She didn't know why the man hated her so much. The more she thought about it the more she became convinced that he was the one who'd helped the prisoner and found a way to have her take the blame. She just hoped Pauline was right and no one would believe him; people knew her better than they did him, after all.

'Dot and Vi are downstairs. Can they come up?' Pauline said.

Lily smiled and nodded. It was nice to know that her friends were standing by her, although she was surprised that Vi was there. She'd thought the girl didn't like her.

Pauline popped downstairs to get them, and when they entered they both looked as though they'd rather be anywhere else. 'How you feeling, love?' Dot asked solicitously.

'I've been better,' Lily said bravely. 'Thanks for coming.'

Dot shuffled her feet while Vi went over and handed Lily an envelope. 'Matron told us to give you this,' she said. 'Not that we wouldn't have come anyway. As if you'd do something like that,' Vi said. 'We've had our differences, but still . . . I believe in being fair, and what's happened to you ain't fair.'

Lily looked at the envelope and her stomach sank. Why couldn't Matron have come herself? Surely she'd want to check on the health of one of her nurses after she'd been attacked. 'What's this?'

Vi shrugged. 'I have a feeling it's not good. She had a face like thunder when she gave it to me. Open it, then. Let's have a look.'

Glancing uncertainly at the others, Lily slit open the envelope and took out a single sheet of handwritten notepaper.

Dear Nurse Castle,

On the orders of Dr Ramsay, I have been asked to inform you not to return to work at the Casualty Hospital for the time being.

Please be assured that I have no faith in the accusations being levelled against you, but for the moment, it is felt that your presence would cause unnecessary controversy amongst some of our military patients.

I will be in touch as soon as the situation is resolved.

Lily let the paper drop to the eiderdown, staring sightlessly at the door. That was that, then. Her nursing dreams lay in tatters, and all because she had been in the wrong place at the wrong time. Matron could claim to support her all she liked, but actions spoke louder than words. Same went for Dr Ramsay.

Pauline snatched the paper up and read it. 'That bloody cow!' she exclaimed. 'How dare she say that! "Controversy amongst the military patients!" What's she on about! NO one believes it.'

Dot cleared her throat. 'Actually, a few of them were quite vocal after Lily got taken off this morning. And then apparently this lawyer fella turned up asking questions, saying your mum had hired him, Lily. Matron was spittin' feathers. So was Dr Ramsay. Thrown out on his ear the lawyer was. But not before he'd had a good chat with Sister Mackenzie and Sister Murphy. That's what I heard anyway.'

Bless Mr Wainwright, Lily thought. At least he believed her. As for Matron and Dr Ramsay ... their lack of faith when they'd seen what had happened to her hurt. 'Can you all just go now,' she said faintly. She wasn't sure she could stand to hear any more. 'You too, Pauline. In fact, would you mind sleeping in Marianne's room tonight?'

Pauline's eyes widened. 'You don't want me here?'

'It's nothing personal. I just need time on my own.' But it wasn't only that. She *knew* Pauline was hiding something from her, and until she found out what it was, she wasn't sure she could trust her. What if Dick Brown had been involved and she knew something but wasn't saying? Did he hold some sort of threat over her? Is that why? Because if there was anyone in the hospital she'd lay money on being sneaky enough to help that prisoner escape, it was the odious porter. She just didn't know why.

'In which case,' Pauline said tightly, 'I'll pack me bags and leave. I won't stay where I'm not wanted.'

'Suit yourself,' Lily said. 'But don't nick my hairbrush.' She lay down and pulled the eiderdown over her head. She really didn't care what anyone did, she thought as she listened to the sound of Pauline throwing things into her suitcase. She just wanted to be left alone with her misery.

'You can come and stay in our room, Pauline. There's space on the floor, if you don't mind bunking down there,' said Vi. Lily was vaguely surprised at the girl's kindness. She couldn't work her out at all.

'Maybe I will. I'd rather that than be at home on my own tonight. Especially with a prisoner on the loose.'

'We'll wait for you downstairs, then,' Dot said. 'Bye, Lily. Try not to worry. Me and the other girls will be making sure that people know you had nothing to do with it.'

Lily's throat was too tight to make a reply, and after a moment, she heard the door open and shut as they left. With tears leaking from her eyes, she lay listening to the sounds of her friend packing. Finally, she heard the door open again, and she pulled the blankets off her face to see Pauline standing in the doorway. 'Bye then, Lily,' she said in a small voice. 'I really am sorry.' Then thankfully she left and Lily was alone at last.

Breathing a sigh of relief, she turned onto her side and stared at the brightly coloured wallpaper, thinking about Pauline's final words. Why would she apologise? Unless she had something to apologise for. Maybe she'd been right in her suspicions that Pauline knew more about this than she was letting on. She sighed miserably. It looked like this incident might well have cost her her job, her friend, and the first man she'd ever met who made her feel truly excited. No, more than excited, she realised. Much more than just excited.

The thought of Charlie sent a surge of anger through her. She'd thought he felt the same. But the first sniff of trouble and she hadn't seen him for dust. She sat up and pushed the covers violently away from her. Well, she wasn't going to stand for it. She was going to give that man a piece of her mind whether he liked it or not.

∞

Ten minutes later, Lily was dressed in baggy slacks and a warm jersey; since that morning the weather had turned and it was now pouring with rain.

'Lily?' Her mother was in the sitting room with Marianne and Edie, and, at the sound of her footsteps, she rushed out to her. 'Are you all right, love?' she asked gently. 'I saw Pauline and those other two leave. Where have they gone?' She regarded Lily anxiously.

'I asked to be left alone.'

Nellie gripped Lily's arm tightly. 'Did that girl say something to upset you?'

'No, *I* said something. I asked her to leave. I need space to think.' She shook her mother's hand off her arm. 'And that means space from you, too! Oh, and in case you're wondering, Dot and Vi brought me a letter from Matron telling me not to go back to work.' She gave a short bark of laughter. 'Controversy amongst the military patients.' Just saying the words, understanding that this meant people believed she was responsible for what had happened, brought the sting of tears to her eyes again.

'What?!' Nellie's face went red with indignation. 'How bloody dare she? You've been helping out at that hospital for years, and suddenly she can't trust you! Well, I'm not having it.' She stalked towards the stairs.

'Where are you going?'

'Up the hospital. I'm not sitting by while my daughter gets bad-mouthed all over the town.'

'For God's sake, Mum, leave it, will you? Don't you think I've got enough to deal with without you shouting your mouth off?'

Nellie paused. 'Shouting my mouth off?' she said then quietly. 'Is that what you call me defending my daughter? Doing my best to protect you?'

Lily sighed. 'But you won't be protecting me. You'll be getting people's backs up as usual.'

'Oh, that's lovely, that is. Is that what you thought I was doing when I fetched Mr Wainwright and came running to the police station? You think he came out of the goodness of his heart? NO! I have to pay him!'

'Mum, stop.' Marianne got up and put an arm around her mother's shoulders. 'Why are you having a go at Lily? None of this is her fault.'

'I will pay back every penny, Mum,' Lily ground out. 'The last thing I want is to have you holding this over my head for the rest of my life.'

Ignoring the devastated expression on her mother's face, Lily ran down the stairs and stormed out of the back door, hesitating for just a moment, before running down Castle Street and then flying across Market Square.

∞

'Here we go again,' Edie said as Marianne led their mother back to her chair.

Nellie sat down and put her head in her hands. 'Oh God. Gladys is right. I need to learn to control myself. I didn't mean to shout. It's just been a hell of a day.'

Marianne regarded her mother as she sat hunched in the chair. She looked diminished somehow, and she couldn't help feeling that this had more to do with her visit to Jasper than the situation with Lily. Usually, in times of crisis, Jasper was always there, giving comfort with his good-humoured solidity, but she'd never seen him as angry as he had been today. It frightened her a little, because Jasper was a fixture in their family, and if he was no longer around, everything would start to crumble. Especially their mother. She'd got it wrong all these years, she reflected. She'd always considered her mother to be the strong one, but she realised now that without Jasper there to back her up, Nellie was lost.

Another thought came to her then. If Jasper and her mother had truly fallen out, did that mean he'd no longer be there for the rest of them? Would he even come to her wedding? She felt horribly guilty worrying about that when her sister was going through hell, but if this continued, she might end up getting married without Jasper or Lily there. And she wasn't sure if she could go ahead if that was the case.

∞

Lily approached the bridge that led to Drop Redoubt with trepidation. She could see the soldiers standing to attention by their sentry box, and she wasn't sure if they'd let

346

her pass. Would they recognise her from when she was there with Charlie before? she wondered. And if they did, would they have heard what had happened at the hospital? Taking a deep breath, she straightened her shoulders and marched on. The rain was coming down heavily now, and her hair hung in a dripping plait down her back as she approached the soldiers.

'I'm here to see Dr Charlie Alexander,' she said with far more confidence than she felt.

They regarded her sceptically. 'You got your pass?'

She dug in her pocket for her identification – something all residents had to have to be allowed to enter Dover now – and held it out to one of them. He took it and looked at it silently. 'I seen you before. You're that nurse what came here with the doctor.' He hesitated and looked at his colleague. 'Castle . . . You Bert and Jim's sister?'

She nodded.

He handed the papers back decisively and shook his head. 'Nope. Sorry, can't let you through. Saw Bert earlier. Heard all about you. He swears you're innocent, but even so, it's more than our job's worth.'

'I *am* innocent!' she cried desperately. 'Please, let me through.'

He shook his head. 'Best I can do is get a message to the doctor.'

Her shoulders sagged. It was unfair to argue with them; they were just doing their jobs and in their position she'd probably say the same. 'Can you tell him to meet me at the kissing gate at the top of Cowgate Steps? I'll be waiting.'

She trudged back down the hill and sat at the top of the steps, staring out over the cemetery. It was appropriate that she'd wait here, she thought. Considering everything she'd hoped and dreamed of for her life seemed to have died today.

She sat for what felt an eternity as slowly the rain stopped and the sky cleared, but the evening sun did little to warm her and she shivered as the wispy clouds slowly turned pink. She sighed. It seemed he wasn't coming, which shouldn't surprise her. After all, he couldn't be seen to spend time with a woman accused of being a traitor. Just then she heard footsteps and jumped up, turning expectantly. Charlie was jogging towards her, but in the gloom she couldn't make out his expression. She watched his approach and was heartened to see the concerned look on his face. But then her heart soared as he got close and he grabbed her, wrapping his arms around her.

'Are you all right?' he whispered into her damp hair. 'I'm sorry I couldn't see you sooner. I was operating.'

Lily's eyes filled with tears. 'I'm sorry about dinner,' she said with a small laugh as she sagged against him.

Charlie snorted. 'There'll be other dinners. But didn't I tell you not to get in any more trouble?'

'You're not going to ask me if it's true?'

'Of course it's not true!'

'Thank you. I thought . . . I thought when Bert said you couldn't come that you believed it.'

'Oh, darling. I might not have known you long, but I feel like I really *know* you. Does that make sense? The only reason I couldn't come was because when I got the message I was gowned up and about to operate on some poor sod who got shot in the chest.'

Lily nodded against his jacket, shivering as cold droplets of rain trickled inside her collar.

He pulled away and looked down at her face for the first time. 'Christ!' He stroked her bruised jaw gently. 'If I could get my hands on that bastard, he wouldn't last long. Bert didn't mention you were hurt.'

'It's nothing. Well, nothing compared to the fact that my life has gone down the khazi.' She attempted to smile, but her teeth were chattering so badly, all she could manage was a grimace.

Charlie pulled his jacket off and swung it around her shoulders. 'We need to get you home. Don't want you ending up in there.' He nodded towards the cemetery.

'I can't go home,' she whispered. 'I've had a fight with Mum and I can't even look at her right now.'

He frowned. 'Lily, no good ever came from hiding. And whether you like it or not, you need your mum right now.'

'No! I'm not going home!'

He thought for a moment. 'Look, let's go and sit down in Barwick's Cave. It should be empty right now.' He guided her back up the hillside towards a path that led directly down to Snargate Street.

As they were walking, the distant droning of planes made them stop and stare out over the sea. In the distance, the sky was black with aircraft, and they watched in horror as they advanced towards them.

349

'Those are bombers!' Charlie exclaimed, pulling her urgently down the hill. 'We need to get to safety.'

Hearts in their mouths, they started to run as what seemed like hundreds of Dorniers and Heinkels roared towards the coast. The air raid siren began to wail and, as they neared the entrance, a stream of people were already scrambling to get inside the cave.

Lily hid her face against Charlie's shoulder, unwilling to be noticed, but people were too intent on getting to safety to even look at them. At the mouth of the cave, Charlie stopped and stared at the sky. The noise was deafening now as wave upon wave of enormous planes roared overhead, and the familiar sound of explosions carried towards them.

Charlie swore. 'I need to get back,' he said. 'I'm so sorry, Lily. Will you be all right?'

Her heart sank at his words, but she knew she couldn't keep Charlie from his duty.

'I'll be fine. But, Charlie, why are there so many?'

He shook his head. 'I don't think they've come to bomb Dover. My guess is they're headed for London.'

Lily gasped. 'Are you sure?'

'It's been on the cards for a while. This is what they've been aiming for. It's just the RAF have managed to keep them over the south. But they're not going to stop this.'

He was shouting over the roar and, around them, others, too, were staring up at the huge aircraft flying over them.

'Gawd preserve them!' someone shouted. 'Mark my words this is the beginning of the end.'

'It's quicker if I go through the tunnel. I promise I'll come to see you as soon as I can. Trust me.' Charlie gave Lily a hard kiss on the lips, then pushed his way into the crowd.

Without him, Lily suddenly felt exposed so she ran in the opposite direction. The only place she felt truly safe at the moment was home. No matter that she'd argued with her mother, Charlie was right; she needed her right now.

∞

'Thank God!' Nellie jumped up and grabbed Lily's shoulders as she ran into the basement. 'Don't ever run out on me again, Lily. Promise.'

Lily put her head on her mother's shoulder, wrapping her arms around her soft waist. 'I'm sorry, Mum,' she whispered.

'Oh, love. You've got nothing to be sorry for. It's me and my big mouth. You know I just want the best for you. For all of you. Now sit down and have a cup of tea.'

She bustled to the table where Donny, Marianne and Edie were sitting, Donny feeding birdseed to Polly.

'What's going on out there?'

Lily dropped into a chair. 'There're dozens and dozens of them, Mum. I've never seen so many bombers. Charlie thinks they're headed for London.'

'Those poor buggers,' Nellie gasped. 'Those poor, poor buggers.'

They lapsed into silence. But finally, Marianne cleared her throat. 'Given everything that's happened today, and

351

what with Jasper, and the fact that there's only two weeks till my wedding, I think I'm going to talk to Alfie about postponing.'

'What?' Edie exclaimed, shocked.

'You can't, Mum! I won't let you!' Donny shouted. 'And if you do, then it'll be *your* fault, Gran, for being so mean to Jasper!'

Lily stared at Nellie in consternation. 'But why would that stop the wedding? You're often mean to Jasper. He knows you don't mean it.'

Her mother didn't meet her eyes. 'Don't be daft, Marianne. Jasper'll be there. He wouldn't let you down for the world. He wouldn't let any of you down.' She put her hand over Lily's and gave it a squeeze.

'Is this my fault?'

'No!' Nellie said forcefully. 'None of this is your fault, Lily. *None of it.*'

Lily nodded, shocked at her mother's vehemence. 'What then?'

Nellie ignored the question. 'As for you, Marianne, you postpone the wedding, you let *everyone* down. The whole neighbourhood's clubbed together to sort the food, and God knows we all need a good party. But, worst of all, you'll break your little lad's heart. And Alfie's.'

Marianne fiddled with her cup. 'But that's just it, isn't it? After what happened this morning no one'll even come to the party. And I just thought . . . Well, it won't be much of a celebration, will it, if you and Jasper aren't talking to each other, and with everything going on with Lily.'

352

'That lot out there might have their brains in their arses right now, but once they've had time to think about it, they'll see their mistake. Anyway, with Mr Wainwright on the case, it'll be cleared up in no time. The man's got a brain as sharp as a tack. Nothing, and I mean *nothing*, is going to stop you marrying your man.'

'Mum, you still haven't told me what happened with Jasper.'

Nellie waved her hand. 'It'll blow over. Don't worry about it, love.'

'You sure about that?' Edie asked sceptically. 'Didn't look that way to me.'

'Of course I'm sure. And, Marianne, you cancel the wedding over my dead body.'

Nellie still wasn't looking at her and something told Lily that this was more serious than her mother was letting on. She glanced at her sisters, who shrugged in unison and then looked away from her. Tomorrow, she thought, she would go to see Jasper. Maybe he would give her a straight answer.

Chapter 35

Contrary to what Nellie had expected, the café was busy the following morning, although she noted that a few of the regulars from the market didn't come in as usual. She didn't want to admit it, but their absence hurt. She'd known these people all her life and she'd assumed that at this time of crisis for her family, they would be supportive. But it seemed she was wrong. And with no Jasper or Gladys, Nellie realised for the first time that she really could be on her own. Bert's face had been like thunder when he'd left yesterday, and when Lily found out the truth, she doubted she'd be much more forgiving. Soon, she might find that she'd lost her children as well as her friends.

Hopefully the wedding might bring the community back together. People had already donated bits of food and surely that, if nothing else, would remind them that they all needed to stand together. Nellie stared out of the window as Tom Burton, the cobbler, who would normally pop in for a quick cup of tea before starting work, walked past without even looking in. Suddenly, anger started to burn within her. How dare they do this to her family! She wasn't going to stand for it.

She stomped to the door and was about to yank it open, when Jasper's voice came to her. *Nell, love. When will you learn to think before you speak?* Gladys's comment, too, replayed in her mind. *Your Don's better at controlling himself than you.* Slowly, she let go of the handle. They were right. Maybe it was time to just wait and see. People would come round; their lives were too closely bound for them to stay away forever. Castle's Café had been at the heart of this community for years. So just this once she'd take her friends' advice and ignore her impulses.

She walked back behind the counter, smiling graciously at a couple of sailors who had come in for breakfast. 'Hello, my loves. What can we get you? Full English, is it? Or perhaps you'd like something sweet.' She gestured to the rock cakes and scones sitting under a glass dome on the counter. 'Sit down and make yourselves comfortable and I'll be right over to take your order.'

'Are you all right, Mrs C?' one of the men asked, looking at her curiously.

'I'm perfectly fine, thank you.'

'Not what we 'eard,' one of them cackled. 'One minute it's black market, the next it's 'elpin' Krauts. If it weren't for the fact the grub's so good and cheap in 'ere, we'd have been down the Pot and Kettle.'

Nellie ground her teeth as the smile on her face froze, then she took a deep breath. 'Talking of pots and kettles, lads, I heard all about the fight in the Oak the other night. Was it one of you that was locked up for being drunk and disorderly?'

'Bit different from betrayin' your country, though, ain't it?'

'Right.' That was it. Nellie slammed her hand on the counter. 'Out! You can't go throwing accusations around and expect me to serve you.' She marched to the door and opened it with a bang, while others around her stopped eating to watch.

One of the sailors held up his hands. 'All right, Mrs C. We don't mean nothing by it. Just sayin' what others are sayin'. We know Lily's a good girl.'

'OUT!'

They stared at her for a moment, before reluctantly leaving the café, their expressions surly. Nellie slammed the door shut behind them, took another deep breath then turned to face the rest of the customers. 'Enjoy your meals, everyone,' she said, smiling stiffly.

Then, back rigid, she walked back to the counter. 'Don't look at me like that,' she muttered to Polly, who was regarding her with her head on one side, her gaze unblinking. 'I tried, didn't I?'

∽

Upstairs, Lily remained in bed. With no job to go to, she felt rudderless, as if her life no longer had meaning. She lay staring at the ceiling, her mind going back over the last day. It felt like a lifetime since she'd been arrested, since that man had left her unconscious and tied up. The events played in her mind like a film, but one she took no pleasure from. One of the images that kept replaying over and over was that of Pauline slapping Dick Brown. Was that because she knew Dick was involved or was Pauline telling the truth when she said it had nothing to do with him? There was only one way to find out.

Lily threw back the covers and dressed hurriedly in the clothes she'd worn the day before. She needed to talk to them both.

Lily wound her way through Dover's narrow back streets, staying away from the thoroughfare, reluctant to bump into anyone she knew. But she couldn't avoid the main street completely and soon she had to cross the High Street. At a shout behind her, Lily paused, debating whether to turn or not; she really didn't want to see anyone right now.

'Lily!' The voice came again and she glanced furtively over her shoulder. It was Mary Guthrie and the look on her face was so sympathetic and understanding that Lily nearly burst into tears.

'Lily, love, are you all right?' the woman said as she hurried over to her.

Lily sniffed. 'I'm fine, thanks, Mrs Guthrie.'

'Just so you know, I don't believe a word of it. Utter nonsense. If there's anything I can do?'

'There's nothing. Thank you.' She took in the woman's kind, careworn face; the marks of grief clear to see. 'How are you bearing up?' she asked.

Mrs Guthrie nodded as she tried to smile. 'Not too bad.' She paused. 'Jim came to see us the other day. He seems . . . he seems different.'

'He's taken Colin going missing very hard.'

'Yes. Those two were closer than brothers. Is it true that Jim and Reenie Turner are walking out?'

Lily was surprised by the question. Mrs Guthrie wasn't a gossip, but then, she supposed that Jim was like a second son to her.

'It seems he is.'

Mrs Guthrie gave a tight smile. 'I see. Well, I wish them both happiness. No doubt I'll see them at Marianne's wedding.'

'I expect so.'

'Good luck, love. I'll be keeping you in my prayers.'

Lily watched as Mary Guthrie went back into the bakery, feeling warmed by the woman's support, but puzzled by her attitude towards Jimmy and Reenie. But then it was hardly surprising that she'd act a little oddly. After all, Jim was still here, whereas, no matter what his mother wished to believe, it was more than likely that Colin was lying in an unmarked grave somewhere in France.

She sighed sadly, picturing Colin as she'd last seen him in January – tall, blond, with a sweet, shy smile. Was it really only nine months since he and Jimmy had come home on leave? Such a short space of time and yet everything had changed. Suddenly, her own problems seemed paltry in comparison to so many others who'd had their lives turned upside down with no hope that it would ever return to normal. She lifted her head and straightened her shoulders. She had nothing to be ashamed of and it was time to stop behaving as if she did. She refused to hide herself away any more.

When she arrived outside the hospital, though, her confidence started to drain away. Staring through the railings, she wondered what she should do. The girls would be in the canteen right now on their break, so should she just brazen it out and walk in? Or should she loiter outside hoping that Pauline would come out at some point?

She crept up the long driveway, keeping close to the bushes on the left-hand side, grateful that it was quiet. Ducking past Matron's office, she scuttled round the side of the building and was rewarded by the sight of Pauline, Dot, Vi and a few of the other nurses huddled outside talking quietly.

She walked up to them. 'Hello, girls,' she said as casually as she could, though her heart was thumping.

'Lily!' Pauline gasped. 'You shouldn't be here.'

'Just wanted to check up on you all.' She nodded towards the Nissen hut. 'Any more escapes last night?'

'I don't know how you have the barefaced cheek to come here when you should be in jail!' one of the nurses said in disgust. 'If you don't leave in the next thirty seconds, I'll find someone to remove you.'

'Oh, get over yourself, Beryl,' Pauline snapped. 'She's bloody innocent, and well you know it.' She threw her cigarette down and took Lily's arm. 'Over here.'

Lily allowed her friend to lead her over to the shrubbery that bordered the lawn, affording them a small amount of privacy.

'I'm sorry I asked you to leave, Paul,' Lily said. 'I was upset. Will you come back?'

Pauline shook her head. 'You're all right. Mum and Dad'll be back in a couple of days, and I've been given a temporary bed at the nurses' home.'

'You don't sound too pleased about them coming home.'

Pauline avoided her eyes. 'Course I am. It'll be good to sleep in me own bed.'

Lily examined her friend's face. She was pale and she looked exhausted. Was this because she had a guilty conscience? Or did she have a hangover as usual? Or perhaps a combination of both? 'Why did you slap Dick Brown's face yesterday?' she asked bluntly.

Pauline's startled gaze came back to her. 'I already told you.'

'Yeah. But see, I don't think you were telling me the whole truth.'

Pauline shuffled her feet before sighing. 'The truth is, Lil, I can't tell you. Or rather, I *won't* tell you. It's private business. But please believe me, it weren't nothing to do with what happened with that Kraut. Honest.'

'Every time I see you with Dick, you look scared and upset. So if it weren't that, why can't you say?'

'Because it's none of your bloody business, that's why,' Pauline snapped. 'And, if I were you, I'd take Beryl's advice and leave before anyone else spots you.'

Lily felt anger spark in her as she watched her friend walk away. No way was she leaving here without answers.

360

She needed to speak to Dick. She took a step forward, ready to shout down anyone who stood in her way. But then she stopped. What she needed now was patience. Dick would come out of the back sooner or later to stick something in the bins or run an errand. She'd wait. And the minute he stepped foot outside she'd beat the truth out of him if she had to.

To her surprise, she didn't have to wait long as, within minutes, Dick appeared, strolling towards her, hands in the pocket of his hospital coat. 'Well, well, well. A little bird told me you were loitering around. Thought I'd come out to see how you're doing.' He sucked his teeth. 'Dreadful business yesterday. You'll be glad to hear they've taken them all away—' he nodded at the hut '—and locked 'em up safe and sound.' He tutted when he caught sight of her face. 'That's a nasty bruise that is. Shame it didn't work.'

Lily regarded him suspiciously. 'What do you mean?'

'You know, knock the girl out so it looks like she weren't involved. But seems you got your pretty face bashed up for nothing. We all saw him with his hands all over you that day and now people are wondering what you and him got up to in that hut. Still, it's only a matter of time till they catch up with him, considering how sick he were meant to be, and then we'll hear the truth from the horse's mouth. Unless you and your mum have him holed up somewhere. Maybe that big basement of yours?'

Lily took a deep breath, refusing to rise to the bait. 'Did you give him Ipecac?'

Dick laughed softly. 'You're barking up the wrong tree there. I got no love for the Nazis. You, on the other hand . . .' He raised his eyebrows. 'Although that strange old fella was round asking all sorts yesterday. Spent a bit of time in Matron's office. Pushed his luck with Dr Ramsay, though. The man had him thrown out on his ear. Your mum must be richer than I thought if she can pay for a lawyer.'

'Did he speak to you?'

'Oh, he spoke to me all right. And I told him to sling his hook. He's got no right to question anyone when the culprit's already been caught bang to rights.'

'You know I had nothing to do with it,' she snarled. 'Otherwise why would the police have let me go?'

'Do I?'

'Why did Pauline smack you one?'

He raised his hand reflexively to his cheek. 'You saw that?' He grinned, his teeth yellow in the sunlight. 'Me and Pauline have an understanding, is all. I felt she weren't fulfillin' her side of the bargain. But don't worry; we're back on track now. Better than ever, in fact.'

She frowned. 'What are you talking about?'

He tapped his nose. 'Ah, that's for me to know and you to find out. Which maybe you will, when the time is right. Anyway, must get on; some of us have jobs to do.' His eyes raked over her. 'Though mine is a sight more boring now you ain't there to brighten me day.'

Lily grimaced as he walked away. She didn't want to believe him, but he'd sounded so convincing that she was starting to doubt herself. But even if she was wrong about his involvement in the escape, there was definitely something threatening about that man. She just couldn't fathom why, or what he held over Pauline. What did he mean by they had an 'understanding'?

'Nurse Castle!' Lily jumped as she saw Matron Watson striding towards her. 'I think my instructions were perfectly clear,' she said sternly. 'You are to stay away from here until the matter has been resolved.'

'But I haven't done anything wrong.'

'So you say. And, personally, I'm inclined to believe you. But for now, you're barred from the hospital. And that includes the grounds.' She hesitated. 'But like I said in my letter, I have every confidence that we'll be welcoming you back soon.'

'How do you know? Have they found the prisoner?'

She shook her head. 'I can't say more. But please, leave now. I'll be in touch one way or another in the near future.'

Lily knew she had no choice but to go, so without another word to Matron she walked away.

Chapter 36

Lunchtime at the café was not quite as busy as usual, which was just as well as far as Marianne was concerned. With no Gladys to help, it would have been impossible to stay on top of things. As it was, she'd had to persuade Donny to do the washing-up and she could hear him now, clattering the plates on to the draining board as a way of making his displeasure known. With the schools shut, the council were again putting pressure on parents to send the children away, and if they didn't, they were expected to teach the kids at home. How were they supposed to do that? The schoolbooks had been sent to Wales with the evacuated children, and Marianne had never been one for learning. Lily had helped a bit, but everyone had enough on their plates doing their jobs and keeping their households going, without then having to teach the kids as well. She sighed. The sooner the school in the caves that Mrs Palmer had told her mother about started, the better. Until then, the children would continue to roam free, learning a lot about planes, and death and destruction, but not much about anything else.

She was distracted from these gloomy thoughts when the back door opened.

'Marianne!' It was Alfie.

She flew into his arms, standing on tiptoe to kiss his lips.

'Are you all right, love? Bert's filled me and Jim in. Sorry I couldn't come yesterday, but it was a bit . . . Well, we were on high alert. Turns out they were right. But it was London that took the flack this time.' He examined her face. 'You look tired. How's Lily?'

'Gone out. And Mum's behaving strangely – all smiles one minute and bursts of temper the next. She's had a run-in with Jasper, who's now holed up at the forge and says he won't be coming back. Something's happened with Gladys as well because she hasn't come in.' Her eyes filled with tears. 'Oh, Alf, I know I shouldn't think of myself right now, but what if Jasper won't come to the wedding? I suggested to Mum we postpone but she wouldn't hear of it.'

Alfie drew back. 'Postpone?'

'With no Jasper and no Gladys, Lily living under a cloud and the neighbours not talking to us, it's not much of a celebration, is it?'

'Mum, Gran said no!' Donny came out of the scullery, his hands dripping water on to the floor. 'I've been practising "The Wedding March", and you can't not get married cos that's not fair to Alfie cos then he won't be able to adopt me.'

Alfie smiled down at Marianne. 'You can't fault the boy's logic. Come on, love. It's not as if the wedding's tomorrow, is it? In a couple of weeks, Lily's problems will be sorted and you know Jasper – he can't stay angry with your mum for long.'

Marianne shook her head. 'I'm not so sure. He seemed like a broken man yesterday. And when Mum came back, I've never seen her so upset.'

'Alfie, my favourite son-in-law-to-be,' Nellie called through the hatch. 'Get your fiancée to serve you up a plate of pie and mash and come in here and talk to me.'

He quirked an eyebrow at Marianne. 'She don't seem too bad to me.'

'Give it time. She'll blow up about something in a minute.'

Alfie looked thoughtful. 'Listen, I don't mean to worry you, but something's up with Bert as well. He was in a right mood last night, which isn't like him. I put it down to Lily's trouble, but I think it's more than that.'

Marianne sighed. 'You see? Who wants to go to a wedding when there's so much else going on?'

'I do!' Donny piped up.

'Get back to the washing-up, Don, and stop listening to other people's private conversations!' Marianne snapped.

Donny's head drooped and he disappeared back into the scullery.

'That were uncalled for,' Alfie chastised.

Marianne huffed. 'The boy has no discipline, and he's *my* son, so I'll talk to him how I want.'

Alfie's eyes widened and he stepped back; he'd never seen Marianne lose her temper before. 'I see. So all that stuff about me being a proper dad to Don, that's just talk, is it? Maybe all these reasons you have to postpone have more to do with you having second thoughts than what happened yesterday. And if that's the case, you need to tell me now.'

Marianne's eyes filled with tears. 'Oh, Alf, I'm sorry. I didn't mean it.' She tried to pull him in for a hug. 'Honest, I didn't.'

He stood stiffly in her embrace, then nodded. 'Fine. But you have to understand that once we're married, Donny is *our* son. We will be bringing him up *together*; are you sure that's still what you want?'

She nodded. 'I want to marry you more than anything in the world and I can't wait for you to be Donny's dad,' she whispered.

He put his arms around her. 'Thank God for that. Because that's what I want too. Hey, Don,' he called.

Donny poked his head out, his expression sulky.

'Don't worry, mate. The wedding's on.'

He nodded. 'Good. And, Mum, I will accept an apology when you're ready.' Then he disappeared again.

Alfie smiled. 'Please try not to worry, love. This is going to be the best day of our lives, I promise.'

∞

Lily knocked on the door of the forge, her brow creased with concern. It was so unlike Jasper not to be open; even when he wasn't there, his apprentice would be. Things between her mum and him must be worse than she thought. She knocked again, and when there was no answer, she stepped back and looked up at the open window on the first floor.

'Jasper!' she shouted, causing people to turn and look at her. She ignored them and tried again. 'Jasper, it's Lily.'

Finally, she was rewarded by the sight of Jasper's bushy head poking out of the window.

'What's happened?' he asked anxiously.

'Let me in.'

His head disappeared and soon he opened the door, pulling her into a hug. 'Are you all right, love? Is it your mum?'

'I'm fine.' She stepped back and looked up at his face. His eyes were red and his face was unshaven. 'But I'm not so sure about you. What's happened? Why aren't you talking to Mum?'

He looked away. 'That's between me and her. But, Lily, I want you to know that if there's anything you need – anything at all – you come to me and I'll help. I don't care what it is. Even if it's to go to some fancy school to learn to be a doctor. I'll sell the forge if I have to.'

Lily was taken aback. 'Why would you do that?'

He shook his head. 'Cos I can. Cos I love you like you were me own.' At her startled look, he added, 'I love all of you as if you were me own.'

'And we love you like a father.' She put her arms around his large waist, resting her head on his chest. 'But Marianne is talking about postponing the wedding cos you might not come. If you loved us like your own, you'd never do that, would you?'

Jasper looked at her aghast. 'I told your mum, and I want you to tell Marianne, I will be there. With bells on.

Nothing and no one, not even your mum, will keep me away.'

'Was it because of me? Whatever you and Mum argued about?'

He shook his head. 'Nothing you could do or say would drive me away, love, I promise. But you should go. You need your mum right now.'

'I need both of you.'

'And you have us. I'm just around the corner. Go on. Everything'll be all right.' He pushed her gently towards the door. 'An' I'll see you soon.'

Searching his face, she could see that she wouldn't get any more out of him, so, with a nod, she turned to leave. Then she stopped and looked back at him. 'Same goes for you, Jasper. You need anything at all, you come to me, all right? If I can help, I will.' She blew him a kiss and walked back to the café, slipping quietly in through the back door and up the stairs, ignoring her sister's calls, as she rushed to her bedroom and threw herself down on the bed.

Whatever Jasper said, she couldn't shake the feeling that she was the cause of the rift between her mother and him. She sighed deeply. Despite her determination, she'd not learnt much today after all. It seemed the more questions she asked, the more confused she became. She turned over and lay on her side, wincing as her bruised jaw touched the pillow. So now what? she wondered. Would she just have to lie here until everyone else sorted it out for her?

She jumped up again and started to pace. In only a couple of days, it felt that not only had her job been turned upside down, but her family was coming apart at the seams. She only hoped that Marianne's wedding would bring them all back together. It was a small hope, but better than nothing, she thought, as she flopped back onto the bed. She should try to think of something good, she thought. Charlie's face came into her mind and she smiled slightly. He, at least, seemed steady as a rock. Yes, if nothing else, at least she had him. For now.

∽

Lily sat up, startled, as she heard her name called. Outside the sky was darkening, so she must have been asleep for a while.

'Someone to see you, love.' Her mother's voice floated through the door.

Immediately, she thought of Charlie, and she jumped up, running a brush quickly through her hair before dashing down the stairs. She stopped short in the doorway of the sitting room, disappointed at the sight of the woman wearing a familiar blue dress and glasses on a chain round her neck sitting primly on the edge of the flowered sofa, not a hair out of place as she sipped from one of her mother's best teacups.

'Matron,' she said faintly.

Matron Watson stood up and held her hand out. 'How are you, my dear?' she asked solicitously.

'No different to the last time you saw me. You know, when you told me to leave the hospital?' she said bitterly.

Matron ignored her comment and looked at Nellie who was sitting in her chair watching the scene avidly.

'Would you mind if we had a word alone, Mrs Castle.'

'Please stay, Mum,' Lily said quickly. If Matron was going to sack her, she wanted her mother here to back her up.

'I ain't one of your nurses and this ain't the hospital. If my daughter wants me here, then this is where I stay.' Nellie folded her arms and settled further back in the chair.

The woman's lips thinned with annoyance, as she gestured for Lily to sit. 'As promised earlier, I have come to apprise you about the events of yesterday. And I have also come to issue the strongest possible apology on behalf of the hospital.'

Lily's heart leapt with hope. 'They've caught the prisoner? He's told them I'm not involved?' she whispered faintly, but her question was drowned out by her mother.

'A *strong* apology?' Nellie mocked. 'Don't you think you owe her a bit more than that?'

'Mum, please,' Lily murmured faintly, as she sat down in one of the armchairs. 'Let her finish.'

'Not only has the prisoner been caught, but Mr Wainwright has been working diligently on your behalf and has taken his findings to the police. As a result, an arrest has been made and you have been fully vindicated.'

'Dick Brown?' Lily asked.

Matron looked puzzled. 'Why do you mention him? As far as we're aware Richard Brown had nothing to do with this.' She took in a deep breath. 'It seems we have had a traitor working in our midst. Dr Ramsay has been found

371

to be a Nazi sympathiser, and he fabricated the prisoner's illness in order to keep him at the hospital until his broken leg was healed enough to escape.'

'*Dr Ramsay!*'

Matron nodded. 'He has connections in Germany that we were completely unaware of. His house has a radio with which he has been communicating with someone. Apparently, Felix Muller is from a very prominent and wealthy family, close to Hitler—'

'Bloody man!'

Matron turned and stared in bemusement at the parrot.

'Shut up, Polly,' Nellie snapped, while Lily started to giggle.

Matron turned back, her lips twitching. '—and who paid very good money for Dr Ramsay's help.'

Lily sat back. 'Blimey,' was all she could think to say. 'He's one of them four statues then.'

Matron stared at her. 'Pardon?'

'Them Nazi-lovers. Like that rat, Moseley.'

'Oh, you mean fifth columnists? Yes, it appears he is. And we have Mr Wainwright to thank for his arrest. He put two and two together and realised that the prisoner couldn't have faked such a serious illness without a doctor's help. So I've come to say that you are free to return to work. In fact, I, for one, will welcome you back with open arms. You have the makings of a very fine nurse indeed, Miss Castle.' She stood up.

'And that's it, is it?' Nellie said.

'I'm not sure what else needs to be said.'

'Oh, I think there's plenty more to say. For a start, I want a full written apology published in the *Dover Gazette*. Front page is my preference. You've turned my girl's life upside down with your accusations. And look at her face! Why are your nurses not properly protected? Particularly when they're expected to look after dangerous Nazi prisoners. So if you think your words are enough, then you can think again. And Lily isn't returning until I see that apology in the paper. In fact, Lily will be taking a bit of time to recover from her ordeal.'

'I don't think—'

Nellie stood up. 'Tomorrow, I will send a man called Ron Hames to see you. He works for the *Gazette*. He'll know what to do. And only then will she return to your hospital. I'll show you out.' She gestured to the door, and, looking perplexed and a little annoyed, Matron followed her.

Lily sat mutely, staring into space, her mind in turmoil. She could hardly believe it was all over, but even so, she didn't feel the euphoria she had been expecting. Rather, the prospect of going back to the hospital filled her with dread. And now her mother had made matters worse by issuing demands that Matron probably couldn't meet.

As soon as Nellie walked back in with a triumphant smile, Lily exploded. 'For God's sake, Mum! You could have ruined my chances at the hospital for good!'

'Stuff and nonsense! It's the least they can do. And as for that Mr Wainwright, he can have free meals for the rest of his life. The man is solid gold. Come on, girl, stop looking so sour! This calls for a celebration.' She raced across to the kitchen and took down three glasses. Pouring a generous measure of sherry into each glass, she hollered up the stairs, 'Marianne! Get your arse downstairs now. We've got some celebratin' to do! And I don't mean your wedding.'

Cackling, she downed her drink in one and poured another. Lily, meanwhile, sat quietly. She felt stunned that a doctor had turned out to be a traitor. And not only that, he'd been willing to throw her to the wolves without a second thought. But, most of all, she was confused. If Dick wasn't responsible, then what was the meaning behind his strange, threatening behaviour? Rather than relief, she felt renewed dread. She'd been so sure the man must have been involved somehow, but now she knew he wasn't, she wondered what else was coming round the corner.

Chapter 37

Nellie was as good as her word, and the next day, she sent Don round to the offices of the *Dover Gazette* with a note for Ron Hames. He arrived at the café at lunchtime with good news.

'Thanks for the tip, Mrs C. Was only too happy to help. Had a bit of a wrangle with the old battleaxe up at the hospital, but she gave in in the end, and their apology will be in the papers day after tomorrow. They want to keep the good doctor's name out of it. Had to give my solemn word not to name him.' He grinned and tapped his nose. 'Don't mean I can't make it clear enough, though, so don't worry on that score. It's my civic duty to serve up the truth, the whole truth and nothing but the truth to the good citizens of this beleaguered town. Speaking of serving up?' He looked at her hopefully.

Nellie nodded her satisfaction. 'All right, I reckon you deserve a bite to eat on the house. Just this once, mind. You're doin' me a favour, but by my reckoning this is as much a favour to you as it is to me.'

'Ah, you drive a hard bargain, Mrs C. And you're right, the boss is right pleased with the scoop. Just think, your girl's name could soon be on everyone's lips.'

'Just as long as they're good words, Ron. That's all I care about.'

The journalist leant on the counter, taking off his helmet and running his hand through his greasy black hair. 'Anyways ...' he said. 'While I was up the hospital, I got accosted by a sleazy bloke by the name of Dick Brown. Said he had a juicy morsel of info about a certain family that runs a café in the town. Anything else you'd like to tell me?' He raised his eyebrows at Nellie, who stared back at him blankly, although her stomach had dropped.

That man again, she thought. Had Pauline told him something?

'Seems like I've hit a nerve. Anything you'd like to get off your chest?'

She took a deep breath. 'I got no idea what you're talkin' about. And yes, there's something I want to get off my chest. Like you said, you need to stick to reportin' the *truth*. Not idle gossip from some bloke I don't even know.'

The man grinned knowingly. 'Fair enough. And I see your Marianne's cooked my favourite cottage pie, so ...' He clamped his lips together and buttoned them. 'My lips are sealed.'

Nellie frowned as she watched him take his usual seat by the window. She just hoped Pauline hadn't opened her big gob and that her secrets wouldn't come out before she'd had a chance to speak to the kids. She sighed. Not so long ago, she'd been looking forward to the wedding. She'd even made herself a new dress – one that reminded her of a kaleidoscope with its swirls of reds, pinks, purples and greens all merging into each other. But with things as they stood, she felt that black would be a more appropriate colour. For while it would be the happiest day of Marianne's life, it could very well be the day that would break her own heart.

∽

On the day the apology was due to be printed, Lily got up early and raced across the square to the news kiosk next to Perkins' Fish.

'Two copies of the *Dover Gazette*, if you don't mind, Mr Gallagher,' she said to the old man standing behind the counter. One was for her mother, the other she intended to take to work with her the next day. Something she was alternately looking forward to and dreading.

Mr Gallagher smiled around the pipe sticking out of the corner of his mouth. 'I always said it were a load of codswallop.' He held up the paper he was reading, opening it to the third page, where a headline stood out:

'Casualty Hospital apologises to nurse wrongfully arrested after prisoner escaped'

Lily stared at the man disbelievingly. 'Did you really? Don't remember you popping over to offer your support.'

The man looked shamefaced. 'Well, I couldn't, could I? Not till I was sure.' He reached under the counter and brought out a battered-looking chocolate bar wrapped in distinctive purple paper. 'Have this by way of an apology. Been savin' a few, special like.'

Lily looked at the box of fresh chocolate bars on a shelf behind him then back at the battered offering. 'How long have you been saving this? Since Armistice?'

He sighed and put the chocolate back, taking down one of the new bars. 'Fussy little madam, ain't yer? But I suppose I owes you. 'Ere, fancy me knowin' someone in the papers.' He chuckled, revealing toothless gums.

Lily smiled weakly. 'Yeah, aren't you the lucky one.' Nodding, she took the papers and the chocolate and skipped back to the café.

'It's here!' she shouted, waving the paper above her head as she raced through the door. 'A full apology.'

Nellie rushed over and snatched the paper from her hand, tearing open the pages.

'All right, you lot,' she shouted over the breakfast hubbub. 'Listen to this.' She cleared her throat. '"The Casualty Hospital have issued a full apology to Miss Lily Castle, eighteen, of Castle's Café, Market Square, Dover. Early in the morning of the seventh of September, Miss Castle was on night duty at the hospital where she is a trainee nurse, when she was attacked by one of the German prisoners and left unconscious while the man made good his escape. She was later arrested on suspicion of aiding and abetting the enemy. All charges against Miss Castle have since been dropped thanks to an investigation by Mr Harold Wainwright, of Wainwright and Wainwright Solicitors in the High Street.

Hospital staff have been left shocked at the discovery that there has been a Nazi sympathiser working amongst them. Miss Castle has now been reinstated and will resume her training forthwith. It begs the question: why did the police not discover this for themselves? When this reporter asked Inspector Forrest, he declined to comment.'"

Nellie smacked the paper back down on the counter. 'Oh, nice touch, Ron Hames. I'd like to know that and all. But they're not the only ones who owe Lily an apology,' she said loudly, glaring around at the customers.

'But we never accused her of anything. Sure, I've always had a powerful fondness for the girl.'

Nellie nodded at the soldier. 'You have always been a perfect gent, Sergeant O'Malley. In any case, I can forgive those as haven't known Lily since she was born. But there are others—' she glared at Lou Carter, who was sitting at a table by the window '—who should have known better.'

'Mum,' Lily hissed, her face red with embarrassment, 'leave it, will you?'

Lou Carter stood up then. 'No, she's right, love. I'm happy to hold me hands up and say we was wrong. It was just in the heat of the moment, you know.'

'Heat of the moment?' Nellie exclaimed. 'Don't talk rot. You just couldn't help gettin' involved in the scandal, could you? Even though she saved your life the day before.'

Lou flushed and looked away. 'Don't push it, Nell. I've said I'm sorry, ain't I? I never really believed it, truth be told. And your Rodney's speech convinced most of us.

379

Better than Churchill, he was. But by then, well . . .' She shrugged. 'I suppose we all got a bit carried away.'

The door opened then and Roger Humphries walked in, his helmet under his arm. He'd not been in the café since Lily's arrest, and the sight of his weaselly face and wispy moustache infuriated Nellie. Folding her arms, she counted to ten as he approached the counter, trying her best to control her temper.

'Lily,' he said obsequiously. 'I'm delighted to hear that you have been cleared. Of course, I never believed a word of it and, thanks to the local constabulary, justice has well and truly been served.'

Lily stared stonily at Roger. She'd not forgotten how he'd spoken to her when she was brought in to the station. She shot a glance at her mother, and saw she was about to explode. Well, he deserved it. But she'd rather it came from her. 'I think you better turn round and go straight back out again,' she said. 'Because after the way you spoke to me, you're no longer welcome in here.'

His eyes widened and he looked at Nellie nervously.

'You heard her. Hop it.' Nellie pointed at the door.

'But you must understand—'

Suddenly, Marianne came out of the kitchen, her blue apron dusty with flour and a tea towel over one shoulder. 'Didn't you hear what Lily said, Roger? You're not welcome here, so get out!'

Roger's face paled. 'B-b-but you can't mean that? We've been friends for years. Why, we were even courting before you got your head turned by that trumpeter.'

Marianne laughed. 'Don't flatter yourself. We were *never* courting. And if you want the truth, I was only nice to you cos I felt sorry for you. But I don't any more.' She walked to the door and opened it. 'So, like Mum said, hop it. And don't come back.'

Roger stalked towards Marianne, pausing to stare hard into her face, before hissing, 'You'll regret this.' He glanced back at Nellie. 'Or rather, your mother will. Because I know she's up to no good and sooner or later, I'll get to the truth.'

Marianne's face blanched, but she held her ground. For years the man had pestered her, and she'd let him. Well, soon she'd be a married woman, and it was about time she started sticking up for herself and her family. As Roger stepped out of the door, she slammed it behind him, then turned back around, dusting her hands together. 'Right. Anyone else? Cos like Rodney said, if you're not for us, you're against us, and we don't take kindly to those that slag us off.'

The café was dead silent as people stared at Marianne in shock. Lily glanced at her mother, eyebrows raised, but Nellie was watching Marianne, a slow smile spreading across her face as she started to clap. 'At bloody last the worm turns.'

Marianne pointed a finger at her mother. 'And don't you forget it, Mum,' she said. 'Cos I have had it up to here—' she held her hand above her head '—with the temper tantrums and the outbursts and the grudges. And that includes whatever you've done to drive Jasper

381

and Gladys away. So you better sort that out, cos I don't want my wedding ruined because you can't keep your gob shut.'

She flounced into the kitchen and started to clatter the pots and pans around.

Lou Carter gave a cackle of laughter. 'I never thought I'd see the day that girl said boo to a goose. But, by God, I'm glad I did.'

Marianne stuck her head through the hatch. 'As for you, Lou Carter, it's about time you stopped gossiping. If I see you out there one more time with your gaggle of cronies gathered round you, then you'll have another burnt stall to deal with.' She withdrew her head, her chest heaving. What had happened to her? she wondered. Just the other day she'd snapped at Alfie, and now she was taking on Roger and Lou. She took a deep breath as she realised her hands were shaking. Was it the pressure of the wedding? But it couldn't be. She loved Alfie and couldn't wait to marry him. So why did she feel so wound up and tense? She put her hands on the table and bent over it.

'Marianne?' It was Lily.

She looked up and smiled as her sister came into the kitchen and gave her an enormous kiss on the cheek. 'Thank you,' she said. 'For sticking up for me, and for giving Roger, Mum and Lou a piece of your mind.'

Marianne gave a laugh. 'Is she cross?' She nodded her head towards the café.

'Nah. I think she's just stunned. And you were right to have a go about Jasper and Gladys. She's not said any more to you about what it's all about, has she?'

Marianne shook her head. 'Not a word. But whatever it is, it must be bad for them not to be talking to her.' She sighed. 'And only ten days to go before the wedding. I can't help feeling it's a bad omen. Perhaps I should have called it off after all.'

Lily kissed her again. 'Don't be daft. How could you keep a bloke like Alfie waiting?'

Marianne's eyes went dreamy. 'He is lovely, isn't he?'

'Couldn't have picked better myself.'

'Not even Charlie?' Marianne said with a sly wink.

'Better for you, I mean. So no more talk about calling it off, all right?'

Marianne nodded. 'So long as there's no more drama, that's all I ask.'

Chapter 38

At the hospital the following day, Lily made straight for the canteen where a noticeboard for staff announcements hung on the wall. Glancing over her shoulder, she noticed people were watching her furtively, so she pulled out a drawing pin from the cork board, whipped out the article from her pocket and pinned it swiftly over a notice about an upcoming dance and another about air raid procedures. Then, head held high, she went and stood in the queue for tea.

'How come *you're* back?' a voice said behind her.

She whirled around to see the nurse who had told her she ought to be in jail behind her. 'Oh, haven't you heard?' She smiled sweetly and nodded towards the noticeboard. 'I've been cleared.'

'Yeah, I heard all right. But I still say it's a bit fishy. I mean, weren't you and Dr Ramsay sittin' all cosy in his office after it had happened?'

Lily sighed. It seemed no matter what you did, there were always people ready to believe the worst about you.

'Leave it out, Beryl. Why can't you just accept that Dr Ramsay was a filthy Nazi? Or maybe you're one of them too?' It was Vi, and Lily felt a flood of warmth towards her. They'd never been the best of friends, but she'd stood up for her when few others hadn't.

'I'm just sayin' there's no smoke without fire, is all.'

'Well, the smoke was coming from Dr Ramsay and that's all there is to it.'

There was a buzz behind her and Lily glanced over her shoulder and grinned as she saw a group of people standing around the noticeboard. She nudged Beryl. 'Tell you what. Why don't you go and have a read of that? Might put your mind at rest.'

Vi giggled. 'You got some gumption, I'll give you that, Lily. Sticking that up there.'

Lily shrugged. 'Saves me having to repeat myself. I'll just send them all to have a look.'

Dot joined them then. 'Well, you've caused a bit of a stir. Wouldn't be surprised if Matron had a word with you about that.'

'She wouldn't dare, after what they did to me. So, while she's still feeling bad about it, I intend to get away with as much as I can.' She looked around. 'Where's Pauline?'

Dot shrugged. 'She were off sick yesterday, and seems she might be again.'

'Doesn't she live in the same house as you now?'

Vi shook her head. 'Moved out a couple of days ago. Her mum and dad came back, so she packed her stuff and we've not seen her since.'

Over the course of the day, Lily was touched at how much support she received. It seemed that while she'd been feeling isolated and condemned there were plenty who hadn't believed a word of the rumours about her. The one fly in her ointment, as always, was Dick.

'Well, well. Here she is again, like a bad penny.' He chortled. 'I told you I weren't involved, didn't I? You should have more faith in me.'

Lily narrowed her eyes at him. 'I don't trust you as far as I can throw you. You might not have had anything to do with the prisoner, but I know you're up to something.'

He tutted. 'That ain't no way to speak to a friend.' He paused. 'Anyway, all's well that ends well. Bet your sister's happy. Would have been a shame to have this hanging over you when she got married.'

Lily frowned at him. 'What do you know about that?'

He shrugged. 'Pauline mentioned she was goin' to the party after. Said I could join her if I wanted.'

'You're not invited,' Lily hissed, vowing to have a word with Pauline. Why would she invite him? Just the other day she'd smacked him round the face. Something wasn't right.

'I reckon I can worm my way in. I'm part of the community after all.'

'*Worm*'d be about right for you. And for your information, the party is for our friends and neighbours. You're neither.'

He grinned at her. 'We'll see, eh?' he said as he walked away.

Lily fumed for the rest of the day, and determined to pop in on Pauline on the way home.

As soon as her shift had finished, Lily hurried to Pauline's house on Queens Gardens. It was a small terrace, two-up, two-down, in a row of similar houses, with front doors that opened directly on to the street. Lily knocked and smiled as Annie Elliott opened the door a crack and peered round. 'Hello, Mrs Elliott, I've come to see how Pauline is.'

Without a word, the woman pushed the door to and went back inside. Lily stepped back in surprise. Pauline had never been one to invite people to her house, and her mother was a shadowy figure who seemed to keep herself to herself, but on the few occasions she'd met her, she'd never thought of her as rude.

When Pauline came to the door, she stepped outside and ushered Lily up the street a little way.

'The girls said you were ill.'

'Bit of a gippy tummy, that's all,' Pauline said.

'Is your mum all right? She was a bit strange when she came to the door.'

'She's just anxious. Dad's in one of his moods again so I can't stay long. Don't want to leave Mum alone with him.'

Pauline looked dreadful: her eyes were bloodshot and her face pale. 'Would he hurt her?' Lily gasped.

Pauline stared back at her, her expression blank. 'What do you think?'

'Is that why you're not in work?'

Pauline nodded.

Lily was shocked, but suddenly a few pieces of the puzzle that was her friend fell into place. 'Does he hit you?' she asked quietly.

Pauline shook her head. 'Never. The bastard. No matter what I do or say, he's never laid a bloody finger on me. It's always Mum.'

'But why's he cross tonight?'

Pauline sighed. 'She overcooked the chops, apparently.'

Lily put her hand on her friend's arm. 'I'm sorry, Paul. I had no idea.'

'Yeah, well, not many do. And anyway . . . these last couple of days you've had enough on your plate. Hospital's been buzzing with the news about Dr Ramsay.' She gave a humourless bark of laughter. 'And to think, I even considered him as a possible husband. But seems like he's done the impossible.'

'What's that?'

'Managed to be worse than Dad,' she said flippantly. 'And that takes some doin' I can tell ya.' She turned to go back inside.

'Wait! Dick said you invited him to the party after the wedding,' she said accusingly.

Pauline gasped. 'I never!'

'He says he's going to come.'

'He can't! No! You mustn't let him!'

Lily shook her head. 'I'll tell the boys to keep an eye out for him. You ever gonna tell me what's up between him and you?'

Pauline shook her head. 'Not if I can help it. But, Lily . . .' She hesitated. 'You've been a true mate. I would never want to hurt you, I want you to know that.' Then she turned and walked back to her house, leaving Lily with a sick feeling of dread in her stomach.

Chapter 39

As the wedding drew closer, life settled back to normal at the café – or as normal as it could be without Gladys or Jasper. But even so, Marianne grew more and more anxious as the big day approached. And now, on the night before her wedding, she was a bundle of nerves. Carefully, she went over everything in her mind. Nellie had done a beautiful job of the wedding cake. It was a two-tier rich fruitcake, decorated with the purest white royal icing. She'd even managed to pipe pink rosettes around the edge – not quite as Marianne would have done it, but, all the same, it was very pretty – and on top she had placed the ceramic bride and groom that had been on her own wedding cake over thirty years before. Now, the cake stood on the counter, ready for Marianne and Alfie to cut tomorrow in front of their friends.

As for the rest, Lily, who'd just arrived back from work, had pushed the tables and chairs to the side in preparation for the party, and they were now groaning under the weight of the food. For the last couple of weeks, everyone invited had been donating some of their rations, so Marianne had managed to make sausage rolls and pork pies with some pork from the butcher – who was now keeping his own pigs. And first thing the following morning, Mary Guthrie would be bringing round several freshly baked loaves so that they could make dozens of rounds of fish paste, spam and egg salad sandwiches.

Ethel Turner had promised to bring some potato salad, the Perkins would be bringing a whole salmon, and Marianne had baked dozens of scones. Donny and Fred had been tasked with going blackberry picking the previous week and had returned with two enormous baskets of fruit. So much, in fact, that she had been able to make jam tarts as well. All of this had been done while still cooking for the customers every day, and she had to admit that she was exhausted. But there would be plenty of time to rest during the two days' leave that Alfie had managed to get. They had booked a little bed and breakfast in the country, and she couldn't wait to spend two glorious days alone with him, away from the noise and turmoil of Dover.

All that remained was the dress, and Daisy was due to arrive any minute for a quick fitting. She hadn't seen her old friend since she'd left Dover shortly after the birth of her little girl, Marguerite, in June, and Marianne wasn't sure if she was more excited about seeing her friend or the dress.

'What'll I do if I don't like it?' she fretted to Edie, who had taken the day off from the garage to help with preparations.

'Daisy's got the best taste of anyone I know. I bet you'll look like a fairy princess,' Edie reassured her, as she took a dish of sausage rolls out of the oven.

As if Marianne's thoughts had conjured her friend, a cheery voice shouted out, 'Hellooo!' and a tiny figure with white-blonde hair and wearing a slim-fitting blue skirt and a pink jersey, walked into the kitchen carrying some tissue-wrapped packages.

'Daisy!' Marianne rushed forward to give the woman a hug, not noticing she was still holding a knife covered with blackberry jam and managing to get a blob on Daisy's shoulder. She pulled away. 'Show me!' she said eagerly, reaching for the dress.

'Oh, no you don't. Upstairs with you, madam. Can't have the bride walking down the aisle with jam all down her dress.' She stared at her shoulder pointedly.

'Sorry.' Marianne wiped at the blob with a tea towel, managing to smear it even more.

Daisy laughed and smacked her hand away. 'Leave it for gawd's sake. Not as if I'm not used to having food all over me. Maggie's a right little bugger for bringing up her milk. Anyway, don't you want to see what your clever Auntie Daisy's made? It might not be quite what you were expecting, Marianne. The dress you sent was nice and all, but well . . . I reckoned I could do a better job.'

'Daisy!' Marianne protested. 'I hope you didn't go to too much trouble.'

She grinned at them as she skipped towards the stairs. 'Don't be silly. I wanted to make you something special. Something you could pass down to your daughter when you have one. Which I know you will. So chop-chop. Let's make sure it fits.'

Eagerly, the three girls whipped off their aprons and followed her upstairs.

As they passed the sitting room door, Marianne stopped short at the sight of her mother, sitting in her favourite spot by the fire listening to the radio with a glass of sherry in her hand and tears pouring down her face.

'What's wrong, Mum?' Marianne rushed over to her. 'Is it Jasper? Is he not coming?'

Nellie hastily wiped her face and shook her head. 'Oh, those poor little loves. And what about their parents? They thought they were doin' the right thing getting their babies to safety, and now look. Whoever's idea it was to send kiddies over the ocean in the middle of a war only needs to stand on the seafront here to see it's a bloody stupid idea!' Just then she noticed Daisy. 'Oh, Daisy, love. You got the right idea, sitting snug in the country with your little one.'

'What's happened, Mum?'

'Bloody Nazis bombing a ship full of little children. Thank God our Don's here, safe with us.'

There was silence in the room, as the women contemplated the tragedy. It seemed every day brought a new horror, and no matter that the wedding they were all looking forward to would bring joy, as always it would be tempered with fear and sorrow.

'Sorry, girls. Didn't mean to put a damper on the evening. Let's see the dress, then, Dais.'

'Not till Marianne's had a look. You three wait here, while I get it on her.'

Once they'd gone, Lily put her arm around her mother. 'Don't cry, Mum.'

'But it's so unfair!' she wailed. 'Losin' your child is the worst thing that can happen to a parent.' She started to sob, and Lily looked at Edie in alarm. This was so unlike their mother, but then, just recently, with Jasper and Gladys's defection, her mood had been uncertain.

'I think those tears have more to do with your row with Jasper than anything else, Mum,' Edie said. 'So why don't you go round there and make the peace right now. Otherwise it could ruin Marianne's wedding.'

Nellie shook her head. 'This has *nothing* to do with that stubborn old man. I've made my apology to him, and he's chosen not to accept it.' She glanced up at Lily and squeezed her hand, her tone softening. 'But he will, love. He will.'

They sat in silence for a while as the newsreader burbled on, talking of more air raids on London. Lily wished she could just turn it off; the night before a wedding was meant to be a time of celebration, a time to forget what was happening, just for a while, and enjoy themselves.

She was distracted from her gloomy thoughts by footsteps on the stairs and Nellie gasped as Marianne appeared in the doorway. 'Oh, love . . .' Her eyes welled up again. 'Just look at you.'

Lily gazed at her sister and could only agree. She looked beautiful. The dress was made entirely of white silk, and fitted her sister's small, hourglass figure to perfection, falling in gentle folds to her feet. The sweetheart neckline emphasised her generous bust, while tiny covered buttons ran down the front, and long sleeves ended in a point on her hands. Around her waist was a blue silk plaited belt, which hung down almost to the bottom of the dress and on her head was a hairband covered with silk roses, from which a long veil trailed behind.

'But where did you get all that silk?' Edie gasped.

Daisy winked. 'Let's just say it was a donation from Hitler.'

'Bloody man!' Polly interrupted.

Nellie threw a cushion at the cage. 'Bloody bird, more like,' she grumbled as the others giggled.

'What I was trying to say was, Stan's mate, who's a policeman up our way, gave it me. They have a stash of the stuff. All from pilots that have bailed out.' Daisy grinned. 'It's a bugger to sew, but worth every pinprick.'

'You are a magician,' Edie said in admiration.

'Well, you ain't seen *your* dresses yet. Come on.'

They followed her upstairs, where two matching dresses in blue silk, the same colour as Marianne's belt, were lying on the bed. They were slim-fitting, falling to just below the knee, with large bows tied at the waists.

Once Edie and Lily had their dresses on, the three sisters stood in front of the mirror, their arms around each other.

Daisy clapped her hands. 'Now that's what I call a family. Look at you.' She went out and called down the stairs. 'Mrs C. Get up here now!'

Nellie lumbered up the stairs and stood in the doorway, staring at her three daughters. Edie so dark, with hair like her father; Marianne, with her chestnut hair loose and rippling down her back; while Lily's head shone golden in the overhead light. Tears came to her eyes again and she held her arms out. Wordlessly, the girls went to her, and the four stood together, arms around each other for several moments as Daisy looked on with a smile of satisfaction.

Finally, Nellie stood back and wiped her eyes. 'I might get things wrong now and then, but, by God, I produced beautiful children.'

'Not just you, Mum,' Lily admonished. 'You had a bit of help, and whatever else he was, Dad were a good-looking bloke.'

Nellie stared at Lily, her expression strange. 'Yes, I suppose I can't take all the credit,' she murmured. 'But enough of that. Get changed and I'll come and help with the preparations.' As she turned to leave, she stopped. 'Tell you what, though, Marianne, it's lucky folk'll be distracted by the dress when you walk down the aisle, cos our Don ain't no Alfie when it comes to the trumpet.'

'Mum!' Marianne gasped, but she couldn't help laughing. Her mother was right. Donny's enthusiasm for learning the trumpet was not matched by his talent, but he was so excited to play at her wedding that no one had the heart to refuse him. 'Don't be mean. He's doing his best.'

Nellie grunted. 'I just thank God we got a break from him practising today. He gives the Waffa a run for their money when it comes to noise.'

∞

Much later that evening, Marianne and Nellie had gone upstairs while Edie and Lily put the finishing touches to the tables. They were surveying their handiwork with satisfaction when there was a knock at the front door.

Edie slipped behind the blackout curtain and peered through the glass. A tall figure loomed outside.

'Who is it?' she called.

'It's Greg,' the figure called back.

'Who?'

'Canadian pilot, we had a little run together.'

Edie gasped. She'd forgotten all about him, but, curious, she unbolted the door to let him in.

'What are you doing here?' she asked more abruptly than she'd intended. As he came through the blackout curtain, Edie was struck once again by the bright blue of his eyes as they met hers.

'Well, I came into Dover with some guys, and as we drove past the garage, I thought I'd stop in and say hello. But your boss told me you were here so . . .' He trailed off as he noticed the wedding cake. 'Oh. Are you getting married?' He sounded disappointed.

Edie blushed. 'Oh, no! No. No, not me.'

He nodded and smiled. 'So that's a no, is it?'

Edie reddened even more, embarrassed by her awkwardness.

Lily, who'd been watching the meeting with interest, intervened then. 'Don't worry, she's still single. Not even a sniff of a boyfriend.'

Edie threw a furious glance at her sister. 'Shut up, Lily,' she hissed.

'Ah. The infamous Lily Castle. Very pleased to make your acquaintance. And sorry to hear about your run-in with the Nazis.'

'So what's your name? Seeing as my sister hasn't seen fit to introduce us.'

'Greg Manning,' he said. 'And I'm hurt that you seem to have forgotten me,' he said to Edie, who looked away; she *had* forgotten him, but now that he was standing in front of her, she couldn't imagine how he could have slipped her mind.

'Well, Greg Manning, we're having a bit of a party tomorrow for my other sister's wedding if you'd care to come and join us.'

Greg raised his eyebrows. 'Maybe I will,' he said with a lazy smile. 'As long as Edith doesn't mind.'

Edie huffed. 'My name is *Edie*, and if you want to join us, don't let me stop you. But I still don't understand what you're doing here.'

He shrugged, looking bashful. 'I just wanted to ask—' He caught the challenging expression on Edie's face. 'Uh, make sure you're all right.'

'As you can see, I'm fine,' Edie said, turning to walk back to the kitchen.

Lily ginned at Greg. 'Don't worry, she's not really angry. That's just the way she is when she's nervous.'

Greg's eyes were following Edie's progress, but at Lily's words, he glanced at her and smiled. 'If that's the case, then I'll definitely come tomorrow.' He grinned. 'But I can see you're busy, so I'll leave you to it. Goodbye, Edith,' he called, and laughed when an indignant voice floated back through the door. 'It's *Edie*.'

'I guess I'll see you tomorrow then.' He tipped his hat as he left and Lily bolted the door behind him, before rushing back to the kitchen.

'Who was *that*? And how do you know him?' she asked avidly.

Edie shrugged. 'Just some man.' She explained how they'd met. 'You shouldn't have invited him! This is Marianne's wedding for her and Alfie's friends, not some free-for-all for every Tom, Dick and Harry.'

'Oh, stop moaning. Charlie's going to come down as well, so he'll blend in just fine. Anyway, that's not the point. *What* Polish pilot?'

Edie shrugged. 'That's just it. I didn't know him. I mean, I did. At the dance, we had a little kiss and a dance, but I never saw him again. It's just so sad. If I'd realised I'd have made more of an effort.'

'Huh. If you tried to comfort every sad, lonely service-man in Dover, you'd get yourself a reputation,' Lily said. 'You're right, though. It *is* sad. But then, maybe it was meant to be; if that poor man hadn't died, you'd never have met Greg.' She clapped her hand over her heart and fluttered her eyelashes. 'It's all so romantic.'

Edie stomped out of the kitchen, without another word, leaving Lily giggling quietly to herself. Her sister was so easy to wind up.

Chapter 40

Marianne woke early, her stomach in knots, and peered round the blackout curtain. The moon was hanging low in the lightening sky as it made its way beneath the horizon and the castle was a great shadow looming over the quiet streets. It looked like it was going to be a beautiful day.

Lying back down, she gazed at the gorgeous dress hanging on the cupboard door. Did she deserve this happiness, she wondered, considering the chaos in the world? Was it wrong to snatch a moment just for herself? Sometimes, as the casualties around Dover mounted and the news from London worsened, it felt that people had become inured to the lives that were lost. No, she thought, that wasn't right; they were just better at hiding the hurt. Better at carrying on as though nothing untoward was happening. And how would it be, she wondered, if one day it was one of her loved ones who died? Could she still keep calm and carry on?

Beside her, Lily stirred and opened her eyes. For this final night before her wedding the three sisters had slept in the same room again, like old times.

'Happy wedding day, sis.' She smiled sleepily. 'Do you want a cup of tea? Breakfast in bed?'

'Just tea. No food. I think I'd be sick if I ate anything.'

Lily sat up. 'What's up?'

Marianne sighed. 'I don't know if I deserve this.' She gestured at the dress.

'Your dress?'

'No. Alfie, the wedding. This happiness.'

Lily threw back the covers and went to sit on her sister's bed. 'Why wouldn't you?'

'It just doesn't seem fair. How can I be so happy when there are people like the Guthries and the Masseys who will never be happy again?'

Edie sat up then. 'Honestly, Marianne, do you have to think so deeply about everything? Life is full of tragedy and heartache. Take the happiness while you can. You don't know what lies around the corner, so hold it close, enjoy every moment, and cherish Alfie for what he brings *today*. Don't waste time worrying what might happen tomorrow.'

Marianne smiled. 'You've got a wise head on those shoulders, Edie. You're right.'

'And the first thing you're going to enjoy is a bath.' Lily got up. 'So sit there while I go make the tea and Edie runs the bath.'

Marianne sat back against the pillows. 'Go on then. Do you think I should check on Jasper later; make sure he's coming?'

'Don't worry about him. He said he'd be here so he will be. Just relax. Me and Edie'll take care of everything,' Lily said.

Marianne sighed. They were right. Today of all days she needed to trust that everything would turn out all right.

∞

By twelve o'clock, the food was laid out on the tables; Marianne was getting ready upstairs, helped by Daisy and her sisters; Donny, in the grey suit with a pale blue tie that Nellie had bought him, had been scooped up and taken to the church by a nervous Alfie – looking handsome in his khaki dress uniform, his buttons shining and his hair carefully slicked back – for a last quick rehearsal with the trumpet. Jim and Bert had been with him, but though Jim had popped in to say hello, Bert had stayed outside the back door. Nellie had gone out to find him leaning against the wall smoking a cigarette and though he'd nodded at her, he'd avoided her eyes. She'd waited a moment, but then turned and left him to it.

Though they were closed today, the café was still a hive of activity as people popped in to wish them well and to leave small presents for the bride and groom: pots of jam, some bottles of beer, and an awful lot of teapots. Nellie chuckled at the sight of them. Fancy bringing a teapot for a girl who works in a café.

'Any chance of a quick peek at the bride?' Tom Burton, the cobbler, asked Nellie, as he placed a small shoe ornament on the table.

'Are you joking, Tom?' she asked. 'Why would she come down for you, and not for anyone else?'

The man looked sheepish. 'I just loves a wedding,' he said. 'Maybe cos I never had one of me own.'

Nellie smiled. 'You're a sentimental old fool.'

'Bleedin' heck, Nell. Did the paint factory explode over ya or something?' Lou Carter entered at that moment and put her hand to her forehead to shade her eyes.

'What? You don't like it?' Nellie did a twirl, admiring again how the bright colours swirled together like a kaleidoscope. 'I made it meself, if you must know, from some curtains I got cheap at Turpenny's. And if only you'd asked, I'd have made you something an' all.' Lou was wearing a shapeless black dress, under her beige work coat.

Lou looked offended. 'This is me best dress. I just change me hat depending on the occasion.'

'If you say so,' Nellie said as Ethel and Phyllis came in, both wearing their Sunday best, Ethel carrying a brown-paper-wrapped package. They'd be at the church today, while their husbands stayed behind to hold the fort.

'Mornin' all,' Ethel called out merrily. 'A beautiful day for a weddin'.' She stopped short at the sight of Nellie, her mouth dropping open briefly. She recovered quickly, however, and deposited her package on the table. 'Just a little somethin' for Marianne's bottom drawer.' She shook her head. 'It's like when I married my Brian. Off he went to war the next day and there was me stuck with me mum and dad for another three years. And me a woman of twenty-nine! Just like your Marianne, eh? And my Reenie.'

403

Bless her. Always thought she'd be with us forever after that upset with her mum and dad. But looks like we might have some happy news soon, eh, Nell?'

'Wouldn't that be a turn-up for the books?' Nellie smiled, but in her heart she wasn't at all sure about Jim and Reenie. People tended to make rash decisions during wartime; eager to snatch what happiness they could in case it was their last chance. But then in some cases it was, so who was she to criticise?

'I like your dress,' Ethel said unconvincingly.

'Thanks, love. I feel the mother of the bride has a duty to look her best.'

A couple of soldiers came in then and stared at Nellie. 'Jesus, Mrs C,' one of them said, 'you should have a health warnin' on that thing.'

'We are shut, Private!' Nellie snapped. 'For a weddin', if you must know.'

The man held up his hands. 'I forgot. Wish Marianne the best.' He backed out, straight into a woman wearing a blue dress with a feathered blue hat and carrying a large bouquet of red roses.

'Here she is,' Nellie cried. 'My fellow angel of the caves.' Since Mrs Palmer had covered for her with Roger, Nellie wouldn't hear a word said against the woman, despite the fact that she frequently enraged people with her organising and bossiness.

'Good morning, Nellie. I come bearing gifts,' she tittered. 'Gladys is busy arranging flowers at the church and she asked me to bring these for Marianne.'

Nellie's smile slipped. She'd hoped that on this day of all days, Gladys would have set aside her anger and come to support her family. But then, Gladys could be a sanctimonious old cow at times. Then she shook her head, ashamed of the thought. She shouldn't blame Gladys; she should have known that if Gladys said she wouldn't come back until Nellie had told everyone the truth, she meant it.

'Is everything all right?' Mrs Palmer said as she set the bouquet carefully down on the counter.

Nellie nodded. 'Why on earth wouldn't it be? Have a cup of tea, love,' she said, picking up a cup and saucer.

'No, I can't stay. I've promised Gladys I'd go back to help. Although I won't deny it was a relief to get away from young Donny's trumpet, bless him. I must say your boys are looking very handsome today, and Rodney said to let you know he'd arrived.'

After a quick cup of tea, Ethel and Phyllis left as well, and Nellie was alone in the café. She glanced at the clock. Surely he'd be here soon? Footsteps on the stairs sounded and Daisy came in, looking beautiful in a pink suit with a large boxy jacket and a slim skirt. There was a rosebud in her buttonhole and the outfit was completed by a pink hat with a small veil, underneath which, her white-blonde hair was curled into an immaculate victory roll.

'She's all set, Mrs C. And the most beautiful bride I've ever seen.' She smiled happily. 'Oh, it's wonderful to be back. The country is all well and good, but nothing beats being in Dover, with the sea on the doorstep and my friends around the corner.'

'And we miss you too, love. Where you off to?'

'I've got to give Maggie a quick feed before the ceremony, or she'll be yelling her head off. I'll see you there soon.'

Nellie watched Daisy as she skipped down the road towards New Bridge, a bright spot of colour standing out in the crowd of khaki and blue. A sound behind her made her turn her head quickly as Jasper walked into the café and her heart leapt as she drank in the sight of him, realising how much she'd missed him over the past couple of weeks. Normally, Jasper would come straight to her, a smile on his face. But today he stared at her silently, his eyes moving over her dress. For the first time she felt self-conscious. Did he think it was too much as well? He'd never criticised her colourful dress sense before. In fact, he'd once told her that he loved the fact that wherever she went, she brought colour to the scene. She smiled uncertainly and he nodded back. His cheeks, usually covered in bristles, were smooth and she could see a shaving cut on his chin. His shirt collar stood up stiffly around his neck, the points digging into his jowls, and around his neck was a pink silk cravat, with a small silver horseshoe pin. Under his arm he held a helmet, which he'd painted to match his light-grey suit. At least some things never changed, she thought with a faint smile, the man never went anywhere without his tin hat. But what the hell had he done to his hair? Usually bushy and uncontrollable, it had been cut short and slicked down with brilliantine. She didn't like it. She preferred his bushy head and bristly cheeks. But he'd done this for Marianne, to show respect for her big day, and the thought of the effort he'd put in made her heart clench.

'You look . . . really handsome, Jasper,' Nellie said.

'And you look colourful as always.'

She couldn't tell from his expression whether that was a good thing or not. 'I've missed you,' she whispered, surprising herself; she hadn't intended to say that.

He raised his eyebrows. They'd been trimmed as well. 'Have yer?'

She nodded.

'Good.'

Lily came down the stairs then, calling over her shoulder. 'Marianne! Jasper's arrived!' She threw her arms round his neck. 'Thank God you're here,' she said, planting a kiss on his cheek. 'Ooh, smoother than a baby's bum.' She stared at his outfit. 'Crikey, Jasper! You've pushed the boat out.'

He grinned. 'Only the best for Marianne.' He held Lily slightly away from him, taking in her blue silk dress. 'Don't you look a picture!' He looked up the stairs as Edie followed Lily down. 'Both of you.'

Lily twirled around. 'Do you like the dresses? Daisy made them. But wait till you see Marianne.'

Jasper stood at the bottom of the stairs and watched as Marianne walked carefully down. He let out a long, low whistle. 'Oh, Marianne, love. You look . . . You look just like your mum did on her wedding day.'

Marianne laughed uncertainly. 'Is that good?' she asked.

'Oh, yes. It's good.'

Nellie felt her heart leap with hope. Perhaps she'd be able to get him to change his mind. Maybe they could go back to the way they were, and she'd never have to tell Lily the truth.

But then she remembered Bert's expression when he confronted her and realised that now he knew – as well as Pauline – she had no choice.

'So what's the form?' Jasper asked. 'Should you three go on, then me and Marianne will give it five minutes and follow behind? Give you a chance to get in position?'

Nellie shook her head. 'Let's go together,' she said. She went to Marianne and kissed her on both cheeks. 'I'm so proud of you, love. And so happy that you've found Alfie. You couldn't have done better.'

Marianne's smile wobbled. Suddenly, she collapsed against her mother. 'Oh, Mum, why am I scared? Is this normal?'

Nellie rubbed her daughter's back. 'Course it is, love. You should have seen me on my wedding day. Felt sick as a dog till I got to the church door and saw your dad at the end of the aisle and remembered why I was doing it. Because I loved him. Just as you love Alfie.' Nellie's eyes rose and she stared at Jasper. He flinched slightly and looked away.

Marianne nodded against her mother's shoulder. 'I love him so much, Mum, that I think I'd die if anything happened to him.'

'Course you wouldn't. You're stronger than you think.'

Marianne stood up, wiping her cheeks as Jasper put his arm around her. 'Come on, Marianne. Chin up. Today's gonna be the best day of your life.'

She smiled. 'I know. And I am happy. I really am.'

Nellie kissed her again then pulled the veil down over her face before handing her the enormous bouquet of roses. 'Come on then. It's time to put Alfie out of his misery.'

Marianne let out a little laugh. 'He knows I'd never let him down.'

'Not right now he doesn't.' Jasper took her arm. 'If I don't miss my guess, the lad'll be standing at the front of the church fiddling with his tie, mopping his brow and turning around every five seconds to see if you've arrived.'

'And not only that, you've got a young boy who's itching to play his bloomin' trumpet and the sooner he starts the sooner it'll be over.' Nellie chuckled, as she picked up her large black bag and walked towards the front door, Edie and Lily following closely behind.

As they stepped out onto the pavement, they moved to the side, making space for Marianne and Jasper. It was a warm autumn day, and to their left, the sea was sparkling under a bright blue sky and the market square was bustling with Saturday morning shoppers. As one, everyone turned and cheered as Marianne walked out on Jasper's arm. Lou Carter let out a loud wolf whistle and soon a chorus of 'Here comes the bride' was ringing around the square.

Nellie waved regally, while Marianne smiled shyly at the crowd. 'See you all later,' Nellie called. 'Come over whenever you like, the party'll be going on long into the night.'

The singing and whistling continued as the wedding party started to make their way up Cannon Street. But they'd only taken a few steps when a loud crash made them jump and turn towards the seafront. In an instant, the happy shouts turned to screams as the now familiar whistle of a shell soared over their heads.

As one, everyone froze, and a second later, an explosion ripped through the air, making them duck, hands above their heads.

Crouching, Lily took a swift glance behind her and gasped. The view down King Street was obscured by dust and she heard the loud roar and rumble of a collapsing building.

'Shells!' Jasper screamed, digging in his breast pocket for his whistle and slamming his helmet on to his head. He grabbed Marianne and Lily's arms. 'Get to the basement!' He thrust them back into the café. 'You too, Edie!' He grasped her round the waist and pushed her into the doorway. 'And you, Nellie.' He turned to grab her, but he was too late because Nellie was already running down King Street, the colours of her dress fading as she disappeared into the cloud of dust.

❦

Nellie's heart was thumping as she paused by Townwall Street and squinted down New Bridge. She could hear a man shouting for help, and she quickened her pace. As

410

she reached the corner of Liverpool Street, she stopped and gasped. Where once the Grand Hotel had stood in all its Victorian splendour, there was now a jagged, smoking ruin. For years the hotel had been the place to go when you wanted a bit of a treat. She and Donald had spent their wedding night there and they'd had dinner there the night before he joined his regiment in 1914. Back when she thought she would love him forever. She stared in shock at the twisted metal and bricks. Already, firemen and ARP wardens were trying to reach people trapped beneath the rubble.

'For God's sake, Nellie.' Jasper caught up with her, puffing hard. 'Get to shelter.'

But Nellie barely heard him, because she'd caught sight of a man with bright-red hair, a pram beside him, who was desperately digging at the bricks of a collapsed wall, screaming for help.

She gasped. 'Stan!' She ran towards him and her heart dropped as she saw a slim pair of legs poking out from the rubble, a heavy section of wall obscuring the pink of her jacket. She fell to her knees and began to help him, oblivious to the wall teetering over them.

'It's Daisy,' he sobbed. 'We was just walkin' up when the shell came. She pushed the pram at me and I couldn't get to her.' The pram now stood in the middle of the road, the baby's screams adding to the noise and confusion.

Nellie heard Jasper shout at someone to get the baby to safety, and then he was beside them, helping to pull the bricks away as, slowly, the bright pink of Daisy's suit became visible. Stan stopped and stared at it, before collapsing on top of her prone body.

'Dais! Dais, wake up, darlin'. Come back to me!'

But Daisy's body remained still. Nellie looked up at Jasper, tears running down her own face and he shook his head. Just then, Derek came running out of the Oak, stumbling across the road to get to his son. Dropping down beside him, he put his arm around him. 'Come on, now, Stan. Let Jasper do his job.'

Stan turned his face into his father's chest. 'I can't leave Dais, Dad. She needs me.'

'Maggie needs you more. She needs her dad. Come on now.' Derek's face crumpled as he stared down at his daughter-in-law's bright figure and he bowed his head briefly before helping his shocked and heartbroken son up and leading him back to the pub.

Nellie, meanwhile, continued to dig. Others had joined them now, and slowly they were managing to get the rubble off Daisy's body.

'For God's sake, Nellie. At least put this on.' Jasper whipped off his helmet and thrust it onto her head. 'You'll get yourself killed.'

Nellie looked up at him. 'I didn't think you cared,' she said.

Jasper stared into her eyes for a long moment, before he knelt down beside her and began to dig.

Suddenly, a groaning above them caused Jasper to look up. 'Get away! The wall's comin' down!' he shouted.

He grabbed Nellie's arm. 'Bloody stubborn old woman!' he said, as he pushed her away from danger. 'Why won't you ever listen to me?'

Nellie landed with a thud and screamed as the wall collapsed, burying Daisy once again. Jasper took a step back, but he was too late as a brick hit him on the head and he crumpled to the ground.

Nellie tried to rush forward to him, but someone caught her round the waist. 'You have to get away from here!' the man shouted. 'Leave it with us!'

She knew he was right; she was only getting in the way of their efforts, so she retreated to stand against the wall of the Oak, her eyes never leaving the crowd of people as they tried to dig out Jasper and Daisy. Suddenly, she realised that she was still wearing Jasper's helmet. She took it off and turned it over in her hands. The fact that he'd painted it to match his suit made her heart ache. And that he'd given it to her, even though he was far more likely to need it. If she'd just gone to the basement, maybe he wouldn't be lying there right now. She started to sob. How had she let this wonderful, selfless man slip through her fingers? Why had she rejected him for all these years? Denying him the joy of fatherhood, and Lily a father who truly loved her. She'd wasted so much time. Nellie put her head in her hands. 'Please God, give me more time,' she whispered brokenly. 'Just a little more time.'

Chapter 41

For a moment the three sisters stood in the café, staring at each other in shock, as outside the crashes and booms of the shells made the windows shake. The door burst open again, and a stream of people pushed past them, making their way to the basement. Others were coming through the back door, and their urgency galvanised Marianne into action as she threw down her bouquet, jostling through the crowds and out onto the pavement.

'Marianne, don't!' Edie shouted, following her sister and trying unsuccessfully to grab her gown and drag her back to safety. But Marianne had the strength of the desperate. All she could think as she sprinted up the road, ignoring the screams of people around her, was that she needed to get to Alfie and her boy.

Lily stood frozen to the spot, barely noticing the people running past her as she stared at the discarded bouquet, the deep-red petals strewn around it like drops of blood. Then another crash brought her to her senses and, hitching up her tight dress, she sprinted after her sisters, uncaring that the tops of her stockings were visible. It took only a minute to get to the church, and she could see Marianne was already turning in to the gates, her veil trailing behind her, Edie close on her heels.

Lily skidded through the arched doorway. The beautiful stained-glass window that stood above the altar had smashed and sunlight flooded through the hole, glinting off the coloured glass and throwing rainbows around the walls. On the steps by the altar, Alfie, Marianne and Donny stood in a huddle, their arms around each other, while Rodney was trying to usher them through a door that Lily knew led down to the crypt.

'Lily!' It was Mavis. 'Have you seen Daisy and Stan?' she asked urgently.

She shook her head.

Jimmy came up to her. 'Get downstairs, for Christ's sake! Where the hell is Mum?'

'She ran off! I don't know,' Lily replied.

Jimmy swore and called out, 'Bert, Rod, Alf, get over here. We have to go!'

The men ran past her, as Lily walked down the aisle, her heart in her throat. Alfie was trying to extricate himself from Marianne's grasp as she approached them.

'I knew something awful was going to happen,' she sobbed. 'I just knew it. We should have waited, Alf.'

Alfie looked harried as he tried to comfort Marianne while Donny stared up at them in fear and bewilderment. 'Take her, will you?' he said to Lily. He bent towards Donny. 'Mate, try not to worry, eh? Me and your uncles are going out to help, but I need you to look after your mum.'

Donny nodded solemnly and took his mother's arm. 'Come on, Mum,' he whispered. 'I'll look after you now.'

Marianne grabbed on to her son and tried to hold him close, but he wriggled free. 'Mum! Come on!'

Marge took Marianne round the shoulder as well and led her towards the door, while Reenie took Donny's hand. Lily stood for a moment, staring round her in shock. The pews had been decorated with small bunches of flowers, and on either side of the altar, Gladys had created the most beautiful arrangement of roses, lilies and begonias.

Edie took her arm. 'We need to get downstairs,' she said.

'Look at those beautiful flowers,' she said brokenly. 'We were so happy just a few minutes ago.'

'I know, love. Come on. You need to stay strong for Marianne right now.'

Lily took a shuddering breath and nodded, allowing Edie to lead her towards the wooden doorway to the right of the altar. Downstairs, the crypt was cold and damp, and while Phyllis and Ethel tried to keep up a deliberately cheerful chatter, Mavis sat between them in silence, her fingers twisting nervously on her smart blue skirt.

'Are you sure you ain't seen Daisy and Stan? They should have been here by now,' she asked again, and Lily could only shake her head.

'Did you see where the shells hit?' she asked.

'Not exactly. But it was down on the seafront, I think,' Edie said. 'Try not to worry, Mavis. Daisy and Stan'll be in the basement at the pub having a drink right now.'

Mavis smiled stiffly. 'Yeah. Course they will.'

Marianne, meanwhile, was still sobbing while Donny patted her back, murmuring, 'Please don't cry, Mum. You can get married later, can't you?'

Gladys raised her voice then. 'Reverend Johnson, why don't you lead us in prayer.'

The man nodded and cleared his throat, while the others bent their heads solemnly. It was better than doing nothing, Lily reflected, so she folded her hands and started to pray harder than she ever had in her life: for her mother, for Jasper, for Daisy and Stan, and for everyone caught in the eye of the storm.

∞

It was more than an hour later when the all-clear sounded, and the small group came out of the church, blinking in the sunlight. As they approached Market Square, Lily saw with relief that the shops and buildings around the square were still standing, though many windows were smashed, and a bus had toppled onto its side, but when they walked down to New Bridge she could see that the view towards the sea had forever changed. The majestic Victorian Grand Hotel had gone, leaving a gaping hole. The barrage balloon that had so recently replaced the one shot down a couple of weeks before was also missing. An ambulance raced past her, and she stared after it; she needed to get to the hospital, she realised. They'd need all hands on deck after an episode like this. She just hoped she wouldn't find her mother there. Or Jasper.

Without another word, she turned and walked swiftly back up the road. She wasn't dressed for nursing, but she could have a quick scrub and find an apron, and she'd be good to go.

By the time she reached the gates of the hospital, she was sweating and her hair, that had been so carefully styled that morning, was hanging around her shoulders. She gathered it impatiently at the back of her neck and tried to wind it into a knot, but it just fell out again, so she tossed it over her shoulder and approached the door.

'Well, you look like you've bin in the wars,' a mocking voice said.

Dick Brown was leaning against the sandbags chatting to an ambulance driver, while in the drive, Pauline was helping a man with a bleeding leg hobble towards the entrance.

'Leave it out, Dick,' she muttered.

'Come to see your dad, have you?' He tutted. 'He looked in a bad way, so best prepare yourself.'

She stared at him in confusion.

'Oh. You didn't know? He got hit on the bonce. Didn't look good.'

'My dad's dead. Has been for years.'

'Tall bloke with greyish blond hair and blue eyes, always hangin' round the café in his ARP uniform.'

'That's not my dad,' Lily said absently, pushing past him into the entrance hall.

'You sure about that?' Dick called after her. 'You don't look much like your sisters and brothers, do you? Or your mum, come to that.'

'Shut up, Dick!' It was Pauline.

At the panic in Pauline's voice, Lily stopped and turned as her friend came through the door, her arm around the injured man.

'Don't listen to him, Lily. He's full of it.'

'I wasn't going to.' She stared at Pauline, wondering why her friend refused to meet her eyes. 'Pauline?'

'Can't stop,' Pauline gasped, as she hurried into the entrance hall.

Behind her, Dick laughed. 'Galling, ain't it? When your friends keep secrets from you. But much worse, don't you think, when it's your own mum and dad?'

'Pauline?' Lily called after her friend.

Pauline looked over her shoulder; her face was as white as a sheet.

'Is this true?'

'I can't talk, for God's sake, Lily.'

Lily's eyes darted between the two of them, and suddenly a cold sweat broke out over her body and her stomach started to swirl. Could this be true?

She stood very still, trying to picture her father – the shape of his face, the sound of his voice – but she couldn't. And was that any wonder? Because she didn't remember him ever addressing a single word to her. She knew he'd talked to the others sometimes, especially

Edie, who was the only one of them who seemed able to make him smile, but if she tried to join in he'd stop. Her mum had always told her not to take any notice, that her father wasn't in his right mind and it wasn't his fault, but now ... 'Pauline?' she cried again, but her friend ignored her as she scurried as quickly as she could towards the stairs.

She looked back at Dick who quirked one eyebrow. 'Don't tell me you didn't know,' he said with a smirk.

She whirled round and ran outside, retching into the sandbags. Maybe her mother had lied. Maybe it wasn't the war that had caused her dad's mental illness. Maybe it was the knowledge that he'd been betrayed by his wife and his best friend? Oh God, was it her fault he'd become such a monster? She spat onto the ground and stood up, wiping her mouth. No. None of this was her fault. This was all down to her mother. And Jasper.

With tears blurring her vision, Lily forgot about her desire to help, and even her worry for Jasper; all she knew was that she needed to get away. Run as far as she could from the dawning realisation that the two people she had always trusted the most might have been lying to her for her entire life.

⁓

Nellie sat slumped on a hard chair in the corridor, waiting for news. They'd taken Jasper immediately to the operating theatre, and she was refusing to leave until she knew how he was.

She looked up hopefully when someone called her name. 'Mrs C?' It was Pauline, looking pale and shaken. 'How's Jasper?'

Nellie shook her head, her lips trembling. Pauline sat down on the seat beside her. 'I saw Daisy come in,' she said.

Daisy! Shame flashed through her as she realised she'd put the poor girl completely from her mind. 'Is she . . .?'

But she knew the answer before Pauline had the chance to shake her head. She'd watched her poor lifeless body being lifted into an ambulance. Seen a devastated Stan, holding little Maggie tightly against his chest, whispering, 'It's all right, love. It's all right,' into her hair as she wailed. But his eyes had told a different story. Nothing was all right. And it never would be again.

Nellie put her head in her hands and Pauline stood and patted her awkwardly on the shoulder. 'I'll get you a cup of tea.' Nellie hardly heard her as the girl moved off and she forced herself to sit up straight. She needed to be strong. Marianne would need her. And if the worst happened, then her children would once again know what it was like to lose a father.

∞

It was a couple of hours later when Dr Toland emerged from the operating theatre. 'Mrs Castle? You shouldn't be here.'

'I just need to know . . . Jasper?'

'Mr Cane is unconscious, but I'm hopeful. Now, please. Go home.'

'I want to see him.'

'You can't. But try not to worry; someone will sit with him until he comes round.'

'If you don't mind, I'll wait a little while.' The thought of returning home not knowing whether Jasper would live or die was too much to bear.

Dr Toland sighed and walked away, looking too exhausted to argue. Nellie sat back and leant her head against the wall, steeling herself for a long, long wait.

Chapter 42

Lily ran blindly down High Street, not sure what to do. She couldn't face going back to see her sisters, not with this new realisation weighing heavily on her shoulders. So where? But in her heart she knew there was only one person she wanted to see right now. Charlie. And if he was busy, well, she'd just roll up her sleeves and help him. She needed the distraction of work right now, and she knew he'd welcome another pair of hands.

She was out of breath as she approached the bridge where the sentries stood. This time, though, they recognised her and allowed her to go straight through and somehow she managed to find her way to the tunnels that led to the small hospital.

When she opened the door, she saw that the six beds were full, and Charlie, looking harried and exhausted, his white coat bloodstained, was bending over one of the patients while an orderly bandaged the injured man's chest.

He looked up in surprise as she came in, his eyes widening at her bedraggled appearance and tear-stained face. 'Lily! I'm sorry . . . I can't—'

She held up her hands. 'I know. I want to help. Let me get an apron and have a quick wash and I'll be with you.'

He smiled gratefully. 'My office, back of the door, there's a clean white coat. Stick that on. Then wash up and get over here.'

For the next few hours, Lily did whatever needed to be done, grateful that the work drove all thoughts of what Dick had said to the back of her mind. At one stage, she helped Charlie in the operating theatre as he removed shrapnel from an unfortunate soldier's face. When that was done, she cleaned down the room, sterilised the equipment, then returned to the ward where she checked dressings, handed out painkillers, and generally tried to bring some order to the room.

She wasn't sure how long she'd been there when Charlie approached and took the broom she was holding from her hands. 'I think it's time we both had a rest,' he said. 'And you can tell me what's happened.'

His tone was so gentle and his expression so caring, that tears came to her eyes. Charlie took her arm and, after issuing some orders to the orderlies, led her up the stairs to the roof where they'd first had lunch a few weeks before. He laid out a rug on the grass, and urged her to sit down, pouring a cup of tea from a Thermos flask and then wrapping a strong arm around her as she leant into his shoulder.

'Is everyone OK?' he asked.

Lily shook her head. 'Jasper.' She started to sob. 'I don't know if he's alive or dead.'

'I'm guessing the wedding didn't happen?'

Haltingly, Lily recounted the events of the day. 'When I went to the hospital . . .' She hiccupped. 'I went to help. But I bumped into Dick Brown outside the door and he said—'

She stopped and drew her knees up to her chest, resting her head on them, her tears soaking into the blue silk of her dress. How could she still be wearing it? she wondered. This morning felt like years ago, and now she no longer knew what to do. She couldn't go home – she just couldn't face her mother and though she felt guilty for abandoning her sisters, they had each other, she reasoned. And her brothers. She pictured each of their faces; Dick was right. She didn't look like any of them and, for the first time in her life, she felt like she no longer belonged with them.

Charlie said nothing, just tightened his arm around her as he waited patiently for her to continue.

Finally, she blurted out what Dick had told her, and how Pauline's guilty expression and panic had seemed to confirm the truth. 'They've been lying to me. I always thought of Jasper as my dad. I always *wished* he was my dad. And now I know he probably is . . . I always thought my dad ignored me cos that's what he was like. But no; he ignored me because he *hated* the sight of me.'

Charlie dropped a kiss on her hair. 'He wouldn't have blamed you, sweetheart. He just hated what you represented.'

'And how is that different to him hating me?' She sniffed and rubbed her nose with the back of her hand. 'I can't go back,' she whispered. 'Can I stay here tonight?'

He gazed down at her, his expression serious. 'Are you sure?'

She nodded. 'I just need a bit more time.'

He sighed. 'Tell you what, you can stay in my bed. There's a spare cot in the ward; I'll bunk down on that.'

'You won't get in trouble for having me here?'

'I'm pretty much my own boss, so don't worry about that.'

'Thank you.' She dropped her head on his shoulder, and together they gazed out as the sun sunk towards the sea, leaving a pink sky streaked with grey reflected in the rippling water below them.

Finally, after the sun had disappeared completely, and Lily shivered against him, he stood and helped her to her feet, leading her back down the stairs. He opened a door next to his office, revealing a small room with a single truckle bed, a grey blanket pulled tightly over the mattress, a wardrobe, a desk and a hard-backed chair. Charlie led her to the bed and pushed her onto the mattress, then knelt down to remove her shoes. He held them up. 'Are you telling me you've been running round Dover in the middle of a raid in three-inch heels?'

She smiled wanly. 'I didn't even notice.' She put her arms up and tried to undo the zip at the back of the dress.

'Let me.' He grasped her shoulders and turned her around, then pulled the zip slowly down, before turning his back while she removed it. She smiled slightly when she saw him standing stiffly with his face to the door.

'I have underwear on, you know.'

426

'I know,' he said. He walked to the wardrobe, took out a shirt and threw it over his shoulder to her. 'Put this on.'

She did as she was told. 'You can look now.' She yawned widely, slipped under the blanket and lay down. God, she was tired. 'Charlie, I need to know how Jasper is,' she whispered.

The mattress dipped as Charlie sat on the side of the bed and smoothed her hair back from her face. 'I'll go down to the café now and see what I can find out. Try not to worry, my Lily. And no matter what, your mother loves you and so does Jasper. You have a wonderful family.'

'I used to think so,' she said. 'But it's all been built on a lie. Everything's different now, don't you see?'

'Is it, though? It's the same scene, just from a different angle.'

She shook her head. 'No. The players have changed. They're not who I thought they were.' She rubbed at her eyes. 'Nothing's the same.'

Charlie didn't reply, instead he sat quietly, stroking her hair until her eyes closed and her breathing deepened, then he leant over and kissed her cheek, before leaving the room.

Chapter 43

Edie sat on the sofa, her arms around a tearful Donny on one side and her sister on the other. Marianne hadn't said a word since they'd left the church and now she sat dry-eyed and staring straight ahead, still wearing the beautiful wedding dress that Daisy had made for her. Downstairs, Reenie was clattering around in the kitchen as she made tea, while they waited for Marge to return to let them know what was going on. She'd been gone for over an hour now.

Where the hell was everyone else? she wondered desperately. She hadn't seen her brothers or Alfie since they'd run from the church, and Lily had gone to help at the hospital, seemingly uncaring that she was still wearing her bridesmaid's dress. She would have expected her mother or Jasper to have returned by now, but neither of them had made an appearance and she couldn't help fearing the worst. Her arm tightened around her sister's shoulder, her heart going out to her. Poor Marianne; what should have been the best day of her life had turned into a nightmare.

With her other hand, she smoothed Donny's wayward hair and kissed his forehead.

'Do you think Gran and Jasper have died?' he asked in a small voice.

'I'm sure they're fine, love,' she reassured him. 'They're probably just helping everyone. You know what they're like.'

He nodded against her shoulder and sniffed. 'Gran's always helping people,' he said. 'Even when she's cross she helps people. So's Jasper. 'Cept he's never cross. I wish he was here now.' He started to sob again, and Edie had to swallow back her own tears.

'No!' Edie's head came up as she heard Reenie's cry and she stood up. 'Stay there, Don, and look after your mum,' she said, as she hurried to the sitting room door.

She peered down the stairs and nearly fainted with relief as she saw Alfie's worried face staring up at her. 'What's going on?' she hissed, anxious that Donny wouldn't hear as she went down the stairs towards him.

'How are they?' he asked urgently.

'Donny's heartbroken and Marianne's just sitting there. Please tell me what's happened.' She could hear Reenie sobbing and her stomach swooped with fear.

'I need to go to them.' He started to move past her but she grabbed his arm.

'For God's sake! I need to know!'

Alfie took a deep breath. 'The Grand's gone and . . .'

Edie gasped. 'What?'

He shook his head. 'Daisy . . .' He swallowed. 'Daisy's dead.'

Edie slumped against the wall. 'Tell me you're lying,' she cried.

429

He shook his head sadly. 'There's more. Jasper—'

'No!' she shouted. 'No, no, no, no!'

Donny came out and stood at the top of the stairs. 'Are Auntie Daisy and Jasper dead?' His voice rose with fear as he spoke, and Alfie sprinted up to him and grabbed him by the shoulders. 'Jasper's alive, Don. He just got hit on the head.'

Edie gasped with relief. 'Mum?' she asked in a small voice.

He sighed. 'Your mum's at the hospital with him.'

Edie covered her mouth. 'Is it serious?'

Alfie's expression told her everything she needed to know.

Dazed, she went into the kitchen just as Jim and Bert came in, their uniforms grey with dust, their expressions sombre, closely followed by Rodney, his arm around Marge, who was crying against his shoulder.

Reenie threw herself into Jim's arms, and he held her tightly against him, kissing her hair as she sobbed against his chest.

Edie was barely able to comprehend what had happened; how the day had turned from one of happiness and celebration to this. Bert led her to a chair in the café, where she sank down and put her head in her hands. The others joined them and they sat, a silent, heartbroken group in their dusty wedding finery, staring at the tables full of food and gifts.

'Will he live?' Edie asked in a small voice.

Nobody answered, and fresh tears came to her eyes as she slumped forward, her head on the table, and sobbed out her grief for the man she loved like a father, and the sweet, beautiful woman who just that morning had danced around them as she did their hair and make-up, insisting they couldn't leave the room until she was satisfied that they looked good enough to do justice to Marianne's big day.

∞

Marianne allowed Alfie to take her in his arms, but she sat stiffly. She'd heard everything that had been said, but she felt numb. She stared down at her lap, at the bright white of her dress. Daisy would never have come back to Dover if it weren't for her.

'Marianne,' Alfie whispered. 'Talk to me, love. Please.'

She shook her head. She had no words. If only they'd postponed the wedding like she'd suggested, Daisy would be alive right now and Jasper would be sitting at a table devouring a plate of sausage and egg while he teased her mother. A rustling behind her reminded her that Polly was there. She turned to look at the bird. Polly's bright yellow eyes stared unblinkingly back at her. She let out a quiet squawk, then put her head under her wing. It was as though she, too, knew that their lives had been irrevocably changed.

'Marianne,' Alfie whispered again. 'Please.'

She turned to him. His face was so close to hers; his beautiful lips downturned, his skin pale and dirty, but his eyes, as always, were full of love. Right now, though, she felt it was a love she didn't deserve. Her mind went back to the dance a year ago, just as war had started. It was the day she'd fallen in love with him. But three of the people who'd been there that night were now dead. Was it her fault? she wondered. If she and Alfie had never met would they all still be alive? Colin and John probably wouldn't be. Their deaths had been tragic, but not her fault. Daisy, though . . .

She turned her face away and stood up. 'I'm going to lie down.'

Alfie started to stand too, but she stopped him with one word. 'Alone.'

Briefly, she stroked Donny's cheek, then left the room without a backward glance.

Donny put his arm around Alfie. 'She's just sad about Auntie Daisy,' he said. 'Maybe after a little sleep, she'll feel a bit better.'

Alfie swallowed and tried to smile, but his throat was tight. Quickly, he pulled Donny to him, and stroked his hair, not wanting him to see the tears in his eyes. This boy was the son of his heart, but he had a terrible feeling that his dreams of a family had been destroyed just as surely as the Grand. Because the look on Marianne's face as she'd stared at him just now made him wonder if she'd changed her mind. If all this tragedy had driven her away from him.

Chapter 44

It was nearly dark when Nellie made her weary way back from the hospital, her heart heavy. Jasper was still alive, but the doctors couldn't tell her whether he'd still be with them in the morning. There was nothing she could do, and Matron had almost bodily thrown her out. Now she had to go back and face her children, because even though Jasper might not survive, she'd made a solemn promise to him and it was time to tell the truth. To tell them just how much Jasper meant to her, and just how closely he was entwined with their family.

She stopped in the middle of the market square and stared down King Street towards the sea, shocked again at the gaping hole left by the Grand. Her eyes turned in the direction of the Oak, but it was hidden from her view. She'd seen Mavis, Derek and Stan at the hospital earlier. Stan, his eyes hollow with grief, clutching little Marguerite to him as though she was the only thing keeping him from breaking apart altogether. And she probably was. She'd hugged Mavis, trying to convey her sorrow, but there was just too much of it. So they'd pulled apart and she'd left them as the baby started to wail for her mother.

Her heart broke as she thought once again of the last sight she'd had of Daisy, dainty and beautiful, the pink hat bobbing up and down as she'd skipped across the square. Just as she'd seen her do so many times over the years, since she was just a tiny child, wobbling uncertainly as she clutched her mother's hand. She swiped at the tears that had once again started to fall. She had to be strong now. If this community was going to survive, it needed them all to stay stalwart. And it would, she knew. There'd be more tragedies to come, but they'd get through, one way or another. She wasn't so sure about her own family though. She took a deep breath and headed for the door.

It was a silent group that greeted her. All her children except Marianne and Lily were sitting at a table, Marge and Reenie too. It seemed that those two might well be part of her family soon, she mused.

The group looked up as one when she came in, the same question in all of their eyes.

'He's still with us,' she said as she walked towards them.

Rodney jumped up and helped her to a chair.

'Where are Marianne and Lily?'

'Marianne's upstairs with Alfie, Don's asleep,' Rodney said.

'Lily?'

'I thought she was at the hospital with you,' Edie said. 'She went there the minute we left the church.'

Nellie's heart lurched. 'She wasn't there.' She'd seen Pauline though. Had that girl decided to tell Lily the truth now that Jasper was at death's door?

She stood up. 'I need to find her. I have something to tell you all, and I need her here.'

'What's that then, Mum?' Bert asked challengingly. 'Don't tell me you're actually going to tell us the truth?'

The others stared at him in bewilderment, but Nellie ignored him as she went to the door. In the dim light, she saw a figure loping over the square towards the café, and with a start she realised it was Charlie Alexander. With a feeling of dread, she stopped and waited; from what she could see of his expression as he approached, he was not bringing good news.

Charlie pushed open the door. 'Hello, Mrs Castle. I thought you'd like to know that Lily is safe with me. I've left her sleeping up at Drop Redoubt.'

'What? But she's an unmarried girl!' Nellie exclaimed.

Charlie looked at her levelly. 'She's perfectly safe with me. But she was given some unexpected news, and didn't feel strong enough to come back.'

Nellie took a moment to grasp his meaning, but then she gasped. 'What news?'

Charlie's eyes never left her face. 'I think, maybe, you have a very good idea what it might be.'

Nellie swallowed hard. 'But who . . .?'

'Some man called Dick Brown.'

That man again. 'But how did he know?' Her shoulders slumped as she realised. 'Pauline.'

Charlie shrugged. 'I have no idea. But I think you need to give her some time.'

'Mum, what the hell is he talking about? And why hasn't Lily come home?' Rodney asked. 'She should be with the rest of us right now.'

Charlie walked over to the table and held out his hand. 'I'm guessing you're Rodney, the only Castle I've yet to meet.'

Rodney shook the hand absently but his eyes were on his mother.

Bert stood up. 'Right, well, seeing as I already know what you want to tell everyone, I think I'll walk back with Charlie,' he said abruptly.

'Sit down, Bert,' Nellie said shortly.

'I don't want to be here.'

'I said, *sit!*'

Bert sat down and folded his arms, his expression sulky.

'Thank you, Charlie, for letting me know. Please tell Lily that Jasper's still alive.'

Charlie knew when he was being dismissed, and he nodded at her briefly, before leaving without another word, relieved to get away from the tense atmosphere.

'Marge, Reenie, I don't mean to be rude, but would you mind giving us a little privacy?'

The two women stood, shooting a bewildered glance at Nellie as they left.

'Go and get Marianne and Alfie, would you, Bert?'

'Sit down, stand up; make your mind up, will you?' Bert said truculently, but he did as he was told.

Soon a blank-eyed Marianne came downstairs. She'd changed out of her wedding dress and was now wearing her customary shapeless jersey and skirt. Behind her, Alfie looked shattered, and Nellie noticed that Marianne shied away from him when he tried to take her hand. Another problem, she thought. But one for another day.

Once they were all seated, she took a deep breath and began to speak.

There was a stunned silence after she'd finished, but finally Edie said quietly, 'Why are you telling us now? You've kept this secret all these years, so why now?'

Nellie swallowed. 'Pauline found out. She overheard me and Jasper talking the day Lily got arrested. And so Jasper said . . . he said we had to tell her. But now it looks like Pauline got there before me.' Nellie rubbed her hand across her eyes. 'Jasper's always wanted her to know. Wanted to marry me. But I-I just couldn't. After your dad . . .'

Edie stared at her. 'After Dad what?'

'You know what I mean.'

'Was that why? Was that why he did what he did? Because he *knew*?' Edie said accusingly.

Nellie looked away. That fear had always been with her too. That it was her fault Donald had deteriorated so badly he eventually took his own life. That living with the evidence of her betrayal had been the final straw. And of all her children, Edie was the one who had taken his death the hardest; it had changed her from a happy little girl, into a morose, bad-tempered child. And even now she was an adult, Nellie was aware that she still hadn't fully recovered from the trauma.

Marianne, who had remained silent throughout, her brow furrowed, stood and left the room, while Alfie watched her helplessly.

'Go after her, Alfie. Stay with her. You're as good as married in my eyes and she needs you. Don't let her push you away. She'll regret it for the rest of her life otherwise.'

'And you'd know, wouldn't you, Mum?' Bert said sardonically. 'Anyway, now that the secret's out, I'm off. You coming, Jim?'

Before Jimmy could reply, Rodney slammed his hands on the table. 'I can't believe this!' he shouted. 'After the way you treated Marianne when you found out about Don's dad, now you're telling us that you and Jasper— Poor bloody Lily. No wonder she doesn't want to come home! Did you never *think* what this would do to her if she ever found out?'

'Of course I did!' Nellie screamed back. 'I've thought of nothing else!'

'Then why didn't you bloody tell her? You should have married Jasper and given us a real dad! One who wanted us, loved us, treated us with kindness! But you've shut him out all this time. How could you, Mum? How could you?' Rodney put his head in his hands, wishing, to his surprise, that Marge was there. She was one of the few people who seemed to grasp that despite his outward confidence and control, sometimes he needed support as well. Why had he never appreciated that before?

Jimmy stood up to follow Bert, but he paused briefly and put a hand on his mother's shoulder. 'I think I understand, Mum. Sometimes a lie seems like the best way, doesn't it?'

She nodded, staring blankly at the table. 'Yes. I'm sorry.'

'What the hell are you talking about? Of *course* it's not the best bloody way,' Bert hissed fiercely at his brother.

'Life's not always that simple though, is it?' Jimmy responded.

Bert snorted. 'Course it is. Either you're living a lie. Or you tell the truth.'

Jimmy didn't answer as he pushed past his brother and walked out of the door. Rodney stood then, too. He wanted to talk to Marge. 'I'll be down to visit Jasper when I can,' he said shortly. He looked over at Edie. 'You know where I am if you need me.'

Once Rodney had gone, Nellie reached out a hand towards Edie's where it was resting on the table. 'I really am sorry, love. I know how your dad's death—'

Edie pointedly moved her hand away from her mother's. 'You don't though, Mum. You haven't got a bloody clue. Now if you don't mind, I'm going to bed. First thing in the morning, I'm going back to the garage.' Back straight, shoulders stiff, Edie walked to the door and went upstairs, leaving Nellie staring around the empty café. How was it possible, she wondered, as her eyes travelled over the food- and gift-laden tables, that she had lost everything in just one short day? Oh Jasper, she thought. Please don't give up. Because without you by my side, I don't think any of them will ever forgive me.

Alfie watched as Marianne slumped down on the bed, wondering how he should approach her. Nellie was right. He couldn't let her push him away. Today had been terrible, but they needed to move forward together. He sat down beside her, keeping his hands on his lap, not sure she would welcome his touch.

'Well, that explains why she's blonde,' he said, and could have kicked himself for being so crass.

Marianne sighed. 'At least Jasper's alive. But Daisy . . .' She started to cry, great heaving sobs, as the tears that had been caught at the back of her throat all day broke free.

Alfie pulled her into his side, breathing a sigh of relief that at last he might be able to get through to her as her tears soaked his shirt.

Marianne cried for a long time as she thought of the man who had always been there for them. And her friend, her beautiful friend who just a short time ago had got her dearest wish of having a baby. And now it had all been snatched away, and her little girl would never know what a wonderful woman her mother had been.

Finally, her sobs quietened to hiccups, and Alfie moved away. 'Love, let's get you out of these clothes and into something more comfortable.'

'Don't leave me, will you, Alfie?' she said.

'I'll be right here in the bed next to yours.'

'No.' She stared up at him with tear-drenched hazel eyes. 'No. I want you in my bed with me,' she whispered.

'Are you sure?'

'This was meant to be our wedding night. If nothing else, let's have that.'

Alfie bent down and kissed her deeply. 'I love you, Marianne. I will always love you.'

'I love you too.' She pulled at his shirtfront, until he lost his balance and fell on top of her. Suddenly, she needed him with an urgency that pushed aside the grief and guilt that was haunting her, and she chose to ignore the quiet voice in her head that told her she didn't deserve it. Didn't deserve Alfie, or the happy future that he offered her.

Chapter 45

Lily woke the next morning as Charlie placed a cup of tea on the floor beside the bed.

'How are you feeling?'

She sat up and pushed the hair away from her face. Her head was thumping and she felt sick with the memory of all that had happened the day before. 'Awful,' she croaked. 'Have you heard anything?'

'Jasper's holding his own, but he's in a coma. I telephoned the hospital early this morning.'

Lily checked her watch and pushed aside the covers. 'I have to get to work.'

'No.' Charlie put a hand on her arm. 'You need to rest today.'

'You don't understand. I need to keep busy. And while I'm there, I'll be able to see Jasper.'

He nodded. 'But don't you think you should go and see your mum first?'

'I have to go home to change, but I've got nothing to say to her.' Lily couldn't think of anyone she wanted to see less right now.

'I saw Jimmy. They all know.'

'Are they angry?' she whispered. She and her brothers and sisters had always been close, but with this news, suddenly she didn't feel one of them anymore. She was the cuckoo in the nest.

He nodded. 'With your mum. But not Jasper, it seems.'

'But he lied too.'

'He didn't want to. They blame your mother.'

She nodded. 'I need to go,' she said again. 'I shouldn't be late after everything that happened the other week.' She gave a bitter laugh. 'It all seems so long ago. I thought that was the end of the world, but how simple those problems were, compared to now.' She sighed. 'I'm sorry, Charlie.'

'What for?'

'Ever since I've known you it's just been one thing after another.'

Charlie laughed softly. 'Life certainly isn't boring with you around.'

'Do you still like me?' She sniffed against his shoulder.

He looked down at her, his dark eyes serious. 'I more than like you, Lily Castle. Much, much more than like you.' He kissed her and she melted against him. Charlie was the only good thing to have happened to her in months, and she wasn't sure how she would have coped yesterday if not for him putting her to work, distracting her, then looking after her so tenderly.

'And I more than like you,' she said eventually. 'Much, much more. But I still need to go to work. Which means I need to go home.'

He nodded. 'Do you want me to walk back with you?'

'You've got patients to see to. And I'm a big girl. I'll be fine.'

He kissed her one more time then left her to get dressed. Lily stared at the door long after he'd shut it, wishing with all her heart that she could stay in this room with Charlie for the rest of her life.

∞

Thankfully, as it was a Sunday, the market square was quiet as Lily emerged from Cowgate Hill. Glancing quickly in both directions to ensure no one would see her, she scuttled across the square and round to the back door, acutely aware of the fact that she was still wearing the blue silk dress, thoroughly ruined now, of course, but she didn't care. She never wanted to see it again.

She tiptoed up the stairs, pausing briefly on the landing, praying that her mother wouldn't hear and come out to accost her. But Nellie's bedroom door remained shut and, breathing a sigh of relief, she continued up to the next floor. She was surprised to see Edie in the bedroom. After Pauline had moved in, she'd tended to sleep in the boys' room with Marianne when she stayed. But perhaps Marianne had wanted time on her own last night.

Edie sat up as soon as she came in. 'Oh, Lily, thank God you're here. Are you all right?'

Lily nodded shortly. 'I'm just here to get changed then I'm off to work.'

Edie hesitated. 'Mum told us. About Jasper.'

'I know.'

'I'm sorry.'

'Not your fault. None of us knew.'

Edie didn't say any more as Lily went to the wardrobe and took out her uniform dress, then walked out to the bathroom to wash. It was as if they no longer knew what to say to each other, Lily thought in despair. There had never been a time in her life when she'd felt uncomfortable with her sister, but now their relationship felt different.

When she got back, Edie was standing by the door, her dark hair in a plait down her back, her white nightdress skimming her toes. Without a word, she grabbed Lily's shoulders and hugged her tightly. 'You know this makes no difference, don't you?' she said, almost as though she had read Lily's mind.

'Not to you maybe,' Lily said, standing stiffly against her.

'It wouldn't matter if your dad turned out to be Hitler. Us six have always stuck together. And we always will.'

Lily sniffed. 'Even if I'm not a proper sister?'

Edie let her go. 'You wind me up more than anyone I know – except maybe Bert. You make me laugh, you make me scream, you nick my clothes and you've always, *always* been there. If that don't make you a proper sister, then I don't know what does.'

Lily laughed tearfully and hugged her back. 'Thank you.'

'Are you going to talk to Mum?'

'No. But I do want to know how Dick Brown and Pauline knew something about me that I didn't even know myself.'

'Pauline found out and must have told him,' Edie said.

'But how? And why did she tell *him* and not *me*?' She thought back to what Pauline had said, that no matter what she'd never meant to hurt her. Was this what she meant?

'She heard Mum and Jasper talking when you got arrested.'

Lily started to get dressed with jerky movements. 'That still doesn't explain why she told that creep. She knows I hate him.'

Edie shrugged. 'Does it matter?'

'Yes, it bloody matters! She's meant to be my friend, but instead she's gossiping about me behind my back. Telling people secrets that have nothing to do with her.'

'I did warn you.'

'Oh, for God's sake. The last thing I need right now is I told you so!'

Edie laughed. 'See what I mean? True sisters, no matter what.'

Lily began to brush her hair, a reluctant smile coming to her lips despite everything. 'Fat lot of good it's done me.' She twisted the blonde strands and pinned them into a bun. Then she pulled her cape from the wardrobe and swung it around her shoulders. 'Will you be here later?'

Edie shook her head. 'But you know where I am if you need me.'

'You reckon I can move in with you?'

'Not sure that'd be fair on Mr P.'

Lily sighed. 'I expect you're right.' She opened the door and tiptoed to the top of the stairs. Peering down, she saw her mother lurking at the bottom, her hair covered with the yellow scarf, her pink dressing gown clutched around her.

'Lily,' she called weakly up to her. 'We need to talk.'

Steeling herself, Lily walked down the stairs towards her and, pausing briefly, she said, 'I disagree.' Then she continued down to the ground floor and let herself out of the front door.

∽

As she approached the hospital gates, Lily caught sight of Pauline ahead of her and her temper surged.

'Oy! Pauline!'

Her friend turned and her face blanched as Lily walked towards her. 'Lily . . .'

'Why did you tell Dick about Jasper being my dad?' Pauline reached a hand out to her, but Lily stepped back. 'Do you know how I felt yesterday? Finding out like that?'

Pauline dropped her gaze. 'I'm so sorry,' she whispered. 'You're a true mate and I'm so sorry for what I done. But I had no choice.'

'Of course you had a bloody choice!' Lily snarled. 'You could have kept your mouth shut, or you could have told me. Instead, you blab off to that disgusting man. And I don't understand why.'

'I didn't have no choice, Lil,' she repeated, her tone flat.

Lily stared at her friend in bewilderment. Pauline looked dreadful: her face pale, her eyes bloodshot and a crop of spots had broken out on her chin. She sniffed at the air. 'You been drinking again, Paul?' Lily leant forward and reached into the pocket of Pauline's dress, pulling out a hip flask. 'You're gonna get in real trouble if you get caught with this. It's six o'clock in the bloody morning, for God's sake!'

Pauline snatched it back. 'I don't care. I don't care if they sack me. I hate it here. And now Mum and Dad are back and . . .'

'Has he hurt your mum again?'

Pauline shook her head. 'Not with his fists at any rate. You don't know what he's like, Lily. He's horrible. You're lucky, you always had Jasper but me and Mum, well, we have to live in the house with that man. And I'm sorry you had to find out about Jasper like that but you couldn't have asked for a better dad. He's certainly better than your other one.'

'What do you know about him?' Lily asked in wonder.

Pauline shrugged and looked away. 'Just what you told me.'

'Oy, Pauline! I want a word with you!'

Both girls spun round to see Nellie standing there wearing a lime green cardigan, pink blouse and red skirt with a yellow sunflower pattern.

'Why have you been gossipin' about my family?' she screamed.

Pauline narrowed her eyes at Nellie. 'Maybe if you'd told the truth from the start, there'd have been no gossip for me to tell.' She turned to go, but Nellie caught her arm.

448

'Oh no you don't, girl, you owe me an explanation.'

Pauline shook her hand off. 'I owe you *nothing*,' she hissed. 'If anything *you* owe *me*!'

Nellie stared at the girl, her mouth opening and closing in indignation. 'You've been living under my roof, eating at *my* table. And ...' She paused for a moment as a thought struck her. 'Of course! It was you who told that bloody Dick person about the stash in the basement, wasn't it?'

'Pauline!' Lily gasped.

Pauline looked at Lily. 'I'm sorry. I really am. But I'm not sorry about *you*!' She pointed at Nellie. She turned and walked away. At the gates, she looked over her shoulder and shouted, 'Tell Matron, I quit.' Then she disappeared along Union Road.

'If it weren't for what happened yesterday, I'd wonder what she had against you, Mum. But now—' she shrugged '—well, it could be anything.'

'I swear to you, Lily, I've not got a clue what her problem is.'

Lily examined her mother's face. The cardigan cast a green tinge over her face, and her eyes were sunken and shadowed. She looked ridiculous, Lily thought, with her lurid clothes and her big stupid black bag, and she suddenly wanted to hurt her. Make her feel even one-tenth of the pain that had been inflicted on her by her mother's lies. 'I'll never believe a word you say again. And take some advice: start dressing your age. You're an embarrassment.'

Then she turned and stalked round to the back of the building.

∽

Nellie pushed blindly through the doors of the hospital, her daughter's words ringing in her ears. She hadn't always dressed like this. When Donald was alive, she wore sober colours like all the other matrons. But after the initial shock of his death, God forgive her, it felt as though a weight had been lifted from her shoulders; like the light had come back into her life. And the best way she had found to express this was through colour. She looked down at her skirt and suddenly she wanted to rip it off. Lily was right. What place did all these bright colours have in her life right now?

'Mrs Castle?' It was Matron Watson, and Nellie wiped surreptitiously at her cheeks and turned to face her.

'You know it's not visiting hours,' the woman admonished her.

'Please, can I see him? Just for a moment? You owe my family that much after what you put us through.'

Matron sighed and nodded. 'Just to warn you that he's still unconscious. But go downstairs to the men's ward. Someone will show you where he is.'

Nellie needed no further urging and she sped towards the stairs. 'I'm here to see Jasper Cane. Matron said I could,' Nellie said quickly to the nurse at the desk by the door.

The woman led her to the end of the ward, where the blue curtains were drawn around a bed. Holding her

450

breath, Nellie stepped through them and stared at Jasper. His head was swathed in bandages, and once again his face was covered in bristles. He was breathing steadily, a brown tube going from his hand to a bottle of clear liquid hanging at the head of his bed.

She sat down in the chair beside the bed and took his hand. 'Wake up, old man,' she whispered. 'I need you. Lily needs you. Our beautiful, stubborn daughter is behaving just as I would if I was her. She needs your calm strength to guide her back to me.' Jasper's eyes flickered beneath his lids, but his body remained still.

She sighed and laid her head on the rough blanket, his stomach rising and falling beneath her.

'I see he's still out of it.'

Nellie sat up and looked around in surprise. 'What are *you* doing here?' Everywhere she went at the moment, this man always seemed to be lurking in the background.

Dick Brown didn't reply, instead he folded his arms across his chest and stared up at the ceiling, painted grey like the rest of the building, the light dim in the window-less room. 'This used to be the workhouse.'

Nellie fought back her instinct to stand up and slap the man's smarmy face.

'This is where I started my life.'

Nellie narrowed her eyes, but her breath started to come faster as her stomach churned.

'Didn't stay here long, though. Middle of the war, they didn't want the kids here.' He laughed shortly. 'No one

451

wants orphan kids anywhere. We're just a nuisance. See this?' He gestured to a small scar by his eyebrow. 'Want to know what happened?'

Nellie shook her head. 'I want you to leave.'

'I'll tell you then. I got fostered with a fishmonger who fancied having a kid to do all the labour for him. But, see, he didn't really like kids. Just wanted a slave. And when I was eleven, the bloke weren't happy with the way I cleaned the winders. So he beat me black and blue and threw me in the gutter.'

Nellie felt sick. This man was hateful but then was it any wonder if that's what his childhood had been like?

'Sent me back to the orphanage and I vowed that one day I'd find out who my real parents were, so's I could make them pay for abandoning me. So here I am. Back where I started. You know what else is here?'

Nellie didn't reply.

'Records from the workhouse. They didn't know what to do with them when the hospital took over so they stuck them in a little room out of sight. But I found them. Want to know what else I found?' He dug in the pocket of his beige coat, brought out a long, folded piece of paper and threw it on the bed.

Nellie stared at it. She didn't want to know what it was.

'Go on,' he urged. 'Take a look.'

Tentatively, she reached out a hand and picked up the paper, before taking a deep breath and unfolding it. It was a birth certificate.

'Read it out to me,' he demanded.

In a shaky voice, Nellie complied. 'Richard Donald Brown.' She paused and gulped.

'Go on.'

'Mother: Annie May Brown. Father—' She stopped, unable to continue.

'I want to hear you say it.'

'Father: Donald James Castle. Date of birth: 23 May 1916.'

Nellie stared at the date, her eyes blurring, her mind whirling. The same day as Jim. She thought back to when Jimmy had been conceived. Donald had been home on leave in August 1915. It had been a magical time. The weather had been so warm and she, Donald, Marianne and Rodney had gone for a picnic on the cliffs. They'd sat on a tartan rug, she remembered. She wondered where that rug was now. She hadn't seen it in so long. The children had clambered over the father they barely knew, while he'd tickled them until they cried with laughter, and then carried them home, one on each broad shoulder, as they yelled at him to go faster. She'd thought her heart would burst with love. The year he'd been at war had been hard as she'd tried to make ends meet, look after the babies and keep the café running. That night, Donald had made love to her so sweetly, whispering in her ear about how lucky he was to have her waiting for him.

What a fool she'd been. What an utterly stupid woman. She tried to remember more about that brief leave. He'd come home with Jasper, she remembered, and she'd shooed Donald out of the café during the day, telling him to take advantage of the good weather. She looked at the man lying pale and motionless in the bed. Did he know that Donald had fathered another child, and kept the secret, uncaring what happened to the poor bastard? And to think she'd kept Jasper at arm's length and denied him his daughter all these years because of her guilt. Her husband deserved everything he got, she suddenly thought viciously. All those wasted years ... all those tortured nights wishing things could have been different, that that night had never happened. That Donald would die. Well, she'd got that wish in the end, much good it had done her. Because the guilt that she had betrayed her vows when her husband needed her most had never diminished. Well, this was the end of it. How many more little Castle bastards were there running about the world? France was probably populated with the poor buggers. She refused to waste any more time on futile regrets.

She folded the paper, and handed it back to Dick. The man was revolting, but even so she felt sorry for him; it was Donald's fault that he was here now, twisted and bent on revenge.

'Well, now you've dropped your bombshell, I think it's time you left.'

Dick smirked. 'I don't think so.'

'I don't know what you expect from me.'

'Don't you? I can think of a few things. Like, oh, I don't know, maybe a share of that precious café of yours.'

Nellie smiled grimly. 'Then you'll have to think again. The café belongs to Rodney, lock, stock and barrel.' Donald hadn't even seen fit to leave her that. She swallowed back the tears that were suddenly clogging her throat and stared into the man's eyes. There was nothing of Donald in him. But he did have the look of Donald's worthless brother, Jack. He'd died in the first wave of fighting back in 1914, but he'd been a nasty piece of work. She'd always thought she'd got the good brother; but it seems that they were two sides of the same coin. And now this weasel of a man stood before her with a smug smile on his face, as though he'd achieved some sort of victory. Well, maybe he had. Now he'd transferred some of his hurt, maybe he'd be less bitter. But he was repugnant to her: he represented the deepest betrayal of her memories; everything she'd believed about her and Donald's relationship before he became so ill had been a lie, and now all her certainties were gone. Is this how Lily feels? she wondered. Like the earth has shifted and she no longer knows which way is up and which is down? No wonder she hates me.

She stood up and gathered all the courage that had seen her through the long difficult years since the last war had started; twenty-six years of battling, she thought. And no end in sight. 'So now you've shown me this you can leave. We have nothing more to say to each other.'

Dick narrowed his eyes. 'I think we have a *lot* more to say.'

'Like what?'

He looked uncertain for a moment. 'Like you owe me. I don't care who owns the café, I reckon you're pulling in a nice little profit, and I want some of it.'

'I can't help you there. Everything that place earns belongs to Rodney. He checks those accounts every month, so he'd know if anything was missing.' This was a lie. Rodney trusted her implicitly. He barely even remembered that the café belonged to him.

'Well, then, I'll just have to go ask him, won't I? About time I met my brothers and sisters properly. I thought at least I'd got to know one of them in Lily, but turns out I was wrong. My father wasn't the only one doing the dirty. You were at it and all. You two were obviously made for each other. Still, luckily, turns out that dear *Annie* provided me with another sister.'

Nellie's breath caught. Of course. Annie Brown, who later became Annie Elliott. Pauline's mother. That little cow, she thought fiercely. How dare she go after Donald! She stood up abruptly and thrust the curtain aside.

'Get out! Now! Make do with the sister you do know. For what she's worth.'

'Maybe I will. Problem is, they ain't got a penny. But don't worry, I'll come and pay my respects to the rest of the family one day soon.'

He left then, and Nellie collapsed back on the chair. She knew he'd do it, as well. Which meant she'd have to talk to them first. And after the revelations of yesterday, she wasn't sure how they'd take it.

'Oh, Jasper, what am I going to do?' she said softly, taking hold of his hand. 'Did you know?'

There was no response and Nellie smiled grimly. Even Jasper, the one man who had never let her down and had stood steadfastly by her for years, wouldn't be able to help her out of this one. She stroked his cheek. He needed a shave, she thought. His beard had always grown quickly. 'Why did you give me your helmet, you foolish old man? When will you learn that I'm not worth saving?' She lay her head on his chest and closed her eyes. She had no tears left, but the steady beat of Jasper's heart gave her comfort.

Chapter 46

It wasn't until much later in the day that Lily had a chance to look in on Jasper. She'd been avoiding it until now, partly in case her mother was there, and partly because she felt that if she didn't see Jasper lying helpless and unconscious, maybe she could pretend it had never happened. She could imagine that when she got home that night, he might be sitting upstairs having dinner with them, as he had so often over the years. But she couldn't put it off forever, so while the others made their way to the canteen, she approached the men's ward with trepidation.

Sister Murphy was on duty at the desk and she came around it the minute she saw her. 'I'm so sorry for all your troubles, Lily,' she said with a kind smile. 'After everything that happened with Dr Ramsay, and now this awful tragedy at your sister's wedding. It just doesn't seem fair.'

Lily nodded. 'How's Jasper?'

'No change, I'm afraid. But his heart is strong. As long as his brain's not too badly damaged, he'll pull through.'

Lily blanched at that. 'What do you mean?'

'You should be prepared for the fact that even if he does wake up, he may not be the same man you knew before.'

Lily nodded. She knew a head injury could lead to terrible brain damage and she wasn't sure what would be worse: Jasper never waking up, or him being irreparably damaged in some way.

She walked to the end of the ward and peeped through the curtain to make sure her mother wasn't there. But Jasper was alone, lying peacefully on the bed, his arms on top of the grey blanket, which was stretched tightly over the mound of his stomach. She slipped in and sat down beside him, taking his hand.

'Why didn't you tell me?' she whispered. 'Why do you *always* do what Mum wants? I always wished you were my dad, but now I know that you are, I don't know whether to laugh or cry. Because you lied to me. All my life, you've been lying to me. I thought you were someone I could rely on.' She sniffed. 'I need you to wake up so I can be properly angry with you. Because I can't be truly angry until I know you're all right. But just so you know, don't think you can get away with this by lying in a coma.' She gave a laugh and put her head on his chest, listening to the strong beat of his heart. 'Did you hear me, Jasper?' She waited, but when there was no response she wiped her eyes, stood up and slipped back out, her heart heavy.

As she walked to the door, she was astonished to see a line of people standing outside the ward. She nodded as she noticed Ethel and Phyllis. Gladys was also there. But there were many, many others. Some in ARP uniform, others who worked at the market.

459

Sister Murphy was standing in front of them with her hand up. 'I'm sorry, only two at a time. Please could some of you go away and come back another day,' she called.

'What are you all doing here?' Lily asked Phyllis.

'Looks like we all had the same idea. We're here to see Jasper.'

'All of you?' Lily squeaked.

One of the ARP men nodded at her. 'What's Dover without Jasper?' he said simply.

Tears came to Lily's eyes again. She might be angry at him, but Jasper had the biggest heart of anyone she knew. And here was the proof. He was loved far beyond the small circle of her own family, and there weren't many that could say that. Just for a moment, Lily felt warmed. That was her father, she thought. A man respected and loved wherever he went. Unlike the man she'd always thought of as her father who had left behind a legacy of sorrow and grief. She smiled at the man who'd spoken. 'You're right,' she said. 'Jasper is a very special man.'

It made it all the more infuriating that she had been kept in the dark all these years. She may have softened towards Jasper, but she was very far from forgiving her mother.

❧

When Lily got home later that evening, she slipped the key to Jasper's flat from the hook by the back door. He'd always insisted that if they needed him, or needed a place to shelter, then they could just come and go. But of course they never did. Now, though, she felt the overwhelming urge to be close to him, away from her mother and sister. Somewhere she could think.

The smell of hot metal and the heat of the coal fire had always represented safety and security to her, because it was Jasper's smell. But when she stepped inside the forge, the fire was out, and the smell was muted.

She walked up the stairs and sat on the threadbare chair by the fireplace. It was lumpy and uncomfortable, the cushions moulded to a far larger frame than hers. She wriggled, trying to get comfortable, the scent of Jasper all around her. She wished she could stay here forever, away from everyone. She stared around the dismal room. She'd offered to redecorate it once, but Jasper had refused. Said Clara had chosen the furnishings, so they always reminded him of his wife. She smiled sadly. Poor Jasper. His wife dead soon after the war, and the only child he'd had wasn't even aware of it. And so he'd lived here alone, snatching at happiness as and when he could, creating a family from the community around him; a family that, if today's queue of people was anything to go by, truly loved him.

He had gifts, she realised, far beyond his cleverness with metal. And her mother was a fool for not letting him fully into her life. It made her blood boil to think of all those wasted years. She brought her knees up to her chest and clasped her arms around them, trying to pretend it was Jasper she was holding, but it was no good, her legs were too bony and would never be a substitute for Jasper's large stomach. She put her head on her knees, inhaling the scent of him in the room. Her father's scent, she thought. That wonderful, generous man. Her father. The tears came suddenly and she wept as she wondered what she would do if she never got the chance to tell Jasper how much she loved him.

Chapter 47

A week later, on a cold and blustery autumn day, a sad procession made its way through the market square to St Mary's Church. Stan, with Marguerite in his arms and supported by his parents, Derek and Mavis, walked at the front, and as they progressed, members of the market community silently fell into line behind them. Today, for one hour, the shops would be shut and the stalls empty, because Daisy was one of their own. Before the war, she'd run the second-hand clothes stall and there weren't many who hadn't taken advantage of her skill with the needle. And while she wasn't the first death to hit their community, she was the one to hit hardest.

Nellie stood outside the café, all six of her children ranged around her, the boys holding their caps to their chests. It was a bittersweet moment for her, because it was the first time her children had been together since the dreadful day a week before. Aside from Marianne, they had all kept their distance, although she knew that they visited Jasper whenever they could. As for Lily, she'd not spoken a single word to her since she'd told her she was an embarrassment.

There had been no change in Jasper's condition, and Nellie wondered how long he could survive being fed through a tube. Already his frame had diminished, the blankets across his large, barrel-like stomach seeming to get lower each time she saw him – strictly in visiting hours now that she'd had to reopen the café.

At least Gladys had returned. She looked round at her friend who crossed herself as Stan walked by. Across the square, the Turners and the Perkins stood together, Phyllis holding Freddie's hand, while Wilf Perkins had his arm around Reenie as she sobbed into his shoulder. She wondered why it wasn't Jimmy comforting her, as Rodney was with Marge, but then it was none of her business, and Jim hadn't even seemed to notice.

She glanced at Marianne to see how she was bearing up. To her surprise, her eyes were dry as she watched the procession. Beside her Donny was crying and she clutched his hand tightly. Alfie held his other hand, but his gaze was fixed on Marianne. Nellie sighed. Maybe once Daisy was laid to rest, Marianne would set a new date for the wedding. It might seem unfeeling but that was the reality of life. You had no choice but to keep moving forward.

And that was what she would have to do. After the funeral, she needed to speak to her family again. Since Dick Brown's revelation, she'd not slept as she thought back over the years of her marriage to Donald. She'd loved him deeply, only wavering, to her eternal shame, when he'd been so sick. Whether he'd loved her or not, she no longer knew. And now Donald's secret past had come back to haunt her, and she needed to gather her family about her, remind them that they needed to stick together. But, most of all, she needed them on her side. Because she had no idea what Dick might do next, and she wasn't sure she could deal with it on her own.

The end of the line passed them, and Nellie moved forward, followed by her family. And soon the silent procession arrived at the church, where Reverend Johnson greeted them sombrely.

Marianne had asked to speak, and as the time drew nearer, she fiddled nervously with the piece of paper on which she'd written the poem she'd chosen. It was for Marguerite, who couldn't speak for herself, but who one day would know that these words had been said on her behalf.

When the time came, Reverend Johnson nodded at her and she walked up the aisle, her legs trembling. As she stood at the lectern, she looked over at Stan, whose face was wet with tears as he clung to his daughter. 'Stan,' she said. 'You must know how much Daisy loved you; you were the very centre of her world, the sun around which she spun. And since she had Marguerite, her happiness *shone* out of her. Today, I want to read something on behalf of Marguerite, the daughter Daisy had waited for for so long, and loved so much that her last thought was to protect her, no matter the cost to herself.' Marianne stopped and wiped her eyes. Finally, she cleared her throat and began.

465

'O mother-my-love, if you'll give me your hand,
And go where I ask you to wander,
I will lead you away to a beautiful land –
The Dreamland that's waiting out yonder.
We'll walk in a sweet posie-garden out there,
Where moonlight and starlight are streaming,
And flowers and birds are filling the air
With the fragrance and music of dreaming.

'I'll rock you away on a silver-dew stream
And sing you asleep when you're weary,
And no one shall know of our beautiful dream
But you and your own little dearie.'

Her voice failed her then, and she couldn't go on as the tears started to fall. 'I'm sorry, Daisy,' she whispered as she stumbled down from the lectern, straight into Alfie's waiting arms.

❧

Mavis and Derek had laid on some sandwiches and tea afterwards in the basement bar of the Oak. Once again, the community had dug deep, although having already donated food for the wedding, the fare for the funeral was much more sparse. The wedding food had been given to the WVS, who had distributed it amongst the caves and any that needed it after the vicious shelling the town had been subjected to.

Stan sat quietly at a table, saying barely a word. His freckles stood out starkly on his pale face as he sat with Marguerite on his knee. The baby was staring around her in wonder, clutching a rattle that someone had given her and every so often letting out a yell. Stan seemed barely to notice. Marianne went and sat down beside him, stroking the child's silvery tufts of hair.

'Did she really love me that much?' Stan asked Marianne without looking at her.

'It was always you for Daisy, Stan. You know that.'

He nodded, his Adam's apple bobbing as he swallowed back the tears. 'And her for me,' he murmured. 'Why did you say sorry?'

Marianne's hand stilled on the baby's hair. 'Because it's my fault,' she whispered. 'You and Daisy would never have come back if I hadn't been getting married.'

Stan shook his head. 'That's daft talk. Daisy had been itching to get back here.'

'But she wouldn't have done it on that day.'

'Maybe not. But who's to say what would have happened on any day she came back.' He stared across at Alfie, who was watching them anxiously. 'Are you going to set another date?' he asked.

'How can I? After what's happened.'

Stan sat silently for some time, and Marianne was about to leave when he said, 'You know, Dais worried about you all the time. But when Alfie came along, she stopped. Said you didn't need her worry any more.'

Instead of replying, Marianne took the baby onto her knee, letting the child play with her hair.

'So, if you don't sort it out soon, I won't be able to rest thinking of my Dais up in heaven fretting over you as well as me and Mags.'

Marianne rested her chin on the child's head. 'I just don't have the heart to do it now.'

Stan snorted. 'Then you're a fool. You think if I'd have seen the future that I wouldn't have married Daisy? Knowing I'd only have her a short time?'

Marianne shook her head.

'Exactly.'

She waited for him to say more, but he just took Daisy from her. 'She needs a feed and a change,' he said shortly. Then he stood up and walked up the stairs.

Alfie joined Marianne. 'Are you all right?'

'Not really.' She put her head on his shoulder and sighed. 'I'm sorry. I never meant to hurt you, Alf.'

'I know, love.'

'Do you still want to marry me?'

He laughed softly. 'No.'

Her head jerked up and she stared at him in dismay. But when she saw the warmth in his eyes she relaxed and smiled slightly. 'Me neither.'

They sat for a while in silence. Finally, Alfie said, 'Maybe you and me can slip away quietly one day with Don and get married at the town hall.'

She nodded against his shoulder. 'Just you and Don. That's all I need. Let's not tell anyone else.'

Alfie's heart leapt with relief as he tightened his arms around her and kissed her forehead. 'I have to leave now. I'm on duty in an hour. Will you be all right?'

She nodded. 'I think so. As long as we still have each other.'

'Always,' he murmured.

Chapter 48

No one stayed at the wake for long. Usually, there would be singing and celebrating long into the night, but today few had the heart for it, and as Nellie led her family outside, she stopped briefly and stared at the ruins of the Grand and the scene that had so recently torn all their lives apart. 'I need you all to come back with me,' she said without looking around. 'There are things that need to be said.' Then, without checking to see if they were following, she walked up New Bridge.

The look on her mother's face suggested to Marianne that she had something serious to impart. 'Don,' she said, 'go and ask Mrs Perkins if you can play with Fred for a bit, will you?' He didn't need asking twice, and as he scampered away, Marianne looked around at her brothers and sisters. 'Will you come? Please?'

Lily sighed. 'Not like I've got anywhere else to go, is it?' As far as she was concerned, it didn't really matter what their mother had to say, she wasn't sure she could ever forgive her.

By the time they arrived at the café, Nellie had already put the kettle on and laid out cups and saucers. She stood silently as they came in, only Marianne and Jimmy giving her a tentative smile.

Once they were seated, Nellie drew in a deep breath. 'I've had enough of the lot of you treating me like I'm some sort of criminal. I lied. I was wrong. But did I do it to hurt you? No. Did I do it out of malice? No. So you lot will have to find a way to forgive me, like it or not.'

'So, you want me to just pretend it never happened? Go back to the way we were?' Edie asked. 'Because that's not possible, Mum.'

'Maybe not. But I'm still your mother. I'm still the woman who raised you, loved you, worked my fingers to the bone for you.'

Bert snorted. 'Not that again. You do know most parents do that for their kids, don't you? Seeing as they can't do it for themselves.'

'Mum's right,' Jimmy said. 'Forgive and forget. Move forward. Jasper's life is hanging in the balance. Do you think he'd be happy to see us like this?'

'I forgot,' Bert said snidely. 'You're the one who seems to think lying's fine.'

'Oh, grow up, Bert!' Jimmy fumed. 'Not everything is neat and tidy, black and white.'

'Lily?' Nellie looked at her youngest daughter, who was pale and wan in her black dress. 'You're the one most affected by all this.'

Lily folded her arms and shrugged.

Nellie sighed in frustration. 'I just want you all to know that you lot mean the world to me. You're the reason I

471

live. If you want to hate me, then fine. But know this, I could *never* hate a single hair on your heads. And . . .' Her lips trembled as she tried to get the next words out. 'Truth be told, I need you right now. And Jasper . . .' She took a deep breath. 'Jasper needs you too. Don't abandon him now.'

'We were never abandoning *him*, Mum,' Edie said. 'It was only ever you.'

Nellie paled as she slumped down onto a chair.

'Edie,' Rodney said warningly. 'That was uncalled for.'

Edie stared at him mutinously, then sat back with a huff. 'Maybe it was a bit harsh. But we're all reeling. Jasper could die, Daisy's gone and now you're saying we should all just get on with it. Well, right now, I'm not sure I can. I just—'

There was a knock on the window, and they all looked up in surprise. Dick Brown was waving at them. 'Yoo hoo!' he shouted through the glass then came round and opened the door.

Nellie jumped up and ran towards him, pushing him in the chest. 'Get out!' she gritted.

'I just wanted to introduce meself properly.'

'Now isn't the time.' But though she pushed, Dick didn't budge.

'Aw, come on. I heard you'd been going through a hard time and families stick together when things are bad.'

Bert and Jim came forward to help, and Dick stepped back. 'I'd 'ave thought you'd have welcomed me a bit more warmly than this.' He looked at Nellie. 'Haven't you told them the good news?'

Nellie's face went red as she fought to control her breathing. 'Boys, get rid of him. NOW!'

As Jimmy and Bert caught his arms, Dick shook them off furiously. 'This ain't no way to treat your brother, now, is it?'

A stunned silence greeted his words and Nellie's head dropped. 'Please, just make him go,' she whispered brokenly.

'More secrets, Mum?' Edie said. 'How many bloody skeletons can one family have in their cupboard?'

Nellie shook her head.

'Well?' Rodney said. 'Are you going to tell us, or will we have to hear whatever it is from *this*?' His eyes swept over Dick contemptuously.

'Before you stare down your nose at me, mate, you might want to take a look at this.' From his pocket Dick retrieved a folded piece of paper and handed it to Rodney.

Nellie snatched it from his hand, scrunching it up and throwing it to the floor.

Dick chuckled. 'You can try to destroy it as much as you like, but it don't change the truth. I'm part of this family whether you like it or not.'

You could have cut the silence with a knife as all eyes turned to Nellie.

'Who the hell *are* you?' Jimmy asked, his gaze flicking from his mother to the man in front of him.

Dick picked up the paper and smoothing it out, handed it to Jimmy who stared down at it in silence for a moment before murmuring disbelievingly, 'We share a birthday.'

'Aww, do we?' Dick chuckled. 'That makes us twins then, cos that's not all we share. Seems our dad were a dirty dog.'

Nellie moaned, and Marianne went to sit beside her, putting her arm around her mother's shaking shoulders, while Edie let out a shout of sarcastic laughter. 'There is *no way* that our dad could have produced something like *you*,' Edie said fiercely.

Nellie hardly heard her through the buzzing in her ears, surprised Edie seemed to be defending Donald. She'd known she'd have had to tell them sooner or later, but for them to find out like this made it even worse than she'd expected. Drawing in a deep breath, she stood up.

'Right, well now you've shown us, you can leave. We have nothing more to say to each other.'

'But you're wrong, Auntie Nellie – you don't mind if I call you that, do you? See, when I found out who me mum and dad were, I weighed up the pros and cons of letting you all know. But I figured you'd probably throw me out on my ear.' He shrugged. 'I haven't been welcomed anywhere since the day I was conceived.'

Despite herself, Lily felt a flicker of pity. 'Why didn't you just come out with it sooner, instead of all that weird stuff?'

'I wanted info, so I could plan the best course of action. And unlike my poor old mum, you lot are very nice and comfortable, so I'm thinking you should share a bit of that with me. And if you don't, then I'll have no choice but to ask her – or that nasty husband of hers.'

Rodney snorted. 'You've got to be kidding. Why didn't you just ask us sooner?'

'Ah. Well, that was my intention. Then I was persuaded not to. But now I got a bit of a problem that I need you to help me out with.'

'I don't think so.' Rodney nodded at his brothers to take hold of Dick again.

Dick held his hands up, fending them off. 'Oh, I think you will. You see, now that Jasper Cane's all but done for, I need another source of income.'

'What?' Nellie said.

'Didn't I say?' He smiled. 'Best decision I ever made comin' back here. Because my parents weren't the only thing I found in the records. There were a letter. Sent to me!' He laughed delightedly. 'Never had a letter before that wasn't a bill or worse. Sent from the front sometime in 1916.'

He pulled another piece of paper out of his pocket and this time Rodney snatched it from him.

'"To the child of Annie Brown",' he read. '"Should you ever be in need, please come to Jasper Cane, The Forge, Castle Street, Dover."'

'Jasper knew?' Nellie gasped, stunned. Jasper had kept the truth from her? The stupid old fool; he'd been trying to protect her. Her heart squeezed at the thought. He always put her first, no matter what. Even when they were arguing about Lily and he was so upset and angry with her, he hadn't told her.

'Been payin' me every week to stop me spillin' the beans. But now he's near death, and the money's stopped.

And it seems the Elliotts ain't so flush – or at least *she* ain't. So . . .' He held his arms out, palms up, in a gesture of supplication.

Lily's head shot up at that. Elliott? Was it possible that Annie Elliott was his mother? Suddenly the pieces started to fall into place and she began to understand the hold Dick had over Pauline. She opened her mouth to say something, but Nellie spoke before she had a chance.

'He only did that to stop you telling me. But now you have, if you think you'll get a penny out of us or him, you've got another think comin'. Donald's been dead these twelve years, and you can tell whoever you bloomin' well like!'

'Can I? And shall I tell them about Jasper bein' Lily's dad as well? That journalist bloke seemed mighty interested when I spoke to him.'

Lily stood up and stepped forward. 'Like she said; tell who you want. I'm proud that man is my father. He's a sight better than yours at any rate.' She looked around at her siblings apologetically. 'No offence.'

'Ahh. Ain't that sweet. Anyway, seein' as you can't help, I got another visit to pay. Maybe Sid Elliott'll be more obligin'. From what I heard, though, the bloke won't like the fact his wife weren't pure as the driven snow when they married. Quite a temper on him.'

He walked out, leaving a stunned silence behind him. Finally, Rodney sat down next to Nellie and folded his arms. 'Please, Mum, just promise me there are no more bloody secrets. I don't think I can take any more.'

Nellie shook her head. 'I'm sorry. I'm so sorry.' Then she got up and fled the room, Marianne hot on her heels.

Lily, who had been sitting like a statue, suddenly got up from the table and ran for the door.

'Where are you going?' Bert called after her.

'Pauline's,' she said, and yanking open the door, she started to run, desperate to get there before Dick Brown. Because from what she'd learnt about Sid Elliott, Pauline was right: he *would* kill Annie Elliott when he discovered the truth.

Chapter 49

The streets were busy as Lily frantically pushed her way up Cannon Street, screaming at people to get out of her way. She kept thinking of Pauline, of her drinking and her fear, and of how that despicable man had manipulated her. From the little she had found out in the last few days, Sid Elliott was a violent man, and Pauline had spent her life trying to deflect his anger and protect her mother. No wonder she'd turned to drink.

As she neared the turning for Queens Gardens, she spotted a familiar figure and breathed a sigh of relief. Not once in all of her life had she been pleased to see this man, but right now he seemed heaven-sent.

'Roger!' she yelled. 'Roger, I need you.'

Roger spun round when he heard her voice. 'Is this some kind of joke?' he said, as she caught up to him.

'Please. You've got to come. I think Sid Elliott's gonna hurt his wife, Annie.'

Roger frowned. 'What? How do you know?'

Lily caught his arm and started to drag him along the road. 'Just bloody come, will you?'

Roger put a whistle to his lips and blew hard as he ran, hoping to attract some help. Much as he'd love to make an arrest, he wasn't sure he could fight a man on his own.

Lily turned right off Cannon Street and raced down Queens Gardens to Pauline's house.

Inside, she could hear shouting and banging, then a woman screamed. The door was ajar so she pushed it open and gasped. Lying curled in a foetal position at the foot of the stairs was Annie Elliott, while Pauline desperately tried to stop her father from kicking her.

'Halt! You're under arrest!' Roger shouted.

Sid Elliott stopped for just a second and looked up, his face twisted with rage. Then he spat on his wife's body and ran out of the door, barging past Lily and Roger, while Pauline rushed forward and knelt beside her mother, lifting her head and cradling it in her lap.

It was only then that Lily noticed Dick. He was standing out of reach watching the scene with a smirk. When he spotted Lily, he shook his head. 'Dear, oh dear. I hope she's all right.'

A cold rage started to rise in her and she grabbed Roger's arm. 'This man has been attempting to extort money from my family as well as from the Elliotts. Arrest him.'

Roger looked uncertain as Dick laughed. 'Prove it, love. I were just here to check on me poor old ma.'

A noise at the front door made them all turn and Lily's heart leapt with relief as her brothers came in. Rodney had put on his officer's cap and buttoned up his jacket, and even to Lily – who had no respect for any of her brothers – he looked impressive.

'As an officer in the navy, I am more than happy to back up my sister's claim. That man has been blackmailing Jasper Cane, and now he can no longer pay up, he's turned to our family. You would be shirking your duty to let him walk free.'

Rodney spoke with such authority that Roger leapt forward and grabbed Dick's arm, twisting it behind his back. 'Richard Brown, I am arresting you for . . .' He looked at Rodney uncertainly.

'Extortion,' Rodney said, rolling his eyes.

'That's right. Extortion. A very serious crime and one that can have you put away for some time.' He fumbled at his belt as he tried to release the handcuffs.

Bert sighed and stepped forward. 'For God's sake, man! Give him to me.' He put his arm around Dick's neck, holding him firmly while Roger continued to struggle with the cuffs.

'Gerroff.' Dick tried to break free, but being restrained by Bert was very different from being held in the constable's puny grasp.

If it weren't for Annie Elliott lying at the bottom of the stairs, Lily would have giggled. Instead, she knelt down and took Pauline in her arms. Her friend's head dropped onto her shoulder and she started to weep.

'Shh,' Lily whispered. 'It's all right now.' As she waited for her to stop crying, she examined the woman in front of her. Mrs Elliott hadn't moved since she'd arrived, but her entire body was shaking with shock. Lily leant forward to smooth the woman's dark hair back from her forehead and flinched as she saw her face; one of her eyes was swollen shut, while a cut on her cheekbone was bleeding, the blood running down to her puffy lips.

'Can you tell me what happened?' she whispered.

'Dick ...' Pauline gulped. 'I've done everything he asked,' she wept. 'I'm sorry, Lily. I'm so sorry.'

'It's not your fault, Paul. But we need to get a doctor for your mum. Maybe get her to hospital.'

'No!'

Lily jumped as Mrs Elliott made her voice heard for the first time. 'No hospital.'

'She won't go. She never will,' Pauline whispered.

'You can't stay here while your dad's still on the loose. It's not safe.'

'We can go to Mrs Butler next door—'

'No!' Annie Elliott said again. 'I don't want my neighbours to see this.'

'For God's sake, Mum, it's not as if they don't know!' Pauline shouted in frustration.

Tears started to leak from the woman's swollen eye and Lily stroked her back. 'All right, Mrs Elliott. We won't.'

She looked up at her brothers.

Jim sighed. 'You know where the best place for her would be, don't you?' he said.

Lily nodded. Because despite everything that had happened and all the shocking revelations, there was only one

481

place she could think of to go. 'We need to take her to Mum,' she whispered.

'Are you out of your mind?' Pauline exclaimed. 'After everything you've found out, you think the best place to take her is to your bloody mum?'

Lily nodded. 'She'll be safe there,' she said simply, realising it was true. Whatever her mother's faults, however bad her temper, one thing she knew for sure: Nellie Castle would always try to keep them safe no matter what the threat.

Roger let out a cry of triumph then, and cuffed Dick's hands securely behind his back. 'You're coming with me, Sonny Jim,' he said self-importantly. Then he nodded at the assembled company. 'We'll be needin' statements from all of you later.' Then, with Dick Brown held securely in front of him, he marched him out of the house towards the police station.

Rodney shook his head. 'Jesus wept, that man's an incompetent fool.'

'Don't tell me you're surprised.' Bert chuckled as he bent and offered his hand to Pauline. 'Come on, girl. Let's get you out of here.'

'Mrs Elliott, can you walk?'

The woman nodded and slowly Lily helped her to her feet. But her legs collapsed and she fell against Lily's chest.

'Jim?' Lily said. 'Do you think you could . . . ?'

Jim flexed an arm. 'I reckon I can manage it.' Then he bent down and gently lifted the woman, cradling her against his chest as he walked out of the door.

'You sure you can manage her?' Pauline skipped anxiously behind him.

'No problem. My army kit's heavier than her.' He strode towards Cannon Street, the others following behind, doing their best to ignore the curious stares.

Nellie was still sitting at the table with the others when they entered the café, and she leapt up as they came in. Then her eyes fell on the figure in Jimmy's arms. 'Why the devil have you brought *her* here?' she shouted.

'Mum, they need help,' Lily said desperately. 'It was the only place we could think of.'

Nellie paused and stared at her daughter, who returned her gaze unflinchingly. Finally, Nellie's lips lifted very slightly as she nodded and walked towards Jimmy, patting Lily on the shoulder as she passed.

'Get her upstairs, Jim. Put her on the sofa for now. As for you—' she turned to Pauline '—I think you might have something to say to me.'

Pauline shifted uncomfortably. 'I-I'm sorry,' she said miserably. 'I never meant any harm. But Dick said—' Her face crumpled and she started to cry.

Nellie sighed. 'You should have come to me.'

'How could I?' She slumped in a chair. 'Dad didn't know about Dick. An' he's always so jealous. Mum can't even chat to the butcher's boy at the door without Dad havin' a go. I just knew if he found out about this, he'd kill her. And that's exactly what he tried to do. But now he's run off and there's no telling if he'll try again.'

Marianne brought a cup of tea over. 'I put some sugar in it for you, love.'

Pauline smiled gratefully and sipped.

'And where's Dick now?' Edie asked.

'Arrested by Roger Humphries,' Rodney said. 'Eventually.' His lips quirked. 'Marianne, if you'd married that man, I'm not sure I would have spoken to you again.' He rubbed his hands over his face. 'Christ, what a week: a wedding, a shelling, a funeral, and now a long-lost brother bent on revenge.'

'Don't you *dare* call that man your brother!' Nellie wagged a finger at him.

Rodney shrugged. 'Facts are facts, Mum.'

'I don't care! That man has *no* right to call us family. And I don't want any more said about it!' She went into the kitchen and poured hot water from the kettle into a metal bowl. 'Lily, get the medical supplies. I reckon you'll be a sight better at getting that woman fixed than me.' Then she stalked upstairs.

Chapter 50

Later that night, Nellie crept into her bedroom where Annie Elliott now lay. Pauline was sitting in the armchair by the bed, her head slumped to one side, while the light from the oil lamp on the bedside table cast a dim glow over the injured woman, who was lying with her one good eye wide open, staring up at the ceiling.

Nellie shook Pauline gently by the shoulder. 'Go upstairs and try to sleep, love,' she whispered. 'I'll sit with your mum.'

Pauline looked at her mother uncertainly, but at her nod, she left the room.

Nellie settled herself into the armchair and sat quietly for a moment, conscious of Annie watching her warily. Finally, the woman whispered, 'I'm sorry.'

Nellie regarded her steadily. 'Do you want to tell me what happened?' she asked.

Annie shifted uncomfortably. 'I met Donald at the dress shop where I worked. He came in with Jasper, and bought a beautiful silk scarf. All swirly reds and pinks it were. Said his wife needed some colour. He were that handsome in his uniform, with his blue eyes and his dark hair. I'd always fancied him, truth be told. But he were

485

married to you. And everyone knew it were a bad idea to mess with Nellie Castle's man.'

Nellie snorted softly. 'You didn't seem to.' Nellie remembered that scarf. It *had* been beautiful. Donald had told her it brought out the red in her chestnut hair, and she'd worn it till it fell apart.

Annie shook her head, then winced. 'I were young, Nellie. Young and vain and foolish and my head were easily turned.'

'So, is that when it happened?'

'He came back the next day. And then the next. An' then he waited outside for me one day. Beautiful day, it was. We went walking along the cliffs and he turned and kissed me. He apologised. Said he'd been dying to do it since he first saw me. Said that you'd been cold since he'd come back, and I'd brightened his time. I felt sorry for him.'

Every word she said sent a dagger of pain through Nellie's heart, but she forced herself to listen. 'So cold that you an' me birthed on the same day. Did he know? That he'd left you pregnant?'

She nodded. 'I wrote to him.'

'And?'

'He never replied.' Tears started to leak out of her eyes. 'Me mum and dad told me to leave and not come back till the baby was gone. I had nowhere to go.' She sniffed. 'So I ended up stayin' at the workhouse.'

'Did you contact him again?'

She nodded miserably. 'Wrote and told him I'd had a boy and he was in the workhouse. That I'd had to leave him there, but I'd put his name on the birth certificate so our baby would always know where he came from. I got a reply back from Jasper. He sent that note for the boy, and told me to leave it with the workhouse people to give to him when he was older. Told me he were sorry for what Donald had done.'

'And then?'

'After the baby were born I went home and me dad told me never to mention it again and set up the marriage with Sid Elliott. I've thought of that little baby every single day of his life. Every day. And look what he is.' She started to cry in earnest and Nellie patted her hand.

'Maybe he wouldn't have been that way if only someone had loved him.'

'*I* loved him. I loved him something fierce.'

'But he weren't to know, were he?' Nellie sighed. 'Well, it seems you've suffered for your mistake. Did Donald ever try to see you again?'

'I steered clear. Sid were always so jealous. But he didn't know about Dick. He never knew . . .'

Nellie sighed. 'Donald lied to you,' she said. 'We had a good marriage – or so I thought.'

'What'll you do?'

'I'll look after you till you're better, then I think you and Pauline ought to think about leaving Dover. You got anywhere to go?'

'I got a brother in Scotland. I ain't seen him in years. Sid always said it were too far to visit . . .'

'Well, I suggest you get on a train and go soon as you can.'

Annie nodded. 'I would, it's just ... I ain't got the funds. Pauline's been givin' Dick money and Sid only ever gave me enough for food.'

Nellie sighed. 'I'll lend it to you, then. You can send it back when you're settled.'

'I don't know how to thank you. After everythin' I done.'

Nellie laughed humourlessly. 'Don't thank me. If it weren't for the state of you, you'd not be welcome here and your ears would be ringing with my curses. Folk were right – you should never mess with Nellie Castle's man. Soon as you're on your feet, I want you out.'

Annie nodded then turned her face away and Nellie settled back in the seat and closed her eyes. In many ways, Dick Brown's revelations had done her a favour. They'd brought the children rallying round, but, more than that, they'd shown her again what a good man Jasper was. How lucky she was that he seemed to love her. Whether he still would when he woke up, though, only time would tell.

∽

Lily woke as Pauline climbed into the bed beside her and propped herself up on one elbow. 'You all right, Paul?'

Pauline sighed. 'No. But at least I've finally got Mum away. I'm sorry,' she said. 'For tellin' Dick all your secrets.'

'When did he tell you about being your brother?'

'At the dance. I were so happy, but then he comes up and spills his poison, and . . . Well, you know what happened. I made a fool of meself.'

'And you told him about Mum's stash of stuff? And me being Jasper's daughter?'

Pauline nodded. 'He were always on at me. Said he wanted to get his own back on Mum and your dad for the wrong they done him. Said if I didn't help him he'd tell my dad that he was Mum's son. I swear I didn't know he were gettin' money from Jasper, though. Cos I were givin' him most of my wages as well.'

Lily gasped. 'You paid him?'

'What choice did I have? My dad *woulda* killed her, you know, if you hadn't come by. You got no idea how lucky you are to have Jasper.'

'I think I do now.'

'And even your mum ain't so bad. Least you can rely on her.'

'I know. Always.' Lily still wasn't sure she could entirely forgive her for her lies, but when all was said and done, her mother loved her. And she couldn't pretend any longer that she didn't love her too.

'I love Mum, but I've always had to look out for her. Is it too much to ask for someone to look out for me for once?'

Lily reached over and took her friend's hand. 'You'll find someone one day. You've got a good, loyal heart, Paul.'

Pauline sniffed. 'Anyway, soon as we can, I'm gonna try to get Mum to leave. Save enough money and take her to me uncle in Scotland. I've never met him, but Mum writes to him all the time. Maybe we'll have better luck there, eh?'

Lily laughed. 'Well, it couldn't be worse.'

Pauline started to giggle as the tensions of the last few weeks bubbled up, and soon the two of them were rocking with laughter. Until suddenly it changed, and Pauline's laughter turned to sobs. Lily jumped out of her bed and slipped in beside her friend, putting her arms around her. 'I'll look after you tonight, all right? You just sleep. You're safe now.'

Pauline wept for a long time, but finally her cries quietened, and her breathing deepened. Lily lay for a long time staring up at the ceiling, thinking about all that had happened. Everything had changed, she realised. In just a few short weeks, her life had been turned upside down, and it wasn't over yet. Because Jasper's life still hung in the balance, and she didn't want him to die not knowing what he meant to her. To all of them. Because though she might be his true daughter, for the others, he'd always be the father of their hearts.

∞

It was a few days before Annie Elliott was fit enough to travel, and as she waved her and Pauline off at the back door one morning, Nellie breathed a sigh of relief.

'Thank gawd they've gone,' she said. 'Though why she won't press charges on that nasty husband of hers, I'll never know. Still, now everyone knows what sort of a man he is folk have made it clear he's not welcome anywhere so hopefully he'll pack up and leave soon. As for that Dick Brown, he deserves to rot in that prison cell.' After Dick's arrest, the police had discovered stolen goods in his room. It seemed that he'd been pilfering from hospital staff and patients while he'd been working there, so for now he was being kept in prison until a date for his trial was set.

'It were a good Christian act to put that woman up after what she did,' Gladys said.

'You're not wrong. I deserve a sainthood for that. I don't mind tellin' you there was a devil on my shoulder that was whispering bad, bad things to me. But then, it weren't all her fault.'

'Will you stop being angry now they've gone, Gran?' Donny asked. 'Because it's getting a bit wearing.'

'Don!' Marianne gasped.

'What? That's what you said to Lily the other day. I heard you.'

Marianne blushed. 'I've told you before not to listen in on other people's conversations,' she admonished, casting a quick glance at her mother.

Nellie laughed. 'I'll try, Don. But I won't feel meself again till Jasper opens his eyes.'

'How was he yesterday?' Gladys asked.

Nellie sighed. 'No change. But he struggles when they stick that blinkin' tube down his throat to feed him, which they say's a good sign. It's disgustin' what they have to do. Lily's learnt to do it so she can help and that eases my mind.'

A disgruntled shout from the café had Nellie lumbering back in. 'All right, all right. Gawd's sake, I'll be with you in a minute.'

Chapter 51

The weeks following Daisy's funeral were difficult ones in Dover. Although the fear of invasion had started to recede, the threat of sudden death from shells or bombs had increased to such an extent that permission was given for people to sleep overnight in the caves and water, heat and toilets were installed. The caves really were starting to feel like a home from home now, and there was even talk of holding the annual Christmas party in the large cavern at the back of Barwick's Cave.

Late one afternoon in November, Mavis came into the café. She looked tired and thin, her red hair greyer than it had been, but she and Derek had endeavoured to carry on as normally as possible. By some miracle the Royal Oak was one of the few pubs in the area that remained undamaged aside from smashed windows, and they found they were busier than ever.

'How are you, Mave?' Nellie put a cup of tea in front of her friend and sat down opposite her at the table.

'Oh, you know, bearing up, I suppose.' She smiled wanly. 'Stan writes regular from Shillingford. Poor lad's still in pieces, but Maggie's keeping him strong. By heck, I miss our Daisy, though.'

Nellie patted her hand. 'I know, love. I know. But it looks like you mean business today. So what can I do for you?'

Mavis dug in her bag and brought out a notebook. 'Right, well. It's been a pretty awful year, all told, and with the market square Christmas party cancelled, I've decided to have it in the basement at the Oak. What do you think?'

Nellie smiled. 'I think that's a sight better than the caves. When were you thinking?'

'Christmas Eve seems a good day. We can start early and people can come in and out as they please. And we'll do the usual games for the kids. So, you reckon you can do some food?'

'Tell me what you need, and me and Marianne will do it.'

Mavis licked the lead on her pencil. 'Mince pies, sandwiches and maybe Marianne can make a cake of some sort? And anything else you can think of.'

'I'll make sure we have a few treats for the kids.' She sighed. 'Daisy always drew the pin-the-tail-on-the-donkey picture, didn't she? I'll ask Edie to do it this year. She's not too bad with that sort of thing. Just so you know, though, if Jasper's still out cold, then I'll probably not come.'

Mavis nodded. 'I were up there yesterday and I swear while I was chit-chatting his hand moved. I said to Derek, "If Jasper ain't awake in the next few days I'll eat my hat."'

Nellie shook her head. 'Doc says that don't mean anything. His eyes move under his lids and sometimes his legs twitch. Doesn't mean he's awake.'

'We'll see, eh? I want him at my party by hook or by crook.'

'Don't we all, love. Don't we all.' Nellie raised her eyebrows as Marianne and Donny came and hovered over her. Marianne's coat was buttoned up to her throat, and around her neck she wore a new bright-blue velvet scarf.

'Me and Don are off now,' she said. 'Remember I told you?'

Nellie frowned. 'You never said a word. What about clearing up?'

'You'll just have to help Gladys, and don't pretend you forgot. I've reminded you every day for the past week.'

Nellie eyed her narrowly, from her polished shoes to the top of her head. 'Where are you off to all dolled up?'

'Never you mind. I'll see you later.' She grabbed Donny's hand and quickly left the café.

Mavis stared after her through the window. 'She looks nice.'

'I know.' Nellie grinned suddenly as she got up from the table. 'If you don't mind, I have a few preparations of my own to make. But let me know if there's anything else you need for Christmas,' she called over her shoulder as she hurried into the kitchen and down to the basement. Searching the shelves, she found what she was looking for and took them upstairs. She chuckled to herself as she unpacked the tins and got to work; kids

495

thought they were so clever, but there was no chance they could hide anything from her. Especially when you expected a chatterbox like Donny to keep your secrets.

∽

Marianne and Donny skipped up Maison Dieu Road towards the town hall. Alfie had to be back at his barracks by ten that night, so their plan was to get married and then have a quiet dinner, just the three of them.

'There's Alfie,' Donny exclaimed, racing towards the steps. Alfie scooped him up and twirled him round, laughing with relief when he saw Marianne hurrying towards him.

'I thought you weren't coming,' he said.

'Stupid. As if I'd stay away.' She unbuttoned her coat to reveal a lilac-coloured chiffon dress.

'You look more perfect than you did the first time I saw you in that dress,' he said, bending to give her a long kiss. 'That was when I knew that you were the girl I wanted to marry.'

'Because of the dress?' Marianne asked archly, remembering how self-conscious she'd been about the amount of cleavage it revealed.

'No,' he said, kissing the tip of her nose. 'Because of the woman inside it.'

'That's enough,' Donny commanded. 'Time to get married.'

Laughing, they linked arms and trooped inside.

The ceremony was quick and took place in a small room containing only a desk and four chairs, but Marianne didn't care. As Alfie pushed the simple gold band onto her finger, she could feel tears welling up in her eyes; tears of happiness, but also of deep sorrow. The wedding they had planned had ended in tragedy, and visions of Daisy looking so proud of herself for creating that beautiful wedding dress drifted into her mind. And Jasper. Dear Jasper with his shaved face, slicked down hair and carefully painted helmet, all done for her. A tear dropped onto the back of her and Alfie's linked hands, and he raised her chin gently, staring deep into her eyes.

'Marianne, I know this isn't the day you'd hoped for, but I promise you that for the rest of my life I will do everything in my power to make you happy. And I really will buy you an engagement ring one day.' He looked sheepish.

She laughed tearfully. 'You don't need to get me another ring. This one is all I need. But, Alfie, you already make me happy every day.'

'Then I will make you even happier.'

'And what about me?' Donny said.

Alfie put his arm around Donny's shoulder and gave it a squeeze. 'And you too. Provided you don't complain when I kiss your mother.'

Donny grinned at him cheekily. 'I don't mind really. It makes me glad to see you love her as much as I do.'

Marianne pulled Donny to her and kissed the top of his head. 'But can we get some food now?' he asked plaintively.

As they walked back out through the entrance, they were suddenly showered with petals as a voice called out, 'Congratulations!'

Marianne whirled round to see Edie standing by the door with a bag of dried petals in her hand and a wide smile on her face.

'What—' Marianne looked at Donny, who was carefully looking away. 'Why you little monkey!' she cried. 'This was meant to be a secret.'

He kicked the ground. 'It weren't my fault. Gran made me tell.'

Marianne groaned. 'Not Mum too!'

'Yup. And she's expecting you back home right now,' Edie said, grabbing Donny around the neck.

Alfie laughed. 'Bang goes our intimate little supper then.'

'You didn't really think she'd let you get away with this, did you?' Edie said.

'I suppose not,' Marianne sighed. 'Come on then. We may as well get this over with.'

❧

Lily hurried down the drive of the hospital. She'd managed to get off an hour early – after much wrangling with Sister Murphy – and Nellie's instructions that morning had been explicit. She needed to be home at six o'clock sharp – not a minute later.

'Hello there, pretty nurse.'

Lily jumped as a tall figure emerged from the shadows by the gates.

'Charlie?' Over the last few weeks they hadn't seen nearly as much of each other as she'd have liked. Casualties had been heavy in Dover, and they had both been working almost seven days a week. The last time she'd seen him had been two weeks before when she'd persuaded him to go roller skating. Lily had laughed herself silly as Charlie, his long legs wobbling like a baby giraffe's, had clung to the side as he tried his best to stay upright while Lily, who'd skated regularly for most of her life, had pirouetted gracefully around him. Eventually, he'd leant against the side, folded his arms and refused to move. Instead, he'd watched her show off, until, as she passed close enough, he'd grabbed her round the waist and kissed her for long minutes, until the attendant told them to either get moving or leave. They'd gone to get some fish and chips, and as the rain had finally let up, they'd stood by the railings and stared out at the dark, turbulent sea, keeping a watchful eye out for the telltale flashes of red from across the Channel that would indicate a shell was on its way.

'You looking for another roller-skating lesson?' She smiled wistfully as she put her arms around his neck knowing full well that there'd be no more roller skating in Dover for a while as the skating rink had been hit by a shell and reduced to rubble just a couple of days after they'd been there.

He chuckled. 'I was thinking more along the lines of that meal I promised you.'

'Oh . . .' She sighed. 'How I wish we could go back to that day.'

Charlie tightened his arms around her. 'And I wish I could make everything better for you.' He looked at her pale face and tired eyes. 'Is there no change?' he asked gently.

She shook her head. 'And you do make things better for me, Charlie. You really do. But tonight, I can't.'

Charlie's face fell. 'Oh. Got a better offer?'

'Hardly. Tell you what, why don't you come home with me? We're having a little do for Marianne and Alfie's secret wedding.'

'If it's secret then how come you're having a do?'

'Cos there are no secrets at the café. But it's just me, Mum, Don and Edie. And Marianne and Alfie, of course, when they get back.'

'Perhaps we should do this another time. I don't want to intrude.'

'Don't be stupid. Mum'll be chuffed to have you there.'

He grinned. 'In which case, I'd be happy to come.'

∞

The sitting room was crowded when they entered, the small table loaded with plates of sausage and mash, with the wedding cake sitting in pride of place at the centre.

Marianne, looking flushed and beautiful, was sitting at the head of the table, Alfie on one side and Donny on the other, and Lily's heart warmed. It was the first glimpse of happiness any of them had had since that terrible day two months before. She plastered a smile on her face and went to kiss her sister and brother-in-law.

'You look like the cat who got the cream, Marianne.'

'That's because I have,' Marianne said, taking hold of Alfie's hand.

'You're late!' Nellie said. Then, spotting Charlie, her expression changed as she smiled with delight. 'But I'll forgive you just this once.'

Charlie went over and kissed Nellie's hand, at which she tutted. 'No need to stand on ceremony. If you're going to be part of this family, then just a "hello" would do.'

'In which case, hello, Mrs Castle.'

'Mum!' Lily flushed and cast a sidelong glance at Charlie.

He returned her stare steadily. 'I don't mind at all, Lily.' Then he turned to congratulate Marianne.

Lily's heart lurched. On the one hand, she wanted to jump up and down with joy. But, on the other, his intense stare made her nervous. She was only eighteen and there was so much more she wanted to do before she thought about marriage. Charlie was twenty-six, which sometimes seemed so much older than her. Like now, she thought, when he was looking at her so lovingly. She smiled. 'That's cos you don't know what it's like,' she said lightly, pulling out a chair. 'So, take a seat and let's see how you like it.'

When the meal was finished, Nellie stood up. 'Marianne, it's been a long, hard road for you these last twelve years or so, but this is the start of a new journey – one with a truly good man by your side. So here's to you two; may you have a long and happy life together. Now, there's just one more surprise I have for you. I know you have to get back, Alfie, but that don't mean you two can't have a little bit of privacy. So, go upstairs, loves. I've prepared the room for you so you can have a couple of hours to yourselves. Who knows when the chance might come again?'

Marianne blushed deeply, but Alfie stood up and kissed Nellie's cheek. 'Thank you, Nellie. That's possibly the best present you could have given us.' He held his hand out to Marianne, who took it with a smile.

'But why do they have to leave?' Donny said plaintively.

'Because they do,' Nellie scolded. 'So, eat your cake and shut up.'

Charlie grinned at Lily over his glass, while she rolled her eyes.

'Would you mind, Mrs Castle, if I took Lily off for a little stroll?'

Nellie waved her hand. 'Go! Me and Edie will clear up.'

Edie stood up. 'Actually, Mum, I'm meeting someone.'

Lily turned round at that. 'Are you now? Does he have blond hair, by any chance? And a Canadian accent?'

'That's none of your business. I'll see myself out.' Then she left before Nellie could raise an objection.

'I remember a Canadian bloke. Good-looking lad. Came that day you were arrested.' She stared after Edie, then sniffed. 'Foreign, but I suppose she could do worse. At least he's not German.' She cackled, while Lily hustled Charlie out of the room.

Outside, Lily took his hand and led him up Castle Street. 'I want to show you something.'

They walked a little way up the road until they came to Jasper's forge. Lily took out the key and opened the door. Charlie followed her in silently. Upstairs in the small sitting room, Lily said, 'I come here sometimes when I'm feeling sad. Just so I can pick up his scent. For some reason he feels more alive here than when I'm looking at him in that hospital bed. Mum comes too. Sometimes she sits here all night.'

Charlie nodded. 'I wish I'd known him. He sounds special.'

'He *is* special, and you *will* know him,' Lily snapped. 'Cos he's not going to die.'

Charlie put his arms around her and held her close, but she pulled away and wiped fiercely at her eyes. 'I am so sick of crying,' she said, sitting down heavily in Jasper's chair.

Charlie knelt in front of her and took her hands. 'Even tear-stained and tired you are the most beautiful woman I know.'

'Woman?'

'Yes. Woman. You're brave, clever and resilient. You are definitely a woman.' He sat up on his knees and kissed her, his lips hard and urgent against her own, and Lily responded immediately. Being with Charlie was the only thing that kept the relentless sadness at bay at the moment. She pulled him close and deepened the kiss, her hands going to his shirt and undoing the buttons. Charlie tugged her jersey over her head, his fingers starting to fumble with the buttons on her blouse.

He stopped as it fell open and rested his forehead against hers. 'Do you want me to stop?' he whispered.

'I'll kill you if you do,' she replied, pulling him closer. 'I think we should go somewhere a bit more comfortable.'

He paused. 'Are you sure?'

She nodded and, grabbing his hand, she led him to the bedroom.

Chapter 52

As November gave way to December, people's thoughts turned to how they would manage to provide Christmas dinner with all the trimmings. Although rations were increased slightly for Christmas, it wouldn't be the same as the previous year, Marianne thought wistfully, remembering the enormous goose and mounds of potatoes, along with Christmas pudding *and* Christmas cake. This year she had enough mincemeat put by to make pies for the party, but she wouldn't be able to make fudge for the children as she usually did. And, of course, this year Jasper would not walk through the door dressed as Father Christmas, with the silver bin full of presents on his shoulder.

'Right, is that the lot?' Nellie asked, interrupting her thoughts as she finished packing the last of the food for the party into the large wicker basket.

'Yes. Afraid it don't seem much compared to normal. Still, I doubt the kids'll mind.'

'They won't care a jot so long as they get to play and sing and Father Christmas gives them a little something. I'll see you over there, then. I won't be staying long as I'll be going up the hospital. Don't feel right being at a party while Jasper's still lying there.'

Marianne nodded. 'He'll be missed today.' Over the past months, her mother had lost weight and seemed to be fading away as surely as Jasper, because it wasn't just her stomach that had disappeared, but so had her colour, and she now wore a serviceable black skirt and white blouse every day. Marianne missed the colourful, vibrant, indomitable Nellie.

∽

The basement room at the Oak was a cacophony of noise as the children ran around the large space. Lily was already there with her friends from the hospital, Dot and Vi, and the three of them, along with Reenie, were trying to marshal the children into some sort of order so they could play musical statues. Up on stage, sitting beside Santa's grotto, Mr and Mrs Filbert, who usually sang at the town hall dances, were singing Christmas carols, with Alfie joining in every now and then, when he wasn't down on the dance floor dancing with the children. Nellie smiled at the sight of him. Since they'd got married, Marianne had been like a different person, and for the first time, Nellie felt confident for her future.

A loud wolf whistle from the stairs brought the noise and movement to a stop for just a moment, and Nellie looked up to see Marge standing on the stairs, hands on hips and an exasperated expression on her face. 'If you want to play musical bloomin' statues, then you'll have to get on with it now. Or else Santa won't be bringing any presents for you.'

The children obeyed her with alacrity, as Alfie jumped back on the stage and started to play a version of 'Deck the Halls' on his trumpet that she'd never heard before, while the Filberts looked on open-mouthed with indignation at being upstaged again.

Nellie chuckled as she placed her basket on the trestle table at the end of the room, which was piled with food, as everyone had brought a little something.

'What do you think?' Mavis came over and nodded at the glistening bunches of holly that had been hung around the room.

'Lovely, Mave. How d'you get those leaves so shiny.'

Mavis tapped her nose. 'Dipped 'em in glue and Epsom salts. Little tip Daisy taught me. Works a treat.' She stared at Nellie in concern. 'You don't look yourself, love. I hadn't wanted to say anything before, because I understand what you're goin' through. But Nell, you can't just give up. It ain't like you.'

Nellie gasped in indignation. 'For your information, I haven't given up! But there hasn't been a lot to laugh about these past few months.' She stared around the room. 'But look at this, eh? The kids always manage to take your mind off things. Don't forget to let me have any drawin's they do so's I can hang them round the walls in the café.'

'It's a shame they couldn't have the party in the square like normal.'

Nellie shrugged. 'Things the way they are, I don't reckon it'll be safe for a good few years yet.'

'You sure you won't stay, Nellie?'

Nellie shook her head. 'How can I with Jasper all on his own?'

'It's just . . .' Mavis looked around. 'There's going to be a bit of a surprise later and I don't want you to miss it.'

'Vera Lynn herself could walk through the door, but it wouldn't stop me leaving.'

Mavis blanched. 'How did you know?'

'Know what?' Nellie was busy placing the pies on some plates so didn't notice Mavis's startled expression.

'That's what the surprise is,' she whispered out of the corner of her mouth. 'Your Bert sorted it.'

'*My* Bert?'

Mavis nodded.

Nellie's mind went back to a moment a long, long time ago, when Bert had mentioned that Vera Lynn would be performing at the Hippodrome.

'Apparently, she's doing a week's stint, but tonight and tomorrow she's off, and Bert were asked to show her around. I bet they chose him cos he's so handsome.' Mavis was practically hopping with excitement.

Nellie raised an eyebrow. 'I bet they didn't choose him at all. I bet he marched down to the Hippodrome and demanded to do it.'

'Anyway, he asked if she'd like to come to Dover's traditional Market Square Christmas party, and she said she'd love to! So you've got to stay!'

Nellie shook her head. 'No, love. I'll be better off with Jasper. But you can tell me all about it later.'

'All right. Give him a hug from me, won't you?'

Nellie nodded and, wrapping her coat tightly about herself, went up the stairs and out into the freezing afternoon. Where once Dover had been lit up with lights at Christmas, it now looked like a town full of ghosts, and Nellie was horribly aware of the ruins of the hotel standing stark against the darkening sky. She shivered, and moved quickly on. Further into town, many homes, shops and pubs had been damaged and now lay empty, and her heart broke for the shattered lives each empty building represented, and, for the first time, she started to doubt that things could ever go back to the way they were. Where once she had been determined to keep the community together, now, she realised, it would be enough to just keep them all alive and fed.

Chapter 53

Although Lily tried to keep her eye out for Charlie, it was difficult with fifty kids all clamouring for attention. She clapped her hands and shouted above the hubbub. 'Right, children, who's for the hokey-cokey?' Her voice croaked as she said it, and the children ignored her.

Marge sauntered over, put two fingers in her mouth and gave another piercing wolf whistle, then grinned at Lily. 'And that is how you restore order,' she said, as the kids stopped to stare at her.

Edie raced forward with Dot and Vi and started to organise the children into a circle, then looked over and nodded at Alfie, who began to play. Soon, Lily forgot to look out for Charlie, as for the first time in a very long while, she realised she was enjoying herself.

'Ohhhh the hokey-cokey,' she yelled as the circle moved forward and she came face to face with Edie.

Edie yelled it back to her before being dragged away again, just as the little girl beside Lily broke ranks and jumped into the middle of the circle and, uncaring that it wasn't time, sang, 'Knees bent, arms stretched raa raa raa!'

The room broke into laughter and once again descended into pandemonium as Mavis yelled that it was time to eat.

While the children raced over to get a sandwich and a mince pie, Lily went upstairs to stand on the steps. She wasn't looking out for Charlie, she told herself. She was just getting a bit of air. But it didn't matter what she told herself. Since that night at Jasper's forge, she and Charlie had spent every spare moment they could together, and Lily was uncomfortably aware that if not for him, she'd have found it difficult to get through these last months.

Edie came and stood beside her. 'Looking out for Charlie, are you?'

Lily nodded.

'Is he the one for you, then?'

'I don't know, Edie. Maybe. All I know is he's the one for me right now.'

'You love him.' Edie phrased it as a statement, not a question.

'Yes. I suppose I do.'

'Be careful, Lil. Don't make the same mistake me and Marianne made.'

'You can't compare Charlie to Henry!' Lily exclaimed.

'They're both men, aren't they?'

Lily tutted. 'What about you and that Greg bloke? The pretty Canadian pilot?'

'He's coming tonight, as it happens. Difference being, *I'm* the one in control.'

'You sure about that?'

'Oh, yes. My heart is quite safe; I'm just not so sure about yours.' She stroked her arm. 'So take care, all right? I don't want to see my baby sister get hurt.'

Lily tutted. 'I'm all grown up now, Edie. I don't need your advice.'

Edie looked sceptical. 'If you say so. Anyway, it's not advice. Just a friendly warning.'

Lily huffed in annoyance and turned to go back inside. Edie had always acted superior when they were growing up, just because she was a little bit older. She'd thought that was all behind them, especially considering what the family had been through recently. But clearly not.

Charlie arrived soon afterwards, and Lily's heart leapt as she saw him bound down the stairs, Jimmy by his side. The minute he saw her, he pushed through the throngs of children. 'Where's the mistletoe?' he said urgently.

Lily pointed towards the centre of the room, and he dragged her towards it and kissed her soundly.

A chorus of objection came from the children, and they pulled apart laughing, while Alfie started to play, 'I'm Sending a Letter to Santa' with Mrs Filbert doing her best to warble along.

This was Derek's cue to make his appearance, and he hopped onto the stage with the dustbin, causing such a screeching to rise up from the children that the adults retreated to the back of the room, hands over their ears.

Lily spotted Jim, his arm around Reenie, standing by the bar watching the performance on the stage and dragged Charlie over to them. Since Daisy's funeral, the only time she'd seen her brothers tended to be when they made their sporadic visits to the hospital to see Jasper, after which they would pop in to check on their mother. But Lily had been working such long hours that she was rarely home when they visited.

'Derek's good, but not as good as Jasper,' Reenie said.

Lily nodded sadly as Marge and Rodney joined them. 'Who is that delicious man your Edie's flirting with?' Marge asked with a little shiver.

'Some Canadian pilot. But Edie says it's not serious . . .' She watched as the couple retreated to a corner and kissed stealthily. 'But we'll see.'

'Well, if it's not, and she's finished with him, tell her to send him my way.'

A quick glance at Rodney's put-out expression made Lily smile inwardly. Maybe it was finally beginning to dawn on him that he wouldn't find a better woman for him than Marge. About time too.

She leant back in Charlie's arms, feeling relaxed and content. Once the presents were given out, the children would be allowed out, while the adults stayed where they were. Lou Carter sidled up.

'No Nellie today?' she asked. 'I suppose she don't feel like celebratin' what with Jasper havin' all but turned up his toes. Shame. It don't feel the same without them two.' Then she grinned and held up a mince pie. 'Grub's not bad though.'

As she walked away, Lily shouted, 'He's not about to turn up his toes!'

But she doubted Lou heard her as once again Alfie began to play. She looked around the brightly decorated room and sighed. Lou was right, though. It wasn't the same. Every year, the Christmas party was held around the square, with stalls and carols and people wrapped up against the cold. This just felt like a night at the pub.

As the children were ushered up the stairs and told to go and play, Alfie began to play 'Santa Claus is Coming to Town' and people started to dance.

'You seen Bert?' Edie shouted over to Lily as they twirled past each other.

Lily shook her head. It was odd he wasn't here. He'd promised he would be.

An excited murmur went up just then, as Mrs Filbert stopped singing and stood staring with her mouth wide open. Another voice took over – this one a lot more melodious – and as one the crowd stopped and turned to stare. Coming down the stairs holding Bert's arm, was a slim, glamorous woman wearing a fur coat, with a matching hat perched on her blonde hair.

'It's Vera Lynn!' a voice shouted, and a cheer went up around the room as she walked onto the stage, nodded at Alfie, who she knew a little from their days on the band circuit, and continued the song, while Mrs Filbert huffed away and glowered sulkily from a corner.

∞

At the hospital, Nellie sat by Jasper's bed, holding his hand and trying to keep up a stream of cheerful chatter. 'Derek's being Father Christmas this year and, to be frank, he'll not be a patch on you. Cos it don't matter how much padding he puts around his middle, it won't never match up to yours. Though, at the moment—' she patted his stomach reflectively '—even skinny little Derek's got more than you. When you wake up I'm going to stuff you so full of food you'll have trouble fitting through the door.'

Jasper let out a strange gurgling sound, and Nellie sat up straight, staring at his face.

'Jasper? Did you hear me, love? Jasper!'

His lips twitched and she watched his mouth in fascination.

'Are you trying to say something?'

He coughed and his head turned towards her. 'Water.' He coughed again. 'Water,' he repeated piteously, his voice rough and croaky.

Nellie hurriedly picked up the glass by his bed and raised his head so she could bring it to his lips.

'Jasper, you better not be havin' me on right now. I've been waiting for months for you, old man, and if this is just a twitch, you'll be getting a piece of my mind.'

Jasper choked as he tried to swallow. 'Me throat,' he moaned.

She stroked her hand over his neck. 'I know, love. That'll be the tubes.'

He sighed, his eyes still closed as he lay back, his hand flapping on the blanket as he sought hers. She took it hastily. 'Oh, love. Are you really awake?'

'Splittin' headache,' he murmured.

She laughed. 'That'll teach you to take your helmet off in the middle of a shell attack.'

He sighed and squeezed her hand, then seemed to fall back to sleep.

Nellie held her breath, watching every twitch of his face. Then she stroked his head. The hair had grown again, since his operation, and it sprung around his head in short, bushy tufts. All the blond was gone now, and it had turned a pure, silver white, making him look twenty years older, but she didn't care. If only he was back with her, then maybe she'd be able to find some peace again.

She sat back, prepared to wait all night to hear his voice again if she had to.

∞

At the Oak, more people had joined the party as Vera Lynn's singing had drifted up the stairs and people stared in wonder at the woman whose voice had become so familiar to them from the radio. Finally, she paused for a moment and said, 'Bert told me that this would be the best Christmas party I ever attended.'

She was greeted with cheers and Lily glanced over to Bert, who'd not moved from the side of the stage where he had been staring at Vera with a lovelorn look in his eye. At her words, he smiled and preened. Lily nudged Edie. 'He reckons he's got a chance with her. Can't wait to see his face when he realises he doesn't.'

'And it's wonderful to see so many of our brave boys and girls here.' Another cheer went up.

'But now, I want my lovely trumpeter Alfie, who, I'm told, has only recently been married, to get down there and take his girl in his arms. Because I know for many of you, this next song will mean a lot. Especially to the Fifth Buffs, who've been so welcoming to me.' She winked at Bert, who blushed. 'The new year will bring many challenges and separations. But we need to keep our hopes alive. Because you know that one day, one way or another—' she handed some music to Mr Filbert, who smiled and nodded as he took it from her '—we will all meet again.'

The noise was deafening then as Mr Filbert played the opening bars of the song that had come to mean so much to everyone. Then Vera Lynn's deep, husky voice started to sing.

Charlie took hold of Lily's hand and nodded towards the stairs. 'Will you come out with me for a moment, my Lily?'

She nodded and, as they walked up the stairs, she glanced at the people dancing. Alfie and Marianne were swaying together, oblivious to everyone, while Reenie and Jim seemed to be holding an intense conversation, before he bent and kissed her and they started to dance. Marge and Rodney were also dancing, Rodney a little stiff, until Marge said something, and he started to laugh. Edie and her blonde pilot were locked in each other's arms, Edie smiling up at him. Lily wasn't so sure whether her sister's assertion that she was in control of this one was true. Bert, meanwhile, ignored all efforts to get him to dance and continued to stare up at Vera Lynn, stars in his eyes.

She felt a tug on her hand, as Charlie urged her on, and she followed him out of the door.

∞

Somewhere a clock was ticking loudly as Nellie sat, counting each tick and watching Jasper's chest rise and fall beneath the blanket. Soon it would be Christmas Day, she thought bleakly. It would be a Christmas Day like no other with just the family this year, and no Jasper. Suddenly, his hand twitched again and she sat up, staring into his face.

His eyes opened and stared around. 'Nellie,' he croaked.

'I'm here, love.'

'Where?' His hand reached out and she caught hold of it, bringing it to her cheek.

'Right beside you.'

His fingers stroked her skin. 'You really are here. I thought I heard you,' he whispered. 'Turn the light on, love. So I can see your face.'

Nellie stared at him in bemusement. 'It is on.' She bent over and kissed his lips.

'I can't see you,' he said, his voice rising in panic.

Nellie's stomach swooped. 'But I'm here. Right here, love.'

His hand found her cheek again and he stroked it clumsily. 'I can't see you,' he said again. 'Oh God, Nellie, I can't see you. It's all dark.'

Nellie's face was wet with tears as she stared into the blank eyes of the man she loved, but though they seemed to be looking at her face, they didn't meet her gaze as they usually would. 'I can see you, though, Jasper,' she whispered.

'But I want to see your face.' Jasper started to breathe fast in panic as his head started to thrash on the pillow.

Nellie grabbed his face and stilled him. 'But I can see you, Jasper,' she said again.

The curtain was suddenly pulled back and Sister Mackenzie stood there. 'He's awake?' she said, her face wreathed in smiles.

'He can't see,' Nellie wailed. 'Why can't he see?'

The sister's face paled. 'Dr Toland's on duty. I'll fetch her.'

Nellie sat holding Jasper's hand tightly in hers as she waited for the doctor. 'Everything'll be all right, love,' she whispered over and over again.

But Jasper wasn't listening. He'd closed his eyes and was lying still, and if it wasn't for the fact that her hand had gone numb from the tightness of his grip, Nellie would have thought he'd fallen back into unconsciousness.

Finally, as Dr Toland pulled the curtain back and walked in, Jasper opened his eyes and turned his head in her direction.

'Hello, Mr Cane. How are you feeling?'

'Can't see,' he croaked.

Dr Toland pulled a small torch from her pocked and shone it into his eyes. Jasper blinked.

'Hmm.' She stood back. 'Try to rest now, Mr Cane. I just need to talk to Mrs Castle.'

519

She gestured for Nellie to follow her and led her to a small office.

'Is he blind, doctor?' Nellie asked frantically.

Dr Toland hesitated. 'The truth is, I'm not sure. You saw his head turn as I came in – and he looked straight at me as if he could see me. And then he blinked at the torchlight. Both those signs give me hope that his condition might not be permanent.'

'Oh, thank God,' Nellie gasped. 'When will his sight return?'

Dr Toland shook her head. 'There's no way for me to know. The brain is a fragile and complicated thing, and sometimes after a trauma it can behave in ways we just don't understand. I've seen cases before of people who say they can't see, and yet they look at objects or people as if they can. Sometimes their sight returns, and sometimes it doesn't. I'm afraid, for now, all we can do is help him recover his strength and see what happens.'

Nellie stared at her, her mouth trembling. Then she raised her chin. 'He'll bloody see again if it's got anything to do with me.' She turned and left then, and Dr Toland sighed. If it was down to Nellie Castle's determination and devotion, she had no doubt he would. But life was never that simple.

✺

It was a cold, frosty evening, and the moon was full above the sea. Lily shivered and wrapped her arms around herself.

'I wanted to tell you something,' Charlie said.

His tone was so serious that Lily felt her stomach tighten. 'What is it?'

Charlie didn't say anything for a moment as he stared out over the water and Lily waited, her heart in her mouth.

Finally, he took her hand and looked down at her. 'Lily, these past few months have been eventful, and for you, they've been especially hard. But I've fallen for you, sweetheart. Fallen deep and hard. And I wanted to know if you feel the same.'

Lily nodded, tears in her eyes. 'I do, Charlie. I really do.'

Charlie let go of her hand and reached into his pocket, and Lily gasped slightly, knowing what he was about to do and not sure if she was ready to give him an answer. 'You're not going to propose, are you?' she said with a wobbly smile, trying to lighten the mood.

Charlie laughed and looked sheepish. 'I was, actually. You see, the thing is, I'm being posted soon. I don't know where they're sending me but now the threat of invasion has diminished, they want me elsewhere.'

Lily reached up and stroked his cheek, feeling tears rising up the back of her throat. 'Oh no, Charlie.'

'So, will you? Marry me?'

She shook her head then buried her face in his chest. 'You're going away and there's not time to marry. And I'm not even sure I want to. I'm only eighteen. I've got things to do.'

He bent and kissed her hair. 'But . . . you could just promise?'

She pulled away from him and put her hand on her chest. 'You're right here in my heart already. I think you always will be. Write to me. Come and see me when you're here. But don't ask me to marry you. Not yet.'

Charlie sighed. 'I should have known you'd be too independent to be tied down.'

'I didn't say never, Charlie. Just not now. I love you, but you have to do your duty and so do I. I don't want to hold you back.'

Dimly from an open window, they could hear the sound of a hundred voices joining in the chorus with Vera Lynn. They stared at each other. 'It's true, Charlie. We will definitely meet again. I can at least promise that.'

Charlie had tears in his eyes. 'Then that will have to be enough for me. For now. But I will be back for you, my Lily. I promise you that.'

Lily put her arms around his neck, pulling him towards her, her heart breaking at the thought that Charlie would be gone soon. Why had she said no? The thought of never seeing him again was unbearable. 'Do you promise, Charlie?' she whispered against his lips.

'I promise.'

'Because if you don't, I will hunt you down and drag you back to me.'

He smiled against her lips. 'I like the sound of that, sweetheart.'

'Good,' she said then, as their lips met, and for a while, everything around them faded away.

∞

Nellie sat down beside Jasper again, and took his hand.

'Nellie?' he croaked.

'I'm here, Jasper. And the doctor said that your sight will come back.'

'Do you promise?' he asked weakly.

Nellie felt sick. She was lying to him, but he needed hope – *she* needed hope.

She leant forward and kissed his lips, then buried her face in his shoulder.

'Do you promise, Nellie?' he repeated urgently.

She didn't say anything for a moment as Jasper's tears soaked into her hair, while her own collected in a pool at his shoulder.

Finally, she murmured, 'I promise, my love. You will definitely see me again soon.'

Acknowledgements

Writing a book during lockdown sounds like it should be easier, but I found the opposite to be true. Luckily for me, I had several people who helped see me through.

As always, I'd like to thank my agent, Teresa Chris – who is always ready with some no-nonsense and sympathetic advice – and to Claire Johnson-Creek, my editor at Bonnier Zaffre, who listened as I talked through plot problems, and remained diplomatic, even as the deadline for my final draft disappeared into the distance.

Equally, my children: Maddie, Sim and Olly. My daughter has told me she'll be writing a novel about a woman who kills her children so she can finish her book. It sounds like a great concept, so look out for that one soon. Sorry, guys.

Also to my wonderful mother and my sisters. It's been a tough year for all of us, but most especially for my mother, yet even so your support has been invaluable and unending.

I need to say a special thank you to my most brilliant friends Tanita and Natacha, who sent me wine, flowers and chocolate – and not just on my birthday – constantly checked up on me and were always ready to listen to me moan and vent. You two are simply the best.

Finally, I would like to say thank you to the website The Dover Historian, run by Lorraine Sencicle. It is a quite remarkable historical resource, and one that I have mined ruthlessly. And I must mention the invaluable book *Dover at War* by Roy Humphreys, a fabulously useful account of what happened in Dover during the war month by month. Both of these sources have been, and remain, invaluable to me.

·MEMORY LANE·

Welcome to the world of Ginny Bell!

Keep reading for more from Ginny Bell, to discover
a recipe that features in this novel and to find out more
about Ginny's upcoming books . . .

We'd also like to welcome you to Memory Lane,
a place to discuss the very best saga stories from
authors you know and love with other readers,
plus get recommendations for new books we think
you'll enjoy. Read on and join our club!

·MEMORY LANE·

www.MemoryLane.Club
www.facebook.com/groups/memorylanebookgroup

Dear reader,

I hope you enjoyed the latest instalment in the Castle family's story. Dover in 1940 was not an easy place to live, and as far as possible I have tried to make the events around which the story is told as true to historical fact as possible. Some of the dates of events have moved and I have changed some of the incidents to fit the purposes of the story. For example, the barrage balloons were all shot down, however, one did not fall in Market Square. But several fell on buildings around Dover, causing some fatalities when they crashed through the roof of a house. Sadly, it is also true that on the day of the first really damaging shell attack in Dover, one of ambulance men called to Noah's Ark Road, discovered that his house had been destroyed and his wife killed.

In general, apart from the main historical figures of the day, I try to steer clear of using characters who actually existed. But on this occasion I have made an exception. Dr Gertrude Toland was a remarkable woman and there is a bench dedicated to her on Dover's seafront, as well as a plaque commemorating her work at Buckland Hospital. She saved countless lives at the Casualty Hospital during the war and operated for nine days and nights during the Dunkirk evacuation. She continued to work as a doctor in Dover after the war and I have no doubt that she inspired many of the young women she worked with.

One of the joys of doing research is reading first-hand accounts of what life was like during the war, and thanks to Dover being such a dangerous and dramatic place to live, I found quite a few old books and pamphlets with accounts written by people who lived through that time. And this is where I found Polly the parrot. I'm not sure whether she used to swear every time Hitler was mentioned, but during World War I she had been trained to squawk and stamp whenever anyone said 'Kaiser'. As she was still alive during World War II, I like to think that they taught her a new trick to fit with the times.

Finally, for any Dovorians reading this, I apologise for any inaccuracies in the geography of the town and the market square in particular. I have altered it slightly to fit with my own visualisation.

Thank you so much for reading Lily's story and I hope you'll want to come back to find out what fate and war have in store for the Castles next. The

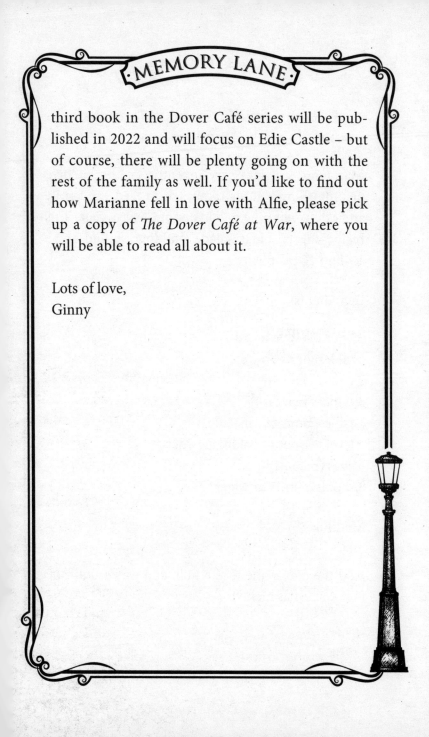

MEMORY LANE

third book in the Dover Café series will be published in 2022 and will focus on Edie Castle – but of course, there will be plenty going on with the rest of the family as well. If you'd like to find out how Marianne fell in love with Alfie, please pick up a copy of *The Dover Café at War*, where you will be able to read all about it.

Lots of love,
Ginny

A Recipe for Marianne's Marmalade Pudding

Marianne is always very inventive in the kitchen, helping those rations to stretch to feed the family and others popping in and out of Castle's Café. This recipe for her marmalade pudding should serve around 12 people.

Ingredients:

12 ounces stale bread
6 tablespoons flour
3 tablespoons sugar
3 ounces margarine
6 tablespoons marmalade
3 level teaspoons baking powder
3 eggs (reconstituted)
3/4 pint of milk or water

Method:

Add the margarine to the milk and warm until the margarine has melted.

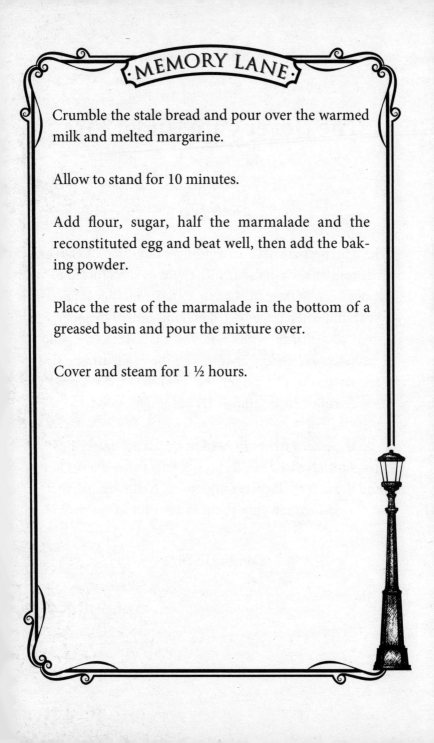

Crumble the stale bread and pour over the warmed milk and melted margarine.

Allow to stand for 10 minutes.

Add flour, sugar, half the marmalade and the reconstituted egg and beat well, then add the baking powder.

Place the rest of the marmalade in the bottom of a greased basin and pour the mixture over.

Cover and steam for 1 ½ hours.

Look out for the next book in The Dover Café Series . . .

The Dover Café Under Fire

Dover 1941

The unexpected arrival of a stranger at Pearson's Garage throws Edie Castle's life into chaos as she's forced to move back to the café. Living with her mother is never easy, but when tragedy strikes, long-buried memories come to the surface, and Edie's world starts to crumble around her. No longer sure who she can trust, she is forced to consider leaving the town she loves – or risk ruining her family's reputation for good.

At the café, a friend in need of a place to stay brings chaos into Nellie's life. But when Edie turns against her and the café itself comes under fire, Nellie realises that her troubles are about to get a lot worse.

Coming in 2022

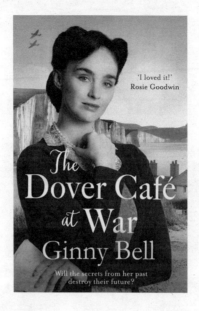

  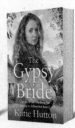